MARCHING ON ZION

A NOVEL BY
JACKSON JARRARD

A Novel on the Utah War

by

JACKSON JARRARD

PRESERVATION BOOKS & PUBLISHING
SOUTH JORDAN, UTAH USA

Library of Congress cataloging-in-publication data:
Jarrard, Gregory Mance "Jackson"

Author: G.M. "Jackson" Jarrard

First edition printed by Printegrity, Lindon, Utah

MARCHING ON ZION

ISBN 979-8-9877629-6-7 *Utah Expedition, 1857-1858 — Fiction 2. Mormon — Utah — History — 19th Century — Fiction.*

MARCHING ON ZION *is a work of fiction based on real people and real events. Care has been taken to tell an historically accurate story based on current research. Direct quotes used in this book based on research discovered during its creation are attributed to the sources in the End Notes and Acknowledgments*

DEDICATED TO CHRISTIE

IN MEMORY OF...

Bodil Mortensen, a 10-year-old Danish immigrant who came west in a handcart company in 1856 without her parents and died from exposure at the Sweetwater. Along with the countless other children and adults who died on their way to Zion, her death was a tragedy. Of the 70,000 or so Latter-day Saints who migrated to the Great Basin from 1847 until the completion of the transcontinental railroad in 1869, some 6,000 died along the way, buried in unmarked graves.

Let us remember their sacrifices and carry on!

The Author

ACKNOWLEDGMENTS

I am indebted to the authors of the books and articles listed in the End Notes whose years of research have brought the Utah War into the light. In particular, the two volumes by **William MacKinnon** (At Sword's Point, Parts 1 & 2) represent a lifetime of devotion and labor to this subject. He began his crusade in 1958 as an undergraduate at Yale University and still continues writing in his 87th year. Another author, **Matthew A. Grow**,PhD, wrote the biography of Thomas L. Kane while seeking his doctorate degree. His revelation of the life and the achievements of Kane as it relates to the very survival of the Latter-day Saints in Utah is monumental. Other writers and researchers, including **R. Devan Jensen** should also be noted; Jensen's story of his third-great-grandfather, William Stowell, a Mormon POW, who was kept shackled in a tent with Johnston's Army during the winter of 1857-1858 gave me food for thought as I tried to breathe life into this episode of Mormon history. All of the publications listed at the end come with my highest recommendations; I hope what you find in this book piques your interest enough to read the other volumes cited in the Endnotes.

Special thanks to Dan Rekow and to his staff at Printegrity in Lindon, Utah, for turning a PDF into a real book.

G.M. "Jackson" Jarrard
August 1, 2025

TABLE OF CONTENTS

Author's Note

"We Claim the Privilege of Worshiping Almighty God According to the Dictates of Our Own Conscience, and Allow All Men the Same Privilege, Let Them Worship How, Where or What They May."

11th Article of Faith,
The Church of Jesus Christ of Latter-day Saints

People of faith accept the fact that human rights come from God. They are not bestowed on men by some benevolent potentate. As the Framers put it, the pursuit of life, liberty and happiness is a universal right. And chief among those are freedom of religion, freedom of speech, freedom of the press (in all its forms) and freedom to peaceably assemble. When those rights are infringed upon, sometimes people flee and sometimes they fight. And, often they do both.

This is the focus of **MARCHING ON ZION**, a story about the stand-off between members of The Church of Jesus Christ of Latter-day Saints in Utah (often called "Mormons") and "Johnston's Army," about one-third of the entire United States Army. It had been sent by newly elected President James Buchanan in 1857 to "put down a rebellion" by the Mormons in Utah who didn't know that they were rebelling. At the time, Kansas was "bleeding"— pro-slavery forces and abolitionists were killing each other over the issue of whether Kansas was to be admitted into the Union as a slave state or a free state. In the presidential campaign of 1856, Republican John C. Fremont had campaigned on the promise to fight "the twin relics of barbarism: slavery and polygamy." He lost, but the Democrats and their winning candidate, James Buchanan, knew nothing could be done about slavery, but polygamy and the Mormons in Utah? That was fair game.

The troops were accompanying Alfred Cumming, who had

just been appointed to be the new governor of the Territory of Utah. He was to replace Mormon leader Brigham Young, and to do so with force, if necessary.

The Utah saga began in 1846 when Brigham Young, the Great Colonizer, "America's Moses," and the Mormons were hunkered down on the banks of the Missouri in Iowa and Nebraska.

In 1953, Utahn Bernard DeVoto's book, **The Year of Decision — 1846** was published for which he won a Pulitzer Prize and a Book of the Year Award. DeVoto brings the caravan of Saints to life in 3D Technicolor in his book as they trudge westward in the Iowa mud.

He describes how somewhere *"between fifteen and twenty thousand people [were] uprooted from their land and seeking a new land. Thousands of wagons, tens of thousands of oxen, horses, mules, milch cattle, beef cattle, neat cattle, sheep, goats. Chickens, geese, turkeys, guinea fowl, ducks, pigeons, parrots, love birds, canaries. Seedlings with their roots bound in sacking, slips from the shrubbery back home, seeds for the harvest to come, the disassembled machinery of flour mills and sawmills, a college, the mysteries of Heaven, the keys to eternity, the Dispensation of the Fullness of Times. Through sleet and rain, through drouth and prairie summer, half-starved and half-sick, dispossessed, believing, and faithful unto the last, Israel traveled the unknown, toward the land of Canaan, in God's faith and for His glory and under the shadow of His outstretched hand, to build Zion and inherit the earth."*

In 1847, the first contingent of pioneers stopped at the eastern edge of the Great Basin near a North American dead sea, the Great Salt Lake. Here under the leadership of their president-prophet, Brigham Young, they began creating settlements in this high desert region. But, the Mormons had very few allies. Ten years later, they were being besieged.

Someone needed to step in and stop this civil war before the Civil War began in earnest in 1861. That someone was Thomas L. Kane, the unlikely hero of **MARCHING ON ZION**.

PROLOGUE

ong after the tragic events of October 1856, the memory of the suffering of the Mormon handcart pioneers on the Sweetwater in Wyoming still linger…cold, forlorn and melancholy. Decades later, an elderly survivor wrote down from memory for posterity, carefully with pen and ink, occasionally trembling but steeling herself, steadying her hand. Like her name, **Patience Loader Rozsa Archer**, endured and survived, always determined to make sure we remember. One of those pioneers buried on his journey was Patience's father, James Loader, a Mormon convert from Oxford, England. In her journal, Patience describes catching a glimpse of her rescuers, who came to dig them out of the snow and take them to safety:

"[W]hat a deplorable condition we was in at that time Seven hundred miles from salt Lake and only nine days full rations that Morning the Bugal sounded to call us togither the captain ask us if we was willing to come on four ounces of flour a day all answerd Yes we had allready been reduced to half pound per day well we return to our tents I had left the remainer of the beef head cooking on the fire the next tent to ours was Br Sam Jones and sister MaryAnn Greening was traveling with Sister Jones and family sister Mary ann was at her fire cooking something I don't what she had to cook I am sure she had but little . we look around towards the Mountains and she called out, "oh Patience here is some californians coming," and as thay got nearer to us I told her no thay are not californians it is Br Joseph A. Young from the valley he was acompanyed by brother Hanks or James Furgeson. I cannot say which it was of those two breathren with there pack animel thay came to our fire seeing us out there Br Young ask

*how many is dead or how many is alive I told him I could not
tell with tears streaming down his face he ask whare is your
^captains^ tent he call for the bugler ... to call every body out
of ther tents he then told the captain Edward Martin if he had
flour enough to give us all one pound of flour each and said if
there was any cattle to kill and give us one pound of beef each
Saying there was plenty provisions and clothing coming for
us on the road but to Morrow Morning we must Make a Moove
from there he said we would have to travel 25 Miles then we
would have plenty of provisions and that there would be lots
of good breathren to help us that thay had come with good
teams and good coverd wagons so the sick could ride."*

The rescuers — men on mounts, others driving wagons
through snow drifts — had rushed into the storm after heeding
the call that their prophet-president, Brigham Young, had delivered at the church's semi-annual conference. Even for him, the
pugnacious, fearless leader of the nearly 40,000 settlers gathered
in the Great Basin, his address was unusual:

*"I will now give this people the subject and the text for the
Elders who may speak to-day and during the conference, it is
this, on the 5th day of October, 1856, many of our brethren
and sisters are on the Plains with hand-carts, and probably
many are now 700 hundred miles from this place, and they
must be brought here, we must send assistance to them. The
text will be, 'to get them here.' I want the brethren who may
speak to understand that their text is the people on the plains,
and the subject matter for this community is to send for them
and bring them in before the winter sets in.*

*That is my religion; that is the dictation of the Holy Ghost
that I possess, it is to save the people. We must bring them in
from the plains, and when we get them here we will try to keep
the same spirit that we have had, and teach them the way of
life and salvation; tell them how they can be saved, and how
they can save their friends. This is the salvation I am now
seeking for, to save our brethren that would be apt to perish,
or suffer extremely, if we do not send them assistance. I shall
call upon the Bishops this day, I shall not wait until to-mor-*

row, nor until next day, for 60 good mule teams and 12 or 15 wagons.

I do not want to send oxen, I want good horses and mules. They are in this Territory, and we must have them; also 12 tons of flour and 40 good teamsters, besides those that drive the teams. This is dividing my text into heads; first, 40 good young men who know how to drive teams, to take charge of the teams that are now managed by men, women, and children, who know nothing about driving them; second, 60 or 65 good spans of mules, or horses, with harness, whipple-trees, neck-yokes, stretchers, load chains, &c., and, thirdly, 24 thousand pounds of flour, which we have on hand."

The Saints responded. In droves.

On November 30th, 1856, 104 wagons loaded with survivors and the remaining foodstuff, blankets and quilts taken to them for their survival arrived in Great Salt Lake City. A month later the final shipment of Saints finally arrived, some 50 wagons worth.

People with barely enough provisions to feed themselves provided for others even less fortunate.

ONE OF THOSE PEOPLE WAS WILLIAM STOWELL, who had in his charge an orphaned boy with no one to care for him. This begins our story:

William Stowell peered down into his overcoat to check on his passenger. The fifteen-month-old toddler was finally asleep. The mustang was a sure-footed animal but was carrying a heavy load. The snow was getting deeper now, but he was certain the clearing was just ahead. They had left the dugout about 3 p.m. and had the weather been more favorable, they would have made it to the fort well before nightfall. Now it was dark — it was touch and go.

They were being peppered by blowing sleet, and it seemed to be growing stronger. Besides its passengers, the mustang was also loaded up with a knapsack of food, clothing and household items — including several tin cups, a serving dish and a frying pan —

that William had salvaged from the orphan's family. He had fashioned a shawl into a girdle that he had wrapped around him and the boy to secure his human cargo. The overcoat was a gift from the boy's deceased father that enveloped both of them. He'd been a large man.

"Thank heavens for small miracles," William muttered as they approached the clearing. Below them in the gully was the glimmer of a fire from inside the tiny cabin where he had just relocated. Two days earlier, he had hung a new door after acquiring a set of hinges from a barn that had burned down. Again, a serendipitous discovery, gifted by the Divine just when it was sorely needed.

Little Wm. Henry Packard was the sole survivor of William Stowell sister's family; no one but William Stowell could care for him. William was now a father. Now he had to find himself a wife, and for little Henry, a mother.

William Stowell and the other Latter-day Saints in the Territory of Utah were discovering that their problems were burgeoning, including crickets, drought and thousands of new converts. New challenges were coming from an unexpected source. In the fall of 1856, despite their rallying cry to fight the twin relics of barbarism — slavery and polygamy — the upstart Republican Party and their candidate, explorer John C. Fremont, lost the election. The new president, Democrat James Buchanan, had no illusions about curing the national plague of slavery. But, polygamy and the unpopular Mormons? They were fair game. Once again, they were in the gun sights of their enemies; in modern parlance, the unpopular sect soon became the tail that wagged the dog, a diversion from the real Civil War that would start in South Carolina five years later.

It was time to start **Marching on Zion**.

Soda Springs

Green

Fontenelle Creek

[Kemmerer]

Bear Lake

Oregon

Bear River

Bear River

Hams Fork

Alexander's March Trail

Camp Winfield

[Granger]

Muddy Fork

Cache Cave
Fortifications

Echo Canyon

[Evanston]

Camp Scott

Fort Bridger

Black's Fork

Smith's Fork

Camp Supply

Weber

River

Wasatch Mts.

Jordan River

Provo River

Uinta

Lake

Provo

THE UTAH EXPEDITION
in Utah Territory, 1857-1858

LEGEND

————	Route of U.S. Army
———	Alexander's March
• • • • •	Oregon Trail
— — —	Sublette's Cutoff

[Present day place names shown in brackets]

SCALE OF MILES

1

A MIGHTY FORTRESS

William Wagstaff watched the irrigation ditch fill up as he cleared a path to his fruit trees. First a trickle and then a stream and finally a flood covered the small orchard surrounded by sagebrush and clump grass. A few dozen spindly trees had taken root in the stony soil; several others hadn't made it through the first winter. He worked his shovel and directed the water from one tree to another.

As soon as he had the means, he would plant more and then maybe some peaches and cherries to add to his little apple orchard, he promised himself. The whole field would be row after row of fruit trees — a bit of Eden carved out of the gentle hillside just below East Millcreek Canyon, the source of the creek that filled his canal.

He turned to his stepson who was playing in the water: "Come on, Willy. Let's finish our chores." The boy had been distracted by a flat-bed wagon that had pulled up over the East Millcreek bridge and emerged through the trees.

"Papa, look it's Christian!"

Willy ran to greet the big woodcutter who jumped down, grabbed the boy, and hoisted him up.

"Willy, you are as big as a stump and just as heavy!" Christian Holz laughed as he set the boy down. He grabbed the elder William by the shoulders and flashed a big smile.

"So, what brings you up from the city, Christian?" William asked as they took a seat on the back of the wagon.

"Actually, I'm driving up Big Cottonwood Canyon to dismantle

the bowery and bring the lumber back once the July 24th celebration is over, and of course, to see Winnie. And I wanted to hear first-hand the mayor's news."

"The mayor?" William asked.

"Yes, Mayor Abraham Smoot. Porter Rockwell, Judson Stoddard and the mayor returned yesterday with Elder Pratt's widow. Made the journey from the Platte in just five days or so."

"...And what news would that be?" William asked under his breath.

"Rumor has it, there's an Army on the way... 'to put down the rebellion,'" Christian replied.

"What rebellion?"

"Well, your rebellion, of course, William. Raising fruit trees, digging canals, and settling on federal land. And, of course, pledging allegiance to old Brigham, I reckon," he said with a wry smile.

"Then I guess I am in good company. And I know enough to stay right behind you and your musket, since you are trained in the dark arts," William replied, trying to put a light spin on it.

"We'll have to hang together on this, William."

"Or hang separately," the older man replied.

With that, William watched as Christian gave his horses a whistle and jerked up the hill towards the canyon where the Saints were about to celebrate the 10th-year anniversary of the Mormon pioneers' arrival. Christian wanted to be there to hear the news firsthand. He looked over his shoulder and caught a glimpse of Willy holding a yacht race in the ditch as the boy urged the lead pine cone on to victory. He felt a shiver crawl up his spine as he wondered what future lay in store for the eight-year-old. And for everyone else in the valley of the Great Salt Lake for that matter.

TENS OF THOUSANDS OF YEARS AGO, prior to the settling of the Great Basin by pioneers made up of members of the Church of Jesus Christ of Latter-day Saints (or "Mormons," (a derogatory nickname given them by their enemies, their eventual destination was a great lake, later named Lake Bonneville, about the size of today's Lake Michigan and was fed by streams from melting glaciers flowing westward out of the canyons from the Wasatch mountain range. Those glaciers filled up and then enlarged the canyons east of the lake as they slowly descended, carving paths down to the valley before eventually melting and disappearing.

In July 1847, the first wagons driven by Mormon pioneers snaked down one of these boulder-ridden, narrow canyons that the Donner Party had followed the year before after exiting South Pass and Echo Canyon. Aptly named Emigration Canyon, it became the main entrance into the Valley of the Great Salt Lake. A few years later, Mormon apostle Parley P. Pratt cleared a wagon road and set up a toll gate further south at what became known as Parley's Canyon. From these canyons, the Saints not only acquired their drinking and irrigation water, but also timber and wild game, especially mule deer.

In 1856, the president of their church and the man they recognized as their prophet, Brigham Young, along with other Saints, celebrated Pioneer Day in the largest of these canyons, Big Cottonwood Canyon, about 18 miles south of Salt Lake City and another 17 miles up a winding canyon wagon road to Silver Lake at the top of a bowl surrounded by 10,000-foot peaks. Brigham was so enamored with its forested canyon walls, lush vegetation and stream-fed lakes that he determined that it would be the ideal place the following year to celebrate 10 years of living in peace and freedom. Thus, early in the summer of 1857, invitations were sent out to gather in the canyon for a three-day celebration.

THERE WERE WAR DRUMS BEATING IN THE DISTANCE. Just the same- no sense in worrying the children. Besides, why ruin the party? More than 2,500 residents of Utah, many of them the very first Mormon pioneers to arrive in the Great Basin, were having a three-day celebration at the top of Big Cottonwood Canyon surrounding Silver Lake to celebrate the tenth anniversary of peace in the mountains.

By Thursday. July 23rd, hundreds of horses and mules, close to 500 wagons and over 2,500 Saints were up in the canyon. Bands were tuning up, wagons were being unloaded and children were frolicking in the cool mountain air. Dozens of campfires were burning as breakfast was being cooked and served. Out in the flat east of the lake, several dozen brethren, Brother Brigham included, were laying down planks for the boweries for evening dancing and serenades.

There was a lot to celebrate — and much cause for concern. Ten years prior to the day — July 24th, 1847 — Brigham Young rolled into the nearly treeless valley filled with clump grass and sagebrush and announced "this is the right place, move on." He had promised that if the Saints' enemies would leave them alone for 10 years, they'd be unable to chase them off their land again. The older pioneers who remembered Ohio, Missouri and Illinois and their desperate flight west knew only too well what was at stake. And they were bound and determined to stay in their mountain homes.

By afternoon, much of the preparation for the weekend celebration had been completed. The Young family retreated to their camping spot just east of Silver Lake. Brigham removed his boots, rolled up his pant legs and stepped carefully through the willows at the water's edge. His five-year-old son Mahonri or Mac rushed over to him and pointed to his right:

"Papa, there's a big horse in the water with horns looking at you!"

"It's not a horse, Mac — it's a moose, a really big deer. Stay away from it."

"You too! Be careful, Papa!"

Brigham smiled at his boy and waded away from the "horse

with horns" and found a boulder at the shoreline, a flat rock that gave him a front-row seat of the lake and all the activity unfolding before them and where he could cool off his feet. Before he realized it, his boy had joined him there. Brigham reached down, put his hand in the water and made a fist.

"Look down, Mac. Is that a clam?"

The boy peered at it; Brigham squeezed his fist, sending a water spout at the boy's face who retaliated, and soon a water fight ensued, drenching both of them.

They sneaked back to the tent to get drier clothes, but they were apprehended.

The boy explained with a grin: "It was a clam, a really big one."

Brigham and Mac were still laughing as they were putting on their footwear at a log near the campfire; Brigham tied his son's shoes.

Mac leaned forward, looking into his father"s eyes: "Papa, why can't we just live up here all the time? It's not hot and dusty, it's pretty and we can have water fights every day."

"For one thing, Mac, we really can't grow food up here. And, in the winter, the snow is way over your head, but we can come up on special days, like this one."

"But, Papa, what if the soldiers come? They couldn't find us here, could they"

Brigham took a deep breath: "Mac, who told you about the soldiers?"

"Emily and George."

"They were just trying to scare you. Don't you worry."

Mac smiled. "I don't worry. Everybody says you know what to do — you'll keep us safe."

Brigham patted his son's head. "Thank you, Mac. I'll do my best." But, he wondered: Is my best good enough?

It was time for this hard-scrabble group of survivors to forget their troubles. The meadows surrounding Silver Lake were filled with weary animals and festive pioneers. Small campfires illuminated the alpine site, the native mule deer were hiding higher up the slopes, wide-eyed with their over-sized ears standing at attention as children played hide-and-seek amidst the pines, oak brush and quaking aspens.

The bowl they were celebrating in was some 8,700 feet high and was surrounded by rugged peaks towering an additional 2,000 feet over their heads. Ribaldry was echoing all around. Firelight illuminated the scene. The looming threat from the east was weighing on Brigham, especially because he didn't know the government's specific plans or timetable. And, he was worried that he hadn't heard from his dear friend Thomas Kane for weeks now. For years, he was the best friend the Saints had who would come to their aid and tell their story to a hostile nation, but ever since his brother Elisha died, Thomas had been in seclusion, and now they really needed him!

Brigham and Heber C. Kimball, his counselor and long-time friend, along with a few other close confidants were huddled inside Young's tent. George Watt, Brigham's secretary and stenographer, arrived to transcribe the minutes of the meeting that they had hastily convened to discuss rumors about a potential invasion:

"Brother George," Brigham inquired, "we did send an invitation to Thomas, did we not?"

"Yes sir."

"But, no response?" George shook his head.

"I realize he couldn't just hire a coach, jump in a steamer and venture across the prairie to drop in for a weekend, but out of love and respect, I wanted him to know that we missed him and still count on his help," Brigham mused.

"It's probably Drummond," Heber interjected, referring to the irascible federal judge and avowed enemy of the Saints who had fled the territory. "That's why Kane's been so quiet, after Drummond's letters defaming him — and us."

"Yes, Old Scratch's favorite emissary, the corrupt judge who called us 'lechers' and had his mistress sit with him on the bench! And, it doesn't help that Thomas' family seems not to be too keen on his championing our cause, but then who is?"

"Senator Houston, our favorite man in Washington, is still with us," Apostle John Taylor volunteered. "He's as wise as Solomon and as smooth as silk, so I suppose two devoted friends are all we have at the moment, along with the Creator of heaven and earth."

"Thank you, John, for setting me straight! We all need our faith bolstered now and then, especially me. So, on to business: George, do you have a final count?"

George Watt handed the president his handwritten note showing the number invited and the number who made the trip.

"Bless their hearts! This is no easy trek up here.Reaching paradise was never supposed to be easy, I suppose. And, it thrills me that a few of our handcart survivors from October's disaster are here. I hope that gives them some solace. Is Ephraim back?"

"Brother Hanks?"

"Yes, of course," Brigham answered but he could see the consternation on George's face. He swallowed and spoke carefully:

"Yes, Ephraim Hanks has returned from Laramie, but without the mail. Remember when Bill Hickman returned from Missouri last month and reported what he learned?"

Brigham sighed: "I suppose we should have taken to heart what he warned us about." George nodded and then continued.

"Ephraim fears that the government has indeed cancelled the mail contract; we'll learn more soon."

The news hit the group hard and then George added:

"And that Mayor Smoot, Brother Stoddard and Porter Rockwell will be here tomorrow with all the details."Brigham paused, then said softly: "I suppose we should brace ourselves for more bad news, but put on a happy face. If they think we'll roll over again, they have another thing coming. Just remember, the Lord will provide."

AFTER WILLIAM WAGSTAFF AND LITTLE WILLY, his stepson, had spent the night counting stars in the wagon, they awoke as the sun broke over the top of Parley's Peak. Grabbing his shovel, William dug a channel from the stream and watched the spindly trees soak in the moisture. That's when he noticed the cloud of dust moving from left to right up on the canyon trail. The boy ran over to William and watched as they counted one, two, three, four horsemen, almost at a trot. They were pushing their animals.

William waved his hat over his head. "Hello!" he yelled. One of them tipped his hat in acknowledgment but they all kept moving.

"Who are those men, Pa?" Willy asked.

"Christian said they would be coming this way this morning: Four horsemen in a hurry," William muttered. To himself, he wondered, "the four horsemen of the Apocalypse?"

Everyone had heard the rumors. Ever since President Buchanan had taken the oath of office in D.C. earlier in the year, news from the east grew more and more ominous. Yes, the Democrats had beaten the upstart Republican John C. Fremont and his party's call for ending the twin relics of barbarism: slavery and polygamy. But, while the Democrats were in no hurry in attacking the former, the latter was fair game. The 'latter' as in Latter-day Saints. Everyone in the territory was talking about it in hushed tones. New immigrants brought copies of eastern papers that sounded bellicose, especially old Horace Greeley's *New York Tribune*. The orchardist looked down at the boy who was dropping bits of flotsam in the stream. It was just a year earlier that the widower had married William's mother, the merry little Mary Stubbs Wiseman, as they made their way on the Mormon trail here to Zion. Now Willy was like his own, would they all have to make another journey? He walked to his horse and wagon as he saw the four riders disappear over the crest of the hill. The boy was engrossed in his naval armada fighting their way downstream. William always loved to spend time in the orchard — like the Saints, he knew they would grow and prosper.

ABRAHAM SMOOT HELD HIS HAND UP to shield the morning sun and caught a glimpse of a series of peaks practically overhead.

"It's quite a sight," he said to his three companions as he slowed down his mount. His mare was foamy in sweat. They had left the Salt Lake City before dawn and had made good time. But they still had miles to go, all uphill. "Think we can make it up the canyon by noon?"

Orrin Porter Rockwell pulled his mount to a stop and patted her on the neck. At first glance, he appeared every bit the wild man his enemies described him to be. Hair down his back, a long beard, buckskin and leather and weapons in plain view. But, Mayor Smoot knew the man, knew his character and trusted him.

"If we don't spend time talking about it," Rockwell replied as he spit, wiping his mouth and beard with a kerchief.

And then he stopped and looked up to his left as Twin Peaks stared down at him.

"I like what I see," he declared.

"What is that?" the third horseman, Elias Smith, asked.

"A mighty fortress. A mighty, mountain fortress." And the Mormon gunman gave his mare a nudge, and she lunged ahead. Mayor Smoot and Judson Stoddard exchanged glances and a grim smile. They were glad Orrin Porter Rockwell was on their side. The four horsemen picked up the pace. After a mad dash of 520 miles in just 20 days, they were to be surprise guests at a picnic up the canyon. Few would be expecting them. Would they ruin the party?

Ahead of them some two miles or so, Christian Holz, who had overnighted in his wagon, turned and caught a glimpse of a cloud of dust as it veered left and moved up the canyon. He wanted to be there when the news broke like a dam. He feared that the art of war that he perfected in Europe and declared he had put away with his "natural man" would soon be resurrected and put to work here in the American West. At least, this time he would have something worth fighting for! He snapped the reins — he wanted to hear the news for himself. As they rode, Smoot feared that the news they were bringing would fuel war hysteria. Orrin Porter dismounted to remove a rock that had lodged in his horse's hoof. Evidence of the wagon train was scattered along the trail up ahead. A child's cap, part of a broken wheel and animal droppings lay before them. Wagon wheels had rutted the trail. Clearly, hundreds of wagons and animals had preceded them. Elias Smith broke the silence:

"There's a host of folks just up ahead that won't like what we're about to tell them," the postmaster declared. "But many, I suspect, knew this news was coming."

"Better us than Buchanan's butchers," Rockwell replied. "Brigham will know what to do. Nobody better to get us prepared." Abraham Smoot thought about his family and his farm and all that he invested in his mountain home and wondered out loud:

"Where else would we go? They'd just follow us, they'll never let us be. It's their 'Manifest Destiny' to drive all before them, the Indians, the Mormons. We're in the way of the fortune they believe is buried in our mountains. Can 40 thousand Mormons stop the determined madness of 60 million enemies who are bent on their destruction?"

Smoot answered his own question for all of them: "Not without Divine help, gentlemen, not by ourselves. Isn't the Lord on our side? Aren't we trying to build His Kingdom? Alone, we cannot succeed. With His help, we cannot fail." They all nodded in quiet agreement. Before they proceeded, they tuned back and took a final glimpse of the valley behind them with little patches of green here and there. Someday, the prophet Brigham had promised, the valley would be filled from north to south, from east to west. The Saints trusted he was right. And then they turned left, faced the canyon trail and pressed on.

2

BUCHANAN IS A TIMOROUS MAN

On the 24th, Brigham and his entourage, along with dozens of others, were busy finishing setting up the bowery for the official event later that day. At an altitude of nearly 8,000 feet surrounding Silver Lake, it was about 15 degrees cooler than down in the Salt Lake Valley. Still in the thinner atmosphere, labor was more difficult than in the city. President Young took a seat on the back of his wagon, took a handkerchief and wiped his brow. Heber Kimball brought him a tin cup of ice-cold mountain water and joined him.

"Thank you. Heber, we're not as young as we used to be, are we?"

"Maybe not, Brigham, but you can still outwork nearly every man in Zion."

"What choice do I have? We go from one pickle to another; we're driven from Ohio, then from Missouri, from Illinois until we landed here. What a beautiful place to be driven to though, isn't it? I suppose when Smoot and Porter arrive, we'll know better what our immediate challenges are. It may be just as Thomas reported in his letter."

Brigham piqued Heber's curiosity: "What was in the letter?"

Brigham thought for a second and then responded: "Basically, that President Buchanan is a 'timorous' man… and that he 'succumbs to outside pressure.' He reminds us how 'all those Yankee editors love to interfere in Utah affairs' and how he has not heart enough to save his friends from that pack of wolves,' as best as I can recall."

"Not a man's man," Heber said.

"Exactly. He would do poorly here."

A mountain jay was hopping from branch to branch just over their heads. Conifers surrounded the lake and aspen groves covered the mountain sides until the pines took over. But, near the top of the peaks all around them, the tree line revealed the jagged outline of the Wasatch mountain range.

Brigham chuckled: "I sometimes wonder if it weren't for that blasted milk cow, would my life be easier? Would I have all these problems including Washington, those Yankee editors and everything else and everyone pressing down on us?"

"What cow?"

"The cow that Mrs. Marsh shared with her neighbor," Brigham explained. Heber looked puzzled.

"Oh, you mean the tussle over the milk strippings that caused the Marsh's to get mad and stomp off, leaving you to be the successor to our beloved prophet Joseph," Heber grinned and then tried to console his friend: "Brigham, it was meant to be."

"Maybe. But, we both know that Martin Luther was wrong: Predestination is a false doctrine — we affect our own future. We are own agents, for better or worse... better if we listen to the Spirit."

He hoped the Saints would be up to the deadly threat that the travelers would likely confirm. *Where was Thomas B. Marsh when he needed him?* Brigham thought. *And where the horsemen?*

AN HOUR LATER, THEY WERE SPOTTED when 17-year-old Caleb Rasmussen and his young companion Hans Berthold were gathering firewood. Four horsemen emerged from a copse of quaking aspens on the trail leading to Silver Lake. Christian was still occupied with finishing his load. They each stacked their materials, balanced their axes on their burdens and peered out of the grove of aspens as the men rode by in a hurry. Porter glanced down at the young men and tipped his hat.

"Isn't that Porter Rockwell?" Caleb asked as they passed by.

"Never seen him up close. But, dey all seem pretty grim," the young German replied and then shielded himself from the sun beating down on them. "Let's hurry up der and see vat ve can learn," Hans urged his friend.

Caleb put his hand on his friend's shoulder: "Let's stay out of sight, not make a fuss."

But, they learned more than they wanted to. Caleb and Hans soon caught up with the four riders and followed them in the direction of President Young's campsite. Smoot's group found Brigham returning to his wagon with a toolbox. Caleb watched as he invited the visitors into his tent. One of Brigham's boys ran out, stopping at several other campsites to spread the news. Soon a dozen of the "Brethren" had joined Brigham and Smoot's foursome in the tent. Brigham grabbed some campstools and shut the tent flap behind him.

Caleb and Hans quietly approached the tent and settled behind a big fir tree. He pulled out a penknife and started to whittle. Hans decided to find himself a perch on the branch of a nearby tree. The young men couldn't hear exactly who was talking, but the message was clear: an Army was coming. A few words from the tent managed to drift to the teens. What Christian had earlier confided to them was now confirmed.

"Apparently General Harney wanted to wait for supplies and reinforcements, but he and General Scott seem to be at odds," a man in a deep voice confided to the others. "Kansas is still in turmoil over the Free-State, Slave-State business, and Harney wanted to stay there — you know, more glory for him. He even sent his adjutant to Washington to get more troops and supplies. A contingent in Laramie is now under his remote command and has been ordered to sit it out and wait for him."

"Wait for him? So, Harney's coming?" Someone asked — Caleb whispered to Hans: "Was that the prophet?"

"Mayor Smoot, just exactly who is this William Harney?"
A British voice asked.

Caleb whispered to Hans: "That's John Taylor." The teens then
scooted in closer to the tent so they wouldn't miss a word.

The mayor continued: "You know, Harney, the Squaw Killer,"
Some call him a hero. Says he prefers war and is adverse to peace.
He has quartermasters all over Kansas doing his bidding, buying
tents and cattle, hardtack, gunpowder, anything and everything
for an Army."

The teens heard another question: "So, how many has he
under arms?"

Smoot answered: "Hard to say. But we do know the names of
several units: the 5th and 10th infantry, 2nd Dragoons and artillery, the Phelps Battery. They are also heavily recruiting immigrants in New York and sending them west."

"To where?"

"To Kansas ...Fort Leavenworth, Now that disturbances are
supposed to be quieting down there, Harney is assembling his
forces there and getting them outfitted. We passed wagon train
after wagon train taking him supplies. Leavenworth is his embar-
kation point, his assembly area."

Brigham was now agitated: "Can we ascertain their intentions?"

Caleb was straining as he eavesdropped. He recognized Mayor
Smoot's voice. He was certain it was Brother Brigham who posed
the question.

"Harney is out for blood and looks to make a name for himself.
He is boasting he wants to hang us all. Even heard say they are
buying all the rope they can get their hands on. But, he is at odds
with General Scott. The troops are a motley lot: Americans who
don't want to make war against their own people and many Welsh,
Irish and Germans who have heard there are a lot of foreigners
here. We're told there are already desertions. They don't appear

to be of one mind. But, we understand that the Missourians are still stirring up trouble against us."

Hans slid down the tree and landed hard. He motioned to Caleb. They huddled under a low branch to discuss what they had heard.

"So, what's the prophet going to have us do: run or fight?" Caleb asked. Hans told him what he had overheard, and then added: "I've come from halfway across *de vorld* and been beaten by Hessian police. I know how to use my musket. If Brigham needs me, I'm fighting."

"But, what if we have to pull up stakes and move on?" Caleb asked.

"Where would we go? Mexico, Canada, Russian Alaska? I'm sure they'll tell us something, maybe tonight after the dance. I trust Brigham and the brethren, don't you?" he asked.

"What choice do we have?" Caleb responded, "We ought to keep this to ourselves for now."

A voice behind them responded. It was Christian Holz, who had also been eavesdropping.

"That's good advice. When the time comes, we might need the help of strong young oxen like you," he said as he put an arm around Caleb.

"You can count on it," Both young men turned and walked back to their campsite and waved to Christian as they left him there. Christian watched them and felt a rush of conflicting emotions as the young men disappeared behind a couple of pine trees. Anger, sadness, faith and apprehension. *Is 10 years in this place sufficient that no power can dislodge us?* He wondered. He had heard Brigham make that promise. Christian realized that he had to muster the faith necessary faith to make his sacrifice.*What about the new settlements that the Church had recently established in Oregon, California and at Fort Limhi up north? Would these outward settlements have to be recalled? And what about*

missionaries in the east, Europe and the isles of the sea? What about them?

He turned back to his wagon and team; they needed a rest, some food and water. So did he.

Later that evening after all the evening meals had been prepared and consumed, the Saints had gathered around a bonfire near Silver Lake. Caleb and Hans found themselves a low-hanging branch. A riser had been placed near the fire and a bearded man stepped forward:

"Brethren and sisters, please gather in and find a seat if you can. We have some road weary travelers who just arrived from the East," a voice called out from the riser.

"Who vas dat?" Hans asked.

"I'm not sure. I can't see."

Dozens of others joined the throng, some pulling themselves up on a tree branch, others on a rock or wagon bed. Hundreds of Mormon men, women and children craned their necks and raised up on tip-toes to catch a glimpse of the speakers and hear what news they had to share.

Far in the back under a Douglas fir, Christian was sitting with Winnie Rasmussen on a boulder with a good view of the proceedings, but nearly out of ear shot. As the crowd was jostling for a better view of the announcement, Winnie turned to Christian:

"So, you brought me out here for a reason?"

He hesitated. "Yes, away from the crowd."

"Because...?"

He took a quick glance at the crowd and wondered if this was indeed their "moment."

"Because you're right: A man does not build a house, a home, for himself. I am good with my hands. I am good with wood. My family name Holz means 'wood' in German."

He swallowed hard. She smiled: "I know. I understand a little German."

"I was thinking that this house I'm building, uh, you know, uh, starting to build...I still have to finish the foundation..."

Winnie watched him sink deeper and deeper, so she threw him a line: "And you're thinking there's room for more than one."

He nodded. She took his hand.

"And you want a roommate, ...someone to keep it neat and tidy, do you? Probably a woman, they're neater and tidier than men."

"I've heard that. Are you neat and tidy?"

"Ask my mother," Winne quipped.

"I plan to, but there's this problem."

She looked him in the eye and demanded an answer:

He continued and pointed at the speaker: "This problem."

She turned her head and saw President Young raise his hands to quiet the crowd. "I'm not sure I understand," Winnie said.

"If they need me, I will volunteer. I will go into the mountains and stay the Army's arrival. It is what I do."

Winnie grabbed his hand:

"What? I thought you cut down trees!"

"Before I cut down trees, I cut down men."

She sat there in stunned silence then found her voice again:

"You once told me how frightful, horrible it was in the war with the Danes, my people, that you would never take up arms again. That you feared for your soul if you did."

"Yes, I said that. But it may not come to that. It's because of you and your mother and... all these people, these Saints... that I will go, if they want me." They slid off the boulder and stepped away from the crowd to find a quieter spot, away from the bonfire and the group. They had some thinking to do and decisions to make.

"Where's your mother?" Christian inquired.

"Let's find out." As they walked into the shadows, more to be alone than to find her mother, the tempo picked up behind them.

Young Turks like Hans and Caleb were all spit and vinegar when Abraham Smoot took the stage,

The black-bearded mayor cleared his throat and for a few minutes shared his impressions with his fellow Saints and tried to calm their fears about a possible invasion — not any easy thing to do. The young men stood on their perch for a better view, and by now, Christian and Winnie had returned without having found the widow Rasmussen. Smoot began speaking:

"The mobocrats in Missouri are very curious about our capabilities here. I think I warned them well when I assured them we could raise 50 or 60 thousand, more or less." Caleb gave Hans a pat on the back. He turned and smiled and gave the mayor his undivided attention..

"From what we saw, we do not believe that those soldiers want to come here. They do not want to shed the blood of Americans; the Germans, the Irish and the Welsh in their company know we have many of their countrymen here, and I doubt they wish them harm. We have it on good authority that many of their number are deserting and making tracks back to where they came from.

"They are pulling some 700 heavy wagons and are barely on their way. We all know better than they do that it can be slow going. And, the weather can stop even the best outfitted trains."

The Saints were eating it up. Christian was pleasantly surprised that he saw no sense of panic. Heber C. Kimball then clarified the First Presidency's official position, erasing any doubt in the members' minds as to their commitment:

"The States evidently commenced a war with us, and are determined to put an end to us or our religion, neither of which they can do, as they have commenced a job they never can accomplish, we may expect a howling from the regions below. The Gentiles never can again put a yoke on Israel, and some funny

times will be seen before they will acknowledge our independence. One thing is certain, the cannot exterminate the Saints, neither can they make them forsake their religion."

Again, Kimball's words were met with hurrahs and applause.

The Saints had learned first-hand that the federal authorities sent west to oversee them had their own agendas. Judges, surveyors, postal officials and Indian agents came and left early, sometimes with the funds they were given to administer their offices. It was not a choice assignment to be sent so far from home, and so, the Utah settlers did not get America's best and brightest to administer federal law in the Utah Territory. Of the eight officials appointed from 1850 to 1856, five fled out of fear or frustration, two died and one was not reappointed. But, the one who did the most harm to the Saints was Associate Justice William Drummond, who campaigned to replace Brigham Young as governor and whose personal life was so offensive that he earned no respect — he had left his wife and children in Illinois and brought with him to Utah his mistress who often sat with him on the bench. When he finally fled the territory, he campaigned continually for the newly elected president, James Buchanan, writing letters to dozens of newspapers, each calling on the government — and a new governor — him — to send the U.S. Army to Utah to "quell the rebellion." Drummond was seen to be the one person most responsible for the crisis about to engulf the Mormons.

Christian looked at Winnie and took her by the hand. He led her through the crowd. Now it was time for them to consider each other.

Finally, she broke the silence: "We need to speak to my mother about our decision."

"I'm not clear as to what our decision is," he fibbed.

"I know what decision is," she said. She stopped and turned to him and kissed him, much to his delight and surprise.

"That is my decision," she announced.

Christian broke into a grin: "I like your choice of words."

They set out to find Sister Rasmussen, Winnie's mother, and break the news as Abraham Smoot completed his remarks. Orrin Porter Rockwell then reassured the Saints of their strength and the rightness of their cause and other members of the Twelve promised deliverance.Sister Mara Rasmussen was standing with her neighbor, the lonely man who allowed her family to use his extra wagon to get up to the festivities. Per Andersen was listening to the speeches and was calming and reassuring Mara:

"Our friends are at work. Dr. John Bernhisel, the Territory of Utah's delegate to Congress, is planning to meet with President Buchanan.. Senator Sam Houston of Texas is in our camp and our great friend and ally Thomas Kane will defend our cause. But that is not all, God will not forsake His people in their extremity. Isn't that right, Christian?" Brother Andersen asked as the young couple drew nearer.

"If we do our part and live up to our covenants," Christian replied as he waited for an opportunity to address Winnie's mother alone.

"Do you know this Kane, Brother Andersen?" Christian asked.

"I know that he was raised up. And I know that President Young counts on him. And so should we."

"What choice do we have?" Christian replied. "But, we can't expect that anything worth having will be easy — it never is."

Christian surveyed the scene before him. A bonfire illuminated the huge throng of Saints tucked into a grove of trees as if they were cupped in a pair of warm hands. That's where it all began, a grove of trees, Christian thought, reflecting on the story of Joseph Smith's first prayer. Now people were once again seeking answers and hoping Providence would smile on them again and show them the path, this time a path to safety and security. The night sky was ablaze with a million points of light. At this elevation, even in July, the air was cool, yet not even a hint of clouds.

No rain could be seen on the horizon. That's why the Saints had to dig canals — to get water from high up in the mountains down into the valleys. There never was enough rain. It made for back-breaking work, but the climate-at least at night in the mountains-was livable, comfortable even compared to the Midwest or the East. Nobody wanted this place 10 years ago. It was a total surprise to Christian when he arrived less than two years earlier — the dry air, the lack of trees, the high-altitude desert — especially after growing up in northern Europe. Now, it seems, outsiders wanted to get their hands on the supposed gold and silver that lay hidden in the rugged Rocky Mountains that surrounded them..

Winnie came up from behind and startled him. She put her arm in his.

"Why can't they just leave us alone?" she asked, not really expecting an answer. "Why does everything have to be so hard?"

Christian squeezed her arm and walked her to her wagon.

"May I call on you after my work here is done," he asked. "You may call on me anytime. You know the address," she said with a smile.

"So you've seen me outside, praying softly and hoping to be invited in," he said with a grin.

"Oh, that was you? When's the occasion?"

"I will drop you a note. Soon. When the president speaks. My neighbor has a very nice carriage."

She smiled, and he walked away.

Now Christian had to find a neighbor with a nice carriage. Miracles do happen. Maybe the Abbotts had room in theirs.

3

DEFENDING THE DOWNTRODDEN

The grizzled old man they called "Hunchie" was screaming, "Where's Mr. Greeley?" In the far corner of the pressroom where the typesetters toiled, picking ascenders and descenders, adding leads and slugs to their composing sticks and looking for just the right drop cap, there was pandemonium.

The editor of the salacious *New York Tribune,* Mr. Horace Greeley, abolitionist and the quintessential newspaper pioneer of the penny-press era, was nowhere to be found. Hunchie had to find him now or they would miss the deadline — trains don't wait.

As Elbert Reinholdt (the "Dutchman') turned to answer Hunchie, the Dutchman stumbled, knocking the composing stick out of Elbert's hand, sending caps, lower case text, leading and Em spacers flying; the opening paragraph of page one's lead-in was scattered all over the floor.

Now, the typesetter's motto, "watch your P's and Q's," took on a whole new meaning as pieces of lead covered the floor. The man who bore the moniker of "Hunchie" earned it (His real name was Fletcher, but no one knew that). He had been with Greeley the longest, learned the typesetting trade 40 years earlier and had been bent over type cases ever since he was a boy, and as a result, now took on the appearance of the bell ringer at Notre Dame.

Fletcher's (aka Hunchie's) florid face was now beet red, the man with more chins than fingers, bellowed louder than ever: *"we have a deadline to meet or Horrible Horace will have your heads!"*

The Dutchman, Bertrand and Francis stood frozen in their tracks. Hunchie felt beady little eyes boring into him: Horrible Ho-

race, their boss, was in the doorway staring at him. The four type-setters couldn't hold it back. First, Francis, then the Dutchman and all four broke into hysterical laughter.

"Horrible? So, that's what you call me behind my back…Hunchie! So, I'm Horrible Horace, am I… Hunchie?" Horace Greeley was trying to repress a smile, then a giggle, then couldn't stop laughing himself. Now everyone was laughing but "Hunchie."

Greeley turned to the man picking up the type: "So, what's scattered all over the floor, Elbert?"

'Unfortunately, sir, it's our page one lead story. I'm sorry, but…"

"That's all right. I hurried back to tell you that we have a new lead. I was at the telegraph office; we are redoing the story. Just pick up the type and resort it and return it all to the type case.

Francis was puzzled, they all were: "What are we replacing it with?"

"This," he said. Greeley handed Francis the hand-written telegram.

"Come into my office and I'll dictate the header for you. It needs to be a banner across the top, something like "American Hero Dies. Brother Retrieves Body. Lies in State in New Orleans."

Reinholdt was shocked: "Well, who is it? Shouldn't we mention his name in the banner?"

Greeley sighed: "Do I have to spell everything out for you people? If we put his name at the top, who will read the whole article? We want to grab the reader — how many times do I have to remind you of that? Force them to read it!

"Well, who died?"

"Elisha Kane, hero of the Arctic, that's who." Greeley walked into his office with Francis on his heels. Everyone was stunned — no one could speak.

"He had a brother?"

"Yes," Greeley said as Elbert was closing the door.

"His name is Thomas, Thomas Leiper Kane."

GREELEY'S NEW YORK TRIBUNE WASN'T THE ONLY NEWSPAPER that reported the tragic death of Elisha Kane. It made headlines all over the east in cities big and small wherever Mr. Samuel Morse's telegraph relayed the news.

In Philadelphia, the Kanes were not the only family that was thunderstruck by Elisha's death. Not far away, the President-elect James Buchanan heard about it early in the morning delivered by his chief aide and advisor James Van Dyke. He and Buchanan's staff had been up late the night finalizing plans for Buchanan's inauguration on March 5th, less than two weeks away.

"Mr. President," Van Dyke said quietly to Buchanan..."

"You can still call me J.B. or Buck, even the old Public Functionary — I'm not the president — yet."

"Just practicing, sir. Problem is, I have some bad news, and I didn't want Harriet to hear it from me. The explorer and Mexican War hero, Elisha Kane, has died. I understand he and Harriet were close" Buchanan was taken aback.

'I had heard he was in Havana and quite ill."

Harriett Lane, the bachelor president's niece, was also to be "unofficially inaugurated" as the new First Lady of the United States. Orphaned years ago and raised by her Uncle James, she had been his secret weapon when he was selected as the Democrat's compromise candidate between the slave-holders in the South and northern Democrats like the Kanes who abhorred the practice. The Buchanans and the Kanes had represented two different camps in Pennsylvania — originally the Kanes had supported former Vice President George Dallas who served under President Polk. While the connection between Buchanan and Judge Kane was "professional," rumors had it that Elisha Kane and Harriet Lane were close. How close? James Buchanan would soon discover that for himself.

"Van Dyke, I haven't even seen her today — she was meeting with the musicians and the caterers. I think she's at the Willard."

"I'll send someone, but in all likelihood, she already knows."

LONG BEFORE THERE WERE SOLDIERS ABOUT TO MARCH ON ZION, more than a decade in fact, even earlier in the late 1830's, the stage had been set for the crisis the Mormon pioneers were facing. Even before the country learned of the Latter-day Saints' practice of polygamy, there were ministers, politicians and newspaper editors — in the name of reform — who were campaigning against the Mormons' millennial view of a theocratic government led by Christ himself.

The critics' perspective ran counter to the Democrat Party's position of local sovereignty or self-government, especially in slave states, where that institution clashed with the romantic notion of human rights, women's suffrage and religious freedom as espoused by such 19th-century thought leaders such as abolitionist William Garrison, reformer Thomas Carlyle, and Ralph Waldo Emerson.

It was a young man, also a romantic and Emerson's friend, Thomas Kane, whose defiance of society's norms and the institutions of the day, specifically the Fugitive Slave Act, led him to devote his life to "defend the downtrodden"— the Latter-day Saints.

Thomas Leiper Kane, at about 5'3"and pushing 100 lbs, was the son of a prominent federal Judge, John Kane, in Philadelphia. Thomas proved to be the Mormons' best, longest-lasting friend who was in the right place at the right time to come to their aid.

To most of the Latter-day Saints huddled up against the Rocky Mountains, it may have seemed they were all alone, that it was them against the world. But since leaving the prairie flatlands and climbing the mountains, they had made a few friends.

Sam Houston was one, best known as the first president of the Republic of Texas, and by 1856, a U.S. Senator representing his state. And Houston's close friend and fellow Texas Ranger, Seth M. Blair, was another.

Blair, a convert to Mormonism, kept Houston in touch with Brigham Young and the Saints, and especially with Apostle George A. Smith, with whom Houston had a close friendship. In 1846, Houston tried unsuccessfully to encourage the Mormons to come

south and settle in Texas, rather than continuing west to the Great Basin. Two other allies of the Saints were Army officers, Lt. Colonel James Allen and Lt. Col. Phillip St. George Cooke, both of whom led the 500-member Mormon Battalion in the war against Mexico.

But, it was Thomas Kane who not only put his reputation, but also his very life on the line to come to the aid of the beleaguered people.

In the spring of 1846, 24-year-old Thomas Kane had read about the Mormons' plight after they had been driven from Nauvoo, Illinois, and had set up temporary quarters on the banks of the Missouri river, one in Mt. Pisgah, Iowa and another across the river in Nebraska. So, when he had heard that the Mormons' presiding authority in the eastern states, Elder Jesse C. Little, was speaking in Philadelphia, Thomas' curiosity got the best of him. He went to the meeting.

Elder Little had been charged by Brigham Young to "make friends and influence people" in the America's biggest, most influential cities — New York, Washington and Philadelphia — and thus, he would hold meetings to encourage more understanding about the Saints and their perceived odd practices.

And, along with Apostle John Taylor who was editing a newspaper in New York, called *The Mormon*, Little was charged, where possible, to raise donations to help the suffering Saints.

This particular gathering in Philadelphia would prove to be significant for the Mormons because of the Saints' dire circumstances in their camps on the Missouri. Later, Kane would confess that the meeting was providential for him as well.

After the meeting, Kane invited Elder Little to his home. It was a typical warm summer evening in steamy Philadelphia, but they found themselves in comfortable surroundings. It had been a long day for the Mormon elder. Thomas was eager to learn more, especially for a young man from a well-to-do family. He put the somewhat older gentleman to ease.

"So, Elder Little, tell me a little about yourself and how you came to be a Mormon preacher."

"Mr. Kane, it's a curious story really…"

"You may call me Thomas — all my friends do."

"And, I'm Jesse, and I'm not really a preacher in the traditional sense. We have no paid clergy in the Church of Jesus Christ of Latter-day Saints. I was called, as they say, by prophecy by men in authority. I was a school teacher, worked in dry goods, as a blacksmith and a wagon builder. But, when I met Elder Parley P. Pratt, everything changed. I'd only been a member a little more than a year. I read the *Book of Mormon* and Elder Pratt's *Voice of Warning* and was touched by the Spirit, and so here I am. Thank you for the invitation by the way — you have a lovely home.

"Thank you, my pleasure," Thomas said.

Little continued: "My charge now is to testify of the restoration of Christ's church and to help the beleaguered Saints camped on the Missouri, to raise funds and tell of our persecution from place to place as we seek a permanent home."

"In Upper California…?" Kane asked.

"Yes, which is currently part of Mexico."

"Exactly. Which is food for thought," Thomas mused, "Authorities are looking for able-bodied men…"

"I believe I know where you're going with this…"

"I know people in the administration, President Polk and Vice President Dallas. They are looking for men to help secure California. Do you think your President Young would entertain discussions about helping supply troops to support the effort?

"We should find out," Little replied.

They did.

That day in 1846 at Thomas's home, the two men talked for hours, making Elder Little miss his next speaking engagement. For the next few days, they planned their strategy that took them to Washington D.C. and then by train to St. Louis. And in those efforts to enlist more men to help fight in the Mexican-American War, Thomas Kane became more thoroughly caught up in the Mormons' plight. His was to be a life-long journey working as as an advocate for the Church, but he never looked back.

At the time of the ensuing conflict with Mexico, Kane had ambitions to be appointed to some prestigious position in the West, maybe a governorship or similar position.

Eventually, he did find himself in the White House with President Polk, an old friend of his father's. He told his brother Elisha that "we must not be meek and mild if we are to inherit this earth." In other words, don't be timid in the presence of a president! He wasn't.

He played his part well. The next day with Senator Lewis Cass of Michigan accompanying Thomas, Polk agreed to have the State Department draft a letter endorsing Kane's efforts. But, the process was going at a snail's pace until Kane reminded the administration that while the "Saints are true-hearted Americans," the British may try to befriend them (due to uncertainty about who owned the Northwest Territories — 54'40° or Fight was still fresh in voters' minds. This threat sealed the deal. Colonel Stephen W, Kearny received his orders to march on California and the Mormon Battalion was born.

Little and Kane took different routes from St. Louis, but met again at the Mormons' temporary settlement on Potawatomi land here Kane would finally meet President Brigham Young and come to learn more about and become devoted to the people the world called Mormons. As Kane stepped down from the mail coach, Elder Little recognized the small dark man; Little and Kane had taken separate routes from St. Louis to Council Bluffs. They had some disagreements earlier, but realized they were both essential to their success.

"People are waiting for you," Little said with alacrity. Thomas followed him down a muddy trail closer to the river.

This was hardly the setting for a prophet and his counselors, their meeting place was not much more than a log hut, but it provided some shade from the summer sun. Jesse Little introduced Thomas Kane to Willard Richards and Heber C. Kimball, the president's counselors and to the famous man himself, President Brigham Young. It was a warm welcome.

"So, you're the young man who has written about the Battalion — very persuasive, indeed," Young said as he pumped the young man's hand; it was meetings like this first one that prompted Thomas to write home about how he appreciated the Mormons, these hardy men with their soft hearts and their hard hands.

"Yes, and we hope they have their intended effect," Thomas said. "I do carry some correspondence for you and the colonel from the president, so I suppose my visit here is official and I hope welcome. I believe your willingness to provide some of your best young men for this military adventure in California will not only be a demonstration of your patriotism for which you will earn the administration's confidence and provide needed funds for your journey, but also provide you some breathing room from those who wish you harm,"

President Young agreed and added: "We pray that our men will march in step as good soldiers and prove their worth in spite of what many of us believe to be Senator Benton's intention to take troops and pounce upon our women and children and sweep them out of existence."

After the initial introductory meeting, Kane mingled with the Mormons for the next few days visiting various encampments accompanied by an officer in the battalion, Henry G. Boyle. On one occasion, they came upon a Mormon praying in the woods; Boyle later reported what Kane had told him to his superiors:

"Thomas told me that he never listened to a prayer so contrite, so earnest and fervent, and so full of inspiration. We had involuntarily taken off our hats as though we were in a sacred presence... As Kane stood there I could see tears falling from his face,

while his bosom filled with the fulness of his emotions. And for some time after the man had arisen from his knees and walked away towards his encampment, the Colonel sobbed like a child and could not trust himself to utter a word. When he finally did get control of his feelings, he first words were: 'I am satisfied: Your people are solemnly and terribly in earnest.'"

But after a few days, Kane's frail nature got the best of him. Little reported his condition to the president:

"Our friend Thomas is not doing well; he has a very high fever and is not entirely coherent. What should we do? I believe his lying at the point of death."

"What does he need" Brigham asked.

"For one thing, he wants the military doctor in Leavenworth to assuage concerns from outsiders about his 'cause of death;' that it was of natural causes…"

"And not us? So, he's more concerned about what others may think of us than he might die?"

"Exactly."

"I need to see him immediately!" Brigham declared. "I'll get an urgent message to the Army doctor, not to spare horse flesh, but to come as rapidly as possible," Young said.

In the tiny hovel of a hospital, Latter-day Saint nurses cared for him by day and by night on the banks of the Missouri, fighting off mosquitoes and cooling him off. After a couple of days, after visits from the president, his fever broke, and he was speaking with his care-givers.

"President Young told me about your Patriarch Smith, John Smith, that he could give me a blessing," Thomas asked as he propped himself up.

"He should be here soon," his nurse replied.

Later that afternoon, the patriarch of the church and uncle of Joseph Smith did arrive and blessed him saying that "angels had been protecting him and defended him and that not even a hair of head would fall by the hands of an enemy and that his name would be held in remembrance by the Saints for generations."

Then, to Thomas' surprise, since he was not yet married, Patriarch Smith promised him that he would "marry and raise sons and daughters who shall be esteemed as the excellent of the earth." These blessings, Smith said, "would be conditional upon his continued service to God."

Six weeks later, Thomas Kane was back in Pennsylvania, and according to his family, returned "with a constitution altered and certainly more flesh, more equanimity of spirit than he has had since boyhood." Upon his return, he reported to President Polk that the president's "wise and humane policy toward the nation," combined with his own efforts had secured Mormon loyalty to the nation and personal devotion to the president.

By virtue of his making acquaintance with not only the federal officers leading the Mormon Battalion, including Col. Phillip St. George, Thomas also made friends with both the Army as well as with many battalion members, including 16-year-old Lot Smith, who in 10 years would cause grief for the Utah Expedition marching on Zion.

True to his word, Thomas Kane kept up his public relations activities for his isolated friends in Utah, hoping that the "Saints would create a new Puritan commonwealth through the principle of cooperation carried out on a grand scale."

By 1857, Polk was gone, and like Joseph of old, Kane realized there was a new pharaoh in town. Buchanan was now in power. Brigham Young had appealed to Kane to represent the Mormons as the non-voting delegate in Congress; he declined, and Mormon John Bernhisel was appointed in his stead.

But by now, the heat had been turned up, and Thomas Kane found himself in the middle of a bonfire again. For ten years, letters between Brigham and Thomas filled their in-baskets. He and President Young promised to keep up their correspondence with each other and did so for years. And they did.

"HENRY, PAPA'S HOME," CYNTHIA SHOUTED TO THE BOY who put his collection of pine cones into his cap and ran out from behind the barrel. What did Papa have in the bag?

William Stowell, who had adopted his deceased sister's orphan son, William Henry Packard, had found himself a wife and the boy a mother. Stowell scraped his boots off on the remains of a stump, unbuttoned his coat and carried the surprise inside their tiny cabin. Suddenly, the bag came alive, moving around on the table.

The 8-year-old whom his stepmother Cynthia called "Henry" was fascinated with what Stowell had carried in.

"Papa, what's in the sack?? A cat?"

"Henry, do we eat cats?"

"Only if we're really hungry, but I'm not that hungry."

Cynthia smiled.

The boy approached the bag and touched it, and it lurched at him and he jumped back.

"So, are we going to eat it?" Little William Henry smiled. "It's not a cat, is it, Papa?"

William shook his head. Now the boy was really excited.

"It's a puppy!"

"Do we eat puppies," William asked.

"Never! So, what is it?"

"It's not a puppy," William assured Henry. "But, it's for dinner."

"But, it's still alive!"

"It won't be alive when we do. It has feathers, but we'll have to take them off first," William said.

Cynthia smiled at this conversation, but knew her husband needed to satisfy the boy's curiosity:

"OK, William, let the cat out of the bag. What is it, a chicken?"

"Kind of. It's a sage grouse. I'll be back in a minute. Maybe there's something we can put with it. Cynthia, can you start a pot of water boiling? Got to get all these pin feathers out." She was already in the process. He grabbed a hatchet and a butcher knife and left to do his grisly business. She was peeling turnips and cutting up an onion when there was a knock at the door.

It was Bishop Peterson.

'I thought I saw William return. Gone to the privy?" The bishop could barely speak.

"No, he'll be right back — he's slaughtering a grouse. Why, what's wrong?"

"I need to speak with him. Got some bad news…" the bishop said, unable to contain the terrible news he had come to share.

"About his brother?" He nodded. Cynthia put the paring knife down and sat at the table. She motioned to him, and he took the other chair, and they waited for William's return.

She forgot about the grouse.

4

THE POWERS THAT BE

There's post for you, Mr. Bernhisel," the clerk said to Utah's territorial delegate to Congress. Bernhisel thanked the young man, walked downstairs, unlocked the door to his office, took the stack of mail, and stepped inside the confines of his claustrophobic basement office in an ancient brick building half a block from the Capitol. He looked around, fumbled in the darkened room illuminated by a peephole of a window, lit a candle and sighed.

"Jonah, indeed!" He laughed at his own description of himself that he had recently shared with Thomas Kane who asked him a fortnight ago in Philadelphia how it felt to be Utah's only representative in Washington. They were huddling in Kane's home.

"As the only Mormon anywhere in sight, I feel like I'm trapped in the belly of the beast, living in the lower abdomen of a dungeon-like cavity like...like Jonah where I'm being slowly digested. At least Jonah was lucky enough to be vomited up on the seashore after just three days," he confided to Kane. "I am a modern version of the Old Testament prophet, deposited here against my will with no visible means of escape! That was his final answer — and he was sticking to it, he said, moaning to Kane, his rueful answer turning to laughter.

"At least you can laugh about it," Thomas said at that time.

But, now things were looking even darker inside the beast.

That was weeks ago. Bernhisel missed Thomas. He loved the man just as Brigham and all the Saints did. Maybe there's a letter from him! He pulled the chair over to his roll-top desk, lit the oil lamp so he could actually read his mail and sort through his correspondence: Hmm, a letter from his sister. A report from Elder Taylor in New York. Ahh, and a fat envelope from Salt Lake City: **The Office of the President.** He checked it to see if it had been opened and resealed. Didn't look like it. The oil lamp was illuminating the room now. Yes, it was morning in Washington D.C., but the basement window was more like a porthole in a steamer or the peep hole in a prison door. He continued sorting.

"Finally, here it is, a letter from Philadelphia!" He said aloud addressing his non-present friend:

"Thomas, what new intrigue have you uncovered for me today?" He used his penknife to cut the envelope open. He felt something rub up against his leg. That would be Drummond, the official territorial Tomcat, Bernhisel's only living assistant, whose main job was to stalk, catch, kill and consume unwanted rodents.

Bernhisel wished he could send Drummond — the cat, not the justice — against larger prey. Would that be wrong? Such a long list. The cat had dropped his catch on Delegate Bernhisel's boot.

"Good job, Drummond!" Bernhisel said — now go have supper! He scratched the cat's ears, and the feline padded away, the catch in his jaws.

The feline Drummond bore the same name as Justice William Drummond, the vagabond, dissolute whoremonger and associate federal justice for the territory of Utah now missing from action after defaming the territory and its leaders before fleeing. Thomas muttered that it defamed the cat to call it Drummond, but Bernhisel defended the choice because the rust-colored Tabby looked a lot like the justice, only brighter. And thinner.

"Let's see what you've has been doing — or not doing — since you retreated into your mountain hideaway. Why have you been so reclusive?" Then it hit him: Verastus. No wonder his letters had stopped coming. Maybe the letter will explain it. Bernhisel ripped open the envelope and began reading.

Mr. Horace Greeley, newspaper pioneer, and in his own mind innovator and champion of the First Amendment, had heard about Albert Gallatin Browne Jr., or who Greeley referred to as Mr. Fancy Pants, the young man who was fidgeting outside his door. Browne was a recent graduate of the University of Heidelberg and an alumnus of Harvard Law.

"You can quit pacing about and come in now," Greeley commanded from inside his cluttered office, stacked high with books, recent copies of his *New York Tribune* and piles of the competition's "rags" as he called them. A friend of a friend had suggested to the irascible Mr. Greeley that he should at least talk to Browne before dismissing him out of hand, despite his his involvement years earlier with his Abolitionist friends who slew a Southern sympathizer. "Just talk to him, Horace," his friend said. Browne took a seat.

"So, Albert, is that how I should address you, or should I call you Herr Doktor Professor Browne?" Greeley asked with a smirk.

"No, sir, Albert is fine," Browne said with a laugh.

Greeley continued: "So, why would you want to do something as 'low brow' as working as a newspaper correspondent for one of the 15 publications like ours currently still selling newspapers in New York City? Are you wanting to keep a low profile from the Anthony Burns matter, hoping to get far away from that episode?"

"No, I was cleared of any implication in that affair..."

"...while you were in Europe..."

"Yes, that's true, but I still oppose the Fugitive Slave Act..."

"And, an Abolitionist?" Greeley asked wryly.

"Well, as you know, I did attend school with many forward-thinking Europeans, liberals like myself, opposed to social injustice. I arrived after their failed attempt at revolution. The princes held sway. The monarchs still hold all the cards. We have our problems, too."

"Like the twin relics of barbarism, polygamy and slavery?"

The young man showed his concern for the downtrodden: "Exactly!"

"I read your vita." Greeley said and then pressed him:

"But, why leave the comforts of civilization to venture into the West?"

"Manifest Destiny, sir. Manifest Destiny. That's where things are going, where fortunes...and history are made."

Greeley smiled; he got the answer he was looking for: "Then, you should pack your bags, get some comfortable clothes, boots, a warm coat, maybe a sidearm and plan on leaving this week for Kansas."

Browne smiled. "You will not regret it, sir."

Greeley grunted. "No, I will not and neither will you if you keep your nose to the grindstone, as long as you stay one step ahead of Mr. Bennett at the Herald. The pay is $2,000 annual plus expenses. Can you live on that?"

"Yes sir!'

"Then, take the next train to Fort Leavenworth and keep me apprised of the war that is about to happen."

"War, sir?"

"Yes, Albert, the war before the war. It will be good practice for you. Keep the missives coming, Browne. I expect something weekly. Good luck to you. Now I have a paper to publish."

ONLY A FEW PEOPLE RECOGNIZED THE GREAT MAN awaiting the arrival of Utah Delegate John Bernhisel secluded in the far corner of the gentleman's club overlooking the Potomac on Georgetown's Water Street. That was fine with Texas Senator Sam Houston.

After all, Chesapeake oysters in the shell were still in abundance this late in the spring of 1857, and he enjoyed feasting on them in solitary. As a man from a land of little rain accustomed to dusty trails covered in cattle, this was a delicacy few of his countrymen enjoyed, and he was not opposed to indulging himself in this pleasant pastime.

Let Bernhisel arrive when he's good and ready, thought the senator, and his wife Margaret's absence meant that he could order a pint of Pilsner stout or a glass of Chablis without her even raising an eyebrow. She warned her husband countless times that eating raw oysters were likely a cause of bathsore fever, but he had dismissed that as an old-wives' tale.

"Senator, more of the same?" The waiter knew the man — he was a regular.

"Just a Pilsner, please, Hammond," Houston replied.

At that moment, Bernhisel spotted his friend in his favorite spot luxuriating in his usual choice of shellfish, **genus crassostrea, family ostreidae**. He joined the man whom most Texans recognized as their Founder, the first president of the Texas Republic and now just one of a few dozen United States Senators, but whose unique skills and instincts had been honed to perfection after more than two decades in the Byzantine world of American politics. Bernhisel knew this, as did Brigham Young, Thomas Kane and their allies. One could not have a more loyal friend skilled in the dark arts required for survival in Washington than Old Sam.

Bernhisel spoke: "Sorry, Senator, it took me awhile to hail a hansom, especially in the rain."

"So, it's raining?"

"Yes sir, it is, in Washington fashion. Is Blair coming."

"He should be here shortly. Want an oyster? I've had my fill — consumed an entire congregation of them." Bernhisel declined; he was familiar with bathsore fever. Houston let another shellfish slide down to its final resting place: "Any news from the West?" Bernhisel hesitated as he reflected on his last voluminous package of mail from Utah:

"Brigham's still brooding over the trouble that that the old reprobate Judge Drummond created with his basketful of lies; his whereabouts are still in doubt since he and his little brightly colored mistress flew the coop from Utah. And, he's not the only one: Our friend Colonel Thomas L. Kane is planning on meeting the president face to face and sharing with him Brigham Young's well wishes, and of course, concerns, especially in light of the tall tales by Drummond and others. You and he are just about all the friends we have."

"Happy to help, and how is my old friend, George, the Bear?"

"The bear? Oh, Elder George Smith. He still has his doubts about the prospects of peace. His people in the southern settlements have a much harder time of it — they're so dry and isolated. Did you hear from Blair?"

"I certainly did. And, he's doing his best to share the Mormon's story," Houston replied as he pulled a letter from his coat pocket. "He's persuasive, especially because of his service with the Texas Rangers — he's working the delegation. Listen to this, he says *'we are unheard, we are condemned without cause; we have been disenfranchised as traitors; we are branded as fanatics; we are cursed as dogs — we are to be hung! Our wives ravished by the mercenary soldiers under the stars and stripes, our daughters by the United States officers, our cities pillaged, our fields laid to ashes, our altars and temples polluted...'"*

"So, how many others sympathize with Blair?" Bernhisel looked at the oysters then thought better about it.

Houston paused and leaned forward to share his latest news: "Making friends now days is difficult with all the fake news being printed about your people. And, it may get worse before it gets better. So, I have friends who reported to me about a telegram from your erstwhile Utah attorney general John Hockaday to President Buchanan's inside man, James Van Dyke. I suppose you know that Hockaday was a partner with Bill Magraw in their mail contract — its cancellation upset Hockaday nearly as much as it did Magraw."

Bernhisel nodded. This was old news to him.

"Yes I know. And, we're grateful your support."

Houston continued: "But, then my sources tell me that Hock-aday spent hours trying to convince Van Dyke to strike back at the Mormons, then continued the conversation with the president. Wish we'd had a mouse in that meeting. Somebody else needs to have a conversation with Van Dyke — he's a reasonable fellow, I think."

"Maybe Kane?"

"Sounds like the best candidate," Houston responded then pushed his bowl of shells to the side. Apparently, the Potomac was now oyster-free.

Bernhisel opened his satchel and extracted a handful of letters, sorted through them and handed the senator two of them, one from Utah and one from Pennsylvania.

"Well, we're striking back. Take a look at the latest edition of Elder John Taylor's tabloid, *The Mormon*," Bernhisel said as he handed him the copy.

He watched the Texan consume the documents with as much relish as he did the shellfish and then Houston commented:

"Well, well, it seems as if the boiler is ready to explode, unless we find a way to turn down the heat… if at all possible, if only we knew what was on 'Old Buck's' mind — if anything."

"Old Buck?"

"Our esteemed President of these 'Dis'united States of America, that "Old Public Functionary" as he calls himself, the one and only James Buchanan,"

Bernhisel shrugged: "I tried to discern that when he I had my momentary meeting with "Old Buck," as you call him, but I was handed off to Secretary Thompson as fast as a three-dollar bill. And, we both know how badly that turned out: He labeled all of us as seditious. So, you're right: the boiler will soon be boiling over, I fear. I worry I'm the one who started it all."

"It started long before you," Houston assured him. There are people who benefit from all the turmoil — we know who they are."

At that very moment, the clattering of a horse's hooves on the paving stones outside caught their attention, followed by the door being flung open as a man in a poncho made a grand entrance.

"It's Brewster, my secretary," Houston said. "This portends something sinister." The wet man walked over to their table.

"Senator, can we have a moment?"

"We're among friends here, Brewster: This is my Mormon colleague, Delegate Bernhisel."

"Fine. Then he might as well hear this news, too."

Houston called to the waiter: "Some coffee for the man, please." The senator turned to Brewster: "Proceed."

Brewster sat down, took a sip of his coffee and pulled a document from his coat: "Gentlemen, I'm afraid the other shoe has dropped. Buchanan finally decided something — he released this."

He began to read:

"The hostility to the lawful government of the country has at length become so violent that no officer bearing a commission from the Chief Magistrate of the Union can enter the territory or remain there with safety..."

Brewster cleared his throat: "And, he continues announcing that General Scott will issue orders to marshal a force to accompany a new governor and remove Governor Young."

The men stared at each other in silence. Finally, Bernhisel spoke: "I will ascertain Thomas Kane's thoughts on these matters since he has now returned from Havana."

"His brother's death made headlines all over the country," Houston added.

"Yes, and I'm sure the Kane family now just want to stay to themselves. But, I hope to find out more when Thomas and I meet soon, very soon."

"Please convey my sympathies," Houston said as he stood to leave. It would be months before the two of them would meet again as the Utah Expedition would begin plodding west.

WILLIAM, CYNTHIA AND WILL were huddled together at the cemetery where Elder William Stowell had just dedicated the grave of his brother. A few other members of the little settlement and a couple of friends and other family members were offering their condolences to the Stowell family, far from grandparents who lived up north. William had been called to Fillmore, but with the orphans, they hoped to return to Ogden, closer to family.

Death had been stalking the ill-clad, hungry pioneers recently. Immigrants were arriving, often in destitute conditions, a drought and crickets had taken their toll and infectious diseases were finishing the awful business, and sadly.William's half-brother, Dan, a widower, had died, turning his children into orphans.

For every death, it seems there's a birth — and for the Stowells, there was at least one on the way: Though she was already a fine mother to her and William's adopted son, Henry, at 8, she would become a mother in her own right once she gave birth to the baby she carried who was almost ready to make its debut.

But, William and Cynthia had other challenges, practically insurmountable ones standing right in front of them: their five orphaned nieces and nephews. They loaded their newest members of the family into the wagon, arranging the straw and quilts. Cynthia wrapped up the two smallest children up and carried them to sit with her and William on the driver's bench; she left the others under the supervision of Dan, oldest orphan behind them.

"Everybody cozy?" Cynthia asked the children. It was gray and chilly, but thankfully no rain or snow. Cynthia turned and inquired of their young passengers.

The orphans were still in a state of shock; their father had just been buried. Three sets of tear-filled eyes blinked back at her.

"We're fine, thank you, Aunt Cynthia," Will whispered.

William whistled and snapped the reins: the horses lurched ahead. Their three-hour wagon ride back home had begun.

Cynthia had tried to get the older children to join her in song and rhyme for an hour or so without getting a lot of participation. The little ones in her care were now asleep.

She whispered to William: "Now what? We need more room and more help." He shook his head and shrugged his shoulders.

"I'm constantly praying," he replied… "hoping the Lord has an answer."

Cynthia straightened her shoulders and took a deep breath:

"Maybe I do: I know someone, known her family…great family, been friends for years now."

William looked at her quizzically.

"Her name is Sophronia, little younger than me. Haven't you thought about that…?"

"About what?"

"A plural wife."

"I wasn't about to bring it up. Maybe your mother could help."

"She has a brood of her own still at home and as you know, she's some distance away."

"If you're all right with it."

"I brought it up, didn't I? Let's meet her on Sunday after church."

"We're both going to court her?" He didn't know whether it was a joke, so he stifled a laugh. Then, he knew she was deadly serious. *How can we take care of the baby, little William Henry and now my brother's orphans,too? That's seven children!*

He didn't know what to say, but Cynthia took the lead:

"It's a family decision, and I don't know what else we can do. Do you?" Sunday was still five days away. William would just have to dwell on the idea. *What strange times we live in*, he thought.

5

KANSAS IS STILL BLOODY

Thomas Kane and John Bernhisel hadn't spoken in weeks, just had exchanged cryptic letters in case of unwanted readers. The two had had a lengthy and a heart-felt conversation, the first since Thomas had returned from Havana with his brother Elisha's body months earlier. They were trying to cheer each other up, but it was an exercise in futility. After their last meeting, Thomas had sent Brigham a note at Bernhisel's request about the new president, James Buchanan, that he "was a timorous man, as well as just now, an overworked one." Now what?

That was the question in search of an answer that Utah's delegate to Congress hoped to wrangle out of Thomas Kane when he arrived. Bernhisel found himself in a smokey men's club in an exclusive section of old Philadelphia with a mug of hot cider.

The waiter stirred Bernhisel out of his funk.

"Anything else, sir?"

"Some honey, just a bit to sweeten the cider," he replied. "Oh, and another saucer of shortbread."

The waiter complied. Bernheisel picked up the well-read copy of the *New York Herald* and opened the paper to Bennett's editorial excoriating the Mormons. He assumed Thomas had seen it, but then Kane had been consumed with settling his brother's affairs. And, Bernhisel had had his own setbacks. Another article on the same page reminded him of it: the appointment of Jacob Thompson as James Buchanan's Secretary of the Interior. The meeting with Thompson had been a disaster, and he hoped Thomas could help him draft a letter to Salt Lake City with at least a nugget of good news, a sliver of hope that Brigham and the brethren could hold onto.

He heard footsteps behind him. It was Thomas Kane, all 5-foot 3-inches of him. Bernhisel stood and gave his friend a hug.

"You are a sight for sore eyes," John exclaimed.

"Sorry, I'm late. Been stewing over Drummond and doing some reading. Seen this?" Thomas held up an identical copy of the Herald.

Thomas read a snippet out loud: *"The Utah excrescence calls for immediate and decisive action. That infamous beast, that impudent and blustering imposter, Brigham Young and his abominable pack of saintly officials should be kicked out without delay and without ceremony."*

"And then there's Drummond. He is convinced he is making a name for himself with his dodgy dialectic," Bernhisel added. "So, he's still stirring up trouble even though he fled the coop..." Thomas noted.

"All while taking the eggs with him," Bernhisel added.

Thomas was puzzled: "How so?"

"He left with the money allocated to fund the court along with his mistress."

"So, there's no silver lining?"

"Just wait and see what John Taylor is about to publish in New York. His little newspaper, *The Mormon*, will shed new light on our erstwhile whore-mongering associate justice. He has a couple of sources in the administration who told him that Drummond met with the Cabinet and has hopes of being appointed governor replacing President Young, but with an Army escort..."

"And, if he's not successful...?" Thomas asked.

"He's threatening to 'take down Buchanan and his administration' by exposing the president's Utah blunder," Bernhisel said as he motioned to the waiter to bring Thomas a menu.

Thomas acknowledged the waiter and then added: "But, he is

the blunder along with Judge Kinney, the surveyor and even Secretary of War Floyd, despite his warnings that sending the Army to 'march on Zion' so late would sentence them to a long, cold winter in Wyoming." And, then Thomas whispered the latest gossip circulating among his Abolitionist friends: "The Southerners in the administration want to move the Army as far west as possible — use your own imagination as to why they want to do that."

Bernhisel nodded and motioned to the waiter to refill his mug and then added: "I heard that Secretary Floyd told the Cabinet, according to my sources and I quote, that *"the Mormon settlements lie in the grand pathway which leads from our Atlantic States to the new and flourishing communities growing up upon our Pacific seaboard... and that 'they stand as a lion in the path...' defying civil and military authority and encouraging the Indians to attack emigrant families."*

Thomas shook his head: "That's their official line. But, there are all kinds of motivations, mostly greed and bigotry, but in Buchanan's case, fear and ignorance. They call Buchanan 'a Doughface'..."

"A what?"

"A Doughface, a Southern sympathizer, but I think he's just feckless, a single, lonely man who fears he might make a mistake," Kane said. "Others make decisions for him — he is pulled in many directions by people with their own selfish motives."

Bernhisel agreed: "Brigham said so himself when he observed that the government does not foresee the evil they are bringing on themselves, not only by driving this people into the midst of the savages of the plains, but by ignoring a bigger problem: slavery."

Before they departed, they decided Thomas would draft a letter to Brigham to warn him what storms were on the horizon, but also offering a sliver of hope that common sense would prevail, that John Taylor's revelations about the true, corrupt nature of Judge Drummond would reach those in power, but for now, they would each retire for a season. They both needed a rest.

DAYS LATER, AS THOMAS AND ELIZABETH KANE were preparing to pack up and retire to the mountains of western Pennsylvania, Thomas was rewriting his letter to Brigham Young.

"I don't know if I should say anything about Bernhisel's rebuff by Secretary Thompson and the nearly violent reaction Thompson had regarding the Utah Territorial legislature's demand for statehood; it was 'impolitical'… it was throwing kerosene on a fire to douse it."

Bess walked over and sat down near Thomas's roll-top desk; she had packing to finish, and the baby was waking up.

"Thomas, just write what you know, don't speculate. Finish the letter so we can pack the carriage and leave. Read to me what you have so far: I'll wager it's likely perfect."

"All right. If you validate it, I'll mail it: *'Dear President Young: We can place no reliance upon the president; he succumbs in more respects than one to simple outside pressure. You can see from the papers how clamorous it is for interference with Utah affairs. Now Mr. Buchanan has not heart enough to save his friends from being thrown over to stop the mouths of a pack of Yankee editors.'*"

And the rest is well wishes, greetings to my Utah friends and so on."

"Just mail it, Thomas. It's fine and to the point." It would the last letter to Utah he would send until the end of summer.

IN WASHINGTON, IT WAS MORE THAN JUST HOT AND HUMID, more like a sauna. Inside the exclusive men's club, there were beads of perspiration all around, but not so much from the humidity as from the game at hand. Four men in dark suits sat around a table, drank whiskey, smoked cigars and eyed each other suspiciously. This particular

game of chance could make enemies of even the best of friends.

"I will see you the Territory of Oregon and raise you California," the banker said and pushed over the rest of his "investment."

"Robert, you are always raising the stakes," his brother Henry, the Keystone State's treasurer, sighed. "You are never satisfied!"

"Are we talking card games here or politics," a federal judge with all the chips responded, peering over his spectacles.

"What's the difference? You cheat no matter what." They all laughed.

"Business, politics, war, cards. In the end, isn't it all the same? Isn't it all about winning?" he said with a smile as he laid down four kings.

"I'm out," said the banker. The others surrendered, too, and railroad executive Robert Magraw gathered up his winnings. All in all, it had been a good night and, it wasn't even over yet. After the banker and the physician left, the two Magraw brothers finished their drinks.

"I got a letter from Bill. He's still chafing at the bit over the Mormons and his mail contract," Henry said.

"Well, he shouldn't. Their contract has been cancelled, too. That should stir things up back in Utah. Now they won't be able to read everybody's mail. Maybe he can get the mail route back and a new contract from the Army. Now that they're on the move, there ought to be more government dollars to be rounded up. His brother picked away at the last of the peanuts and put his glass down.

"Well, they ought to be a little worried about Harney and his entourage."

The older brother leaned back in his chair: "They're not doing much marching yet. Harney's still in Leavenworth and Bill's on his way to meet them. Kansas is still bloody."

"Seems his letter to the president did the trick. Never thought he was much of a man with letters."

Robert laughed: "Bill's a mad bull when he's riled up — at least he's out on the Plains somewhere he can't embarrass the family. He lost the mail contract to the Mormons because they underbid him. He has no one to blame but himself. But that is bad news form old Brigham and good news the for boys from Missouri like Senator Benton and his people. They want to make sure that the old lady in the White House doesn't lose his nerve. I told the Senator not to worry, but he keeps pushing. Their fight with the Mormons has never stopped even though they chased them out. They suspect the Mormons will try and return; they say it's part of their deluded theology."

Henry smiled: "Buchanan may be an old lady, but he's 'our' old lady. Like Pa always said, better to own one than be one."

Robert retorted: "Well, as state treasurer, then, who owns you?"

"Why the people of the Commonwealth of Pennsylvania, that's who!" he laughed.

Both of the brothers enjoyed themselves immensely at that comment. Then Robert shared a confidence with his brother:

"Tomorrow, Benton and some of his Missouri friends insist we talk. You should come."

"Old 'Manifest Destiny Benton,' that old Puritan? What can't wait?"

Robert leaned over to his brother and spoke softly: "He feels Buchanan needs some 'buttressing.'"

"Buttressing?"

"Buttressing. He's getting a little weak-kneed over this whole expedition. Harney makes him nervous; Harney makes General Scott nervous; you could say they hate each other. Anyway, Benton has some ideas. He received some correspondence from Fremont."

"Fremont! Everything Fremont does is for Fremont. He lost the presidency to Buchanan last year, but in.four years, who knows. The two of them view the Mormons as an impediment to their grand plan — they think 'Manifest Destiny' is THEIR destiny."

"I'm sure they realize there's money to be made outfitting the U.S. Army. And, there's gold and silver in the Mormons' mountains. He's Benton's son-in-law. He does the old man's bidding."

"Who's taking advantage of whom? Fremont knew exactly who her father was when he proposed to the old man's daughter. If it weren't for the Southerners, he'd be president now. I don't fault him for marrying wisely." His brother broke into a wide grin.

"What?!" Robert demanded.

"Marrying wisely can advance one's career, can it not?"

Irritated, Robert stood up and put on his dinner jacket: "Are you coming to lunch tomorrow or not?"

"You didn't answer my question," Henry said, still grinning. "And you didn't answer mine. Coming or not?"

"I'll be there. Just confide in me, your brother, do you really enjoy the company of the president's niece?"

"She's an excellent choice on all accounts. Her familial connections are frosting on the cake," Robert smiled.

"What kind of frosting?" Henry asked, but knew the answer.

This time Robert smiled: "An ambassadorship to King James Court."

"London? England? Who'll run the railroad?"

"It runs itself." Robert bragged.

Henry Magraw grabbed his brother by the shoulders and laughed: "So where do we lunch tomorrow, brother?"

"The gentleman's club on Lafayette Square. Be there at half-one."

"Not very discrete," Henry cautioned his confident brother.

"Benton has a room reserved. It'll be a very hush-hush event."

The two brothers left the club and headed out into the rain. For the Magraws of Pennsylvania, things were looking up. Maybe there was even hope for more government contracts for old Bill, their hard drinking, murderous brother who was on the trail west, constantly looking over his shoulder for the Nauvoo Legion.

NOT EVERYONE IN UTAH TERRITORY, or The State of Deseret as the Mormons called it, was obsessed with the arrival of an Army over 1,000 miles away. Others like the growing William Stowell family who had moved back to Ogden from Fillmore after William had taken a second wife — Sophronia, as Cynthia had urged him — had more immediate problems, like getting enough food for their children. Of the nearly 40,000 Mormon settlers in Deseret in July of 1857, only about 2,500 celebrated in the canyon; others like the Stowell's weren't invited, were too far away or probably didn't have the means to join the party in the canyon. William, Cynthia, Sophronia and their numerous children had recently made a nearly 200-mile pilgrimage to to Ogden from Fillmore to be close to family. They hads settled in a two-room cabin at Bingham's Fort, which was not much more than a closet in the corner of the ramshackle stockade between the tinsmith and the milliner.

Cynthia Stowell was queued up at the post office waiting for her turn, In a sling asleep hanging below her left arm, Miranda, one of her twins, was starting to fuss. Mrs. Thompson, the part-time post mistress, whispered: "Let me check, Cynthia dear, and see if we have any post from Salt Lake...from your mother, right?"

Cynthia nodded, leaning on the counter with her free hand, while gently rocking the infant in the sling, hoping the baby would remain still. She brushed her hair away from her face, but looked away, trying to conceal her puffy eyes. The older woman behind the corner was shuffling through mail and then shook her head. Resigned that there was nothing for her, Cynthia turned to leave, but Mrs. Thompson put a hand on her shoulder.

"Wait a second. There's no mail, but this was left for you," she said, handing her a small bag. "This isn't mine...I, uh ..." Cynthia muttered.

"It was left for you."

"What is it?"

"I didn't look inside. It's definitely for you'

Then the older woman looked at the baby and asked: "How's her little sister?"

"Sophronia has her...she's trying to settle her down. Both of the babies are pretty colicky."

"How's Sophronia doing?"

"Growing, getting bigger...baby's due in two or three months. But, with six orphans who sorely miss their parents and the twins, the three of us have our hands full. Thank you," Cynthia whispered as she looked in the bag. Then tears began trickling down her face:

"Who left this for us?" "

"I can't recall," the postal clerk fibbed, knowing the exact contents of the package: corn meal and dried beans. Now tears flowed freely in Bingham Fort's tiny post office.

There would be Johnny Cake and bean soup tonight in Stowell's tiny two-room hovel, thanks to a kindly post mistress who had more corn meal and beans still in her cabin and a heart willing to share what she had. It's time to count our blessings, she reminded herself.

AT BINGHAM FORT IN OGDEN VALLEY, William Stowell returned to the growing family anxiously awaiting him. He tied up his mare in front of the stockade, shook the dust off his boots and cleaned them on the ledge outside before opening the gates.

Three young pioneers ran to him: "Uncle Bill, you're back," his five-year old niece yelled as she jumped into his arms.

Her brother pointed to some blood on his hands and shirt.

"Are you hurt?

William set his niece down. He leaned down to the towhead staring up at him.

"No, it's not my blood," he ruffled the boy's hair to put him at ease. "Had to stop a fight before it got out of hand."

Cynthia hurried over to him and took his hand: "William, what happened?"

He grabbed a tin cup full of water from the rain barrel outside their door, and they all hurried inside.

"Where's Sophronia, he asked as he sat at the table and took a drink.

"She's at the creek, gathering watercress — she'll be right back; William, there were some visitors here this morning…it was very unpleasant."

"I know. We met them — they're traveling south to California."

"Brother Winchester tried to explain that we had no grain to sell. You know the letter Brother Brigham sent, that we had to keep our wheat and corn for hard times, but they were insistent… yelled at us, said we were squatters…"

"Aunt Cynthia, what's a squatter?" William Henry asked.

"Never mind, we're not squatters," Cynthia answered and then asked William: "So, what happened?"

"Brother Webb pulled one of the Arkansans off his horse after their animals helped themselves to his vegetable garden. They each threw a couple of punches until I stopped the fight."

"Good for him! What's an Arkansan?"

"Someone from Arkansas, honey. They're just passing through," William explained. "There are more than a hundred of them with wagons and animals. Bad timing, if you ask me."

Sophronia had just returned with a basket full of watercress. She took one look at her husband and gasped:

"William, what happened? Is this your blood?"

"No, no, not mine. It's a long story," he said, and pulled both her and Cynthia to him as the children joined the group hug.

"We're in this together," William said. "We will be fine."

Little did he know what lay ahead for his family. Soon Governor Brigham Young would declare a state of emergency and activate the militia. Only a miracle could stop what was coming, a miracle by the name of Thomas Kane.

6

A CONSPIRATOR BEHIND EVERY TREE

The Magraw brothers, Henry and Robert, were the first to arrive at the upscale dining suite at Lafayette Square. Henry ordered an appetizer and was about to order a glass of brandy when his brother reminded him: "Benton is a tee-totaler, part of the new abstemious temperance movement."

"Probably a templar, too," Henry said.

"So, go easy on the brandy."

"I'll have some wine. He'll just have to live with it. Who else is coming?"

"We'll know soon enough," Robert said. Just then His Excellency, the former senator from Missouri, Thomas Hart Benton, made his entrance with what appeared to be two "border men." They're probably roughnecks from Missouri, Henry thought, whom neither brother recognized. Accompanying them was the Virginian, and Buchanan's confidant, Robert Tyler, former President John Tyler's son.

"Gentlemen, meet the Magraw brothers, at least two of them," Benton said. "Apparently, Bill is still out west wrestling with the Mormons."

"We're well acquainted," Tyler said.

Robert and Henry both noticed that Benton failed to immediately introduce his fellow Missourians.

Tyler noticed what Henry was drinking: "What, no ale?"

Henry gestured at the fine surroundings, avoiding eye contact with Benton's strangers. "Does this look like a place for ale?"

"Brandy, maybe," Tyler responded with a thin smile.

Benton had the suite prepared regally, fine china, new linen and expensive silverware. Out of the corner of his eye, Robert was certain he saw one of Benton's cohorts put a butter knife or two in the pocket of his coat. Henry wondered how recently either of them had bathed and exchanged a glance with his brother as if it communicate his disdain.

Robert broke the ice: "So, Senator, do we have a specific agenda today?"

Benton cleared his throat: "Buchanan's reticence to act."

Henry responded: "Harney has his Army, he's mobilizing, he's marshalling his forces. What's the problem?"

One of the ruffians spoke up: "Harney's just sitting there. If he don't hurry, winter's goin' to be right on top of 'em. Ever been out there?"

"Can't say that I have, why?"

"It's a helluva place. Ask the Mormons who got caught out there in the wilds of Wyoming last year; two hundred or so of them died, froze to death."

"Damn shame that was, too," Tyler said... "that only 200 did."

With that comment, everybody had a good laugh.

"Regarding the Army just standing around and waiting for General Harney, the problem is that Kansas is still bleeding — they have to stop it," Henry said. "Plus General Winfield Scott and Harney are having this cross-continental cock fight that Harney can't win. Been talk of replacing him. He didn't even want the assignment in the first place; he wanted to stay in Kansas and 'pacify' things there. That man has a lot of blood lust from what I hear..."

"That's why Harney's the perfect man to lead the expedition," Tyler added. The Magraws bristled. Henry whispered to his brother, "What's Tyler's agenda?"

Tyler continued: "Listen, what I told the president in April still stands: if we want to end this 'Negro-mania' and draw attention away from all this abolitionist trouble in Kansas, Buchanan needs to stay the course and push for Utah. The Republicans fell right into our hands with all this 'twin relics' business. The country may be split on slave-state versus free-state, but when it comes to Mormons, everybody wants them gone! The Army needs to get moving — no time to waste. And, we ought find funds for more."

A knock came at the door; it was time to order. By now, every man had worked up an appetite. Robert noticed that Benton had been unusually silent and distant during Tyler's tirade.

After their meals arrived and each was a little more inclined to renew the conversation, Henry Magraw broached the delicate subject of slavery carefully since Tyler's father, President Tyler and a Virginian had slaves of his own.

"Tell me, Senator Benton, as a slave owner yourself, where do you stand on Douglas' settler rights?"

"You mean 'squatters' rights? First, let me correct you, I am no longer a slave owner. Slavery is an anachronism that will die out naturally. I say let it. The modern age and American industry will replace all that back-breaking labor. Let the black man return to where he came from."

"You mean where he was kidnapped from," Henry said as he attacked his cutlet. That drew a dark glance from one of Benton's 'bodyguards.'

"Let me set a few things straight: From the Atlantic to the Pacific is one country: rivers, forests, plains and mountains. And right here..." Benton exclaimed as he took a steak knife and drove it into the table top for effect "is a squalid bunch of squatters, an infernal group of rabble that should be, in Mr. Tyler's words — what was that word you used, extirpated?..."

Tyler was caught up in Benton's fomentation: "Extirpated, yes, that was the word I used."

"Extirpated. Eliminated. Know this: they are allied with the Redman. Did you know that the Shoshones and Utes distinguish us from them?"

"Them?" Robert asked.

"The Mormons! They call us 'Mericats' and them Mormons.," Benton continued. "The Mormons feed them, teach them. Together, they are sitting right in the middle of the crossroads between Kansas Territory on the East and Oregon and California to the west." Benton gestured to one of the Missourians who threw a map on the table, practically on top of Henry's plate.

"Old Hickory would know what to do-he'd treat 'em like the Cherokees!" Benton was referring, of course, to his old mentor, President Andrew Jackson, Robert reminded himself. He knew his brother was getting as uncomfortable around these rustics as he was. But they served a purpose.

Robert Magraw knew what Benton had in mind: a trail of tears, but for Americans, white people like themselves? Robert exchanged a glance with his brother, as if to ask: "what's he planning?" He knew it was time to ask him-if he could get a word in edgewise.

"Look at the size of the territory they have seized-and might I remind you," Benton continued, "they never paid for. Such an impediment must be pulled up and dug out for America to achieve its destiny," Benton declared with a sweep of his hand.

The Magraws exchanged a glance as if to say, "what kind of madman have we found for an ally?"

Henry cleared his throat and felt as if he were in school; if Robert wouldn't ask, he would:

"It seems to me like everything's going according to plan. Can't we just let nature take its course?"

"It needs a little nudging," one of the Missourians spoke up and then was waved away by Benton.

"Who needs a little nudging?"

"That granny in the White House," the frontiersman sneered, "'Cause we're doing our part."

Robert was growing impatient.

What was the point of this meeting? What was he referring to?

"Look, Harney is mobilizing, he has more troops on the way to Leavenworth, his quartermasters are acquiring supplies as fast as they can," he replied.

Benton spoke up before one of the Missourians could: "We hear that Scott is trying to cut Harney down to size; they can't stand each other. It's turning into a cockfight, and the old rooster wants to hang on to his hens. General Scott has the president's ear..."

"So, do we," Henry interjected.

"Well, can you talk to him? If Harney's an obstacle, maybe somebody else ought to lead the expedition," Benton suggested. "Scott doesn't like the whole idea, but he might like it better if Harney stayed in Kansas; Buchanan fears he could get out of control like he did in Florida," Benton said.

"Florida?" Henry was puzzled.

"You know, where he earned his nickname, the 'Squaw Killer?'" Robert reminded his brother. Now Benton was clearly growing impatient with the banker and the railroad baron. He locked his jaw and tried not to let his contempt for them show, but time was running out.

"Listen, gentlemen, the Army needs to get to Utah before snow flies. There are moves afoot by one your own people and others in the Senate..."

"You mean Douglas and Houston?"

"And Judge Kane's boy; he's been writing letters and trying to get the President's ear..."

Henry smiled: "Writing them is one thing, reading them is another."

"Fine, fine." Benton interjected. "At any rate, use your influence to make sure Scott or Douglas or Kane including Attorney General Van Dyke — or anyone else who hasn't the stomach for a fight doesn't get to Buchanan," Benton said as he slowly stood up.

"We're doing all we can. Tell me, Senator, what's your contribution?"

One of Benton's "aides" jumped himself into the conversation:

"Sometimes nature takes its own course. If you've been to the Missouri docks lately, hundreds are pushing west everyday. And sometimes they're driving their teams to Oregon, sometimes to Sacramento to see if they can find some more gold, and some are even going south right down to California, right down the Mormon trail, people from our parts and Arkansas, folks who have no love at all for the Mormonites. And, you never can tell what might set off a powder keg, what's more … "

Benton gave his countryman a look that stopped him in mid-sentence and took over the conversation:

"… What's more, Secretary Floyd is pressing the president to talk to our contacts in the House to pass a measure for another division for the Army; more men are needed if indeed rumors are true about the number of Mormons guarding their mountain passes. And, here's a compilation from the Gunnison expedition, one that my son-in-law sent me some time ago," Benton said as he handed a leather folder to Robert Magraw. "It will raise some red flags."

The Magraw brothers shared a knowing glance: What have these country boys cooked up?

Benton continued: "Just remember, old Brigham is sitting on some very valuable land, as rich in gold, silver and copper as anything in Nevada and California. And do you know what he's doing, besides gathering himself a harem, that is? Trying to grow cotton and sugar beets! He's like a dog in a manger, sitting on all that wealth. making alliances with the Natives. It's our manifest destiny, and he has to go!

With that, Senator Benton and his Missouri entourage stood up and left the room. Tyler tipped his hat and followed them.

After they were all gone, Henry noticed much of the silverware

had disappeared with them. Robert had other things on his mind: he was thumbing through the geologists' reports and notes Benton had given him.

"I think maybe we have underestimated Mr. Benton and his homespun crew. I'm going to do some reading tonight, and on the weekend, we should talk more about this. I thought it was just some kind of bloodlust, some old score he had to settle. I thought he was like our brother and had been wronged by the Mormons.

"No, these are facts that speak for themselves. Gold, silver, lead, tin, copper. Not to mention what can be made with a nice freight contract with the Army! I think I like the sound of Manifest Destiny, our Manifest Destiny," his brother added for effect.

The brothers exchanged worried glances.

After Tyler left, Robert took his brother aside:

"Henry, I can't read his mind, but it appears to me that the Tylers don't share Benton's opinion that slavery will just go away, that progress will end that evil practice. What if Tyler wants the Army as far away from Washington as possible? If one 'relic of barbarism' was eliminated, wouldn't slavery be next? I think for Southerners like him, they want to keep things just the way they are."

Henry nodded: "That explains Secretary of War Floyd's position as well. Maybe we're all just being played by the slavers."

The Magraws made their way carefully out the door; there was no sense in being associated with Benton's rabble or what sinister plans they may be a party to. But before they parted company, they agreed to talk about it soon.

And Robert determined to spend a quiet evening at the White House with an old family friend, James Buchanan, president of the United States, before Van Dyke, Sam Houston or Kane gave him cold feet.

Things must proceed as planned. There was gold, silver and copper to be mined; there was money to be made in Utah as long as it didn't get out of hand. Tyler must be watched!

WHILE SAMUEL MORSE AND PARTNERS were starting to make headway east of the Mississippi with their new invention, the telegraph, and were already planting poles and stringing wire, elsewhere news still traveled no faster than a pony could gallop. But, in Mormon Utah, everybody was already wired; word of Brigham's speech was spreading far and wide. The 24th was a Friday, and by Sunday, the Stowells and their neighbors were gathered for worship services, the word was out.

And, the word was war, even if it was quietly whispered. It was a warm August day as the Stowells wrestled with their brood during church services. So far, there had been no open discussion at home regarding William's role in defending against the Damocles' sword hanging over the Mormons.

In other quarters, the sword was generally only supposed to threaten those in power — at least that's the classic view of how it was portrayed in Eastern newspapers. The Mormons were merely caricatures, dim-witted sheep doing old Brigham's bidding as notables like Benton and Buchanan described them. The Stowells and their fellow Mormons saw the sword threatening all of them.

Problem was that those calling for a March on Zion had no idea who they were dealing with. In the Great Basin as the pot started to boil, no one could foresee what the reaction might be. That would also include the wagon train from Arkansas that was moving slowly southward stirring up trouble and resentment along the way. Many Mormons had other things on their mind: survival. But, soon William and thousands of others would discover that fight or flight wasn't really a choice — they had run out of places to go. So, it would be a fight,

The Stowells and their fellow congregants were singing the closing hymn, *"In the Outward Church Below,"* an old Protestant favorite. Thanks to Brigham Young's recent campaign of reformation and repentance it was a timely choice. He and others inferred

that their troubles were the result of their unrighteous behavior.

His wives noticed the look of amusement on William's face as he bellowed out the verses:

Though in the outward church below
The wheat and tares together grow;
Jesus ere long will weed the crop,
And pluck the tares, in anger, up.

As the second verse began, Cynthia gave William a wifely elbow. The second verse hit a little closer to home. The two young women exchanged puzzled glances. Then Sophronia gave him an elbow of her own.

"Ladies, don't pick on me," he whispered through a smile. "I like this hymn." He was getting elbows left and right.

"What's so funny, William?" Cynthia whispered back.

"It's not humorous, it's ironic."

The congregation continued the hymn through all three verses:

Will it relieve their horrors there
To recollect their stations here
How much they heard, how much they knew,
How long amongst the wheat they grew!

Then, as the members concluded the last verse, William muttered: "This is the ironic part."

But though they grow so tall and strong,
His plan will not require them long;
In harvest, when He saves His own,
The tares shall into hell be thrown.

After the benediction, the women were all ears and knew they had him where they wanted him.

"Don't you see, ladies? The world out there thinks we're the tares. But, in the end, where will all those so-called Christians who chased us here find themselves?"

The fourteen-year-old, Will, who had been watching the flying elbows, provided the answer:

"Uncle William: Surprised! In hell and on fire!" He laughed at his own answer.

William nodded: "Smart boy."

As the Stowells were leaving their pew, Henry was puzzled:

"But Uncle William?"

"Yes, Will."

"What does 'ironic' mean?"

"Ask Aunt Cynthia."

She put her arm around the boy: "It's an unexpected surprise that changes everything."

"Like Aunt Sophronia?"

"Yes, in her case, a happy, joyous surprise."

Irony was following the Stowells outside to their wagon as most of the congregation was filing out of the modest little meetinghouse when Brother Ingraham stopped William as he was loading the smaller children into the back of the wagon.

"Brother Stowell, there's someone from Salt Lake who wanted to speak with you briefly. Do you have a moment?" Ingraham turned to the Stowell women:

"It will just take a minute; we'll have him back to you shortly."

Cynthia and Sophronia looked worried. The children in the back of the buckboard were busy trying to catch a stowaway mouse as William returned. He was taciturn, sober, not smiling. The mood had changed from playful to anxious.

William snapped the reins to get the horses moving. He didn't say a word.

Neither did his wives. The day was getting hotter. And so was the mood in their conveyance.

"William, say something," Cynthia said as both wives stared at their husband.

"I have a new responsibility."

"Well?" Sophronia said.

He cleared his throat and looked away. "I've been asked — um — called — to be an adjutant."

The oldest boy, Dan. perked up: "What's that, Uncle William?"

"It's a staff officer to a commander — somebody who takes orders and gives them to other people, writes letters and so forth. I'm assigned to Major Joseph Taylor's battalion and have to start training soon…after we bring in the corn and finish threshing the wheat; the potatoes can stay where they are for now."

He whistled at the team, and they picked up the pace. The wagon was bouncing along now as they turned the corner towards home.

"And you said 'yes,' with all of us counting on you?" Cynthia pressed him. He sighed and turned to the two lovely young women staring at him:

"Don't we always?" They rode the rest of the way to their cozy little corner in muted silence. He had dropped one shoe — he knew the other shoe would drop with a thud very, very soon.

He didn't want to think about it.

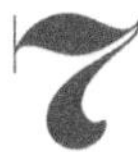

7

CHOOSE YOUR WEAPON

Wars are not only fought with powder and ball, sword and shield. Lead is still used, but is cast unto various other forms: upper case, lower case and the occasional dingbat. Combatants rarely have the pleasure of peering into their adversary's bloodshot eyes as they plunge an ascender or a descender into their opponent's vital parts; such a delicious victory is unavailable to them as their foes are frequently a continent apart.

Bill Magraw had written his share of letters, but he was no Shakespeare and certainly no correspondent. However, since the well-dressed journalist across the table from him was paying his bar bill, he was more than happy to express his thoughts about those damnable Mormonites and was looking forward to the war on paper he would wage against them ..

His interviewer was none other than Albert Gallatin Browne, Jr., the cocky and confident correspondent for the *New York Tribune* whom mountain man Jim Bridger simply called "Doc." No, this was not a medical doctor, just a PhD from the University of Heidelberg, who was nevertheless happy to be addressed as an educated man of letters by the likes of lowbrows such as Magraw or Bridger. Doc fit him perfectly, Browne thought to himself. He pressed Magraw for details about his letter to President Pierce.

"So, do you keep regular correspondence with Pierce? Did you hear back from him, Browne asked.

"Not since Buchanan took the reins of government, but my brothers tell me that Old Buck has the letter in his possession."

The saloon they were drinking in sat on a side street outside

Fort Leavenworth and now, 10 o'clock at night, the remainders occupying the smoky pit were rough men who could hold their liquor. Browne recognized Magraw as one of them, but he needed to keep him coherent. Ply him with liquor, yes; leave him in a drunken stupor, no. Browne had a deadline to keep; old man Greeley expected another installment by early next week, and the mail stage was leaving at 10 the next morning.

"Can you paraphrase for me ...?"

"Paraphrase?"

Browne took a breath: "Summarize, shorten..."

"All right, then. I just told the truth as I saw it with my own eyes," Bill said.

"Which was..."

"That these Mormonites, these fanatics, knaves, when they made their first appearance among us ...

"Which was where?"

"Missouri. Independence, Liberty, Far West...anyway, they're like locusts. They multiply. You see one, then another."

"But they did have their comeuppance," Browne interjected.

"Comeuppance?"

"Their own locust invasion in the Salt Lake Valley, they're always on the verge of starvation."

"Serves 'em right, too. Anyway, their numbers increase daily with Dutchmen, Scots, Danes — you name it — joining their ranks all the time. These pretenders, these deceivers, they act as if God speaks to them, and even claim that they receive communications and revelations direct from heaven, to heal the sick, to work miracles like those wrought by the inspired apostles and prophets of old. Everybody knows that's all over with in this day and age. We're good Christians...

"For the most part..."

"Yes, for the most part, we have the Bible, and they pretend to have one of their own, a golden Bible, if you can believe that."

Browne smiled: "Don't worry, I don't.

Magraw returned the smile: "Of course you don't. You're an educated man."

Browne smiled more broadly: "Yes, it was a long road. Speaking of that, your mail contract, the Mormons took that from you, right?"

"Yes, they did. Stole it. Underbid us by half! It's not right. We'll get it back, mark my word. And, I appreciate all you could do to help us accomplish that. We can't trust them to deliver the mail safely and securely."

"You think they read your correspondence?" Browne leaned forward.

"Of course, everybody does that."

Browne was enjoying this conversation. Another glass of bourbon could help him leverage a bit more information from this frontiersman. He scribbled a few more notes and discovered his ink was running dry. So, was his allotted expense for the week. *Mr. Greeley will love what I have gleaned from Bill Magraw,* he told himself. He still had to rewrite everything neatly for next week's report from the Utah Expedition, he concluded. It was time to let Bill Magraw enjoy his last shot in peace.

Mr. Greeley's correspondent paid the bar tab and thanked his inebriated "anonymous source," still lost in his bourbon glass, and turned to leave.

"Is that all you need, Mr. Browne? Because there are others with even better first-hand accounts than mine."

Browne stopped: "Like who?"

"The judges, Drummond and Stiles. They've both flown the coop. Don't know where Drummond is, but Stiles, an erstwhile Mormon, came east. Look around. I'm sure I saw him. He had himself a lucrative side business that old Brigham shuttered up… a nice hotel for gentlemen and young ladies. He's none too happy either. And, Judge Drummond, he is a colorful character. Turns out, the sassy woman he pawned off on everybody as his wife, ain't! She made a name for herself in the capital city "speaking circuit." She's a real looker — they make a real odd couple," Magraw said as he held up his nearly empty glass.

Albert dropped a couple of coins on the table and motioned to the bar-keep. Stiles and Drummond, huh? He'd have to ask around. He'd heard that Drummond was Brigham's nemesis. Sounds like a great source, if only he could find him. In the meantime, he proofread the article he was able to craft from his conversation with Magraw. He liked to use the butt of short pencil and began scribbling:

"Magraw said that 'there is but one alternative. Either the laws of the United States are to be subverted and its Territory appropriated by a gang of traitorous lechers, who have declared themselves to constitute a 'free and independent State' or Salt Lake City must be entered at the point of the bayonet, and the ringleaders of the Mormon rebellion seized and hung. Whether the entrance can be effected this year is a matter of great uncertainty. My own opinion is that it cannot.'

Satisfied with his ending, Albert Browne signed it, deposited his masterpiece in an envelope and sealed it. Now where was that stamp? He'd get one tomorrow.

IF BROWNE COULDN'T FIND JUDGE DRUMMOND, neither could anyone else. He was finally safely out of Brigham's grasp and out of the public eye, faraway from the likes of Albert Browne Jr. Drummond had found it difficult to conceal his libidinous debauchery from the Mormons whom he had hypocritically labeled "lascivious" because of polygamy. Ada Carroll, the woman whom he had passed off as Mrs. Drummond was really a Capitol City woman of the night who accompanied him to Utah, as he abandoned his wife and child in Illinois with no means of support. It didn't bother him a bit. He was on an adventure, thanks to the funds he absconded before he left,.

New Orleans was as far from Great Salt Lake City as you could get in 1857, figuratively speaking. From the comfort of his love nest on Bourbon Street, the judge went to work, doing all the damage he could to the Saints of the Latter Days. Like Albert Browne Jr., the corpuscular judge was also in Horace Greeley's employ, sending him the occasional letter. But he was also freelancing with the New York Times, using the nome de plume of *Verastus, the teller of truth.* Hypocritical though it might be, nevertheless he collected a handsome fee for his "revelation" of Mr. Kane's support of Brigham Young and his subservient people.

It was almost midnight, and Ada was complaining:

"How long will you continue to write?"

"*The Times* editor expects this as soon as I can finish my … revelation," he said with a laugh.

"Ahh, so now you're a prophet, too… there are so many these days."

"And, you, my dear, are as entertaining as you are beautiful. Almost done. I have to rewrite this last page, let it dry and mail it in the morning. Did Mrs. Shakespeare nag the Bard of Avon when he was penning a masterpiece?"

"I don't nag, and as you know, I'm not your wife. Only wives nag. I seduce, I flatter, and I make you happy. Come to bed."

"I can finish Othello in the morning," the judge said with a lusty smile, and he blew out the oil lamp.

If the old reprobate Judge Drummond thought he was the only one whose prose would go public, he miscalculated and underestimated his Mormon adversaries. In Manhattan, apostle John Taylor also understood that the written word does indeed have sharp edges. He was the editor of **The Mormon**, an advocate for the LDS church, its leaders and its teachings. Taylor determined along with his second-in-command, William Appleby, to unwrap the real Judge Drummond and let his readers learn exactly what kind of rascal was spreading outrageous lies about Utah and its people.

THE HAND-CARVED SIGN WAS BARELY VISIBLE in the gaslight as three weary travelers dropped their bags on the boardwalk of a seamy New York City sidestreet. Shopkeepers were closing up shop for the night, throwing wash water and scraps into the gutter. A fruit vendor swept peelings and cores away from his cart, folded up the sides and pushed it away. An orphan apple rolled toward a barrel but not before one of the three, Günther Brandt, one of the three German-speaking veterans fleeing the continuous European wars, grabbed it and stuffed it in his knapsack. Smoke and soot from New York tenements filled the air, making it not only difficult to breathe, but hard to see clearly in the hot summer night.

The smallest of the three unfolded his tattered note and pointed up ahead. *"Da ist der Schild,"* he exclaimed. (There's the sign). We've found the place."

"Endlich" (Finally), his comrade responded wearily.

They trudged the final few yards to the *Gasthaus zum Jägershof,* a Bavarian beer hall and inn frequented by travelers and *Landsmänner*-countrymen-like themselves who craved something of the Vaterland far from home.

One such genuine article was sweeping the floor, cleaning up what appeared to have been a profitable night. She gave the three veterans a shy smile and continued her chores. A few chairs were already on their resting places, upside down on the plank tables. A fire still smoldered in the hearth below the watchful eyes of a black boar that had seen better days.

"Good evening boys, but we're closing," the bearded innkeeper apologized, The big Prussian stuck his ham-sized fist out and introduced himself:

"I'm Günther Brandt, sergeant major in the First Grenadiers, and we were told that the innkeeper here was a friend of fighting men and a good Prussian. Are you that man?"

"Ja," the innkeeper responded, "I am indeed. I'm Herr Horst," and dropped into an arm chair by the fire.

"Who are your friends?" Horst asked.

"Carl-Heinz Wilcken, artillery man and this is our cook, Dieter Kant," the tall blond German said pushing his way forward. The innkeeper smiled and gave Wilcken a pat on the back.

"Helga, get these boys something to drink and whatever you can find in the back. They look like they've come far."

The barmaid smiled at Günther with a grin revealing missing teeth and hurried off to her duties. His comrade gave him a good-natured poke in the ribs as Helga walked by that didn't go un-noticed by Herr Horst.

"My daughter likes you, but then she likes most strangers from home," said Horst, "But I remind her that the travelers generally come here with nothing. Am I right?"

"Not nothing, we can pay for our meal. We were on our way to Argentina when we discovered our tickets only brought us this far...to New York City. We don't plan on staying. We just want to work enough to earn our steerage to South America," Carl Heinz said.

"The beer, the bread and whatever scraps Helga can find in the kitchen are on me, Horst said. "We had a good night. Thanks to the Irish. They are everywhere. And that is the problem. They work for nothing; they fight with each other, they fight the Amer-icans, and they despise the English. That's why they seem to tol-erate us. They like German beer," Horst explained.

"So, what's the problem?" Dieter asked.

"There will be no work here for you. The Irish control every-thing. And what they don't, the Americans do. But, you have drilled, been trained in the dark art of war, am I right?"

Günther laughed: "We're Prussians, Herr Horst!"

"Not me. I'm from Schleswig-Holstein," Carl Heinz declared. "The Prussians think they own everything."

"But you fought with us. Hessian, Sachsen, what's the differ-ence?" Günther retorted. "One day, it will be one country,

Greater Germany. Mark my word," Günther thundered. Carl Heinz crossed his arms and looked away.

"One country under the Prussian boot is what you mean," Carl-Heinz replied. The innkeeper threw his arms up in the air. Helga returned with a pitcher of beer and a plate of bread, sausages and cucumbers. The three soldiers attacked the food, barely listening to the innkeeper's stump speech.

"Petty politics. If we Germans could just get over our childish differences maybe the French wouldn't march back and forth across the Vaterland. Same problems here you know," the innkeeper explained. He continued since the travelers were quite busy feeding themselves.

"The South is in turmoil; they threaten secession if they don't get their way about slavery. And, there's trouble in Kansas..."

"Where's Kansas?" Carl-Heinz interjected.

"Out west, past the Mississippi. Here's my point: The Americans need soldiers, Trained soldiers. And nobody's better trained than the Prussians. Am I right?"

"Jawohl!" this time Carl-Heinz agreed, now taking the Prussians' side. "But, that's why we left Denmark. After the war, there were a lot of Prussian — Germans — left. And the Danes thought, hey, let's conscript them. We're not draft animal! So we left for Argentina. Why can't we get work on the docks or the canal?"

Herr Horst explained: It's a sad story but true: The English set the table in Ireland, and the Irish have been surviving on potatoes, and when the blight killed the potatoes, it took a lot of the Irish along with it. So, they came here to survive and took all the jobs no one else wanted."

"So, what are you telling us?" the cook asked, as the others looked at him baffled.

"It's obvious: We join their Army, the U.S. Army. Isn't that what you're saying, Herr Horst?" Carl said.

"Exactly. I understand they're raising several companies to go out west to tame the Mahotmens or something."

"Mahotmens?" Günther asked.

"Mormonen," Helga explained, correcting her father as she returned with more bread.

"I heard of them. In Germany," Carl-Heinz said. "What have they done?"

"Nothing that I know of, except for taking too many women to wife," the innkeeper responded. "Anyway, I know this sergeant who comes by. I will get you a name and an address. You can look into it."

Herr Horst showed the three travelers to a storage room in the back where they retired for the night. As he made his way up the back stairs, Helga gave him a cross look.

"So how much are they paying you?"

"Who?"

"The Army recruiters, that's who. They seem like nice boys, polite and all. They just needed some help."

Her father scowled: "I gave it to them. I fed them, didn't I? Daughter, I run a business. And I helped them out. I am referring them to the Army. I get $3 each for each recruit, so what? Everybody wins. I win, the Army wins, and the boys get paid. And they get to see the frontier. What's wrong with that? Go to bed and mind your own business."

The innkeeper disappeared up the stairs as his daughter shuttered the store and put out the fire. What did fate hold for the three boys, sleeping in the storage room, she thought? She followed her father up the stairs.

The next day, Helga watched as the three young soldiers spoke to the recruiter while her father helped translate. They all shook hands and appeared to come to some kind of agreement. After the sergeant and the boys left, she gave her father a disapproving glare as he pocketed his "blood money" and served himself a beer.

Later that day, the three Germans boarded the train west. They were on their way to Fort Leavenworth, Kansas, to join General Harney and his venture to put down the Mormon rebellion, thanks to the innkeeper of the *Gasthaus zum Jägershof.*

CARL-**H**EINZ AND **G**ÜNTHER AWOKE WITH A START as the train car they were riding in came to a clattering and clumsy stop.

"*Alle absteigen* (Everybody off)" came the cry from the first sergeant. Along with several train cars filled with new recruits, they had spent the night riding the rails. Hot and sweaty and covered in straw dust matted on their clothing, the new company of volunteers stumbled off the train cars.

"Grab your gear and form up, form up" was the order. The Germans followed the lead of the others, jumped off the train and assembled behind the platform.

A young lieutenant and the acting first sergeant of the motley group of down-on-their luck Americans, recent Irish immigrants, a couple of Welshmen and a dozen or so German-speakers representing a half dozen different principalities stood and waited for their orders, hoping someone would take charge. Finally, the officer and the sergeant sorted out their differences and the sergeant assumed command.

"Atten-shun!" he barked out as if that would settle things once and for all. It didn't.

"All right, form three columns, right here. Spread out, spread out. Drop your duffels and look at me. Now stand at attention!"

By now, those speaking foreign tongues — they were the ones with the military training anyway — got the message. The three Prussian veterans exchanged smiles and sighs as they viewed the pathetic company of men they now found themselves in and clicked their heels and assumed the position of men at war.

"That's what I'm talking about!" the sergeant said as he walked over to Carl Heinz, Gunther and Dieter on the far right flank.

"See, you sorry sorts! These men know something of military bearing!" He looked at Gunther and barked out a question:

"What's your name, soldier?"

"Wie heissen Sie?" Carl Heinz whispered the translation.

"Brandt. Günther Brandt," Gunther replied.

The sergeant turned to Carl-Heinz:

"So, do you speak English?" he asked him. Carl nodded.

"Good. You're a squad leader. Tell me your name."

"Carl Wilcken," he replied. "Artillery."

The lieutenant sorted through the stack of enlistment papers in his folder and found the one he was looking for. He and the sergeant exchanged a few words and the sergeant turned back to Carl.

"So, it says here Herr Wilcken that you were a sergeant major with the Prussian artillery, fought in Denmark and were awarded the Iron Cross. Is that correct?" the sergeant asked, obviously impressed.

"Ja," Carl replied, wishing he could slip back to the third rank and get out of the sergeant's gaze.

"Good. We will make you a squad leader and acting corporal for now. Take charge of your Dutchmen friends here and help me communicate with them. All right?"

He nodded in reply Without any idea of what the word "communicate" meant or half of everything else he had said.

"Dutchmen!" Carl thought. What an ignoramus! The sergeant was now firmly in control:

"All right, men. Stand at ease. The lieutenant is going to share a few things with you, then we'll eat something and be on our way. Then, it's off to St. Louis. Lieutenant?"

The sergeant stepped back and took out his pipe and found a convenient stump as the lieutenant began his oration:

"Men, I will make this brief. We have a long journey before us

— Wilcken, translate this," he ordered.

"I'll try," he said. The petulant, young officer cast him a hard glance. Carl cleared his throat.

"Well?" the lieutenant barked.

"Eine lange Reise... long journey, very long," Wilcken said in German and then begin to "improvise."

"And he has no idea where we are going."

Dieter tried not to smile, and Günther pulled a face, warning him to 'watch it.'

The lieutenant continued: "... some 500 miles to St. Louis, once we get to the railhead and another three hundred miles to Leavenworth, where we will join the main body of troops and join the wagon train."

A voice rang out from the back: "And how far to Utah to teach old Brigham a lesson?"

"Good question. About a thousand miles, I reckon. But, don't get your britches in a knot. We have a lot to do and a lot of preparation before we put an end to the Mormon rebellion. Let's not get ahead of ourselves. We have prairies and mountains to cross. It won't be easy, but I know you're up to it."

"Did you get all of that, Wilcken," the lieutenant asked his translator of dubious ability. Carl-Heinz nodded and with the wisp of a smile delivered his own version in German.

"Not easy, many mountains and prairies...just like Napoleon and his march on Moscow. Except we have no Napoleon," Carl "summarized." Günther replied to Dieter: "And as you recall, when Napoleon made it to Moscow, they had already burned it."

After the lieutenant was finished, the men fell in and set out for the railhead in three ranks with the Germans at the front. There were still 800 miles to go before they arrived at Leavenworth and days to get there by train, paddleboat and foot. And then the real fun — and the marching — would begin, Carl Wilcken ruminated: *What had they gotten themselves into?*

8

"WE HAVE BORNE ENOUGH OF THEIR OPPRESSION AND HELLISH ABUSE..."

Back in the Great Basin, Moscow and Napoleon were also the subject of conversation. Darkness had won the race to the city, and Christian Holz, Brigham's stenographer George Watt and Caleb Rasmussen had unloaded the wagon and were stacking lumber from the canyon celebration weeks earlier at the lumber house at Millcreek. Since it was already dark, they decided to spend the night there before returning to the city in the morning.

From their vantage point on the east bench, the whole valley was spread out before them. The valley was a bit hazy from dust kicked up by a gentle breeze and from the occasional fires from small settlements scattered here and there. To the northeast lay the City of the Great Salt Lake, some ten miles away. Caleb was building a fire near a clump of oak brush and preparing a Spartan meal of biscuits, potatoes and salt pork, which was all that remained of Christian's provisions.

By the time, Christian and George had finished corralling the animals and unloading the wagon, Caleb had their supper ready. Now, it was dark, and the three sat on a couple of logs and finished their meal around the campfire. Cinders flew heavenward to join the sparks of lights already residing there. George set down his tin plate, leaned against a log and put his feet up on a boulder to take in the scene laid out before him.

"In England, especially in the cities, you never saw the stars like this. Too smokey," he said.

"You from London?" Caleb asked.

"No, I spent some time there," George said, "visited the city,

didn't like it much. I'm from Preston, near Machester, farther north. If it wasn't raining, it was about to. But we didn't have to irrigate," he added ruefully.

"It's funny, isn't it?" Christian observed. "We came to a place nobody wanted, built our homes and dug our canals, and now they want us to leave." He turned to George Watt.

"So I suppose Brigham and the brethren have a plan, George. Can you tell us about it?" he asked.

George reached into his coat pocket and pulled out a small notebook stuffed with papers.

"I always keep this handy in case Brother Brigham has something important to say. And, for the past month or so, I have been packing around this correspondence, a clipping from *Harpers*. It's an account of the siege of Sebastopol by William Russell. He described at as a senseless slaughter, and his account appalled all of Britain, who before that were anxious for blood."

Christian replied: "I don't know Russell, but I know about Sebastopol. The Prussian officers discussed it at length during our Danish campaign. We were busy with the Danes while the English, French and Sardinians had their hands full with the Russians."

"So, you know about the Charge of the Light Brigade? Do you know Tennyson's poem?" George asked with a smile as he referred to his little stenographer's notebook.

"I'm afraid not," Christian said.

"I took the opportunity to put it to memory with the clipping as my cue," he said. George stood up and faced the fire and began his performance, as if on stage in London's West End:

Half a league, half a league, Half a league onward,
All in the valley of Death Rode the six hundred.
Forward, the Light Brigade! Charge the guns!
Into the valley of Death Rode the six hundred."
Forward the Light Brigade!
Was there nit a man dismay'd?

Not tho' the soldier knew
Someone had blunder'd:
Their's not to make reply, Their's but to do and die:
Into the valley of Death Rode the six hundred."
Cannon to the right of them,
Cannon to the left of them,
Cannon in front of them Volley's and thunder'd;
Storm'd at once with shot and shell,
Boldly they rode and well,
Into the jaws of Death into the mouth of Hell
rode the six hundred.

They all stared at the fire as George finished his last line.

"Anyway, that's all I can decipher, but it reminds me of those men," George said.

"What men?" Caleb asked.

"The ones who are marching on Zion," George answered.

"If they come in like that, like little lead soldiers, we'll cut them down," Caleb said. "I'd like a chance to do that."

Christian stirred the coals with a stick and then looked up.

"Maybe so, Caleb, but remember, there's an endless supply of them. If we spill their blood, our blood will be required. Remember, in Sebastopol, more died in the winter of '54 and '55 from the cold than died at the hands of the Russians. And in the end, while Great Britain lost every battle, it won the last one, and the Russians retreated," George answered.

"But, Napoleon? He never made it to Moscow," Caleb retorted.

"Oh, but he did," Christian interjected. "But, when the finally French arrived, the Russians had burned it down — so the French had to retreat, go back, but not because of Russian soldiers — it was the Russian winter. We may have the men, but not the ball and powder. No, I suspect Brigham wants us to conduct a stalling action, to keep them at bay until calmer heads prevail, and use the weather as our ally. Am I right, George?"

"I believe you are, Christian. But, we'll found out soon enough. There will be a call to arms and volunteers asked to muster within the month, if not sooner. By then, I assume we will have our orders," George confirmed.

"And it will be to move into those mountains," Christian added as he looked over his shoulder. The three men — the Prussian soldier, the English stenographer and the teen who smelled blood — sat quietly by the fire in the shadow of the mill. Once the coals faded and the moon rose, they all found a place to sleep until the sun once again peeked over the mountains, their mighty fortress.

IT WAS A BEAUTIFUL MORNING WHEN ELIZABETH KANE found her husband in the garden behind the house, tending to his roses. After a day and a night of constant rain, the flowers and the vegetables seemed revived. Her husband did not. He was pale, too pale, she worried. He had been sick for about a day and she was anxious that he get his strength back, Even though he was a small man by any measure, Thomas Kane nevertheless had the soul of a lion, his Bessie thought. He feared nothing and was relentless in the pursuit of something bigger than himself. She loved him for that. But like his late brother Elisha, she worried that he would push himself until he succumbed.

"Feeling better," she asked her husband and handed him a cup of tea. "It's peppermint; it'll settle your stomach."

"My stomach's fine," he responded and snipped off another twig. Elizabeth sat on the garden bench and set the unwanted tea down, patted a spot on the stone seat as if clearing a place for her husband. "Sit, Tom, we should talk."

"Sit? Am I a collie or a schnauzer?"he responded irritably.

"Be a good boy and sit," she said playfully, which drew a slight smile from her husband who was still wearing his night shirt over a pair of dirty dungarees.

Finally, Thomas obeyed, but didn't speak.

She turned and looked into his face: "Speak!"

Now he couldn't resist his wife's charms and started to laugh:

"Sit, speak. Do you want me to roll over, too,"

"Not out here in the garden!" she said, pretending to take on a Victorian air. He put his arm around her and gave her a squeeze.

"You are truly a delight, Bess. What would I do without you? All right, you ordered me to speak, now what do you want me to say? What?"

She grew serious.

"Ever since you brought Elisha — Elisha's body — back from Havana, and after our retreat into the mountains, I have been worried sick that what befell your brother..." she hesitated as she fought back tears, "might also befall you. I can see you're getting back into this fight." She put her head on his shoulder and began to weep.

"What fight?"

She was worried sick: "The one in Utah."

"Bess, Bess, now, now. It's all right. I'm right here."

She regained her composure and looked into his face. "I just need to understand. Your father needs to understand; he says he wants to come over this evening, and as he says, 'talk some sense into you!' We just need to understand, who or what is pushing you?"

"First of all, all I was doing was writing letters. That's all. Maybe a news article or two. And what's frustrating is, most of them go unanswered. I fear they are being intercepted, especially since their mail contract was cancelled. Brigham does, too. Anytime he writes me something, the next thing we know snippets appear in the New York papers."

"So, you suspect someone is feeding all those New York editors sensitive correspondence?"

"Likely it was someone in the presidents office or one of his cronies. Remember the 'call for immediate action' that appeared in the *New York Herald*? The editors are working hand-in-glove with some shadowy figure or figures."

"What immediate action?" Elizabeth asked.

"Military action against the Mormons. The editors say since the Northern Democrats can't go after slave holders, the Mormons are fair game, an easy target."

"But, Thomas, doesn't that make you a target, too? Not only are you an abolitionist, people see you as a Jack Mormon."

"Abolitionist isn't the appropriate term, it's too, too..."

"Radical?"

"Exactly."

He put his hands on his knees and stared straight ahead. The roses were in full bloom: he concentrated on them.

"Those editors: they're throwing fat on the fire and have no idea what they're doing. Especially James G. Bennett, editor of the New York Herald."

"Bennett, Greeley, the lot of them, they're just selling papers," Elizabeth said.

"They've challenged Buchanan *'not to submissively knuckle under to those two patriarchal institutions, polygamy and slavery.'* Greeley called Buchanan out, and with J.C. Van Dyke and Robert Tyler lobbying hard, Buchanan let things get out of control. And the dissolute, whore-mongering Judge Drummond and his accusations and fabrications provided the spark to start the fire; and somebody has to put it out. Now there's an Army marching on Zion."

"Zion?"

"Zion, Deseret, Utah, you know, the Mormons."

"I know. But Zion?"

Thomas turned to his wife: "How many groups of people in our history struck out to tame a wilderness to try their hand at building a perfect society? Remember Plymouth, Jamestown, Providence? As Americans, shouldn't we at least be free to try?

Remember, the Mormons — like the Pilgrims — didn't leave on their own accord. They were driven out."

"You still haven't answered my question."

He stood and turned, grabbed his snippers and continued pruning his roses.

"Thomas?"

She walked up next to him and demanded an audience. "My question."

"Which one, Bess?"

"What is pushing you, you don't believe in angels or golden plates or polygamy, do you?"

"No, of course not. I even have doubts about God."

"Then, what?!"

"Remember when I first visited the Mormons, what was it, 11 years ago?"

"We weren't married then. I was still just a girl."

"Elizabeth, you still are.'

"Go on."

"So, anyway, I went to Iowa originally because I had read that thousands of people were stranded on the plains, bogged down in prairie mud. I followed them to a place called Council Bluffs in Indian Territory; they'd been chased out of their homes."

He continued, but his voice grew husky, and Elizabeth could see there were tears in his eyes.

"And, they had built these huts, these hovels, out of sod and peat, blocks of mud, really. But, they were so orderly. Everyone was working; not an idle soul anywhere. They were bringing order out of chaos. Occasionally, in a tiny window of these prairie cabins — not much larger than a smoke-house — you would see a small vase, filled with wild flowers. Then, one evening, my hosts and I took a short-cut through a small stand of trees, and there kneeling in the underbrush was a man..."

"Who?"

"I had no idea, but he was praying, but not like you hear in a Sunday sermon, but pleading for his family, that they would have enough food to eat, that his children would survive the trip, that they would reach Zion. Funny thing was, Elizabeth, at that point, he had no idea where Zion was. They weren't certain where they were headed, but he was praying they would arrive safely. And when he prayed, it wasn't to some ethereal Being Without Body, Parts or Passions, it was like he was pleading with a friend, or his father, someone whom he knew loved him, begging for help."

"So, you're going to be the one to answer his prayer," she asked as she put her arm in his. "You're going to stop that Army all by yourself? You're not a large man, Thomas," she said, with tears streaming down her face.

"I've been told that," he responded with a smile.

"So, you're going to stand in front of General Harney and his horde and stop them in their tracks?"

"Something like that. But only if Buchanan will see me first."

She absorbed that, then softly replied: "You're planning on going out there, aren't you?"

"Where?"

She stooped to pick up some rose petals and dead twigs and put them in his box of rose stems and then answered: "Where do you think? To Utah? To Zion or whatever you call it?."

He grabbed his young wife by the shoulders and looked in her eyes: "You're the religious one in the family. Remember the story of the Good Samaritan? These people are just like that; they're lying at the side of the road; they need my help and not just the Mormons. Think! There are hundreds, maybe thousands of young American boys out there on the Plains that are being organized into companies and brigades to go fight the Mormons, and that puts them in harm's way, too. Somebody has to do something. Know this: I'm not trying to prove anything to anybody, not trying to make a name for myself, but please believe me, Elizabeth, when

I tell you: You are correct: I am being pushed to do this, pushed!"

"Pushed by whom?"

"You know that better than me."

She embraced him and looked up at him:

"You are a good man, Thomas Kane. I pray for you."

"Pray for all of us."

Captain Stewart Van Vliet stared at the unopened letter that he had just received from General Harney with foreboding. It was the end of the day as he sat in his quartermaster's office in Fort Leavenworth. He had served under the general years earlier in Mexico and then in skirmishes with the Sioux Indians. He anticipated this assignment because Harney's first choice was to keep the troops supplied that were already busily engaged trying to keep the peace in Bloody Kansas. Was Secretary of the Army Floyd anxious to make Utah as bloody as Kansas?

Where was his letter opener? A pen knife would do.

He sliced it open, looked inside and swore under his breath.

"So, Utah it is." Van Vliet read quietly to himself...'take 30 men with mounts and carriages, make your way to Salt Lake City and negotiate with Mormon leaders about the acquiring supplies to outfit the Utah Expeditionary Force with provisions, land, lumber and other materials to build barracks for the 5th and 10th Infantry Regiments, the 2nd Dragoons and 4th Artillery as well as storage, warehousing and barns for horses, mules and wagons..."

Below that were the numbers of men and animals, carriages and wagons for him to prepare the necessary inventory and quantity and then calculate how much of each item would need to be acquired at the destination and the quantity of manufactured items he would need to acquire locally. Damn!

Van Vliet had been serving his country since his graduation from West Point in 1840, and he had earned the accolades and promotions along the way for services well performed, but this felt like punishment.

He called for Sergeant Morgan who was writing a letter to his wife in the adjoining room; Morgan would now have to add a post-script. Wherever Van Vliet went, Morgan was sure to follow.

A month later, his team found themselves in Fort Laramie, a more desolate and unpleasant place than Leavenworth getting briefed about the journey that lay ahead.

A young lieutenant Oscar was reading a report which irritated the captain:

"I can read it myself," Van Vliet said. "Give it to me."

He took a few minutes and then explained to Morgan and his other non-coms.

"We'll leave in the morning, but from what I've ascertained from the expected hostility from the Mormons, I may end up driving the last miles in a light carriage by myself. A contingent of 50 armed men may not like the reception they might have planned for us. One man in a two-horse carriage doesn't pose much of a threat. I am an amiable man, don't you think, Sergeant?"

Morgan laughed: "The most amiable quartermaster I have ever met, sir." The corporal added: "You're no General Harney, that's for sure."

"Comedians, one and all." Van Vliet managed a weak smile. "All right. Then let's get to it."

NEWS OF TROUBLE WITH THE ARKANSAS EMIGRANTS up north came at the same time as Apostle George A. Smith's return to southern Utah. Unlike the Saints who were huddled up against the lush Wasatch Mountains, the Saints in southern Utah suffered more from isolation, drought and harsher living conditions than their northern brethren. So when they heard of the impending arrival of an Army with bad intentions and a wagon train of hostile emigrants, it was a recipe for disaster.

In August of 1857, Brigham Young declared martial law in the old tabernacle that declared that no person or persons could pass through the territory without permission — this was direct at the Army, but it meant everybody, including the Arkansas emigrants. Apostle George A. Smith was charged with taking the news south; he spoke at a conference in Beaver to an anxious audience. Towards the back, the two teenage Ott brothers, Jimmy and Joe paid more attention than usual to Elder Smith's report from Salt Lake. Rumors had preceded him; for a change, they were more interested in the content of his sermon than the young ladies who were in attendance. Like everyone in their little community, the boys worked from dawn to dusk to make the desert blossomed as a rose — no one could drive them off, whether they were the United States Army or emigrants from Arkansas. It was a hot, stuffy day in the clapboard meeting house and everyone was fanning themselves.

They sat next to Carl Roundy, a neighbor and friend, who would rather hunt than farm and often took them on his questionable ventures. They were looking around in the congregation for the Littlefield twins when Elder Smith suddenly got their attention:

"Harney and his horde intend to hang about 300 of the most obnoxious Mormons..." Jimmy Ott elbowed Carl and whispered, "He means you," which made his brother laugh. But, soon, the speech's sober tone removed any reason for the teens to make anymore light-hearted comments.

Smith continued: "Brigham's to be hung anyhow — no trial necessary for him or the principal leaders; and then go through a form or trial for the rest. They are sending out officers, a governor, judges, jury and troops...they expect half of the women to leave their husbands and cut their throats and half of the men to join them..."

It didn't take long for the congregation to become inflamed about what was coming their way, not only the Army, but also the emigrants whose journey through Utah Territory was already common knowledge. They had stirred up trouble in Fillmore about 100 miles further north; news of trouble there reached them a day before. Cedar City was only a day or so away by wagon. And, many of the pioneers, like Elder George Smith, had already experienced persecution and been driven from their homes back East. Like him, they wouldn't let it happen again.

Elder Smith reminded them of that: "As a people, we have been long harassed and oppressed, driven, slain and plundered. I have got through with it. I am one of the proscribed, but greatly prefer fighting to hanging, being naturally so great a coward."

The crowd rose to its feet and voiced its unanimity with the preacher's call with hurrahs and applause.

And, then Elder Smith lowered the boom, which got the attention of the congregation: "If the troops come here among us, and we have to flee unto the mountains, we will haunt them as long as they live, unless they live longer than we do. Will we sell them grain or forage? I say damn the man who feeds them; I say damn the man who sympathizes with them…"

The boys in the back were now resolved; they had to do their part. Communities up and down the mountainous backbone of Deseret were up in arms. And, whether it was the Utah Expedition that was marching on Zion or a group of hostile Arkansas emigrants and the Missouri wildcats traveling with them who called the Mormons squatters and ran their cattle over their gardens and in their fields, they were of the same mind. Like Apostle George Smith, they all preferred fighting to hanging.

The emigrants were doomed.

9

"THE SAINTS WOULD BE SATISFIED EVEN IF IT WAS A BARREN ROCK!"

The officers and the men together with their supply wagons under Capt. Van Vliet's command, who had been on the dusty trail headed west for a few weeks now, thought it would be more of the same until they reached the Salt Lake Valley. But, when they reached the summit and viewed the scene below, Captain Stewart Van Vliet stopped his mount in its tracks and removed his hat.

"Dreshler," he muttered to his lieutenant and the second in command, "this is a sight for sore eyes. Now we can see where the Green River got its name."

The valley was a verdant paradise compared to what they had been traipsing through since leaving Fort Laramie. Baptiste's trading post lay a mile or two below them in the midst of a large Shoshone village. It wasn't exactly civilization, but it had its share of humanity.

"Captain, I think the men might want to spend a bit of time in the trading post and find some kind of liquid refreshment."

"As long as they are temperate," Van Vliet responded. "We need to speak with a Mr. Morehead regarding refreshing our stocks."

"Who is Morehead?"

"Charles Morehead is the agent for the shippers, Russell, Majors and Waddell; he's the man who feeds the Army, and that includes us. Let's pick up the pace."

The fifty men on horseback and their supply wagon and mules hurried down the road to Baptiste's, refreshed themselves, and set out for the next stop" Fort Bridger where the Mormon "Army" would greet them the day after tomorrow, some 50 miles distant.

The plan was to meet up with their escorts there and then proceed down to Big Mountain and then into Great Salt Lake City.

But, Brigham had other plans.

At Fort Bridger, Van Vliet met two Mormons who would accompany him and him alone into the valley, Nathaniel Jones and Bryant Stringham.

"Captain Van Vliet," Stringham said as he introduced himself and Jones to the officer at the trading post, "we understand you are going our way, and we have been commissioned to guide you safely into the valley."

"That won't be necessary; I have my dragoons with me, we'll be fine."

"Sir, the dragoons won't be safe if they venture through Echo Canyon, but you will be with us. President Young gave us word to be at your beck and call since we have had to abandon our mail station at Deer Creek. We can leave at 9 in the morning from here, if that works for you."

Van Vliet hesitated and then agreed. "I have a few things to add to my pack mule here in the establishment so I can be prepared for the last leg of the journey. 9 am then, right here. See you in the morning." Jones and Stringham departed, and Van Vliet had to find a campsite for the dragoons to bivouac until his return from the city.

"Nervous?" Lieutenant Dreshler asked his superior officer later that evening as he men were dismissed.

"I'm only nervous that you will keep the men occupied and busy until I return.

"When will that be?"

"That is the question, now isn't it?"

Three days later, Captain Stewart Van Vliet was no longer worried. Late that beautiful summer afternoon, he and his fellow travelers emerged from Emigration Canyon some five or six miles east of Great Salt Lake City and was greeted by a view that took his breath away. Laid out before him were small patches of green in neat rows along wide streets with cottages and gardens arranged neatly; it reminded him of his native New England. The trees were all small, since the Mormons had planted them just10 years earlier. As he looked around, there was nothing haphazard. A half an hour later, Jones and Stringham left him with an aide to the president at the steps to the Lion House. There was construction underway on the Beehive House next door, and there were workmen and suppliers everywhere. Van Vliet was not only impressed by the neatness of the city, but also by all the activity — Deseret — a beehive — seemed to be the appropriate term.

"President Young is in a meeting with some of his counselors and a visitor from southern Utah; he would like you to join them." The captain followed the man inside and upstairs to a meeting room. The aide announced Van Vliet's arrival.

Besides President Young and his counselors were two members of the Council of the Twelve Apostles as well as Jacob Hamblin, the leader of the mission to the Indians in southern Utah, as well as Delegate John Bernhisel.

Brigham explained: "Perhaps you know that we see the native peoples as descendants of the 10 Tribes, not as enemies, and our doing our best to accommodate their needs and teach them about Christian values and their lost heritage, and President Hamblin is key to that."

After being introduced to the assemblage, the Mormon prophet and the captain retired to a smaller office. Young could see that there was some astonishment expressed by his uniformed visitor and was intrigued. After a brief introduction of who he was and why he was in Salt Lake City, Brigham smiled broadly:

"Captain, do you mind telling me where you hail from?"

"Vermont, sir, Ferrisburg."

"I could discern that from your speech! I like to think I'm also a Green Mountain Boy; I was born down the pike a few days ride from you, in Whittingham. Welcome to the Territory of Utah!"

"Well, that is a pleasant surprise!" Captain Van Vliet's astonishment rose a notch or two higher — he was not prepared for this introduction to the man described in eastern newspapers as an imperious lecher and even worse. Then it was Brigham's turn:

"Before we get down to brass tacks and tackle the dilemma before us, may I offer you some victuals and drink — no alcohol on the premises, but we quite like our cider. I'd like you to meet some of my family and colleagues. There's a wash room around the corner; let me gather up some people and then have a fruitful conversation. Please share with me your purpose for your visit,"

Van Vliet showed him his assignment as quartermaster to acquire both materials to construct billets and a supply depot, but also the Army's requirements to fill the depot and its warehouses.

"We are bringing supplies for 15 months, along with the personnel, some 2,500 officers and enlisted men, as well as civilian support, and of course, Governor Cumming. I also want to ensure you that our motives are peaceful and want to be an asset to the community."

Van Vliet could see that Young had been listening very carefully and was contemplating his response. It was a long and awkward pause.

Brigham spoke softly and finally responded: "I perceive you to be an honest and fair man with the best of intentions, and I wish others in your camp shared your views, but I read the eastern newspapers, our people take note of what politicians like Senator Benton and General Harney are saying about us, that we are dictatorial lechers and our women are enslaved victims waiting to be rescued. We would like to let you see for yourself if these things are true, but we have years of sad experience with the federal officers, judges and military personnel who have visited and lived here. The last two judges, Drummond and Stiles left and took the money Congress allocated for their offices with them. They skedaddled.

Brigham continued: "We are even more concerned about the teamsters and suppliers that would accompany and Army of that size and their lack of discipline. We fear for our peace and safety, so I must decline your request at this time, but we would like you to enjoy your stay; we have comfortable accommodations for you tonight and invite you to dine with us. We also have one request: our delegate to Congress, Mr. John Bernhisel was planning on returning to the East tomorrow, and we were hoping he could accompany you on your return."

And, then the president revealed his immovable position: ""We would like to ward off this blow if we can; but the United States seem determined to drive us into a fight. They will kill us if they can. A mob killed Joseph and Hyrum in jail, notwithstanding the faith of the state as pledged to protect them. I have broken no law, and under the present state of affairs I will not suffer myself to be taken by any United States officer to be killed as they killed Joseph."

Now it was Captain Van Vliet who was in search of words: He did not get the answer he wanted, but he was overwhelmed by how was received and was surprised by Brigham Young and the people he had met so far. His astonishment would grow.

On Sunday, Captain Stewart Van Vliet was the guest of honor as Brigham and several other leaders addressed a large gathering at the old tabernacle. It was a hot, August afternoon.

Apostle John Taylor and the president himself laid out for the audience the situation they were facing and then, as Van Vliet and the congregation witnessed, Brigham was a bit worked up:

"I do not often get angry; but when I do, I am righteously angry; and the bosom of the Almighty burns with anger towards those scoundrels; and they shall be consumed, in the name of Israel's God. We have

borne enough of their oppression and hellish abuse, and we will not bear any more of it; for there is no just law requiring further forbearance on our part. And I am not going to have troops here to protect the priests and a hellish rabble in efforts to drive us from the land we possess; for the Lord does not want us to be driven, and has said, 'If you will assert your rights, and keep my commandments, you shall never again be brought into bondage by your enemies.'

"The officer in command of the United States' Army, on its way to Utah, detailed one of his staff, Captain Van Vliet, who is now on the stand, to come here and learn whether he could procure the necessary supplies for the Army. Many of you are already aware of this, and some of you have been previously acquainted with the Captain. Captain Van Vliet visited us in Winter Quarters (now Florence); and, if I remember correctly, he was then officiating as Assistant-Quartermaster. He is again in our midst in the capacity of Assistant-Quartermaster. From the day of his visit to Winter Quarters, many of this people have become personally acquainted with him, both through casual intercourse with and working for him. He has invariably treated them kindly, as he would a Baptist, a Methodist, or any other person; for that is his character. He has always been found to be free and frank, and to be a man that wishes to do right; and no doubt he would deal out justice to all, if he had the power. Many of you have labored for him, and found him to be a kind, good man; and I understand that he has much influence in the Army, through his kind treatment to the soldiers. He treats them as human beings, while there are those who treat them worse than brute beasts. Well, the enquiry is, "What is the news? What is the conclusion?" It is this — We have to trust in God. I am not in the least concerned as to the result, if we put our trust in God. The administrators of our Government have issued orders for marching troops and expending much treasure, and all predicated upon falsehoods, while every honorable man would have first made an economical and peaceful enquiry into the circumstances. And even now, every honorable man would use all his influence to avert the present unjust and entirely groundless movement against us..."

Brigham's hard-nosed counselor, Heber C. Kimball, was more blunt when he looked as the captain and promised, *"But let me tell you, the yoke is off our neck and it is on theirs, and the bow key is in. The day is not far distant when you will see us free as the air we breathe. We will not be governed one whit by the men that are sent here."*

That warning was seconded by hurrahs from the 2,000 in attendance. Following the service, Van Vliet, now sobered by the reality of the will of the people, had a final meeting with Young and his counselors, who predicted that if federal troops entered Salt Lake City his people would burn their homes, destroy their crops, and return Utah to desert rather than surrender it. Seeing that the Mormons "have been lied about the worst of any people I ever saw," Van Vliet gave his word that he would do his best to stop the troops marching on Zion.

Late that evening, as he was preparing to spend a very comfortable night in a feather bed, not on a bedroll with a boulder for a pillow, he wrote a brief note that he planned on mailing to his wife when he returned:

"We read in the Book of Matthew not to judge others, lest we be judged. I have found this to be true. These people have been slandered and made into caricatures. I have been deceived, the nation has been deceived as to who these people are. They have made the desert blossom as a rose after Christians had chased from state to state to their mountain fortress. I came here to acquire food and supplies for our Expedition, but the Mormons will not permit an Army to march into their settlements and put them under their boot. I am leaving here with nothing, no agreement to supply us with anything…nothing but clarity and a commitment to do what I can to make sure we have a peaceful conclusion to this venture."

Sometimes nothing can be better than the alternative.

The next day as John Bernhisel joined the captain on his return, he found something new: a friend and so did Bernhisel as well as the Saints of the Latter-days, the people commonly disparaged as "Mormons." For them, friends were as scarce, and as dear, as water was in this country.

The original tabernacle on the temple block was said to accommodate 4,000 congregants, but with news about the Army on its way, that would be tested. Thanks to the Abbotts, Christian's neighbor, he was able to find a respectable ride down into the city with Winnie at his side. Christian knew one of the doormen; he met him in Bremen years earlier as a new missionary. The doorman was delighted to see Christian as missionaries always are, to see real flesh-and-blood examples of their evangelical success.

They were on the fourth bench on the right side. It was hot and dry, but President Young was in good form. This time, he had a wider audience than the Cedar City stake president, and in his mind, he probably thought the crisis in southern Utah had been averted, so after a hymn, he got right to the point. It was a hot August day; audience members were already fanning themselves.

The president spoke:

"As was noted in the canyon on July 24th, and some of you were there, it has been ten years since we first arrived in this place, and in fulfillment of prophecy, we have seen the desert blossom as a rose. It has occurred to me that I promised you something then, namely that if the Lord would permit us to live here for ten years unmolested where we could build our homes, raise our crops and our children, then no power would be able to drive us out, with the Lord's help."

A loud cry of affirmation went out from the crowd.

"On that day, Brothers Smoot, Stoddard, Rockwell and Stott had just arrived from the east bearing grave news. A new governor is supposedly on his way..."

Many expressed their displeasure with the announcement, but the president continued. *"...a new governor is on his way with some 2,500 troops equipped with 15 months worth of provisions under the direction of General William Harney who has communicated his intention of hanging many of us."*

Again, the Mormons booed Harney and his bravado but Young finished his statement:

"But, God willing, if Harney and his mob try to cross the South Pass, the buzzards will pick his bones clean!"

A great cheer went up from the Saints as President Young attempted to quiet the group.

"We have been charged with treason. The Prophet Joseph, too, was charged with high treason. When Joseph had his trial when he was imprisoned at Far West, Judge King asked him if he believed the prediction of Daniel the Prophet, that in the latter days the God of Heaven would set up a kingdom which would succeed and finally rule and hold dominion over all other kingdoms. He replied that he did believe the scripture, and for that he was accused of treason. Joseph's lawyer then turned to the judge and said, 'Judge, I think you better write it down that the Bible is treason.' And you know the rest: we were driven out of Missouri; what we were guilty of, we did not know. We lived in Illinois for a few years and again, persecution overtook us. 'Treason, treason, treason!' they cried, calling us murderers, thieves, liars, adulterers and the worst people on the earth.

"Three congressmen called on us in the fall of 1845, informing us that religious prejudice was such that we could stay in peace no longer. One of them, Stephen A. Douglas said: 'I know you, I know Joseph Smith; he was a good man ...and this people are a good people, but the prejudices of the priests and ungodly are such that you cannot stay here in live in peace.'

"We wish strangers to understand that we did not come here out of choice, but we were obliged to go somewhere and here we landed. We considered California or Vancouver Island, but we knew after five years, they would chase us out again. So, this was the best place we could find.

"So, I said, let us stay in the mountains, and we can raise our own potatoes and eat them. We came here penniless in old wagons,

our friends telling us 'take all the provisions you can, for you can get no more!' Take all the seed grain you can, for you can get none here. We did this, and in addition to all this, we have gathered all the poor we could, and the Lord has planted us in these valleys, promising that he would hide us up for a little season until his wrath and indignation passed over the nations. Will we trust in the Lord? Yes!"

Christian and Winnie drew closer together as the congregation shouted their affirmation. And the president turned up the volume:

"We made and broke the road from Nauvoo to this place. Some of the time we followed Indian trails, some of the time we ran by the compass; when we left the Missouri river we followed the Platte. And we killed rattlesnakes by the cord in some places; and made roads and built bridges until our backs ached. For 1,200 or 1,300 miles, we carried every particle of provision we had when we arrived here.

Instead of the 365 pounds of breadstuff when they started from the Missouri river, there was not half of them that had half of it. We had to bring our seed grain, our farming utensils, bureaus, secretaries, sideboards, sofas, pianos, large looking glasses, fine chairs, carpets, nice shovels, and tongs and other fine furniture with all the parlor, cook stoves etc. and we have to bring these things all piled together with some women and children, helter skelter, topsy-turvy with broken-down horses, oxen with three legs and cows with one teat.

You may say this is burlesque. Well, I mean it as such, for we comparatively speaking, really came here naked and barefoot."

The burlesque comment drew some laughter and Winnie smiled as Christian held her closer.

But President Young wasn't laughing:

"I did not devise the great scheme of the Lord's opening the way to send people to these mountains; I had nothing to do with it. No, we came here by faith, not knowing beforehand whither we would go. We had to have faith to come here. When we met Mr. Bridger on the Big Sandy River, he said to me: 'Mr. Young, I would give a thousand dollars if I knew an ear of corn could be ripened in the Great

Basin.' Said I, 'Wait eighteen months and I will show you many of them.' Did I say this from knowledge? No, it was my faith because all we heard told us otherwise, that the land was sterile, its cold and frost. But, we traveled on, breaking the road through the mountains and building bridges until we arrived here, and then we did everything we could to sustain ourselves.

"There is not another people on the earth that could have come here and lived. We prayed over the land, and dedicated it and the water, air and everything pertaining to them unto the Lord, and the smiles of heaven rested on the land and it became productive, and today yields us the best of grain, fruit and vegetables."

He paused for a moment and then concluded:

"You inquire if we shall stay in these mountains. I answer yes, as long as we please to do the will of God, Our Father in Heaven. If we are pleased to turn away from the holy commandments of the Lord Jesus Christ, as ancient Israel did, every man turning to is own way, we shall be scattered and peeled, driven before our enemies and persecuted, until we learn to remember the Lord our God and are willing to walk in his ways.

"Let us remember: We have been thrown like a stone from a sling, and we have lodged in the godly place where the Lord wants his people to gather... **If the Lord should say by revelation this is the spot, the Saints would be satisfied even if it was a barren rock!"**

10

"MARTIAL LAW IS HEREBY DECLARED"

At the conclusion of the conference where Brigham Young spoke so boldly about the impending crisis,, Christian and Winnie held hands, but said little as they walked west along North Temple Street where Brother and Sister Abbott were waiting for them in their carriage. Their frame home was east of where the Rasmussen's were staying, and it was no trouble for them to give the young couple a ride.

Perhaps it was the ride back — in relative silence since their hosts were engaged in a conversation of their own — that Winnie and Christian exchanged glances that communicated that they were indeed a couple, but wouldn't make it official while everyone's future was in doubt.

That was drilled into their minds now that everyone realized an Army had begun marching on their mountain homes; all doubt as to the federal government's intention had been erased. In response, a few days prior to his address, Governor Young, wearing his territorial hat, had declared martial law and sent riders ahead to let the "Federales" know that they were not welcome.

What's more, the residents of the Territory of Utah were advised not to sell or share their stored supplies, especially grains and stocks with any parties traveling through the territory. It had to kept in reserve in case they were driven out again.

Tragically, a group of Arkansas pioneers were on their way south via Idaho and headed through Utah Territory to southern California, thinking all was well in Zion.

It wasn't.

Brigham's martal law proclamation had been posted all over the city and one appeared on a post near where the Abbots were waiting for Christian and Winnie to emerge from the meeting.. They all four paused to read it before driving away:

CITIZENS OF UTAH:

We are invaded by a hostile force, who are evidently assailing us to accomplish our overthrow and destruction....The issue which has thus been forced upon us compels us to resort to the great first law of self-preservation, and stand in our own defense....Therefore I, Brigham Young, governor...in the Territory of Utah forbid:

First. All armed forces of every description from coming into this Territory...

Second. That all forces in said Territory hold themselves in readiness to march at a moment's notice to repel any and all such invasion.

Third. Martial law is hereby declared to exist...and no person shall be allowed to pass or repass into or through or from the Territory without a permit from the proper officer.

Christian and Winnie had to talk; they would need to wait until they had a quiet moment alone — it was complicated.

DAYS BEFORE THE ARKANSANS ARRIVED at the Iron Mission in Cedar City, the Saints had been made aware that they were coming. Their charismatic spiritual leader, and a major in the militia, Mayor Isaac Haight, had been warned, and he was worried.

In fact, from Fillmore where the last confrontation took place, word had traveled up and down the various settlements, and with each iteration, the warning about the wagon train's arrival was repeated and then repeated again, increasing in volume and intensity each time it was retold.

There were even rumors that a militia was marching north from California.It worried 24-year-old Nephi Johnson, a second lieutenant in the militia, and events were transpiring just as his father had predicted in April when news of Buchanan's order arrived. Nephi missed his father. Joel Hills Johnson had left the territory on a mission to Iowa months earlier. Nephi wished his father was there to advise him.

But, Nephi, had his marching orders. He had heard Elder George A. Smith's warning a couple of weeks earlier at a conference that the Army intended on hanging about "300 of the most obnoxious Mormons without 'due process.'" Jokes were flying around about who was the most obnoxious — he and his young friends had nominated a few.

But, now things were getting serious. Nephi had left Tropic a week ago after he had been activated to go to Cedar City to help the militia. His assignment was to work with the Paiutes because he knew their language, and they were on the warpath because of the trepidations of the Arkansas emigrants.

Nothing to joke about now!

Nephi recognized some other militia members hanging around on Main Street in Cedr city. He got off his horse and tied her up by the mercantile. A group of his friends were engaged in a lively conversation.

If the Army was looking for somebody obnoxious to hang, Nephi told himself, there's one standing at the door: Jim Norton.

Nephi interrupted the conversation: "What's happening?"

"The Paiutes are on the warpath, and Mayor Haight and John Lee are all riled up," Norton said.

Nephi tried to calm things down. "These emigrants are ornery because no one will sell them anything, and they run their animals all over the place, and they're on their way here. If you don't calm down, there will be trouble."

Norton was really worked up: "There already has been trouble — a Paiute was killed, another wounded and so was an emigrant.

The Indians said the Arkansans poisoned an ox, and the carcass festered and some Paiutes got sick, some died. They're up in arms, and so are settlers up and down the trail.

Norton continued: "They ran their animals all over, claiming it was 'Uncle Sam's land.'"

"I have to leave, and I don't want you boys to get involved — you go home so your parents won;'t worry," Nephi said. "I have my orders, and if you are needed, we'll call you."

After they left, Nephi and a boyhood friend, John Chatterly, watched as the the teens left in a huff. Nephi could see that his friend was worried.

"Good to see you, Neph', Chatterly said. "I'm on my way to Parowan — hope we can catch up sometime soon."

"What's in Parowan?" Chatterly lowered his voice, since they were standing right outside the mayor's office.

"Mayor Haight gave me this note to take to President Dame in Parowan and, in his words, 'to return immediately with explicit instructions.'"

Now Nephi was worried, too. "John, be careful and cautious. Things might get out of control. Let's talk when you're back," Nephi said. They mounted up and rode off in opposite directions.

Later that evening as he sat on Dame's porch in Parowan, John Chatterly overheard a lively conversation that lasted for at least an hour. One member of the council exclaimed that "turmoil in Cedar City was disturbing, but nothing that called for harsh measures."

When the council had finished, the major's adjutant gave Chatterly a letter that stated that "all possible means should be used to keep the peace until the emigrants should leave and proceed upon their journey."

"Brotherly Chatterly," the adjutant said, "we are counseling peace. Remind your people not to place any serious regard to the emigrants' threats, for they are merely words and 'words are but wind.'"

Chatterly was not consoled. Who would take his counsel? In truth, he was right — Mayor Haight and the other members of his council might listen to him and read the letter.

But John D. Lee would not.

J.C. VAN DYKE AND ROBERT TYLER WERE COMPARING NOTES over coffee in a Georgetown dive on Canal Road awaiting their "secret source" as Tyler called him. These two advisors to President Buchanan were officially on the same team, but their motivations and loyalties were polar opposites. Van Dyke was a Pennsylvanian, a northern Democrat; Tyler, the former president's son was from Virginia, from a slave-owning family. For the moment, their goal was to keep the Union from flying apart. Their visitor's name was Brewster — Tyler invited him, but that's all that Van Dyke knew, but he was "well connected." Van Dyke was ready to leave.

"I have duties to perform, Robert. How long do we have to wait?"

Robert patted his arm: "Be patient; it's worth your time, you'll see. He has been waiting for a telegram from Independence."

They ordered more scones and two more cups of coffee. Van Dyke took another look at his pocket watch and was ready to leave when a burly man in a leather jacket hurried over to their table by the window.

Brewster slid in next to Tyler at the table and waived away the waiter. No coffee for him, but he grabbed a scone, stuffed it into his mouth and pulled an envelope out of his pocket and handed it to Robert Tyler. There was a telegram inside.

"Holy Mary and Joseph," Tyler exclaimed. "This is terrible!" Smiling, he handed it to Van Dyke.

"Well, this is indeed interesting. How did this all come about?" Van Dyke handed the telegram back to Tyler.

"Act of God, bad deeds by men, who knows. But, there were a contingent of Missourians who were traveling with a group of

Arkansans whose bad timing found them traveling through Utah just as old Brigham declared martial law. They've been exchanging blows and even bullets on their way south," Tyler said and then turned to Brewster. "How did you get this information?"

"From a Wildcatter."

Van Dyke was puzzled: "What's a Wildcatter?"

Brewster looked at Van Dyke like he was a schoolboy: "A southern sympathizer from Missouri who made Kansas bleed, stirred up more trouble between abolitionists and southerners."

"And?"

"He likely left Fort Laramie a few weeks ago and arrived in Independence last night. He keeps me updated. I sent a telegram to his employer asking him to send me a note about what was happening…"

"Where?"

Brewster was irritated: "In Utah, of course."

Now Van Dyke was irritated: "What in the hell happened? Who is bleeding in Utah?"

"Too early to tell, but soon there may soon be 100 Arkansans and a smattering of Missourians causing hell in Utah where some 40,000 Mormons are being invaded, and it's not looking good for the emigrants. He wonders if they will reach California without a battle."

"But maybe good news for us," Tyler conjectured. Van Dyke was still puzzled, but Tyler and Brewster shook hands — so far, so good. People will be looking west, not south. They had misjudged the president's man. Van Dyke was no ally.

THOMAS L. KANE COULDN'T SLEEP. At the Kane family retreat, it was raining, a steady, warm summer rain, something his friends in the high mountain desert rarely enjoyed. He walked over to the nightstand, grabbed a small hand towel and dropped it into the basin, wrung it out and buried his face in it. His nightshirt clung to his body; he took it off and patted himself down, trying to relieve himself of the night sweats.

He coughed and then opened both windows, but it didn't help. He braced himself on the window sill and watched the rain come down. There was no relief. Thankfully, September was coming. And October with cooler weather. Maybe by then he would regain his health. His lovely young bride, Elizabeth or "Bess," slept peacefully, but then why wouldn't she? She was so young and so full of faith. Her concern was him and his health. Why worry about problems so far away, about a lost and wayward people who brought their problems on themselves? She took the side of Thomas' father and brothers. The Mormons, she admonished him. Let them be, Thomas — they're making you sick; it's not your fight.

Kane looked down at his pile of correspondence with Brigham Young and the Mormon's delegate to Congress, John Bernhisel. He hadn't written or sent a letter west for a couple of months now, but the eastern newspapers had kept the subject on his mind.

There was a flash of lightening in the distance, followed by a muffled clap of thunder. He found a dry shirt and fumbled around in the writing desk until he found a candle, lit it and pulled up a chair. He sat down, took pen and ink to hand and began composing his first letter in awhile.

After lying low for a couple of months thanks to the malicious hit piece in the *New York Times* that had attacked him for standing up for Brigham and his friends in Utah, it was time to get back into action. His father, Judge John Kane and others suspected the real poison pen belonged to the lecherous Judge Drummond who had been "drummed out" of his position in Utah and had slinked back to Washington City via California and New Orleans, leaving his real name off of the article.

Thomas figured that since the newly installed President James Buchanan owed much of his political success to Judge Kane, maybe a letter from the judge's son would give him some food for thought before doing something reckless.

Never worried that Thomas was a "secret Mormon" as some claimed, Bess was finally at peace now that Thomas had officially expressed himself not only to be a Christian, but now along with her and the rest of the family, a respectable Presbyterian, a gentleman's sect if there ever was one.

Bess padded softly into the study in a quilted rob with a candle in hand to check on Thomas who looked up from his reading.

"Anything wrong, Bess? Just finishing some reading," he said putting the book face down which piqued his wife's curiosity.

He laughed: "Yes, Bess, I am reading the Bible, First Corinthians chapter 29, verse 15, if you must know. Aren't we planning to go to church tomorrow?"

She beamed her approval, but added a balm of Gilead: "If anybody asks you about your Mormon friends, just smile: Our friends and neighbors read newspapers as well as the Bible, you know."

"Don't you pay no mind to anything others may say, here in this little village or in anything printed in the papers. I know I'm in a funk, but that's not why. Elisha is still on my mind; he had unfinished business to do, as we all do. Others may respect me less for my being alone in the defense of a despised and injured people, but I respect myself more for it. I have unfinished work to do as well."

"And I respect you for it, too; you're an excellent writer and lobbyist for them, but it's getting late. It's time for bed," she looked at him wistfully and shuffled away.

Nevertheless, lying next to Kane on the ottoman was a bundle of unopened correspondence from his friends, his Mormon friends, in the West. Maybe his energy was waning, but his friends were in grave danger. He would do what he could do to help them. Maybe later, not now. *But if not now, when? And if not me, who? Who else would come to the Mormons' aid? I'll address that later,* he thought, wrestling with his dilemma.

It was raining, and it continued all through the night.

NEPHI JOHNSON WASN'T A PROPHET — never claimed to be — but his concerns about the Baker-Fancher wagon train of Arkansans and Missouri Wildcatters traveling to California were spot on. As predicted, the emigrants' arrival was apocalyptic. Cedar City residents remembered what their leader Mayor Isaac Haight had said weeks earlier at a town meeting as he recounted the persecutions and deprivations his family had suffered when he was driven out of Nauvoo where he had served as a town constable and body guard to Joseph and Hyrum Smith:

"I am prepared to feed the enemy the bread he fed me!" Among those on hand to hear his speech was a dozen boys in uniform who went by the moniker of "Zion's Avengers." So, when the emigrants trotted into town and stopped at the Deseret Iron Company store, the fuse was lit.

Store clerk Christopher Arthur was behind the counter when two rough-looking men barged inside.

"Is this all you got," shouted the larger man in buckskin.

Arthur was taken aback: "Excuse me? What exactly...?"

The man profaned, complained and threatened Arthur: "What a sorry excuse for a town you have here! Who is in charge here?" His partner had an answer: "He's next door!"

Next door was the partially completed home of Isaac Haight, who was not only the mayor, manager of the Iron Works, and the stake president of the town's congregations. Several of the emigrants, a couple obviously inebriated, were standing outside yelling at him to show himself.

"If you are a real man, come outside and answer our demands. Our people need supplies to continue our journey. Sometime soon an Army of Californians will visit you with vengeance and seize old Brigham, you and your cohorts and put you where you belong!" The mayor slipped out the back door and hurried to Marshal Higbee's office around the corner to get help:

"Marshal, get some men and come to the store," Haight ordered the marshal.

"Isaac, it's just me and my boy," he replied, but grabbed a weapon and hurried over to arrest the perpetrators.

The emigrants were not impressed:

Right in front of the store, the face-off was witnessed by both a couple more emigrants and a dozen townspeople. Weapons were visible all around.

Higbee spoke: "Mister, you and your people need to leave this town, or so help me, we'll have the militia here and force you to leave."

"We can defend ourselves from a bunch of debauched Mormons. You don't scare us! My pistol was used on your so-called prophet Joe Smith — don't think I won't use it again!"

As the emigrant considered his position, he motioned to his fellow travelers, and they turned and rode away. Within the hour, the emigrant train was leaving the city, but not before they stopped by the Morris farm just as Barbara Morris was crossing the street to her corral. Her neighbor, Mary Campbell, later reported to Haight that one of the emigrants stuck a pistol in Sister Morris' face while a boy ran to her chicken coop, grabbed a couple of hens, wrung their necks as the man in the wagon screamed at her:

"By hell, if old Brigham and his priests won't sell us nothin,' then we'll take whatever we need."

The die was cast. The emigrants would have the battle they had been provoking, and the vengeance that had been seething for decades inside the hearts of Mormon settlers in Utah would be sated. The Mormons would live with that shame for generations.

THE BAKER-FANCHER EMIGRANT TRAIN, along with the Missourians and other hangers-on, had been told that a narrow valley north of the Santa Clara river offered a lush respite where their animals could be fed before their departure into the barren desert areas that lay further south on the Camino Real. But, that area of peace and rest turned into something else — a bloody killing field. The emigrants found themselves surrounded with Paiute Indians to the south and Mormon settlers on all sides. A gun battle raged all around.

Nephi Johnson was the interpreter for the Indians and was there under duress. Some of the Paiutes who believed that they had been betrayed by the emigrants by the "poisoned ox" wanted revenge. But, the Paiutes also had reservations. He watched from the hillside as combatants on both sides were wounded, with two fatalities that he had witnessed, an emigrant and an Indian. A sometime friend and sometime adversary of Haight was down at the skirmish line directing the battle. A young man rode up to him: "I'm James Haslam. I was told to report to Major Haight, uh, President Haight. Do you know where he is?" Nephi pointed to a wagon at the edge of the ridge.

"He's observing the battle, up in the wagon." Haslam found Haight nervously pacing around with a notebook in his hand. Haight spoke first:

"Brother Haslam, I am told you are an excellent horseman, is that right?"

He nodded.

"We have a mission for you.," the mayor said, sotto voce. He looked all around to make sure no one overheard their conversation:

"In this envelope is a message for President Young…"

"President Brigham Young?"

"Who else? Of course, Brigham Young!" Haight was losing patience.

"This other note is for militia commanders or local authorities from here to Salt Lake, authorizing them to assist with new mounts along the way. Do you understand what your mission is?"

"To deliver this letter to Brigham Young…"

"And?"

"To no one else…And as fast as I can ride."

"Exactly, day AND night." Haight said with relief.

"I, uh, just have one question," Haslam stuttered.

"Yes?"

"What's in the letter?"

Haight looked resigned: "What do we do with these people?" He pointed at the circle of wagons with more than 100 emigrants cornered inside.Haslam turned and rode off as fast as he could, but just before he arrived at the top of the ridge, he looked back at the scene below and muttered out loud, *"what have we done?"*

11

"SPARE NO HORSEFLESH"

Proclamations were flying all over the place in 1857. Men in power were sending letters, issuing edicts and giving orders. From Washington to Salt Lake City, there was an uproar — peace seemed in short supply and out of fashion. The dozen and a half newspapers in New York City alone were practically running out of ink, all just trying to keep pace with the animosity. Albert Browne Jr. kept his regular messages going to editor/publisher of the *New York Tribune*, the quirky Horace Greeley. His counterparts from the *New York Herald* and the *New York Times* were running low on stamps, too.

But, the peace that "surpatheth all understanding" still found its way to godly people everywhere who had reserved space for it in their hearts and didn't allow it to be driven out regardless of their circumstances, geographic location or standing in life.

Outside Bingham Fort in Ogden, Lt. William Stowell had his mare all packed along with a mule loaded with supplies in tow. He had an appointment with his superior officer, Major Joseph Taylor and the rest of their team. Cynthia and Sophronia took a last look at their uniformed hero:

"William, the uniform suits you," Cynthia declared bravely. Sophronia let her do the talking for both of them. Tears from tots were wiped away and each child took a turn to say good-bye. William's 13-year-old nephew whispered, "I wish I were going with you, Uncle Will."

"I need you stay here and be the man of the house…well, of the Fort. Can you be your aunts' right-hand man?"

The boy nodded, but couldn't speak. His sister, though, spoke for all of them: "Come back, Uncle William!"

"I have God's assurance that I will," William said and got on his mare, waved and trotted away.

With orders in hand from Lt. General Daniel H. Wells to his superior officer, William Stowell took leave of his family, sensing that it would be some time before their reunion. In a dream that he had (which he would later share with his family and friends), he foresaw that he would be captured and taken prisoner by the Expedition, but then saw in vision that he would ride through Echo Canyon and subsequently be reunited with his loved ones unhurt. But, for now, he kept his revelation to himself.

Later that afternoon, William arrived at their prescribed meeting place. Major Joseph Taylor, Wells Chase, George Rose, and Joseph Orton had already arrived. Their team was all assembled.

Taylor addressed his team: "Let's get something to eat, and afterwards, we'll read what General Wells has in mind for us."

William unsaddled his animals, hobbled them, let them graze and got a drink. They found themselves some shade under a pair of cottonwoods not far from the Bear River. Half an hour later, they shared a log as Taylor read their orders:

"Major Joseph Taylor: You will proceed with all possible dispatch, without injuring your animals, to the Oregon road, near the bend of Bear River, north by east of this place. Burn the whole country before them and in their flanks, keep them from sleeping by night surprises; blockade the roads by felling trees and destroying river fords; take no life, but destroy their trains, and stampede or drive away their animals at every opportunity. Take close and correct observations of the country on your route. When you approach the road, send scouts ahead to ascertain if the invading troops have passed that way. Should they have passed, take a concealed route and get ahead of them. Express to Col. [Robert T.] Burton, who is now on that road and in the vicinity of the troops,

and effect a junction with him, so as to operate in concert, Remember, take no life."

"So, we're spies…" Orton muttered.

William answered: "Yes, to spy but not to be spied upon. Tricky business, no?" In other words, they were to find the enemy, but not let the enemy find them. Didn't exactly work out that way.

AFTER TEN YEARS, THE WAGON TRAIL LEADING from Big Mountain and down into Emigration Canyon was finally clear of boulders and stumps. But, now it was rutted from hundreds and hundreds of wagons and handcarts that had rolled down the mountain and onto the floor of ancient Lake. Bonneville. Footsteps made by the thousands of pioneers who had trod the trail didn''t leave such a lasting impression, excepting the ones engraved in the fleshy parts of their hearts. At the entrance to Echo Canyon, Christian Holz and his beloved Winnie's younger brother, Caleb Rasmussen, were among Captain John Winder's company who were on horseback with pack mules in tow. It was late afternoon.

"I don't remember this being such a beautiful place when we first passed through here. But that was a long time ago, and we just wanted to get down into the valley," Caleb said. "And I was just 12 years old. Now look at it. Much greener than down in the big valley."

Christian studied the eager young man saddled up next to him, thinking of the concern Caleb"s mother had shared with him before they left. Like most mothers, she was worried about her son. Caleb knew about the Saints' sacrifices, the persecutions and the shallow graves that littered the pioneer trail. He even helped dig his own father's unmarked grave, somewhere west of the Missouri River. For Caleb, it was payback time. Christian knew about bloodlust. He witnessed it firsthand fighting the Danes. The irony of being in love with a Dane, the winsome Winnie Rasmussen, and now watching over this young Danish man, her brother, was not lost on him. This young descendant of fearsome Vikings, Caleb wanted to get into the fight. Captain Winder's orders were far different from a Viking's order of battle.

Around the campfire that night at a ramshackle place they called "Wickiup City," they got their orders. Their temporary "boomtown" when completed would consist of a few log houses, some Sibley-style tepee tents but mostly wickiups — hence the "town's" name — shelters like the Goshute Indians constructed made of poles, willows and grass with dirt roofs. The next day, construction began.

The young Viking was clearly disappointed; rather than a rifle, his weapon was a shovel.

"This isn't how you fight a war," he muttered to no one in particular. Christian was notching logs for a cabin nearby and overheard Caleb's complaint and laughed:

"Caleb, soldiers have been moaning about orders like these since Roman times. It gets worse than this, trust me. Make some friends, tell a joke."

"This is the joke," Caleb groused.

"Captain Winder said once we have our habitations completed, then the real fun begins," the officer in charge said. His name was Abraham Halladay, an Englishman and a carpenter.

"What's that?"

Halladay laughed: "You're going to love it. The first squad will spend this week digging a zig-zag trench…"

Caleb was confused: "Zig-zag?"

Halladay explained: "Back and forth, like the letter 'Z'. Then, Christian and I will take the second squad and proceed up Pine Canyon across from the narrows, climb to the top and use what materials are available, along with timbers that have been pre-cut and build the breastworks, parapets in other words."

Again, Caleb's English vocabulary was insufficient: "Parapets?" Christian explained: "Shooting sites, places where we can fire down on invaders stupid enough to try to come up the canyon or roll boulders down on them — if it comes to that. But, as always, are orders are clear, Caleb: Take no life."

And, so for the next few weeks in the fall while the weather cooperated, several hundred members of the Mormon militia were busy building defenses: breastworks, entrenchment along the entire bottom of Echo Canyon, some 350 feet apart which, when filled with water, would measure 12 feet wide and six feet deep. And, their most ambitious project would be the dam, a 30-foot-wide and 16-foot-high structure designed to back up the stream feeding the Weber River to force the invaders to march along a narrow edge right below the cliffs so defenders above them could drop rocks and roll boulders down on top of them.

Caleb's blood lust would not be sated. He continued to grumble. The persecutors needed to be taught a lesson! But, the work continued, Caleb did his part, and like so many conscripts before and after him, he groused and moaned every step of the way.

Weeks later, however, the Mormon construction crew was able to look with pride at their handiwork.

Captain Winder and Colonel Jones had the several companies stand at attention on the south side of the canyon; the colonel addressed the men:

"At ease, men: Now, take a look at your handiwork, gentlemen: You know what this means? The United States Army will not be marching in step down this canyon, unless you and I under directions from Brother Brigham, give them permission to do so. We understand that Colonel Albert Sydney Johnston has been named to replace that bloody General Harney; he is on his way to take command of an Army and its supplies that are moving slowly west. And, now we have new orders which will be communicated to you shortly. Take pride in your work — generations to come will remember your contribution with pride. Dismissed!

Christian walked over to Caleb: "Are you disappointed?"

"About what?"

"That you didn't fire your weapon," Christian smiled.

Caleb laughed: "My weapon is a shovel, but…"

Christian pressed him: "But what?"

"What if our enemies never learn their lesson?"

Christian took a seat on the log near the campfire — supper was being prepared: "Caleb, the only lesson they need to learn is what we were taught before we came here."

"Up here in the canyon?" Caleb asked, pressing him.

"No, Caleb, the lesson of peace that we were taught by our missionaries, to do good to them that despitefully use you."

"That's hard for me."

Christian sighed: "So is digging trenches, and worse — digging graves."

Caleb softened: "I know. I did that, somewhere in Nebraska."

Christian put his arm around his angry young friend: "That, Caleb, is a lesson that has eternal consequences."

The next day, Captain Winder delivered them new orders:

"Christian, Colonel Burton heard about your experience fighting for the Prussians. And, they want you and your young friend to report to Colonel Taylor down at the staging area at Mormon Flats."

"You mean Caleb and I?" Christian asked.

"Yes. We appreciate your help here. But, we need your experience in such matters But, we hope it isn't needed."

"You mean killing people…that's why I left my home, you know, but this is my home, our home now — and that's worth fighting for."

"My sentiments exactly," Winder said, saluted him and left.

AN UNEXPECTED VISITOR KNOCKED ON BRIGHAM YOUNG'S DOOR. A sunburned man, covered in sweat and smelling of leather and horseflesh stood on Brigham's doorstep.

"My goodness, brother, who are you and what brings you here?" Brigham asked the man teetering on his doorstep.

"James Haslam, sir, from Cedar City, rode here for two days

with no sleep, at the request of President, rather Mayor Isaac Haight. I have a letter. Among other things, as you will see, it says that the Indians have gotten the Arkansas emigrants corralled at the Mountain Meadows, and the mayor wants to know what should be done."

"Please come in and sit down," the president said. "Rhonda dear," he shouted to his daughter, "can you please get this young man something to drink and a wet towel? Let me have the letter, please."

President Young took it from Haslam and went into the other room. Haslam had collapsed in a large chair in the corner and had fallen asleep,

"Does anybody know where George Watt is?" Brigham yelled. One of the children responded:

"He's around back with the glaziers."

"Can you fetch him, please?"

Five minutes later, his stenographer and personal secretary was standing in front with a small notebook.

"George, can you get a copy of the statement we prepared two days ago when Van Vliet and Jacob Hamblin were here? I want to paraphrase some of that note for an answer we are sending to Cedar City mayor." Brigham Young continued: "There has been a series of skirmishes with a wagon train of emigrants west of Cedar City. Apparently, the Paiutes were involved — several Indians were killed, along with a couple of the emigrants. Haight wants advice — what can we do here?" Brigham asked incredulously as he searched for words.

"George, let's use that letter we prepared and draft one for President Haight. We need to attend to the courier and get him to return post haste!"

George returned a few minutes later with a note summarizing Van Vliet's letter that included the directive to let the emigrants pass in peace with the reminder that *the Lord has answered our prayers and again averting the blow designed for our heads."*

Then Brigham added the following lines to end the letter:

"In regard to emigration trains passing through our settle-ments, we must not interfere with them until they have been first notified to keep away. You must not meddle with them."

Then he added a post script in the form of prophetic advice:

"He (the Lord) has overruled for our deliverance this once again, and He will always do so if we live our religion, be united in our faith and good works."

George then penned the official letter to be signed by Brigham Young for James Haslam to take immediately to Isaac Haight. After he had rested and had been fed and issued a fresh mount, Haslam set off on his return journey to save the emigrants.

"Spare no horseflesh" was Brigham's admonition, and according to the report later put into print, that he "shot off like an arrow down Theatre Hill and was soon out of sight."

THE DIMINUTIVE THOMAS LEIPER KANE DIDN'T FEEL CALM at all on this summer day. He and his family were still in their summer home in the woods, far away from the political frenzy of Philadel-phia and New York. Some New York newspapers were calling for the Army to push right into Utah, even though their commander hadn't yet arrived and supply trains were scattered across Kansas and into Nebraska. Soon men would be marching while he was squirreled away in his comfortable abode in the Alleghanies.

And that made him uncomfortable.

Maybe it was time to come out of hiding and forget all about Drummond's lies.On his way back from the local post office, Elizabeth met him on the porch.

"Your father's inside, pacing, helping himself to your liquor cab-inet, searching your library. He has something on his mind."

Thomas was even more agitated now.

The conversation with his father, Judge Kane, didn't help.

"Thomas, do you consider yourself well read," the elder Mr.

Kane asked his son as he poured himself a glass of sherry.

"Is this a trick question, Father?"

"No trick, just trying to reason with you. Might be a good time to re-read Cervantes. Don Quixote can be very illuminating."

"Ahhh, of course, Don Quixote," Thomas said with a laugh. "So, you think I am tilting at windmills? You think I am the Man from La Mancha?"

Thomas walked to the bookshelf to see if he indeed had a copy of the old masterpiece. He didn't.

"Look at the similarities, son," the Judge Kane said as he settled down with his glass in his son's favorite chair, probably just to irritate him a bit more, Thomas thought.

John Kane didn't mince words:"You're both romantics. You both go charging off to who knows where. Admittedly, your new gelding is in much better shape than the old knight's Rocinante was ... "

"But I have no Sancho," Thomas replied, finding his face flushing but still in control.

"No, you are even more alone than Senor La Mancha. At least he had a servant to do his bidding."

"Yes, but I must admit that I am a bit envious; he did have one person who believed in him!"

The judge felt cornered: "Look, son, I'm your father. I just want what's best for you. This delusion ..."

"So, this is where this La Mancha thing is going? Deluded? You think I'm deluded?"

"I didn't say that, but those Mormons ..."

"Yes, they may very well be deluded. Aren't we all? What did the Apostle Paul say, that 'we are all looking through a glass darkly?'"

"But Thomas, think about all the blood that's been spilled in Kansas. Rushing in to give aid and assistance to the Mormons is like, uh, like running into a burning house. You could end up hated and despised just like them. Or worse!"

"Maybe, but remember: When I went to Iowa ten, 11 years ago, I saw an opportunity, maybe even a governorship. That wasn't to be. But, I learned something more important, namely, that there is a crisis in the life of every man when he is called upon to decide seriously and permanently if he will die unto sin or live unto righteousness. Such an event was my visit to the Mormon camps on the Missouri."

"Yes, I know. I read your account — a tragedy for sure."

"You should have seen it as I did! It was such a spectacle for noble self-denial. And suffering for conscience sake. It made such an abiding impression upon my mind. They had no friends, enemies on every side. I discovered that there was something higher and better than the pursuit of earthly things."

Judge Kane stood up and walked to the bookcase where his son was rearranging the titles, occupying himself rather than lose control with his father and lose an argument he knew he couldn't win. The judge put his arm around his son and pulled him around so they could talk eye to eye:

"I only prefer you stick to letter writing. I had another son who thought himself a hero, and we know all too well what happened to him."

"Nothing will happen to me, I know this. You forget that when I was in their camps and had a bout of consumption, they nursed me back to health."

"Well, it's no secret you have become their patron saint," the judge said with a smile.

Thomas continued: "Maybe so. But I can't put out of my mind the blessing that old Patriarch John Smith gave me, that not even a hair of my head would be lost, that I would be protected and that my name would be held in esteem among their people for generations. Besides when has writing letters become a fatal practice, some kind of death-defying act?"

"That was your mother. I wanted you to live long and live well and make something of yourself," the judge replied.

Thomas held his ground: "Writing letters is one thing: acting on them is something else."

The judge stood and walked to Thomas' desk and held up a copy of the *New York Herald.* Thomas had read the paper earlier.

"Yes, dozens of editors like *The New York Herald's* James Gordon Bennett are calling for Mormon scalps. There are storm clouds in Washington these days. The twin relics of barbarism, slavery and polygamy? They don't dare touch slavery, but polygamy? That's fair game." Thomas said and then paused: "It's coming you know, Father," Thomas said as he walked past his father and opened the window to let in the evening breeze.

"Keep your eye on South Carolina, Father."

"What? What does that have to do with anything?"

"South Carolina. That's where Joseph Smith said the war would begin. He said it in 1832, or rather if you believe the Mormons, prophesied it."

"So do you believe it?"

"Time will tell. And that is a storm no one can stop. But maybe, just maybe, we can stop this one."

"We?"

"I was hoping to enlist you as my Sancho."

"What do you want of your humble servant, Don Quixote," the judge asked with a resigned smile.

"Nothing much. Just a face-to-face, meeting with the president of the United States."

"No midnight rides to the Rocky Mountains?" his father asked.

"Let's hope not," Thomas answered.

Somehow the judge knew he wouldn't stop until he was in the West tilting at windmills. "Well, at least your Sancho could write the good man a letter of recommendation," the judge admitted.

Writing a letter to the president was the least Judge John Kane could do. Thomas would appreciate it — so might the Mormons.

12

"IT'S IN THE MAIL"

The judge suspected, Thomas sensed and Utah's nonvoting Delegate to Congress John Bernhisel knew for a certainty that it wasn't writing letters that made a difference, it was getting them delivered in a timely fashion to whom they were addressed without them being intercepted, read or used as tinder to start a prairie fire. From his last conversation with Thomas, Bernhisel knew that the letter in his hand must be delivered to Brigham Young as fast as possible.

It was Sunday and services had concluded at a rented hall in Philadelphia. John Bernhisel, Utah's nonvoting delegate to Congress still had business before he left the East to return home, but he had an urgent message that needed to be delivered to Brigham Young that couldn't wait for him.

He spotted his courier: a middle-aged man who had left farm and family and spent the last two-and-a-half years in a fertile part of the field: Denmark, preaching the Gospel in that small Nordic bastion of believers. Together with converts from the British Isles, Danes, Swedes and Norwegians made up a larger percentage of Mormons than the home-grown variety.

"Elder Breinholt?" Bernhisel asked the bright-eyed man in the tattered suit coat.

"You found me," he responded with a smile. "Are you our man in Congress? I understand you have a task for me."

"Yes sir. A task and a ticket. Ever had a ride on the railway?"

"Not yet, sir," Breinholt answered with excitement.

"Here's your charge," he explained, handing him a leather

pouch. "Inside is a very timely communication for President Young and the brethren. The tickets inside will take you to St. Louis, then on a paddle boat to Iowa where you will be met and accompanied west. These papers are for the Prophet's eyes only — a lot is riding on this package. Protect it. Lives are at stake, Brother Breinholt. Do you understand?"

He nodded, put the strap around his shoulder and slipped the pouch underneath his jacket. What was inside his coat, Eler Breinholt wondered. What secrets did he bear? Was the letter sealed? *This is intrigueing, but not your business,* he thought.

The returning missionary took a deep breath and prayed for a safe arrival, for himself and his package. Bernhisel would be following him soon; his family in Utah needed him, and melancholy about his inability to change the minds of people in power overwhelmed him. He needed to breathe some mountain air.

A few days later, maybe more like a week, Breinholt's prayer was answered — in part. Elder Breinholt was on a steam-powered paddle boat making satisfactory time on Old Man River. It was exhilarating, he mused, to be part of the modern age, traveling at this rate of speed, much faster than any carriage or animal-drawn vehicle. *What does the future hold?* Already Mr. Samuel Morse's new invention harnessing the power of electricity was sending dots and dashes long distances in an instant! But not in Deseret, not yet anyway.

It was dusk, muggy but not terribly unpleasant. Breinholt had a perch on the second deck, and since there were no prying eyes around, he wondered about the communication in the pouch, inside his suit coat and hidden from view. Except for mosquitoes, he was all by himself. He reached inside, felt for the envelope and sneaked a peek. It wasn't sealed.

He extracted it and opened it, then wish he hadn't. It was brief and to the point:

"Dear Pres. Young: From all I have been told from reliable sources, Buchanan is moving ahead with his reckless campaign. It appears that should a collision take place between the good people of Utah and the detachment sent thither, the news of such an event would produce the most intense excitement throughout this vast confederacy and the tide of public sentiment would set against us with tremendous force."

The rest of Elder Breinholt's journey back to Zion would have him looking over his shoulder and wondering if his journeying would ever end. The distance between Utah and Washington made timely messages impossible — Brigham, the leadership and Nauvoo Legion had already learned that men were marching, but the true nature of the intent was still a big question mark. Wagons and supplies were moving west, but what about Harney and his hostile intent — was it bravado or reality? Can you ever look into another person's heart? But, that's was Bernhisel's assignment — a politician's words often are followed by violence, pain and suffering. Utah's delegate to Congress hoped his message would reach Brigham Young sooner rather than later. The word Gospel came from Old English meaning Good News. What was the word for Bad News?

THE GOOD CAPTAIN STEWART VAN VLIET WASN'T THE ONLY FACTOR that affected Brigham Young's decision to either wait and see what the Utah Expedition had in mind or to prepare to fight while it inched westward. As a man of action and not one to merely "wait and see," Brigham Young had organized an extensive spy network right inside the queue of teamsters, supply wagons and the conscripts.

The superintendent of the Russel, Majors and Waddell Freight Company didn't take references when they hired drovers and other men with strong backs to move supplies for the Utah Expedition. If a young man was willing to put in a day's work for subsistence wages, that was fine and good.

So, when the Campbell brothers Harold and James, showed up at Fort Laramie to hire on to move, load and unload freight, nobody knew their origins, namely, that they had lived — for awhile — in Nauvoo, Illinois.

"That's a lot of bacon, James," Harold said to his younger brother. "I like my bacon from time to time, but not for every meal." They were reloading a half dozen wagons after a broken axle put another one out of the queue.

"Did you see what was in the last wagon?" James whispered to Harold.

"No, why?"

"Rope, Harold. It's a wagon full of rope, and according to Thompson, there are more wagons of twisted hemp just like it."

"For what purpose?"

"Use your imagination, Brother."

Thompson, their supervisor, walked up behind them as he usually did to harass his men and to intimidate them; rumor had it.that he liked to skim wages from men that he accused of "being slackers," but the Campbell brothers were anything but.

"More work, less talk boys — we need to get this line moving again."

"Got a question, Boss: Why all the rope?" James Campbell asked.

"What do you think we'll do when we finally roll into Mormon town, boy? There's going to be some hangings," he said with a laugh. The Campbell boys exchanged worried glances. That was a bit of news they needed to pass on as soon as they had the chance.

Later that evening, they got their chance. Harold packed a few things on his horse, grabbed some hard tack, a sack of salted jerky and his bedroll and filled his canteen. James was cleaning up after their supper and stacking some firewood; the sun had barely set. By the glow of the remaining coals of the fire, Harold reached in his field jacket and pulled out a tattered old map. It frightened his brother:

"Don't let anybody see that — want to be hanged as a spy?"

"Not really. Most of these bullwhackers can't even read. Today, we crossed the Little Sandy. That means straight down the trail is the Big Sandy ..." Harold whispered.

Then his brother added, "Followed after by the Sublette Cutoff where our contacts should be waiting, someone should be nearby, maybe even Ephraim Hanks. He knows this country better than anybody. If not, just follow the trail down to Bear River and then into Mormon country, all the way to Cache cave in Echo," Harold said but then stopped: "I need a story if I'm caught...a reason why I'm riding all alone."

His brother smiled and the looked around: "I have one in my duffel, remember? Sit down."Harold found a log and warmed his hands by the fire. Five minutes later his brother came clatter-banging into view. Harold laughed:

"Grandpa Littlefield's rusty old beaver trap! Too bad all the beavers have already been 'rescued,'" Harold said.

James had an answer: "The bullwhackers don't know that. That's what made Bear River famous all over the West."

Ten minutes later as night took over the caravan's campground, the Campbell brothers shared a hug and a good-bye. With a full moon lighting his way, Harold Campbell could make the Big Sandy and then the cutoff by tomorrow. They said a prayer, and James watched his older brother disappear into the darkness.

Hidden from view from the officers of the Utah Expedition and even from the Saints down in the valley, the staging area for the defense of Utah Territory from its invaders had now taken on the look of a boom town. Hundreds of horses, mule and cattle had been herded into their own corrals onto the pasture now referred to as Mormons Flats. Nearby was the lumber yard where wagon loads of timber, posts and logs for the parapets and barricades destined for the cliff tops in Echo Canyon were beginning their jour-

ney. Other wagons were bringing more pre-cut lumber from the mills down in the valley.

It had been almost two weeks since William Stowell, the children, Cynthia and Sophronia had had their tearful good-byes. A mail courier had taken a small note he had scribbled to his wives down to the valley; he had a a few sheets of paper with him and three remaining envelopes. Postage was a smile and a handshake; he hoped his carefully written message of love, concern and testimony would be of some consolation and would actually reach them. Now there were serious matters to occupy him and the rest of his band of brothers.

The company had occupied a meadow in a copse of pines and oak brush below Hogback Summit along the well-traveled emigration trail the day before. What their animals hadn't eaten was now tromped underfoot — it was time to move on. The Henefer brothers had visited them the past few days bringing them a few fresh items that the Henefers could spare, some eggs and a little milk; the brothers had finished the second cabin a year earlier and were trying to make a go of it five miles or so up the trail. It was the survival of the fittest, no doubt about that.

After moving down the pioneer trail to join the rest of the battalion at Pratt's Pass to join two other companies, William and his comrades were finishing a breakfast of Johnny cakes, flapjacks and coffee. It was at this spot 10 years earlier on July 15th, 1847, that Orson Pratt had found what he was seeking, "Mr. Reid's route," where he discovered traces of wagon tracks of the ill-fated Donner-Reed party that had broken the trail a year earlier. Here at the mouth of Main Canyon was where Pratt's advance party of Mormon pioneers became the first of thousands of travelers to use this campsite on their way to the Valley of the Great Salt Lake.

This gathering place at Spring Creek or Pratt's Pass now had taken on a life of its own; it was becoming a supply depot where the Saints were stockpiling all the necessities of making war, or rather defending against those wanting to make war against them.

William and his superior officer, Joseph Taylor, were awaiting Colonel Burton along with the other members of their contingent to issue orders when they saw mounted men coming into view.

"William, have the men assemble in front of the fire pit; I'll gather our weapons and gear."

"Yes sir." He turned to the motley group of volunteers.and yelled out the order: "Men, fall in, Colonel Burton's riding in!"

Even though it was still officially summer in mid-September, at their altitude it was a crisp morning that called for more than a hand-stitched blouse. The men dropped their tin cups and tossed the balance of their breakfast into the sagebrush, much to the satisfaction of the ground squirrels who appeared suddenly to gorge themselves — fall was on its way, and somehow they sensed it.

Change was in the air, and ground squirrels weren't the only creatures in the wild that felt it. William did. It had been bothering him ever since he and his superior officer, Joseph Taylor, had been told they had a "special assignment." They would soon find out the details. William hoped he could quell the uneasiness that was stuck in his craw.

"Dress right, dress," the First Sergeant yelled out. Men in ranks raised their left arms, looked right, straightened out their columns and rows and then anticipating the order to stand at rigid attention, they did that just as the command, "Ten-shun" was bellowed out.

Major Taylor stood at the front of William's company now assembled below a barren hill with sagebrush and scattering of clump grass. The wagon road and the small grove of trees and Spring Creek that gave life to the small garden spot was across the trail. William was on the front row, left side, with more than 100 men behind him. To their right were two more companies all

arranged like the tin soldiers he had seen other more well-to-do comrades play with when he was a boy, a body of men that now constituted a battalion of the Nauvoo Legion. The order to "Stand at Ease," was shouted out so all could hear it, and Colonel Burton dismounted to address the assembly of Mormon volunteers.

"Gentlemen, take a knee if you wish and listen up: There's not a man among you who doesn't understand what's at stake here. Many of you, like myself, were present in Jackson County, in Davies County, or in Kirtland, maybe even at Haun's Mill who became well acquainted with the evil that resides in some men's hearts. Satan himself has taken root therein. You've seen it eyeball to eyeball.

"Please permit me, if you will, to remind you of what our president, Brigham Young, proclaimed in August after learning of the horde that has been sent to tame us from Fort Leavenworth. Let us not forget President Young's official declaration which stands as our justification and obligation to serve in the capacity in which we now find ourselves. He reminded us that we have been invaded by a hostile force that wants to *'accomplish our overthrow and destruction.' The government has not condescended to investigate the charges that have falsely made against us. We have a right, given to us by the genius of our Founders, to defend ourselves, in the president's words not to tamely submit to be driven and slain, without an attempt to preserve ourselves.*

"*Rather than subject ourselves to an unlawful military despotism, he declared first, 'to forbid, in the name of the,people of the United States in the Territory of Utah, all armed forces, of every description, from coming into this Territory under any pretense whatsoever; second, that all the forces in said Territory hold themselves in readiness to march, at a moment's notice, to repel any and all such threatened invasion; and third, he stated that 'Martial law is hereby declared to exist in this*

Territory ... and no person shall be allowed to pass or repass into or through or from this Territory, without a permit from the proper officer.'"

Immediately, the battalion responded with shouts, hurrahs and applause until Burton had to calm them down. He continued:

"Finally, here are the exact orders as dictated by General Wells; if still available, your commanding officers will have copies for you, which I will read word-for-word for you.

"On ascertaining the locality or route of the troops, proceed at once to annoy them in every possible way. Use every exertion to stampede their animals, and set fire to their trains. Burn the whole country before them and on their flanks. Keep them from sleeping by night surprises. Blockade the road by falling trees, or destroying the fords when you can. Watch for opportunities to set fire to the grass on their windward, so as, if possible, to envelop their trains. Leave no grass before them that can be burned... Take no life, but destroy their trains, and stampede or drive away their animals at every opportunity."

"Gentlemen, a couple more tidbits of news: One of our people who had been imbedded with the supply train recently reported that there are several wagon loads of rope on their way here — use your own imagination as for whom that's intended.

And, second, Ephraim Hanks tells us that the supply trains are scattered all along the wagon trail from Kansas for hundreds and hundreds of miles headed west, along with thousands of beef cattle to feed the Army which is still pouring in. President Young sent a letter to the acting commander, Colonel Alexander, informing him that his presence in the territory is in violation of the governor's order prohibiting his presence here; he replied, politely, that he was following orders of the new president, Mr. Buchanan," Wells said which drew boos from rhe men.

Then, Burton concluded: "That is all for now. Company commanders, please review your specific orders spelled out for you and which have been delivered accordingly. Commanders with questions may have their adjutants direct them to your superior officers. Dismissed."

"Battalion dismissed," Burton's executive officer ordered, which was repeated down the line. The order of battle for each company was now reviewed separately.

Burton's adjutant sought out Major Taylor who motioned William to join him:

"The colonel would like you to take a team of your choosing and move forward to become the battalion's eyes and ears: Find out where the expedition is, its movements and its stores, cattle, supply wagons and so forth. Set up a system to report back to us with regularity on a timely basis. We must know, where possible, their intentions, their movements and their capacity to cause us harm."

"You want us to be, in a word, spies, correct?" Taylor asked.

"In a word, yes. Be watchful, take care and go with safety." The officer handed Taylor his written orders who passed them on to William. They saluted, and then left.

"So, we're spies, Major?" William asked.

"Looks like it, William, but you just don't seem the devious type," he added with a laugh. "Let's get started." They grabbed their weapons and gear and began preparing for the perilous journey.

They left the Spring Creek staging area and depot and headed north through Echo Canyon, a narrow pass with cliffs on either side. Above them, their comrades were busy constructing parapets and concealed spots for sharp shooters.

Taylor's ten-man team with their pack animals found a secluded spot above a stream to spend the night. Darkness came soon as the sun was already behind the cliffs. They set up three tents, hobbled their animals and sat around a small campfire.

Ever since the discovery of fire and the invention of sharp instruments, man found solace in whittling by firelight.

William did.

"Brother Stowell, is there something hidden in your oak branch you want to set free?" Old Henry posed that question with a laugh as he whittled like a madman, watching with envy William's purposeful handiwork.

"Yes, Henry, our boy wants a puppy, and so I'm carving him one," William responded with a grin. "This one won't bark."

Henry leaned over and spoke softly to his younger friend.

"You didn't finish telling me about your dream."

William looked long and hard at the campfire now dying down to a embers. He tossed another log onto the pyre, and then turned to Henry:

"It's kind of sacred, so let's not share it with others, but yes, I did see myself with another man returning to the settlement as we were in Echo Canyon after being released by the Army. Maybe it was just something I imagined, but it seemed real enough. Time will tell." The major walked over and reminded the men that they were leaving at dawn — time to retire. A canyon and an Army were waiting for them.

New York Tribune Correspondent Albert "Doc' Browne Jr. discovered what real horsemen experience much earlier in their rustic lives: saddle sores. The Utah Expedition was still at least 500 miles away from their destination, somewhere in Nebraska Territory but less than a week out of Fort Laramie and Browne was trying to stay hot on their trail, pushing himself out of his comfort zone to get the stories that his hard-driving editor, Horace Greeley, was expecting. As he passed another company of infantrymen kicking up dust, Browne was wise enough not to complain. But, he still had to get off that horse. Albert Browne wore his new moniker of "Doc" proudly, the title given to him by the legendary mountain man Jim Bridger who heard that Albert recently had earned his PhD from Heidelberg University.

Even his German friends addressed him as *Herr Doktor*, but more sarcastically then honorifically. Al;bert Gallatin Browne Jr. was a dandy and everybody knew it. But, saddle sore after saddle sore had slowly earned him a bit more respect.

A light carriage with three of the Expedition's VIPs came along side him. Doc recognized the passengers: newly appointed Utah Territory Governor Cumming, his wife Elizabeth and Judge Delana R. Eckels, named to replace the disgraced Judge Drummond.

"I say young sir, are you not Mr. Greeley's correspondent?" Cumming asked as the driver brought the wagon to a halt. Cumming turned to Eckels: "We have room, do we not?" Eckels nodded.

Browne immediately felt tears coming to his eyes. He was not a religious man in any sense of the word, but he loved justice and mercy, and for a moment thanked God — to himself.

"Why don't you join us? Your name's Browne, correct? Doctor Browne?" Doc nodded.

Gingerly dismounting his nag, he tied her up behind the carriage, grabbed his correspondent's leather bag and climbed aboard. He looked up — *there was shade, a top to the carriage — what a miracle!* A tear or two did make it down his cheek which he quickly brushed aside.

"Water?"

"Thank you," Albert muttered.

The carriage continued on its journey, and after a few minutes, Cumming's curiosity got the better of him.

"So, just between us, what are your thoughts about the expedition?"

Albert paused and chose his words carefully:

"It's a motley group, but newsworthy just the same."

"How so?" Judge Eckels asked.

"Well, there are more foreigners it seems than true-born

Americans: Welshmen, Irish and Germans. And since I studied in Germany, I speak their language and have had some opportunity to speak with them and sometimes overhear their conversations."

"And?" Elizabeth Cumming asked.

"They're not overly impressed with our 'military bearing.'"

"Spit and polish?" Cumming asked.

"I suppose, but that's the Prussians for you. The other German-speakers are not that keen on the Prussians, particularly the Bavarians and the Rheinlanders. The Hessians seem to get along better — they're also more war-like. I was in Heidelberg — it's in Baden, right on the border near Rheinland-Pfalz, rather the Palatinate. If the Germans ever got their act together, they would be formidable. I was there during the 1848 revolution, which the liberals lost and the aristocracy won, which is how I see this current struggle we are in."

"In what way? Which side are we?"

"The liberals, of course, espousing representative democracy against a theocratic despotism."

Cumming mulled Albert's comments for a moment, then responded: "What about popular sovereignty? The Mormons have applied for statehood, were driven from place to place and then in 1847 left the boundaries of these United States to live by themselves. Additionally, when asked, they supplied 500 volunteers to fight for the United States in the Mexican War, calling themselves the Mormon Battalion. Does that sound like something rebels would do? I've been doing a little research about my new assignment. Thought I'd try to keep an open mind."

Albert had no reply, but nevertheless was still convinced that the Mormons needed to make way for progress. Manifest Destiny was the future! Was Cumming like Senator Houston and the little man Kane, a Mormon sympathizer? He better look into that.

After all, Mr. Greeley would want to know, wouldn't he?

13

"IT'S TOO LATE, TOO LATE!"

Lot Smith and his riders had been on the trail for a couple of hours since leaving the Henefer settlement. They picked their way through the Narrows along the creek as mountain peaks loomed above them. Conifers stood like sentinels above them on the mountain sides, but along the river bottom, they found themselves blanketed on either side with willows and Gambel oak, a thick scrub oak that covered the backside of the Wasatch Mountains.

Lot called out to his men behind: "We'll take a break when we get to the Weber! Pass it down the line." A few miles ahead, the Weber River broke away and headed west through the canyon where over millions of years, it had carved another pathway to the Great Salt Lake; ten thousand years earlier, it fed a huge fresh-water lake the size of Lake Michigan, and even earlier as large as Lake Superior at the end of the last Ice Age. Then, at some point, an earthquake or deluge of some kind caused the northwest corner to give way and carve out a canyon near modern-day Twin Falls, Idaho, which became known as the Snake River gorge.

In 1857, these horsemen were determined to make some history of their own: the Utah Expeditionary Force was waiting for them, and Lot and his troops were prepared with some very creative surprises.

About three hours later that afternoon as they moved further up the canyon where it narrows and the crimson cliff tops come into view, they heard a gunshot up above them. Someone on the edge was waving a flag at them. Since it was getting dark, Lot yelled back to his men and the supply horses behind them to bed down for the night. There was always the possibility that there were onlookers from the "celestial heights" — maybe a sniper or two observing them.

Lots' attacking force was spread out along the creek that watered the bottom of Echo Canyon. Joseph Taylor's advance reconnoitering squad, Stowell et al, were at the front of the column and had settled in for the night. A few minutes before dark, Christian Holz and two others joined them at the request of Col. Burton.

"Welcome, brethren. How's the view from up there?" Joseph Taylor asked.

"Hard to move down the trail without being seen. We have about a dozen parapets and defenses built all the way down to the bottom," Christian explained.

Caleb piped up: "And piles of boulders now and then to roll down on the invaders."

Looking at Christian, Taylor asked: "So you fought with the Danes?"

"Actually, I was employed by the Prussians, and they fought the Danes. A messy business. Then I found religion."

"And your specialty?"

"Artillery and marksman, if needed."

Taylor shook Christian's hand: "You're definitely needed! Mighty glad you're on our side."

Christian thanked him, then asked: "So Major, what are our orders?"

"At first light, we'll move forward, find a higher observation point, then Stowell and I will go on ahead and scout out the enemy's location, then when we've spotted them, I'll send him back to take you to our observation point. And, Christian, please assume command in my place until you hear from Stowell. Understood?"

That evening around the campfire, Christian was bringing firewood back to the assembly area and took a seat on a log near William Stowell and introduced himself. They watched cinders fly off into the night sky; William opened a small, tattered Bible and was studying it intently which aroused Christian's curiosity.

"Ever wonder why we're the only Christians who talk about building temples, and even have already begun the process?" Stowell asked.

Christian leaned back, mulled the question over and finally responded: "You know, sometimes we assume that the Protestants are closer to the truth than the Catholics, but having seen many old Catholic cathedrals, you can see similarities to ancient Israel, like the Holy of Holies, for example."

"Yes, and the Old Testament can be very instructive; not only does Isaiah hint at our day, like Zion being established in the 'tops of the mountains,' which by the way is what the name 'Utah' means to the Indians, but elsewhere, even in Psalms, you can read verses that sound familiar. Here's one:" William opened to a verse where the page had been folded over and read a verse aloud:

"*One thing have I desired of the Lord, that will I seek after; that I may dwell in the house of the Lord all the days of my life, to behold the beauty of the Lord, and to inquire in his temple. And here's another one that I not only find revealing, but troubling. It's in Psalms chapter 84: 'For a day in thy courts is better than a thousand. I had rather be a doorkeeper in the house of my God, than to dwell in the tents of wickedness.'"*

"What part do your find troubling?" Christian asked.

"Dwelling in the tents of wickedness…I'm concerned about being separated from family, even if I know I'll return to them. I know I just met you, but I'm concerned about our foray tomorrow into enemy territory, and if something should detain us, I was hoping someone, maybe you, could forward a note to my wives, Cynthia and Sophronia, and let them know I'll be fine."

Christian sat up and leaned forward: "How do you know you'll be fine?"

"Because it was revealed to me."

Christian felt a chill go down his back. Suddenly, he felt a connection with this stranger and a new responsibility to keep his word.

"That's good enough for me," Christian whispered.

"Thank you."

Later that evening as he was extinguishing the campfire, Caleb approached Christian:

"Thank you for everything — thank you for your kindness to our family, especially towards Winnie. I hope when all this is finished, things work out well for you and my sister."

Christian was troubled: "Caleb, what's on your mind?"

The young man hesitated — "You know about the wagons from Arkansas and Missouri that are driving through our land?

"Not much. Just that they're stirring up trouble."

"More than that — they're running their animals, their horses and cattle on Saints' land. They're destroying crops, ruining pastures. The say we're squatters! That this is American land, not 'Mormon' land. And Brigham said folks couldn't come through because of martial law without permission. I saw Hans yesterday. He wants me to join him. I have a musket, so does he. We're going to stop them. They're not chasing us out. We've come too far!

"Caleb, you are assigned to help us keep the Army from coming down Echo Canyon. We need you here," Christian said as he put his hand on his young friend's shoulder.

"I'm sorry. I'm leaving in the morning. Hans is waiting for me on the road west to the valley. It's settled. Somebody has to do something." Caleb said, walking away into the darkness. Christian felt that it would turn out badly for Caleb, Hans and the Arkansas pioneers, but he knew his friend's mind was made up.

What could he do? What could anybody do?

By early September, the leading elements of the Utah Expedition were well past Fort Laramie and making their way across the desolate plains of south-central Wyoming, destination Fort

Bridger, a rallying point to marshal their resources and await the miles and miles of 700 supply wagons behind them spread all the way back to the Nebraska border.

But the Expedition wasn't the only military force with its eye on Fort Bridger. Years earlier, Brigham Young had struck a deal with the old trapper to buy his fort, and Bridger reluctantly could not refuse such a generous offer. After a Mormon posse had chased him off after he sold alcohol to Utes during the Walker Indian war, selling the fort seemed like a good idea. So, when the Utah Expedition put an "X" on the map where Fort Bridger lay, did they know the Mormons owned it?

It didn't matter, because Porter Rockwell and Lot Smith had specific orders regarding the old trapper's hideout:

Burn it to the ground!

Those orders came from Brigham Young himself. Rockwell didn't like it; he had spent many a happy hour there. But, they both realized that the Army could not be allowed to use it as a launch point to move down Echo Canyon and into the valley. It had to be done.

Lot and Porter were mounted at the head of Mormon cavalrymen late that afternoon near the Henefer settlement. They had just filled their canteens, loaded up their packs with bacon, hardtack and what not and attached their bedrolls.

"Before I leave on our little adventure, let's council together.," Lot said. "Come closer." The 50 mounted men huddled around him to hear what their cowboy leader had to say:

"If I may, please allow me to summarize what President Young declared regarding our obligation," Lot said as he pulled a newspaper clipping from his pocket:

"The people are free; they are not in bondage to any government on God's footstool...we have transgressed no law, neither do we intend to do so," but, Brigham explained, *"I am not going to permit troops here for the protection or the priests*

and their rabble in their efforts to drive us from the land that we possess…they say that the coming of their Army is legal — it is not, and they who say it are morally rotten."

"And, finally, Brigham sums up and promises…*that I will not suffer again as I have in times gone by that there shall not be one building, nor one foot of lumber, nor a tree, nor a particle of grass or hay that has not been burned nor left in reach of our enemies."*

Then Lot Smith explained the momentous task before them:

"So, our first assignment is to burn Fort Bridger then Fort Supply, and whatever supplies we cannot take for ourselves will burn with the stockade," Lot said and then added: "Brother Lewis Robison, if you will take a contingent with you, along with matches, and get started. Another team will come with Porter and myself to the northwest passage and watch for whatever troops come that way and burn the grass ahead of them. So Brethren, let's be about our business!"

THE WHOLE BUSINESS WAS DEPRESSING FOR GEORGE A. SMITH. No Mormon who had suffered so much and had so little was happy about destroying property that they had worked so hard for. Weeks later, Smith was on the trail back to Mormon Flats when he encountered an old friend, Jesse Crosby, who had been burning wagons and grass to slow down the Army on the trail.

"Brother Crosby, you smell a bit smokey."

"All of us do. This unfortunate business forced to us to dispose of the property we had either purchased or built ourselves, but we're in step with the prophet and the Saints."

"So, it's all up in smoke. What exactly?"

Crosby sighed and leaned forward in his saddle. Let me count it for you. Let's see, there were 100 or more good hewn houses, one sawmill, one gristmill and one thrashing machine, and after leaving the fort, we set fire to the stockade, straw and grain stacks. We watched the bonfire for awhile and turned our backs on everything we had, and here we are. Have to start over, I suppose."

He continued: "Oh and then we came to a place we just started: City Supply, consisting of 10 or 15 buildings, set all that on fire, warmed ourselves a little and then on our way here, we passed by the ash heap that was once Fort Bridger, and here we are." Sobered, George Smith saluted his old acquaintances and bid them farewell. He later reported to President Young that the value of it all was about $300,000. Such a waste!

WHAT ELSE WAS THE NAUVOO LEGION DOING IN THE FALL OF 1857? For one thing, it was rustling…freeing the cattle being driven west by the Utah Expedition from certain death — giving them their freedom, introducing them to the wide open spaces, the pastures and mountain valleys of the West. Quite a noble effort!

And, rustler-in-chief was the Mormons' most illustrious cowboy, Lot Smith, assisted by its most notorious mountain man and gunman, Orrin Porter Rockwell. At the age of 16, Smith had sweet-talked his way into the Mormon Battalion, a group of volunteers who had been recruited in 1846 by Thomas Kane to undertake the longest march in American history. Smith joined the Army of the West which left Winter Quarters, Nebraska, the Mormon temporary settlement on the Missouri River in July 1846 on their way west to California completing their enlistment a year later. Rockwell was a boyfriend of Joseph Smith's family in upstate New York who idolized the church's founder and vowed to protect him with his life. When Joseph was martyred with his brother Hyrum in 1844, Porter wasn't there — it broke his heart and haunted him for the rest of his life.

Lot and Porter, these two formidable frontiersmen, were the perfect duo to undertake the assignment to prevent the Army from marching into Salt Lake City. Their job: keep the Army at bay in western Wyoming during the winter of 1857-1858 until a peace agreement could be brokered. The first order of business: Find the Army — without the Army finding them. But, as Lot and

his raiders went north to shadow the Utah Expeditionary force, they had an advantage the Army knew nothing about: they had spies embedded with the supply trains watching and reporting their every move.

BY EARLY SEPTEMBER, 1857, THE UTAH EXPEDITION had been on the road nearly two months; in fact, it left Fort Leavenworth and began marching on Zion ten years to the day that the Mormon Battalion had departed from the Missouri in support of the United States of America. This irony was not lost on Lt. Col. Phillip St. George Cooke, who had been the Battalion's commander in 1846. Now, he was commanding the Second Dragoons; his superior officer, Col. Albert Sydney Johnston, did not arrive from Texas until November — the acting commander was Col. Edmund B. Alexander, who many felt was of the same cut of cloth as President Buchanan, "a timorous man."

Added to that, Alexander was unfamiliar with the country, its terrain, and knew little to nothing about his adversaries, the Mormons. But, Cooke did, and to Phil Cooke, the Mormons were not his adversaries, despite his obligation to command the Dragoons (mounted infantry who dismount to fight).

The two officers shared some stew late one night at a campfire near the commander's HQ; the stew was dreadful — Cooke was unsure as to the meat that floated around in his tin; but the potatoes seemed edible.

"Col. Cooke, you don't seem to relish what our mess stewards have prepared for us," Alexander queried.

"It's not a home-cooked meal, now is it, sir? And, I'm not sure what animal supplied us with its parts." They both laughed and tossed their remaining contents into the sagebrush.

"Well, after such a fine meal, let's talk," Alexander said "What do you have on your mind? Tell me about the Mormons, these people we're supposed to quell."

"Honestly, sir, they don't need quelling. When they were asked

to supply a battalion to march on California to free it from Mexico, I was privileged to be their commander. I am here because I was ordered to be. I feel it's my obligation to protect my men and return them safely to their families. Unless we provoke them, the Mormons are wise enough not to pick a fight with 40 million people. We are making war on them, not them on us," Cooke explained.

Alexander was set back a bit by his subordinate's candor: "To be honest with you, Cooke, I am not sure what is expected of us, except to deliver the governor safely to the city, and I am not empowered to do much of anything else until Johnston arrives…"

"Oh, and what fine hands we will be in then, won't we?"

Alexander could taste Cooke's sarcasm, but he moved on.

"I've heard something about one of their commanders, this Lot Smith, the cowboy; you know him, don't you?"

Cooke laughed: "Know him? I raised him," and then Cooke laughed even louder. "He was under my command of the Mormon Battalion for an entire year, and he was fun to watch, almost like a son. Somehow he was able to finagle himself into our battalion at the ripe old age of 16, and even then, this fiery red-head couldn't be tamed. I imagine his parents let out a sigh of relief when they were free of him. I haven't seen even a man twice his age with better skills on a mount; he could get a horse to do anything. It was artful."

"So, we should keep an eye out looking for him, then?"

"Colonel, we won't even see him coming."

JAMES HASLAM'S MAD DASH BACK TO CEDAR CITY was made in record time, but the grisly fact remained, it wasn't fast enough. Brigham Young's letter was explicit — let the emigrants leave in peace. That was the same counsel William Dame and the leaders in Parowan originally communicated to Haight and Lee. But, John D. Lee had another agenda, and perhaps he thought that since he was Brigham's "adopted son" that he could second-guess what the president would tell Haslam. He couldn't.

Haslam knew that the riled up settlers and the blood-thirsty Lee wouldn't have been playing checkers outside the Arkansans' defensive line waiting for his return. In the past week, Haslam had covered 500 miles on multiple mounts as he begged for fresh horses and assistance in order to meet with the prophet and gallop back with his instructions. He had left Salt Lake just after lunch on Thursday — the day before the Friday massacre — with carte blanche orders from Brigham Young for fresh horses at every settlement. He made it to American Fork by 5 p.m. and Provo by 7.

The next morning, he sped away from Nephi on a fresh mustang and by supper arrived in Fillmore. He described that when he reached Beaver he was riding his mount "as fast as his horse could take it." All along the way, he rode broncos, mustangs and even plow horses the entire 250 miles to Cedar City, in all about 70 hours on horseback. Finding fresh mounts was a concern from beginning to end. The ride south took a few hours longer than on his way north. After Haslam finally dragged himself into Cedar City, he first stopped briefly at his home and then set out for Haight's, which was down the street. After a church meeting, Haight walked outside to see if his courier was back. Haslam was already on his way to Haight's, and they met halfway. He gave Haight Brigham Young's note telling him to let the emigrants "go in peace." Haight opened the envelope, looked inside and sobbed for an entire half hour..."like a child" and could only utter, "Too late, too late." Haslam's dash back to Cedar City had been in vain. Soon, the whole world would learn what had happened when he was enroute to and from Salt Lake City.

Years later, Brigham Young admitted that if there had been a telegraph line at the time between Salt Lake and Cedar City, the whole catastrophe could have been avoided. The remains of some 120 Arkansas and Missouri emigrants lay scattered all over at a place called Mountain Meadows. Once the word got out, things got even worse for the Saints of the Latter-days.

14

"IT'S IN HIS NAME THAT WE DO!"

Lot's raiders knew the U.S. Army wouldn't see them coming because the major had made sure of it. The Mormons cavalry had been shadowing the slow-moving expedition as it was snaking across south central Wyoming, staying parallel to the Army's westward advance, watching it but without being seen. Major Lot Smith's mounted men were just waiting for the right opportunity.

When they stopped near a small stream to water their horses, the first sergeant approached the major.

"We were just wondering, sir, what should we prepare for now that we are closing in on the supply trains?"

"I'll tell you what General Wells told me," Lot said. "He said first to approach the wagon master of the supply train and warn him to turn back east or face the consequences. But, if that warning was not sufficient to change their direction, then take the trains by force and burn them."

"But, there's only about 40 or 50 of us, and our supplies are scant," the sergeant said.

"Ahh, yes, I said as much as that to Wells, but he just smiled and said we should "go Indian."

"Sir?"

"To surprise and frighten them into thinking that there are many more of us than there really are...and that 'Uncle Sam' would provide."

The sergeant again looked puzzled.

Major Smith smiled: "Sergeant, our supplies are on those wagon trains..."

The man laughed: "Ahh yes, now I understand: Uncle Sam WILL provide!"

Lot looked ahead to a grove of trees further up the stream and turned back to his sergeant major: "Sergeant, let's move up to that grove ahead, and given the time of the day, we'll stop early tonight and bed down in preparation for an early morning departure. Please ride back and relay those orders."

"Yes sir." And the man turned and followed his orders; the next two days would be the stuff that history is made of.

Some 50 miles to the west of Echo Canyon, William Stowell, his commander Joseph Taylor, Christian Holz and the rest of the "spy squad" had discovered that a forward element of the Utah Expeditionary force was likely preparing a campsite for the night. Joseph Taylor assumed that their foes were their counterparts, forward observers or spies. Taylor and Stowell had Christian stay behind and wait with the others while the two of them went ahead to scout out the situation for themselves. It grew later and later. One of the other squad members came out of hiding and startled Christian:

"Shouldn't they have returned by now?"

"What? Don't sneak up on me like that, *Mensch*!"

"*Mensch?*"

"It's German. Yes, they should be back by now. We ought to see what happened."

The young man volunteered to take a look: "Let me see what I can find out."

Five minutes later, he rush back, panicked:

"We have to get out of here, now! They have them, and they're looking for us."

The whole party slid down an incline of shale and gravel and hurried down to the stream where there was more cover. A half an hour later, they made it back to their campsite. Christian would wait until the next morning to report the whole incident up the

chain of the command. His commander and the adjutant had been captured! He felt like he'd let them down.

AT 4 A.M. THE NEXT MORNING, MAJOR LOT SMITH and his raiders set out west in pursuit of an ox train after discovering its traces the day before. Their animals were rested, fed and watered from their day off, and that was just as Lot had planned, because the the day before they had been on the trail for more the 24 hours.

Early the following morning, the sergeant major galloped back to Lot: "We've found them, sir, about two or three miles ahead. What are your orders?"

It was typical western Wyoming: desolate, high desert. The Wind River mountains loomed directly north, maybe 25 or 30 miles away. It was windy and dry unlike the previous year when some two dozen handcart pioneers were buried in a hastily dug common grave, maybe a hundred miles away.

Lot took charge: "Let's pay them a visit. Half come with me — I'll 'persuade' the wagon master to turn around and return to where he came from. The rest of you get some breakfast, wait just ahead, rest and recuperate." He pointed to a draw to the right and below with a couple of bare cottonwood trees. "We'll meet you all down there.

The master sergeant replied: "All right, Major. Godspeed!"

Lot's contingent caught up with the ox train and its bull-whacking crew within the hour. The horsemen approached the wagon train, and Lot moved ahead of the group where he came across three bullwhackers who were out of their wagons assisting another to reload his wagon after hitting a boulder.

"Sir, my name is Major Lot Smith, may I speak with your captain, please?" The three men, all civilian "bullwhackers," were shaken by the mounted, armed men looming over them.

"He's up ahead, 20 wagons or so, waiting on us; his name is Rankin," the older of the three said.

The horsemen trotted further up the train and cornered the

man in charge, a Captain Rankin. Lot described him as "a large, fine-looking man."

"Are you the man in charge of this train?" Lot asked.

"I am. Who are you?"

"I'm Major Lot Smith, and I'm here to direct you to turn about, and head back from whence you came, sir, to the borders of the United States."

Rankin laughed and defiantly replied:

"By what authority do you pretend to possess to force us to move even an inch?"

"Martial law has been declared in the Territory of Utah, and by the order of the governor, we are authorized to turn away any force entering this territory to unlawfully interfere with our rights to govern ourselves and practice our religion."

Rankin cursed and spit, and challenged Major Sm: "And, how do you plan on enforcing this order?"

"We are equipped to do so, are we not men?" Lot replied, and each of his cavalrymen displayed a weapon. "The balance of our company stands behind us to carry out these orders. We will give you room." Lot and his men backed up to allow the lead wagon and accompanying bullwhackers to make a U-turn in compliance with the order. A half an hour later, the wagon was moving east. So far so good.

Days after Christian and the balance of their "spy squad" had returned to their campsite without their commander, Joseph Taylor and his adjutant, William Stowell, the two prisoners were shackled in a tent somewhere north and east of Echo Canyon. In the tent with them were a couple of soldiers who had tried unsuccessfully to find themselves another form of employment. They bore the marks of their capture and were in far worse shape than Taylor and Stowell. The prisoners had just been brought a greasy gruel, an unknown type of sustenance, but they soon realized that it was that or nothing. Breakfast was now over. The two

Mormons were cautious in their communication with each other.

"That was delicious," Taylor said with a smile to Stowell.

"Beyond delicious," William replied. "Never had anything like it before." Their cellmates exchanged curious glances, but they were in no mood for any kind of pleasantry.

"They're going to hang you two," one of the shackled deserters in the other corner said with a sneer.

"We're not deserters, just prisoners of war," William said. "Deserters are the ones usually hanged."

"Or shot," Taylor added. That quieted things down for a few minutes until a guard entered the tent. He studied his Mormon captives and determined by his epaulets that Taylor was a major and the commanding officer.

"You the superior officer?" He nodded. "You come with me." The guard assisted him and he left. By agreement, Stowell and Taylor knew what "particulars" to reveal to their interrogators, and the process was just getting started. Stowell knew he was next.

While Major Taylor was being questioned by the befuddled and confused Col. Edmund Alexander, William remembered his first dream and then the subsequent message he had received from his unseen sender. His orders were inside his blouse tucked in a leather envelope of sorts.

Better keep that with you, he told himself. *Could need it soon.* He wondered how Major Taylor was doing, and then he remembered Lot's Raiders and their heroic assignment. *Why wasn't he with the Mormons' most illustrious cowboy? Don't dwell on that*, he thought — focus on what lay ahead: Making it back to his growing family and fulfilling his dream of returning as a free man down Echo Canyon. *When would that happen?* Not anytime soon, he feared.

RANKIN DID EXACTLY WHAT LOT SMITH THOUGHT he would do, turn around and then double back. A horseman galloped back to Lot Smith and reported the wagon train's U-turn. Upon the Army's discovery of the raiders' intentions, they rescued their supplies and left the raiders no reasons to raid them again.

But knowing there were at least an additional 700 wagons heading west stretched out for more than 100 miles, Smith asked his sergeant major to fetch Captain Haight:

Horton Haight reported to Lot half an hour later.

"Captain, we have a report that the Expedition's Tenth Regiment is not too distant and is traveling with a herd of mules they don't need, but which we do. Take 20 horsemen with you and grab those mules while we look elsewhere. There must be another wagon train coming this way. There's more fish in the barrel — let's get 'em all!" Haight's horsemen went in one direction, Lot's in the other.

Lot had gathered his team together in a wash with a trickle of water in the bottom, out of view from prying eyes:

"Philips, tell us what you saw."

"One of my forward men saw a huge cloud of dust off to the north and went to see what was there, and sure enough, it's a long train near the Big Sandy."

Lot was excited: "How many did you see?"

Phillips looked to his companion: "We counted 26, but there could be more."

"Good! There's no better place to do our business than at a river crossing," he said. "It will provide us with an excellent opportunity for us to surround and isolate supply wagons, livestock and the bushwhackers and pin them up against the river. How far?" Smith asked. The other two conferred and then answered: "Fourteen, fifteen miles at most."

"Good. Let's leave this afternoon. This is what we've been waiting for." Lot was picking a stone out of his mount's hoof when Boone surprised him near a stand of junipers. The season was turning — after all, it was October — it would be summer one day and winter the next; just ask the handcart pioneers from the year before, the ones who survived.

"Major, we found a company of the Expedition, a light battery on the other side of the Green, but we could slip below them and make it to the island downstream and then follow the wagon tracks and surprise them," Boone said, his white teeth gleaming through his curly beard.

"I like the sound of that; we could use the next few hours and hit him about midnight and separate ourselves from the battery," Lot said.

His men split into two groups, a group of scouts trotted towards Blacks Fork, but Smith's contingent hunkered down on the island until nightfall.

Later that night, Smith sent three mounted scouts towards the Big Sandy that returned awhile later after they spotted their prey:

"Major, there's a lot more of them than we figured," the lead scout, J.P. Terry announced. He continued: "But, even though there are 66 of them, we woke them all up and placed armed guards around them all. They're all waiting for your orders."

"Men," Lot shouted, "let's mount up and go have ourselves one helluva bonfire! Yahoo!"

Lot's raiders hurried over to the camp where a dozen of his men were standing guard over more than 60 teamsters, of bullwhackers, as they called themselves.

John Dawson, the wagonmaster, was seated on a log by the fire with Philo Dibble and Mahonri Cahoon standing guard. Lot dismounted and walked towards the men; Terry pointed out the leader, Dawson, to Lot Smith, who addressed the man respectfully:

"My name is Smith," Lot announced. Are you in charge here?"

The man stood up: "I am. My name is Dawson; Sir, what are your intentions?"

"To burn the wagons and supplies to keep your Army out of our city," he replied.

"For God's sakes, don't burn the wagons," the man pled.

"It is for His sake that we will do just that — we are on the Lord's errand," Major Smith declared.

Several of the teamsters smiled and laughed. A huge man seated on the wagon shouted: "No more bullwhacking, boys!" They were pleased — apparently, they had not taken kindly to bullwhacking.

"Let us save enough to keep body and soul together, sir," the wagoneer asked.

"Your weapons are stacked over by the corral — they're yours after we leave. We'll let you take your supplies and personal belongings, but we're following our orders to keep your Army out of our valley."

Smith took a breath: "All right, two wagons then. Now, let's set some wagons on fire. Men, remove ammunition and other ordinance and let's light up the night sky!"

A big Irishman they all called "Big Jim," the only non-Mormon in Smith's marauders, announced: "It's only right that a 'Gentile' participate in following the governor's orders — you boys shouldn't get all the credit," Jim crowed. "Let me start the festivities." He lit the first wagon.

For the next hour, it looked like Armageddon on a desolate stretch of high desert in Wyoming. Off to the right, some 100 yards away, a couple of wagons were as bright as cordite, almost too brilliant to look at!

"Boone, what is that over there?" Lot asked his sergeant.

"A wagon load of tar rope, Major, ordered especially for President Young and his counselors. They won't be swinging tomorrow."

"Thanks to you and your spies, Boone."

"Thanks to all of us, sir," the sergeant replied.

Just then, a shot rang out followed by a hideous scream.

In the darkness, several men ran to a Legionnaire who was

holding his leg. They carried him over near the fire and tied a tourniquet above his knee.

The ball had passed through the Orson Arnold's leg, broke the femur which was protruding. Philo Dibble, another member of Arnold's patrol, was lying on the ground, then sat up:

"I got shot in the head," Dibble announced, then added: "But, I'm fine."

Another member of their patrol added: "And there's a hole in my hat." A month later, they could laugh about it, but for now, Arnold's life depended on getting him medical care and down into the valley. The next day, Dibble carved his name on a rock, monumentalizing a skull harder than stone.

Before they left, Boone and a former handcart pioneer sat in their saddles on the ridge and waited for Smith and the rest of the raiders to join them under a moonlit sky. The pioneer wiped his eyes, took off his hat and said a short, silent prayer as Boone watched:

"Everything all right, Casey?"

"Yes and no," the man replied in a husky voice. Boone waited.

"Not far from here, just a year ago, we were pushing handcarts and burying the weaker ones by the cord because of starvation and cold. And, now we're burning food and supplies. Does this make sense?"

Boone was at a loss for words, but Casey came to his own rescue: "But Major Lot explained it best, didn't he?" Boone had no answer: "It was for His sake, they died," the rider said as he looked heavenward. And, it's for His sake those wagons are burning."

As they departed, they rounded up some 150 head of cattle and a few horses and pushed them ahead of the column; a contingent of Lot's men herded the animals down Echo Canyon and into the valley of the Great Salt Lake. The rustled cattle and horses would fare better than the ones left behind — more of the Army's livestock would die that winter than would survive. Except for Arnold's wound, it had been a good night's work. Before the Utah War was over, Arnold would be back on a horse, fighting the good battle.

AFTER PUTTING SEVERAL MILES BETWEEN THEMSELVES and the abandoned bullwhackers, Lot's raiders were recuperating after their midnight ride in a secluded meadow when a scouting party trotted into camp. The lead scout was anxious and in a hurry, looking around for his leader. "Where's the major?"

"He's attending to personal matters down in the wash. Here he comes," Boone said.

Smith walked up the slope to where his men were preparing for the day.

Jackson was still on his horse, anxious to leave again: "Major, we found another wagon train. Let's gather them up before we see any help arriving."

Ten minutes later, most of the party was moving back up the Big Sandy. Within the hour, they had surprised another wagon master. His name was Simpson who preferred not to put up a fight.

Once again, the bullwhackers were left with enough supplies to keep body and soul together. So, the fires were lit, the wagons and the supplies burned and the two adversaries went their separate ways, never to see each other again — so they thought.

Terry would later tell his children and write down for posterity the lessons learned on the Wyoming Plains that day:

"A few days later, we had used up our own supplies and wished we had salvaged some before we set the fire, and were on our way down the Green, when we came across Simpson, the wagon master, who had left with his men and two loads of supplies. The major told him of our situation and Simpson replied: "Well, sir, you acted the gentleman with me, and you can have all you want of anything we have."

Terry's lesson to his children: *"Now you know that the Lord can overrule things for good."*

BRIGHAM AND THE OTHER LEADERS HAD HEARD ABOUT THE RAIDS, the rustling and the burning wagons, but weren't sure they were having an affect — until the president received a letter from Colonel Edmund Alexander, the interim commander.

President Young was busy with the the painters and the glaziers behind the nearly completed Lion House when his stenographer George Watt emerged from the building:

"Got an official letter from Colonel Alexander," George said.

"Alexander?"

'He's still in charge until the new commander arrives — he's none too happy, President."

Brigham smiled and found a seat on bench in the garden: "Read it to me — got putty and paint on my hands," he said, wiping them off on his coveralls.

"He's complaining of the 'hostility and rebellion exhibited by the interception of the supplies and the taking of stock and the interference of the mail between the East and the West.'"

Brigham chuckled: "Well, isn't that ironic — we can claim the same thing ever since our mail contract was cancelled. Furthermore, until replaced, I am still the governor of this territory and I did declare martial law, did I not, and decreed that no person may pass without permission of passage? George, would you please pen a reply to the colonel?"

"Saying?"

"…saying that we would assist them in reaching Fort Hall and would supply with they need there so that they may be in communication between the East and the West. Oh, and invite the colonel to come to the city for a parley, promise them a safe escort…something like that. Now, I have some window panes to set. Thank you, George."

"You're welcome. I'll see it is sent off today," Watt said and left.

15

"JESUS CHRIST HIMSELF CANNOT KEEP US OUT!"

The news of Lot Smith's raid on the wagon train at the Big Sandy was spreading all through the Mormons settlements, even if it was no faster than a pony could carry it. And, with Army couriers hurrying back to Leavenworth and its telegraph office, within a couple of weeks, even Buchanan and his minions, along with Greeley and the other editors in the big cities, would be all over it as well. Lot's line that "it's for His (God's) sake we are burning these wagons" would be printed up and down the Eastern seaboard. The word was getting out.

Even in his secluded mountain hideaway, Thomas Kane had heard read about Lot's adventure. His father Judge John Kane did, too, but Thomas had not been able to face his fate — until now. The year 1857 had been terrible for the Kane family. First, Judge Kane's oldest son Elisha had perished as a result of exposure in his Arctic misadventure. It was left to Thomas to retrieve his brother's body and bring it back from Havana, Cuba. Elisha's death was big news all over the East when the country was looking for a hero in such troubling times. Judge Drummond's outrageous articles spreading falsehoods about the Mormons destroying legal records and law books and especially Kane's role in carrying their water kept Thomas out of the fight.

He had had a restless night.

Bess found him out in the barn. He was putting away tools, harnesses and seed and cleaning up their country refuge for the fall; winter was coming and so was the storm, he told his wife.

"What storm?" Bess asked him.

He was putting his favorite saddle up on a shelf and turned to answer her.

"The Utah storm."

"What?"

"I have to get back on the horse."

She was puzzled: "The horse is hitched up to the carriage."

"Not that horse."

"What horse, then?"

"Old Brigham. He needs my help before blood is spilled. I need to quit my pouting and get back into the battle."

"Oh, you're speaking metaphorically…like your friend Ralph Waldo."

"Remember the invitation to their celebration that he sent us last summer?"

Bess thought for a moment and found a seat on a barrel in the barn; the baby had kept her busy all day, but nap time was at hand. She deserved a break, too. Finally, she remembered.

"Oh, it was in the canyon on their 10th anniversary, I'd like to visit there some time with you, that is, as long as we don't return with a second wife for you."

Thomas knew that the "polygamy thing" had been bothering her for some time, and he certainly wouldn't bring it up — it was as inconceivable to him as it was to her, so this time he let it go, except to offer her a "kudo."

"Why would anyone want a second wife when he already had a Bess?"

"Good answer, Thomas," she replied with a smile, but she was not finished. "So, once you climb aboard 'Old Brigham,' then what?"

"I need to go to Washington City and meet with Bernhisel once he's back. I want to follow up and see if father has unlocked the door to the White House before 'Old Buck' makes any more blunders."

"But, you're not going to grab an ox team and a wagon and go "a pioneering to Utah," are you?"

He knew better than to give her a straight answer because at this point, he didn't know if that were a possibility. But, something told him that a trip west was always in the cards; he just wasn't ready to announce it publicly and certainly not to Elizabeth Kane.

NO ONE ENJOYED THE NEWS ABOUT LOT SMITH'S GREAT BONFIRE more than Orrin Porter Rockwell. Normally, taciturn to the point of being annoying, Mormondom's Mountain Man was gleeful. He actually smiled when he saw Lot — almost gave his horse-wise ally a hug.

"Give me the details, Lot. Leave nothing out," Porter urged him as they were huddling with Burton and others on a Sunday afternoon in the Mormon's secret "Cache Cave" in Echo Canyon. Decades earlier, the cave was a trading post of sorts for trappers where they sold beaver pelts and shared stories. Some things never change! Someone had a brought a couple of pies that they were enjoying on a rough-cut table just inside the cave's entrance.

Lot's punchline, that was now almost becoming trite: 'It's for His sake (that we will burn the wagons),' had become a rallying call, and Porter loved it. Then, he shared his ambitious plan with Smith and the others.

"Lot, what's your favorite cut of meat, what steak do you prefer above all others, a tender loin, ribeye, what?"

Lot was puzzled looking at the wild, bearded man across the table from him:

"Are your taking me out to dinner, Port?"

"Yes, you and everyone from Ogden to Provo," Rockwell said with a chuckle.

"Port, you are actually becoming likable — this isn't your style. Spill the beans, what's up?

"One of our scouts spied a huge herd of Uncle Sam's beef cattle

up on the Oregon trail, moving slowly to keep them fat, but I suppose they're eating every blade of grass between here and Laramie. Let's free them from their overseers!"

"Let's introduce them to Mormonism and our way of life," Porter exclaimed with a grin.

Now Lot and the rest of the cowboys and mountain men were laughing; they all loved missionary work! They were about to evangelize 1,400 head of the Uncle Sam's cattle.

WHEN MAJOR TAYLOR RETURNED TO THE PRISONER'S TENT, he startled his fellow prisoner William Stowell who had finally been able to sleep for awhile.

"I'm still shackled in this foul-smelling tent — my dream was much more pleasant," Stowell said to his superior officer. "How did that go?"

Taylor scooted over to him on the dirty scattered straw — no sense sharing their secrets with the enemy.

"Colonel Alexander is swimming in deep water here," Taylor whispered. "When I shared with him 'my troop counts' of 25 to 30 thousand men guarding Echo Canyon, he turned pale. I think he's going to go west and then south and avoid the canyon, but there's no real trail there."

Then Taylor drew closer: "By the way, there's a correspondent with the Army working for a New York newspaper; he just might drop in for a visit. Has a very high opinion of himself. Also, I retrieved your little Bible."

"Thank you, Major! Maybe we can memorize it in our spare time," Stowell said. " Now if we just had a little more light in here."

"And a chair and a table and no shackles…"

"Then, it would be perfect!" William added. Even a little humor, even a darker shade, can help the days pass faster, he thought.

He opened the Bible to a note in the front that Cynthia had scribbled for him, and he opened the book to Psalms, where he had been reading before their capture, and read three verses in Psalms out loud:

"Remember this?" William asked the major and then quoted Psalms from memory: *"Behold, O God our shield, and look upon the face of thine anointed. For a day in thy courts is better than a thousand. I had rather be a doorkeeper in the house of my God, than to dwell in the tents of wickedness. For the Lord God is a sun and shield: the Lord will give grace and glory: no good thing will he withhold from them that walk uprightly."*

"Where is that?"

"Psalms, chapter 84. It's one that we should remember for a long time.

In the other corner of the prison tent, one of the deserters wiped his eyes.

"Thank you. I didn't know you folks read the Bible. I wish I had one."

"You can borrow mine as long as you're here."

"I don't read that well, but I like listening, My ma used to read to us at night," the prisoner said and then looked away.

William and the major exchanged glances.

"I wonder if they know…" William said.

"Who?"

"Our wives, families, that we're here in the 'tent of wickedness.' Did the colonel say anything?"

"It never came up — he hasn't a clue about where he is, what we're doing or even why he's here. Let's hope our people conveyed our whereabouts to the people in charge," Taylor said.

"Let's pray they know where we are, but then where exactly are we?"

"Nobody knows — not even the Colonel," Taylor lamented.

"Let's hope God knows," the prisoner in the corner said.

It was quiet in the tent the rest of the night.

HOWEVER, THERE WAS NO PEACE AND QUIET in the command tent where the acting man in charge, Col. Alexander was having a heart-to-heart with his subordinates.

"Who can give me an accounting of what we have lost from these Mormon raids, both in wagons burned and stock stolen? Anybody?" He waited for a reply. None came. A couple of minutes later, finally, Captain Randolph Marcy spoke: "Only Van Vliet could answer that, in my opinion, since …"

Alexander cut him off: "Captain, Van Vliet is back in Kansas…"

"But only he knows what was on those wagons…" Marcy replied.

"How many did we lose?" Alexander asked.

An officer from the Phelps Battery came to Marcy's defense: "Fifty-two or fifty-three. But, sir, it isn't so much about what was taken, but rather what is left."

"Lieutenant, if I recall, you are a graduate of the West Point Military Academy, are you now?" The lieutenant nodded. Alexander now fuming was searching for answers, but they all knew they had none. "And, you took all the required classes in mathematics, correct?"

He nodded, but then replied: "Sir, we need to take the battle to the Mormons. not just wait…"

"We have our orders as vague as they may be, and we are not to make war on these people," Alexander said in his own defense.

"But, they are making war on us…"

Alexander was now turning beet red:

"So, Lieutenant, visit the bullwhacker in charge, get an accounting of what we have left and how long it will last. Let's put our heads together, maybe even organize some hunting parties and find a solution."

Then, Alexander lowered the boom: "For now, we have to cut our daily rations, maybe even in half, because we are facing a long, cold winter in Wyoming."

IT WOULD GET WORSE FOR THE **A**RMY BEFORE IT WOULD GET BETTER. Early the next morning, days after Porter's and Lot's first meeting, the Mormon militia was preparing for the day when Rockwell's scouts came galloping into camp.

"We found the cows, we found the cows!"

Anyone who was not still up and about was awake now. Great excitement spread through the camp. When Porter's boys first tracked the giant herd, he felt they didn't have enough men to do the job. They did now.

With both Rockwell's and Smith's companies working together, they could smell the steaks frying! Every man and his mount rose to the occasion. Time was of the essence.

As they rode together to where Port's scouts had discovered the cattle, Lot couldn't help himself. Port was his usual taciturn self, darkly brooding about some misadventure, and Lot rightly guessed what was on Rockwell's mind:

"Think we'll find some mules to go along with the cattle we're about to claim for the Kingdom?"

Porter's mood instantly changed — gone were the storm clouds looming over his brow. He broke out in self-derisive laughter.

"Who told you about that?"

"I think it was in the *New York Herald*; I'm sure I saw a copy, describing Lot's fantastic bonfire right on the front page."

Porter was still laughing — now a couple of other riders had joined the audience.

"How did I know that mules had such a love for bugles," Porter countered. Two of his scouts were snickering — they had witnessed the mules' about-face.

"How so?"

"We had them dead to rights…a whole menagerie of mules, some fine ones, not a jenny in the bunch. We were moving them out when their blasted bugler played their daily 'come to dinner' serenade.' I never saw a mule turn around that fast and hurry back to where they came from. I learned my lesson," Porter said.

Lot was laughing out loud now — so were the other riders within earshot. "So what was that lesson you learned."

"Never steal a mule without a bugler at your side!"

One of Porter's scouts came riding back to Smith and Rock-well:

"Shhh, we're coming up on the herd and their keepers. We need to circle around them through that wash to the left and then push them back this way."

Porter and Lot conferred a second and then Lot gave the order: "Let's have six marksman form a skirmish line to block the path to the guards who might want to stop the stampede, but behind cover. They need to be safe, but still seen. Let's move out."

When they came to the top of the ridge, they could see a giant herd of cattle spread out in front of them, as still as dew in the early morning light.

One of the scouts exclaimed: "There must be 2,000 of them!"

Concealed behind junipers and brush, they formed their semi-circle and then let shots ring out as they screamed and hollered and moved against the animals that awakened and got them moving, pushed them down into the shallow wash just as their guards came out of their slumber.

An hour later that huge crowd of men, horses and some 1,400 head of cattle were moving southwest towards Echo Canyon and Mormondom.

WILLIAM STOWELL MAY HAVE BEEN SHACKLED, but the one who was afraid and worried was Colonel Edmund Alexander, the acting superior officer of the Utah Expedition sitting across the small camp table from his prisoner. Born in Virginia in 1802, Alexander had graduated from the West Point U.S, Military Academy in 1823, had served at Fort Atkinson in Council Bluffs, Iowa, in Michigan, Missouri, and in Indian Territory at a time when the western boundaries of the United States were blurry at best. Nevertheless, William Stowell had a distinctive advantage over the man who had him in shackles: Stowell knew why he was there.

The colonel may have enjoyed the privileges of rank, but William could see that Alexander was no General Harney who enjoyed watching others suffer and used his position for his own pleasure, but nevertheless, William could see that the commander was confused.

"Mr. Stowell, it would be to your benefit to cooperate with us; we are here at the pleasure of the president of these United States to ensure that the citizens of this territory recognize and obey the laws set forth in the Constitution. What is your purpose as a lieutenant in the state militia?" Alexander asked.

"It is to repel a mob, sir. It's that simple."

"What mob?"

"The mob outside this tent, the mob in uniform and their supply wagons and hangers-on. We have been harassed by mobs for 20 years now. I know firsthand how the Latter-day Saints have been persecuted, pursued and chased from place to place. It began in Ohio then went to Missouri, from there to Illinois until in the dead of winter in 1846, they were forced to leave their homes in Nauvoo, to cross the muddy prairie floor of Iowa, to winter on the banks of the Missouri. When they left Nebraska territory, they left the borders of the United States to build their homes and their towns on a blank spot…a blank spot no one else wanted. So, when it was reported to us that an Army was marching on our homes and our towns…which we had built out of nothing…our leader said, 'They Shall Not Pass.'" Then, Stowell sat up straighter:

"Sir, when we heard that there was an Army coming from the states under the name of government troops without any legal cause, we regarded the the troops assembled outside as a vile mobocracy. We are fortified — there would be very serious casualties if your troops attempted to enter the Salt Lake Valley."

Alexander leaned back in his canvas-backed camp chair and considered the shackled man who had just delivered such a defiant speech.

"Lieutenant, I am not sure you understand the position your people are in. You are in over your heads here; we have nearly 3,000 armed men, many on horseback with a battery of artillery, the Phelps Battery. It would serve your interests better here not to put on such a show of bravado."

"No disrespect meant sir, and I don't know what bravado is," Stowell countered, "but you should know that if you try to enter the valley through Echo Canyon, it would be another charge of the light brigade, another Sevastopol. Some 20 to 25 thousand sharpshooters, cavalry men and cannoneers, not to mention engineers are there and ready to dislodge tons of rocks and boulders onto your path, stand ready to prevent your entry into the Valley. In addition, changing course and trying to go west then south through Marsh Valley is folly; it is also well guarded. General Chauncey West and his regiment will block your way. I don't know if that is bravado, Colonel, it's just how things are. You'll just have to use your best judgment."

Alexander stood up and called for his aide:

"Sergeant major, take the prisoner back to his billet if you would please."

A rough-cut man in a disheveled uniform entered, grabbed Stowell and practically dragged him as he shuffled out in his shackles. William glared at his captor as if to say "you can't intimidate me."

The guard would have none of that: "Bravado, Lieutenant, is just Latin for bullshit, but you knew that."

Then the guard got right up into Stowell's face.

"And, as far as keeping us out of your holy city, just know this: We will winter in your homes, and Jesus Christ himself cannot keep us out."

Stowell stumbled and fell as he returned to his home sweet home in his tent of wickedness. When Major Taylor looked up, he was smiling. Taylor smiled back.

Their "counter-intel" effort was taking root, even though they were still shackled in a canvas prison.

After Van Vliet and Bernhisel had left Salt Lake City, Brigham Young and his counselors were finishing their collaboration with Jacob Hamblin about their sometime allies, the native tribes up and down the eastern edge of the Great Basin.

Before Hamblin left to return to Santa Clara, Brigham posed a question: "Anyone have a suggestion about how we can re-energize our friend and ally Thomas Kane and determine his state of mind?"

Wilford Woodruff reminded him that with the ending of the XY mail contract, a letter wouldn't do, besides he had heard that Kane was still out of town. The Saints were really in the dark ever since they lost the government contract to move mail between the West and Independence, Missouri.

"Where? How can we find him?"

"Do we have anyone traveling east who could stop in Philadelphia and make an inquiry?" Brighsm asked.

It was growing dark, and Hamblin needed to leave.

"Yes, Brother S.W. Richards is on his way to New York and then Liverpool; maybe we can catch him before he departs," Watt offered.

Brigham responded: "Make it so. I have the sense that we will soon need Thomas Kane's help more than ever."

16

IN A TENT OF WICKEDNESS

Elder Samuel Richards, who had recently been called on a mission to England, had been asked to first deliver a message to Thomas Kane. He reached Philadelphia in the late afternoon and hired a hansom to deliver him to Kane's home, but found only a servant there.

"He and Mrs. Kane are still in the Alleghanies, and while we are not privy as to when they might return to the city, we pray it's soon," the young woman told the Richards.

He was perplexed, but pushed ahead: "Is there some way we can get him word?"

The servant shrugged her shoulders, but then added: "You may want to post them a note…I can get you the address. Please come in."

Richards waited in the parlor for a few minutes, and the woman returned with an envelope, paper and the address. Then and there, he wrote Kane a short message that it was urgent that he contact President Young and that Delegate Bernhisel was coming east and had news to share.

After a stop at the post office, Elder Richards continued on his mission to Liverpool. He had done his part — now would he awaken Thomas Kane out of his hibernation? Brigham needed his defender now more than ever.

BY OCTOBER, THE KANES WERE ALREADY AT THE OUTSKIRTS of Philadelphia just as the terrible news about the atrocity at Mountain Meadows had reached the East Coast. It was first printed in a California tabloid, but now it was national news: the Mormons were

described as evil and as debased as Judge Drummond had char-
acterized them (under his pen name of *Verastus*).

Bess was at first mum on the subject, but soon they would be
back in their comfortable home in Philadelphia, so what would
Thomas now do in regards to his Mormon "hobby?"

The covered carriage packed with the Kanes and their belongings was just five miles or so from the city's outskirts when Elizabeth Kane finally asked the pregnant question:

"So now what, Thomas?"

"What do you mean, 'now what'?"

"Now that so many Yankee editors claim that the massacre at
Mountain Meadows reveals the true nature of the Mormons, does-
n't that give you pause?"

He took a breath: "It doesn't reflect the character of my
Mormon friends. But, it does make my job more difficult, that's
for sure."

"What job? How much are you being paid by the Mormons for
defending them? And, what about your work for the Allegheny
Railroad, helping them acquire more land?"

"The railroad's plans are still on the drawing board. And, far
as the Mormons go, you know exactly what my wages are, Bess.
And, that makes me redouble my efforts, because the death of
those emigrants will only be the first of many, many more to come
if we don't quit making war on our own people. What does Buchanan or anyone else expect when the Mormons read the death
threats from General Harney and others about hanging their
leaders and hear about the wagonloads of rope they're bringing
with them?

"Thomas, I'll repeat my question: So now what...what will or
can you do?"

"Well, Bess, as you recall, our friend John Bernhisel attempted
way back in the spring to meet with Buchanan. But then John was
shuffled off to Secretary Thompson who became enraged at their

legislature's demand for statehood. The Mormons just want to make their own decisions, to govern themselves…that's the Democrat way. But with corrupt and biased judges like Drummond acting all high and mighty that was impossible."

"All right, fine. But, why is this your, no, our responsibility?"

"I suppose I'm more of a Christian than I admit, Elizabeth, I suppose it's because I believe in liberty for the downtrodden. I guess I'm just a hopeless romantic."

Bess looked at him with tear-filled eyes: "I know, I know. I suppose that's why I love you. I should try to be more patient." She left the room — there was housework to do and children to tend.

ONE OF THE ADVANTAGES OF BEING IMPRISONED in a "tent of wickedness" is the lack of prison bars. Major Taylor and William Stowell had been considering when to make their escape, but how? That was the challenge. Being shackled also has its distinct disadvantages. Also, on at least two occasions, they were convinced that their jailers had attempted to poison them, first from servings of a questionable soup and then from wine that they passed on to their non-Mormon fellow prisoners who then demonstrated its effects. So, when Taylor convinced their jailers that Stowell was suffering from rheumatism and they ought to be able to spend the evening near the bonfire with the troops unshackled, that gave them the opportunity they were looking for. Being quite the storyteller, Stowell spun a yarn that had his listeners enthralled just as a herd of cattle was passing by. All that noise gave Major Taylor the opportunity to slip unnoticed away. Fifteen minutes later, after discovering his departure, a search party — complete with bloodhounds — scoured the area unsuccessfully.

The unshackled Taylor had flown the coop!

After nearly freezing to death, Major Taylor was later discovered by a Mormon surveillance party that took him to safer quarters.

Within a week, he was in Salt Lake City, warm and safe. A few days later, Brigham Young was still in a sour mood after hearing about the capture of Taylor and Stowell, thankful that Taylor was able to escape, but determined to get William Stowell back to his family safe and sound. Stowell's story about his adoption of the orphans, his two young wives left with nine children and just a fifteen-year old adopted son to do the heavy lifting added fuel to the fire that was burning inside President Young.

"George, got a minute," Brigham called to his able aide, George Watt, his secretary and correspondent to the world. George got the message and was at the prophet's side with pen and paper. He could tell President Young was worked up, both angry and concerned, but about what?

Brigham got right to the point: "George, I want you to pen a letter and send it to Colonel Johnston."

"What kind of letter, a Christmas card, best wishes on his new assignment?" George said with a smile. Brigham softened a bit and attempted a smile.

"George, you are aware, are you not, that Major Taylor successfully escaped from that den of thieves, but his adjutant is still in their hands. Do you know of this William Stowell?"

"No sir," Watt said now sobered.

"He has two young wives and between them, I think nine or ten children they are caring for, six of whom are orphans they have adopted, and William, is living in horrid conditions, according to Major Taylor, shackled in a tent and covered with lice."

Then with great emotion, Brigham Young managed to spell out what he wanted George to put in the letter: *"If you imagine that keeping, mistreating or killing Mr. Stowell will redound to your credit or advantage, future experience may add to the stock of your better judgment."*

Brigham had been pacing about and then when he had said his piece, sat down. George said nothing, but wrote it down as far

as he could remember and repeated it, then asked: "…future experience…will what?"

Brigham repeated the last part of the sentence: "… *may add
to the stock of your better judgment, something like that.*"

George put pen to paper, refreshed the ink, finished it, dusted
it off and then showed it to the president for his final approval.
Then, Brigham cleared his throat and with watery eyes asked his
aide, "Did we send someone to talk to his wives and children?"

"Yes, I believe Elder Hyde has been charged to pay them a
visit.

Brigham then added: George, please make sure we know that
they are not in need; I will pray for them and their husband, William. This whole matter grieves me. Thank you, George." Brigham
wiped his eyes and turned away. It was time for George to find an
envelope and determine how to get the letter sent to the man who
wished them all dead.

Eventually, the letter found its way to Colonel Johnston who
shared it with others. Unimpressed by Brigham Young's warning
letter, the Chief Justice Delana R. Eckels had prepared a list of 20
Latter-day Saint leaders and notables to indict for treason. The
list had Brigham Young at the top and ended with William Stowell
who was "honored to be included in such grand company." The
new seat of government, temporary at least until they could occupy Salt Lake City, was called "Eckelsville," a ramshackle warren
of dugouts, log cabins, tents, buggies and wagon boxes, quite an
impressive location, a "suburb" of Fort Bridger where Eckels
could administer his brand of justice on such a scale.

Arriving with Eckels and Johnston was Buchanan's choice to
replace Brigham Young as the territorial governor, Alfred Cumming,
the former mayor of Augusta, Georgia, accompanied by his wife Elizabeth and a few servants. Once he had settled, he sent a proclamation to Brigham Young declaring that *"I come among you with no
prejudices nor enmities, and by the exercise of a just and firm*

administration — I hope to command your confidence. Freedom of conscience and your own peculiar mode of serving God are sacred rights, the exercise of which is guaranteed by the Constitution, and ... is not the province of the government or the disposition of its representatives in the Territory to interfere." He then directed all armed bodies to disband and return to their homes. Disobedience to this command, he stated, would "subject the offenders to the punishment due to traitors." As offensive as it may have been to the Mormons, to Colonel Albert Sydney Johnston, it was considered to be too lenient. It was the first of many disagreements between them.

CYNTHIA AND SOPHRONIA STOWELL still had no husband in the house — he was back in irons — but they did have each other. For them, plural marriage was literally a godsend, even if they did have to share a husband when — and if — he was ever around again.

But, where was he exactly?

Except for a visit from a friend on his way to Salt Lake weeks ago before William's capture, they had received no communication about his whereabouts or well being.

So, when the Apostle Orson Hyde came knocking, they feared the worst. After all, their husband was officially at war, there was no one to deliver a telegram — that technology had not yet arrived in Utah. One could only imagine what the young women and the nine children in their care thought when an apostle suddenly appeared at their door.

As he walked in, Hyde was overwhelmed by their circumstances, 11 people stuffed into two small rooms of a tiny cabin, most of the children under five years of age and the two wives pregnant. He found himself a seat on one of the four chairs, none of them matching, next to a tiny, home-crafted table. Tears flowed freely as the apostle explained what had happened to their husband, father and uncle:

"Major Taylor, his superior who was captured with him, sings William's praises. Your husband made it possible for Taylor to slip away in the night by entertaining his captors with his tall tales. When William was interrogated by the general, he made such an impression on the Army that they hesitated to move against us. He told Major Taylor about his dream that he will eventually be released and even saw himself returning down Echo Canyon. Sisters, we are assured that the Lord, knows of his circumstances and will answer your prayers."

Cynthia Stowell thanked him and then added: "We share in that faith — William is indeed a visionary man; he will be guided back to us." But, as is often the case, fulfillment of such hopeful insight always seems to take much longer than is hoped for. It was November, 1857, when Hyde visited them and shared the bad news. They would have to spend a cold, forlorn winter and spring while they waited — and suffered — until they were reunited.

JOHN D. LEE HESITATED OUTSIDE BRIGHAM YOUNG'S RESIDENCE. He was certain the Prophet was not alone — he never was. Wilford Woodruff or another apostle or one of his counselors would surely be close at hand. After the grisly murder of more than 100 emigrants at Mountain Meadows, he wasn't sure how to explain his actions. Both Isaac Haight and William Dame, his superiors in the militia, told him to tell the truth, confess his sins and ask for forgiveness.

But, he couldn't do that, could he? Brigham counted him as a son, even if he were a prodigal, he was certain there would be no fatted calf waiting in the thicket. After all, wasn't this really an atrocity undertaken by the natives, and natives can get restless, can't they, when their people are poisoned, attacked and killed?

For a moment, he recalled his chance meeting with Brothers Samuel Knight and Dudley Leavitt who told him that they would not consent to his plan to get the emigrants to surrender and then take their lives. Leavitt said if there were any killing to be done, "it would have to be fair and square." This was after the initial skirmish when the emigrants had left Cedar City — Lee had gunshots in his clothing but not in his person.

That was evidence enough that there had been a two-way battle, wasn't it?

Should he have listened to Leavitt and followed the belated advice? That made sense, didn't it? It's too late now!

Lee took a breath, straightened out his jacket, combed his hair with his fingers and walked up the stairs.

Outside the President Young's office a few minutes later, several members of the family and staff who weren't invited inside heard Brigham bellow out "they're what? They're all dead? How did this happen…" followed by a mournful cry and sobbing. Finally, one of the children later heard her father yell out in a muffled, hoarse cry… "tell me no more, John, no more!"

Some reports recalled seeing an ashen Lee slither out of the house, his hat pulled down over his eyes and disappear down the street. The worst incident in history perpetrated by Mormons was now out in the open, a gashing wound that wouldn't ever heal and would soon make headlines from California to the east coast and would even find its way into European publications.

It confirmed the calumny circulated by the enemies of Joseph, Brigham and all the Saints about "their unrighteous behavior, their corruption and their evil ways."

How could anyone explain it away? They couldn't.

Within a few weeks, Thomas Kane and John Bernhisel would find their tasks many times more difficult to calm the waters and find some peace for the beleaguered Mormons.

Lee, his co-conspirators and participants in the massacre at Mountain Meadows, kept their heads down and their mouths shut.

The truth was just too terrible to share.

THOMAS KANE AND JOHN BERNHISEL had some catching up to do since they had both been AWOL for the summer. And with the latest news out of southern Utah beginning to appear in newspapers all over the country, there was no shortage of repairs to take care of. Bernhisel had left Utah to return to his responsibilities in Washington with Captain Van Vliet the middle of September; Kane and his family were back in Philadelphia on October 4th.

A few weeks later, at President Buchanan's request, Kane and Bernhisel were together in Washington waiting to confer with the president's inside man, James C. Van Dyke.

Thanks to his father's letter to Buchanan, Thomas was able to speak with the president briefly who gave Thomas no indication that there was such a thing as "Buchanan's Blunder," that all was well in Utah. But, what about the 2,500 troops, the bullwhackers and the hangers-on who were hoping to survive a long, cold winter? What about them? Kane and Bernhisel were hoping for straight answers. They were sitting in an anteroom in a building near the White House, awaiting their meeting with Van Dyke. Bernhisel knew that Kane had been embarrassed by the many attacks by Drummond and the other Federal officials who had fled Utah with their tails behind their legs, barking as they left.

But, it was the death of Elisha that was the hardest for him to bear, but John noticed that Thomas appeared to be invigorated.

"Bess and the children well?" Bernhisel began with some small talk.

Thomas nodded and asked: "Yours?"

John then asked Thomas how he was holding up under the attacks from Drummond and the other officials who fled Utah and needed someone to blame for their failures.

Thomas smiled and responded with some vigor and then explained: "John, while my many attackers disparage me for supporting the Saints and call me all sorts of names, I actually feel better about myself when I do. I know I felt insulted by the administration and withdrew for a season; if you recall our conversation will Bill Appleby who told us he had never seen such an acrimonious spirit against the Mormons before…"

"And the southern Utah killings have since made it worse," Bernhisel added.

"Undoubtedly," Kane agreed, "but in another sense, it reminded some level-headed people to recognize that there could be much more blood spilt on both sides unless we can reach some kind of agreement. On the one hand, we have our esteemed Secretary of War, Mister Floyd…"

"A Southerner and a slave-holder, " John observed.

"Exactly. And then there's Robert Tyler," Thomas whispered, "a fellow Pennsylvanian who a source told me explicitly that Tyler advised the president that *the best way to resolve Negro-mania in Kansas is to quell the Mormon rebellion,* or words to that effect."

"But, thank goodness, your work with Attorney General Black and others have convinced Mr. Van Dyke to take you up on your offer to mediate this crisis," Bernhisel said and then asked: "How does Bess feel about this whole matter then, given her opposition earlier?"

Thomas looked away, paused and then quietly confessed to Bernhisel: "Since Elizabeth and I have come together on our religious differences, rather, since I began examining my own spirituality, or rather my lack thereof, especially since Elisha's passing, I told her that 'I felt pushed' by an unseen hand to come to the Mormon's aid ever since 1846. Then tears welled up in her eyes, and she also confessed that she felt my intervention in the Utah War has been divinely inspired."

Bernhisel was visibly moved by Thomas' explanation, put his hand on his friend's shoulder and added, "Thomas, there are thousands of people in Utah who see your role in exactly the same way; you, my friend, are a Godsend." Then the door opened. It was Van Dyke.

17

WE ARE CONSTANTLY AT DEFIANCE

Waiting requires patience, or do we learn patience by waiting? William Stowell wondered that every day. How long would he remain shackled while his wives and children suffered without him? It was growing colder by the day, and now that the new commander, Colonel Albert Sydney Johnston, had finally arrived, the Utah Expeditionary Force had finally taken stock of how much they had lost from Lot and Porter and company's raids. It was immense. And, not only were the prisoners, but also the enlisted men and the officers were all now on half rations. One can only imagine what the bellicose Johnston had said when he confronted his subordinate Colonel Edmund Alexander:

"Colonel, where were the guards, our troops, when the Mormon rabble burned our food, supplies and wagons? Who was watching over our herds of cattle, the mules and horses when the renegades just drove them off? Where were you?

Alexander felt the hair rise up on the back of neck because he knew that Colonel Johnston knew very well the status of the train of supply wagons and the corresponding location of the men when the raids took place.

"Colonel, I did not plan this expedition any more than you did. Harney himself said that the expedition should have wintered in Fort Laramie and assembled their stores there and waited until spring before marching south into Utah. It was the politicians, as is always the case, who determined to blunder along into this mess. They wanted to take the attention off of 'bleeding Kansas,' but it is still bleeding," Alexander said, defending himself.

"That's why they sent Harney back there. We, sir, are just the sideshow," Alexander added.

"Why didn't we have someone prevent the burning of Fort Bridger or Fort Supply?" Johnston asked, wanting someone to blame — the object of his scorn was standing right in front of him.

"Sir, that's a different question, but the same answer. Our people were hundreds of miles east of where we are now when that happened," Alexander replied, trying to hold his ground, but it was getting slippery.

"We should take the battle to the Mormons; we have the guns and ammo. Our intelligence tells us they are desperate to find powder and lead, not to mention replace their Revolutionary War weaponry," Johnston huffed.

"Easier said than done. The most direct route through Echo Canyon already has parapets and shooting sites on both sides. And 'to take the battle to them' is prohibited in our orders, unless you have orders I know nothing of," Alexander reminded Johnston.

"My orders are the same," Johnston confessed, trying to calm himself down. "So tell me, who is best situated in our officer corp to help us dig into the mind of the enemy…"

"Sir, they are Americans, not the enemy, but they consider us as such. You should speak with Major Phil Cooke. He knows these people; he was the commander of the so-called Mormon Battalion during the War with Mexico," Alexander said.

"Yes, Phillip St. George Cooke, quite the cavalryman, I've heard of him. We will talk," Johnston replied. "But, what about all the rumors that Mormons have infiltrated our ranks, that they know more about what we're doing than most of our men do. Any suggestions?"

"We have one in shackles now; you should meet him."

"Oh, is his name Stowell?" Johnston sneered. "Ahhh, he's the

one that Old Brigham noted in the letter he sent me. He warned me not to kill or hurt him. But, since Judge Eckels plans to try him for treason, then we'll let a jury make that call. I understand that you did interrogate him. Is it true that he escaped along with his superior officer, but then returned of his own accord?"

"That is correct. Apparently, he got cold and hungry."

Johnston laughed at that, but was oblivious to the fact, that in the months to come as the Wyoming winter arrived in full force, the General, a Southern gentleman, would discover for himself what it means to be cold and hungry. He wouldn't be laughing then.

THOMAS KANE WAS PLEASANTLY SURPRISED to discover how supportive the president's inside man, James Van Dyke, was of his acting as the intermediary between the Mormons and the Army. After waiting for at least half an hour, Van Dyke welcomed Kane and Bernhisel into his office and closed the door; this was an unofficial visit, away from prying eyes.

"Thomas," Van Dyke said to Kane as if Bernhisel weren't there, "how are your parents doing ever since Elisha's death?" Kane had met Van Dyke years ago, but only as Judge Kane's son and law clerk, not as a supposed "white knight" for a group of outcast citizens. Both were "sons of the Commonwealth" and residents of Philadelphia.

"My father is stoic, and my mother is bereft," Thomas replied, "which makes them both very wary about my 'quixotic' quest, as my father calls it, to assist my Latter-day Saint friends."

"So, the Mormons, they're not just clients, they're friends?" Van Dyke asked and then motioned to his visitors to make themselves comfortable. So, tell me Thomas, some people call you 'the Colonel?' Like your brother Elisha, did you serve in the war with Mexico?"

Thomas smiled: "No, it was much more mundane. Former Governor Bigler, now Senator Bigler, appointed me as his aide-de-camp a few years ago, and as a result, he wanted a colonel to be at his beck and call. So, I was given the title and rank, but never saw battle, not yet anyway,"

"So, I don't have to salute you?" Van Dyke said with a laugh.

"But, I do," Bernhisel wisecracked.

Kane and Bernhisel took seats on Van Dyke's overstuffed leather sofa; Van Dyke leaned back in his chair behind a massive oak desk. Thomas looked at Bernhisel to make sure his companion knew he was included and then explained:

"Actually they're not clients since there's no fee involved. I'm just volunteering my time, for what it's worth."

Bernhisel smiled at his friend and then addressed Van Dyke: "Mr. Van Dyke, without Thomas, and of course, Senator Houston, we'd be totally friendless, so we rely on his judgment and character. We trust him to be a peacemaker, and we pray you will, too."

Van Dyke smiled: "That's why we're having this little chat. Given the forces at work in this divided nation, it would be great if 'peace could breakout somewhere soon.'"

Thomas leaned forward and addressed their host: "Sir, what's happening right now in Kansas could spread all over this nation, and using the people of Utah, the Mormons as people call them, to divert attention from bigger problems that demand the nation's attention, only exacerbates violence, not reduces it. We know that people in the administration, particularly Secretary Floyd and Robert Tyler, each with his own reasons, have pushed for this military incursion..."

"Thomas, Utah is a territory of the United States, it's not an incursion..." Van Dyke countered.

"But, if Utah were a state, popular sovereignty — a favorite of the Democrat Party — the law would demand that the Army withdraw, because as they see it, it is a posse comitatus."

"Thomas, Utah is still a territory, and the president appoints the governor," Van Dyke replied.

Thomas replied gently: "Yes sir, and judges, surveyors, Indian agents and so forth. But, to date, those appointees have run roughshod over the settlers, the residents, and many like Judge Drummond have abused their offices and used them for their own benefit." Thomas pulled out a newspaper clipping from his valise and handed it to Bernhisel who put it on Van Dyke's desk.

"Sir," Thomas said, "as you know, Captain Stewart Van Vliet visited President Young in September and sat with him on the stand in a conference in the city with upwards of 3,000 people in attendance. And as you can read in the second paragraph, Young reminded the congregation that *"mobs [have] repeatedly gathered against this people, but they never had any power to prevail until governors issued their orders and called out a force under the letter of the law, but breaking the spirit, to hold the 'Mormons' still while infernal scamps cut their throats...we are constantly at defiance of all hell to provide any just grounds for hostility against us...* . You can read the rest at your leisure. But, I do want to point that when Brigham Young promises that *they will burn their homes, tear up their fences and lay waste to their communities that created out of a high desert in the middle of nowhere the last 10 years,'* and then Brigham promised that '*if the Army marches in force into the city. There will be just an ash heap to welcome them.'"*

Kane paused and declared: "Believe me, it was no idle threat. Maybe it sounds like a fire and brimstone speech, but he was deadly earnest," Kane said, then read directly from the account: *"The people are not in bondage to any government on God's footstool. We have transgressed no law, and have no occasion to do so, neither do we intend to; but as for any nation's coming to destroy this people, God Almighty being my helper, they cannot come here."* Bernhisel nodded his assent. Van Dyke was silent for a moment, then spoke: "I suppose you have a plan, otherwise you wouldn't have asked for this meeting," Van Dyke said.

Thomas and Bernhisel shared a glance, and then Thomas said "we do."

"What do you need from the president, funds, letters, what? It has to be unofficial," the president's aide asked.

"I'm not seeking any funds, not one red cent. I'm doing this as just an interested citizen, nothing more. But, I can speak with President Young and acquire his assent to welcome a new governor, but without an armed force marching into Salt Lake City to forcibly seat him. There is one other aspect of my mission that I want the president to understand: Not only is the country divided into two camps, but so are the Mormons — the peace faction and the war faction. Brigham Young is the key to the peace faction. The Saints in the outlying regions, particularly in the south, are not only isolated, they are also more destitute — the climate is drier, life is harder and they feel put upon by all sides."

Van Dyke sat up and took notice of Thomas' "faction" comment. Kane continued: "Furthermore, the Army cannot be billeted in the Salt Lake Valley, but must be posted some distance away. I need a letter that I can carry to Colonel Johnston and Governor Cumming and signed by President Buchanan stipulating that. Their fort must be far enough away to allow the residents to live their lives without being subject to martial law. One last thing, we need a blanket pardon, no charges of sedition or anything like that."

Van Dyke wrote himself a note, scratched his head and then looked up.

"That is a tall order. Maybe you heard that Justice Eckels is organizing a grand jury to indict various leaders and officials for a variety of offenses. That complicates matters."

Bernhisel replied: "We know that."

Then Thomas added a postscript:"That has to go away."

Van Dyke nodded, then added: "You know, Thomas, this mission is fraught with danger. How do you plan on undertaking it?

How will you finance it?"

Thomas shrugged his shoulders: "I don't know for sure, but it has to happen, not just for the Mormons who are braced for an invasion, but for those American boys up north on the plains who are in for a cold, bitter winter."

"So, when do you plan on undertaking this venture."

"After the first of the year, sir, with your assent, and of course, the president's."

Van Dyke stood, extended his hand and smiled broadly: "God-speed to you, young man, I believe you will make history."

Thomas was touched, but not in awe: "Sir, I want to avoid making history. History is often the result of a fool's errand, a mis-calculation like the War of 1812. Or Sevastopol. **A hundred years from now, no one will talk about a war that didn't happen, only about one that did.**"

A FEW WEEKS LATER, THOMAS WAS BUSY SCRIBBLING notes at his desk when Elizabeth came into the office. They had moved in with her parents and her younger siblings. The financial panic of 1857 led to the collapse of her father's business and his deterio-rating health, so she was wife, mother and nurse at a time when Thomas was planning a 6,000-mile venture sailing to Panama and then to California. And, it included a mid-winter jaunt to Salt Lake City and then up to the high plains of southwestern Wyo-ming in the dead of winter. She wanted to know how he was going to pay for it all without dying along the way. Wives worry about such things, bless their hearts!

"Have you done your homework yet, Tom," she startled him.

"My homework?"

"Your mathematics, you know, the arithmetic, about getting to Panama, then California, Utah, somewhere out on the plains of Wyoming, wherever that is. Just wondering how we'll survive… how you will survive."

She gave him a neck rub, looked at him directly sitting on the corner of his desk and managed a weak smile.

"You know, I love you, Thomas…" He found it difficult to even speak to her. Tears filled his eyes. Hers as well.

"There's no question about that, because you know exactly how I feel about you and your family, including your father. These are difficult times for everybody — I pray he will get back on his feet, physically and financially. But"… Thomas hesitated for a moment, uncovered a small, old book that was under a stack of papers in a slot in his roll-top desk and opened it.

"What's that?" Elizabeth asked.

"A small biography of an Italian monk who died more than 300 years ago."

Elizabeth was puzzled and growing impatient. "And?"

"His name was Luca Pacioli, a Franciscan monk and a mathematician, since you asked me about my homework, arithmetic and more precisely accounting," Thomas said carefully since he sensed he was treading in deep water with his wife. "Did you know he is called the Father of Accounting, the inventor of the double-entry system for bookkeeping? He wrote the book, this book…" Elizabeth picked up the small, well worn book, opened it up and set it down. She glared at her husband.

"It's in Latin."

"Yes, I know. I read Latin, learned it…sort of…for my work in law, as a law clerk Latin is important… ."

Elizabeth folded her arms and stared at him.

"The thing about Luca is that he never made much money, he was a monk after all, and one of his close friends was Leonardo da Vinci. But, he changed the world."

"How so?"

"He helped Europeans, the Venetians, the French, the Germans, the British and their Commonwealth dominate trade for the past 300 years or so. His contribution is incalculable.

"Elizabeth, I'm scrounging up all that I can, selling some of my property, liquidating some bonds and working on an advance for a book so that I can fulfill the promise I made to John Bernhisel and by extension to Brigham Young and the Mormons in Utah and to the agreement I made to Van Dyke and the president. Trust me, you and the children will have enough to get by on, to feed and clothe them and I will be able to undertake this journey and return safely to you. I think you know that there is a divine hand at work here — Brigham Young and the old Patriarch John Smith both promised me that I would be protected and watched over if I stayed to true to what I think we both feel is a heavenly duty. I pray you will trust me and accept my decision."

Elizabeth Kane nodded her head as tears flowed down her cheeks, then she bent down and kissed her husband: "We're all counting on you, Thomas, and I will pray like I've never prayed before."

WHILE THOMAS KANE WAS TRYING TO BALANCE HIS BOOKS and make sure he didn't die trying to save the Mormons and the boys in blue in western Wyoming, the troops had more immediate needs: staying warm in the ice and snow while surviving on half rations. Both Lot's raiders and the soldiers of the Utah Expedition did have one activity that kept their minds occupied and hope alive in these dire circumstances: hunting. The Rocky Mountains were alive with mule deer, cottontails and jack rabbits, sage grouse and other critters even during winter, and they were all in the gunsights of combatants on both sides of the Utah War, since those combatants weren't as of yet actually shooting at each other.

After the Army's morning assembly and briefing, the Phelps battery had finished its assignments to police up the area near its defensive gun placements and powder magazines, Carl Wilcken, Günther Brandt and two privates volunteered to scout the country southwest of Camp Winfield where the cannons were situated, as the captain described it, to "look for enemy movements, especially cavalrymen. and if possible, scout out big game, like deer or antelope."

Günther shared his enthusiasm with Carl to do something more than "stack boxes of powder, organize ordinance and polish cannons."

"This is a brilliant way to get out, to escape the captain's nursemaiding and bothersome behavior," Brandt exclaimed.

"Did one of the riflemen bring the carbine with the scope in case we see some game?" Carl asked Brandt.

"Not sure, they're lagging behind — I know the fat redhead was supposed to check it out of the armory," Günther answered. The two Germans were a couple hundred yards ahead of the privates who were both armed and carried the supplies, including lunch. It was a sunny, brisk day, but relatively calm.

"I'll climb up to that outcropping just ahead near the dead cottonwood where I can get a look up at the wash down below; wait for my signal to join me there," Carl told Günther as he climbed up the rise covered in shale. Then, they heard a gunshot.

"Where are those riflemen?" Carl asked. "What are they up to?"

"Don't know. Climb up to the knob, and I'll go retrieve those *'Dorftrottels!'* (village idiots)," Günther said. "I'll be back soon." With some effort climbing up the slippery slope, he found a flat rock under the dead cottonwood and noticed that the pinyon pines nearby were pregnant with pine cones. Their Pawnee scout had schooled them in the fine art of stealing pine nuts from ground squirrels:

"The squirrels pick them for you, you take them and eat. They do the hard work," the red man explained with a smile revealing missing teeth. Carl figured that if he could eat the nuts, they must be easier to open than German *Haselnüsse* (hazel nuts). He found a couple of unopened pinecones (the open ones have already been

stripped clean) and then watched a ground squirrel a few yards down the slope hurry down into his hole. Carl slid down after him, nearly tripping and falling. Sure enough, he found a couple of handfuls and filled a pocket of his day pack. Now he was surrounded by a treasure trove of pine-nut caches, and for the next half hour had nearly filled his day pack. Carl found a log and ate several handfuls of pine nuts and washed them down with water from his canteen. He looked up behind him. His return trip to the knob on the hill looked too steep for his liking, but if he slid down the wash to the stream and back up the right side, it could be quicker and easier, he thought. As he scooted down, he heard a click of a gun being cocked and a voice said, "Put your hands in the air and turn slowly around."

Carl did as he was commanded and saw his captor, a Nauvoo militiaman in a ragtag uniform, but nevertheless well armed.

"Don't shoot, I am unarmed," Carl said in his German accent. Upon meeting the militiaman, Jonathan Layne, Carl appeared relieved, even happy, Layne later reported to his commander, Porter Rockwell. Carl asked for his field jacket and said, "If your men see me in my uniform, maybe they'll shoot me."

Layne smiled: "You are a big son-of-a-gun, and I'm afraid it wouldn't fit. Walk with me to camp. Your war is over."

Carl then grinned from to ear to ear: "Herr Mormon, I've been in war, and this isn't war. Thank you for taking me prisoner!"

Layne was surprised as well as confused. Carl Heinz Wilcken's days as a soldier had ended — at least as an enlisted member of the U.S. Army.

So, they celebrated.

Layne roasted the cottontail he had just shot and shared it with his prisoner.

18

SALVATION IS A FAMILY MATTER

William Stowell's days as a soldier and as a prisoner-of-war, on the other hand, were far from over. He still dwelt in his canvas prison, and unlike, Carl Heinz, he didn't have the pleasure of dining on pine nuts or cottontail. But, on this particular day, he would get a doctor's visit, not from a medical doctor, but rather a PhD from the University of Heidelberg; the illustrious war correspondent for the *New York Tribune*, Albert G. Browne Jr. was making a house call — rather a tent call. And since Stowell's housing arrangements were inappropriate to accommodate an official visit from a person of his stature, the officer in charge cleaned up the prisoner, gave him some food and water, unshackled him for the duration of the interview, took him to the officer's mess tent and sat him down:

"Stowell, be on your best behavior," the sergeant in charge told him.

"I always am, sir," William replied. He waited for a few minutes until Browne finally arrived, but that didn't bother William one bit, since he was for the moment, at least, unshackled, sitting in a chair and had the opportunity to dislodge a large herd of body lice who made their home on his person. He felt "normal," and that was good for a change. He did, realize, however, that afterwards he would be returned to his wretched living quarters.

Browne entered with a small notebook in his hand and a sharpened carpenter's pencil. There was a cast iron receptacle in the corner of the officers' tent filled with hot coals which took the edge off the bitter cold of winter in Wyoming.

Browne introduced himself.

"So, that I have your name spelled correctly, please introduce yourself and spell it for me." Browne asked.

William complied, then waited.

"So, Mr. Stowell, how is it that you are now in the custody of the United States Army?"

"Wrong place, wrong time, I suppose," William answered.

"No, please tell me how it came to be that you are in rebellion against the United States."

"I am not, but rather I am in support of our governor who issued a declaration of martial law against an unconstitutional incursion into our territory," William said defiantly. "This invasion is no different than the mobs in Missouri and Illinois where our constitutional rights of freedom of religion were violated time after time. This is another form of mobocracy."

If Browne had intended a friendly conversation where Stowell would provide the correspondent with a list of grievances against what the reporter considered to be a theocratic dictatorship, he was disappointed.

Stowell didn't care. And, he didn't care for the arrogant "Doctor Browne" either, who thought he would run rough-shod over the young farmer. The interview was off to a bad start and would only get worse.

"How do you earn a living, Mr. Stowell?"

"Farming, for the most part," William replied.

"Family?"

"Two wives, nine children — lots of mouths to feed."

Browne smiled: "And whose fault is that?"

"Fault? There's no fault — I'm not complaining; my brother died after his wife had died in childbirth and I took him as my own, even before I was even married. Then my half-brother Dan died, and his wife was also gone, so Cynthia and I adopted his five

children as well, for a total of six orphans. Then we had a set of twins, Cynthia and I. Then, she introduced me to Sophronia, a friend, who had a child of her own. You got this? Add it all up: That's nine children in total, so far! And, we live in a small two-room cabin, and now the two women and the children are on their own, thanks to Buchanan's blunder. But, it's worth it."

Browne was speechless — for the first time.

"Worth it?"

"To keep your mob out of our towns and away from our wives and children, it's worth it; we happen to subscribe to the notion of, what do you call it, 'popular sovereignty,'" Stowell said.

"Sounds like a convenient arrangement — for a man, but for women, isn't it a different matter?" Browne asked.

"What do you with your orphans, Mr. Browne?"

"What?"

"Your orphans, where do you keep them?"

"I don't have any orphans, don't even have a wife," Browne protested.

"I personally believe that adopting orphans is better than shipping them off to orphanages."

William continued: "Our choice was a matter of survival. "Mr. Browne, in other words, we believe that salvation is a family matter, since we hold that marriages can be eternal. What do you believe?" William continued.

"Salvation? I'm not sure there is such a thing, Mr. Stowell," Browne admitted.

"Maybe that's why you people have such a difficult time with Mormonism. For us, it's just a matter of faith. Sorry if that seems confusing to you. It's perfectly clear to me."

ONE THING THAT WAS BECOMING CLEARER TO THOMAS KANE, especially after the horror at Mountain Meadows and his first meeting with Van Dyke, was that he needed to travel to the West sooner

rather than later. But exactly when? That morning he caught the 10 a.m. train to Washington City to see John Bernhisel. Both he and John were paying the price for their long absence during the summer when all hell was breaking loose. Were they too late? Would there be another catastrophe like Mountain Meadows before cooler heads prevailed?

Not only Bess and his parents, but his brothers Patrick and John Jr. were also advising him to let nature take its course in Utah. "It's not your problem, not your fight!" That's was the refrain from the family. But, a still, small voice was telling him otherwise.

He had a window seat and watched the country side clatter by. There was a soothing rhythm to rail travel, he thought, and the 150-mile line from Philadelphia to Washington D.C. required no transfers. But, there was so many stops to let passengers on and off that it took much longer than he liked. At 30 mph, it shouldn't take longer than five and a half to six hours, but at this rate, Thomas feared, he wouldn't be there until late tonight.

The long train ride would be a chance to catch up on his reading. He opened up his leather catch-all, filled with letters, most of them from Utah. Brigham's were on top. He began reading, then the train jerked to stop.

They had just arrived in Chester, some passengers exited and then a well-dressed man took a seat across the aisle from him. They exchanged glances. *Where had he seen him before?* Thomas thought.

 The man spoke first:

"Excuse me, aren't you Patrick, Judge Kane's son,?"

"Yes and no, I'm the judge's son, but I am Thomas; I clerked for my father."

"Now I remember." Then the man asked: "How are your parents? So sorry to hear about Elisha."

Thomas acknowledged the sentiment and then finally recognized him: he was the editor of the *Pennsylvania Freeman*, an abolitionist newspaper. The editor had once praised Thomas for leaving his father's employ, writing that it "was manly, an act worthy of his heart," and criticized Judge Kane for "prostituting his powers" in his decisions in support of the Fugitive Slave Act.

Thomas went back to reading his letters. As he continued reading, Thomas realized how he had underestimated the effect of the Utah Expedition's effect on the Mormons in their mountain enclave. In a letter Brigham had sent in September, but not one he had read until now, Young wrote that *"we will resist the government's efforts to the last extremity... their efforts to quash our religious liberty...and to hang, shoot, burn and debauch, lay waste and destroy us as in times past."* Finally, President Young invited Kane to bring his family *"to ride out the storm with the Saints when the government attacked."*

"God's vengeance," Young wrote, *"would break upon the whole country...[so]come with all your household and receive the just recompense of daring to speak, act and feel in behalf of an innocent, but much abused people."*

Thomas could see out of the corner of his eye that the well-dressed man across the aisle was still watching him. Each time as he read one letter, put it back in the envelope, return it to the valise and then grab another, his neighbor made note of that. It was becoming irritating. Then, when Thomas dropped an envelope in the aisle, the man picked it up and handed it back to Thomas, obviously making note of the Salt Lake City postmark. Thomas thanked him, smiled and returned it his collection of correspondence.

"Been to Utah?" Trying to avoid a conversation, Thomas nodded. Then, the man said "So, I heard that their so-called prophet once said that there would be a war between the states and that it would begin in South Carolina. Any thoughts on that?"

Thomas was now visibly annoyed and replied brusquely: "Before that happens, I have to stop a real one from actually breaking out right now. Sorry, I'm behind in my reading."

To stop the cold war from heating up, he had to first speak with Bernhisel, then before Christmas, first with Van Dyke again and then with President Buchanan in person. He wished the train would go faster. Time was running out.

IN UTAH, CYNTHIA AND SOPHRONIA STOWELL were more worried about running out of food than a hypothetical civil war beaking out; their husband was already a casualty of the current one. They had mouths to feed, including two more on the way. Where was William, was he hungry, cold, worried about them? Why hadn't they heard from him?

Ever since the visit from Elder Hyde, the two women had made frequent stops at the tiny post office to see if any kind of letter or card had arrived from Camp Winfield where the troops were stationed. Not any so far. But, a newspaper clipping was forwarded to them that appeared weeks prior in the *New York Tribune*, thanks to Horace Greeley's correspondent who was imbedded with the Utah Expedition. Cynthia and Sophronia were not pleased with how William was described, but as they read between the lines, at least he was stirring up things. Sophronia read the clipping to the children:

"Stowell is a thick, heavy-set man, not more than five feet six inches in height, with a rough and obstinate, but not malignant countenance, short and shaggy black hair, and an illiterate expression. He was clothed warmly, and with tolerable neatness, Judge Eckels having personally inspected and provided for his physical cleanliness before the arrival of the Marshal at camp. He listened to the reading of the indictment with composure, and was evidently gratified, surprised to find his name in such noble company."

Sophronia didn't read out loud the whole letter — for one, because the children wouldn't understand, and two, because it would frighten them even more. How would she explain Judge Eckels' indictments for treason? William was the last person listed, and the only one in their custody, but he was in good company. The others indicted included the Church's First Presidency (Brigham Young, Heber C. Kimball, and Daniel H. Wells), John Taylor, George D. Grant, Lot Smith, Orrin Porter Rockwell, William A. Hickman, Albert Carrington, Joseph Taylor, Robert Burton, James Ferguson, Ephraim Hanks, and finally, the Army's prisoner, William Stowell. Joseph Taylor (who, of course, had been captured with William, but had escaped), and Heber C. Kimball (who had died a few months earlier).

Cynthia and Sophronia knew what "high treason" was, but there was no need to share that with the children old enough to understand. They did not need to understand that if found guilty, the defendant could be sentenced to death.

The two pregnant women with the help of the oldest boy, William Henry, who was now 15, were able to harvest the fall crops and prepare for winter. In a letter to a friend who had inquired how they were doing, Cynthia wrote that "we're living on our town lot in Ogden in a house with two rooms for our families. William Henry, our oldest orphan, was the best help we had for our outdoor work. Before the severe cold of winter set in he, with a yoke of steers and a wagon, hauled a large quantity of sage brush from the sand ridge for fuel as he was too young to battle with the difficulties of hauling wood from the canyons."

The boy, she said, *"was, as well, poorly clad and wore a pair of tattered men's shoes until a kind neighbor furnished him a better pair, for which we're grateful. Sophronia and myself worked together and spun yarn which we . . . wove into cloth to supply the pressing wants of the family."*

For the winter of 1857-1858, more than one child under the outstretched wings of Cynthia and Sophronia was shoeless, but thanks to friends and neighbors as well as their fall harvest, they were surviving, but without William. Visitors and interrogators came and went into his prison tent, but it wouldn't be until summer that his dream of leaving captivity would be realized. For him and his captors — as well as for the Stowell family in Ogden — it would be a long, cold winter.

PRESIDENT JAMES BUCHANAN, THAT OLD BACHELOR, America's "public functionary," was earning the reputation as a man who knew who how to throw a party. But, it wasn't a party that Thomas was anticipating; rather, a chance to leave the city with a letter president that would kick open doors for him if he traveled west. James C. Van Dyke, Buchanan's chief advisor and long-time supporter, had been softening the president up in anticipation of Kane's visit, and the president's aide appealed to Buchanan's vanity — before too long, Old Buck began to believe Kane's mission was all his idea.

Van Dyke was punctual. It was past normal working hours, it was nearly dinnertime and the best time to get the president's undivided attention. America's Princess, the bachelor president's niece, Harriet Lane, met him outside the Oval Office.

"How is he doing today?" Van Dyke asked.

"He's in good spirits. We reviewed the guest list for the Christmas Party, and I've been working on the seating arrangements, which can be complicated…must keep Northerners on one end of the table, Southerners on the other end and wishy-washy people in between them, which are now in short supply," Harriet Lane said with a laugh.

"So, is that where you're sitting — right in the 'can't-take-a-position section?'" She smiled and answered:

"No, silly! I'm right by his side to keep order…well, to keep the great man in order. You and the Mrs. will be down near the Senator from Kentucky, not exactly wishy-washy, but a timorous man."

"I have another name to add to the list," Van Dyke said.

"Who is it?"

"Thomas Kane. He's coming on the 23rd with John Bernhisel to meet with Buck about the Mormon problem." He suddenly had the First Lady's attention.

"Good. Looking forward to meeting Elisha's brother. Who's Bernhisel?"

Van Dyke lowered his voice; there were listening ears around the corner: "The Mormon, the delegate from Utah Territory."

"How many wives does he have?" She asked coyly.

"No idea. He lives solitary here in Washington…not many friends here. His family is back in Utah, I assume. He's a good man, though. Thoughtful. But, I'm not inviting him, just Kane."

"How about we seat Thomas Kane right next to Senator Bigler of Pennsylvania? Aren't they friends?"

"Most likely. Thank you for running things so smoothly here in the mansion."

"And, thank you for running the country…and keeping the peace," she said with a smile. She knew he liked her. After all, everybody did. Finally, Buchanan had finished his lamb stew. Van Dyke was now admitted into his presence.

THOMAS WAS PACKING FOR HIS TRIP TO WASHINGTON. Elizabeth was trying her best not to be a worrywart, but someone needed to show some confidence in him since his parents and his surviving brothers were being so critical about what they called "his suicide mission."

Patrick accused him of being indifferent to the health of their parents since their brother's death in February: "You trying to kill them, too?" He asked Thomas indignantly.

And, John Jr. said "you're disregarding the needs of your wife

and four children — you want to make Bess a widow and your three sons and daughter fatherless while she's caring for her sick father?" Both he and Bess we're trying to ignore their criticism. Like most wives, she knew men shouldn't do their own packing.

"You should take your tuxedo, Thomas," she said and then pulled it out of the closet and dusted it off. "Looks like it still fits, maybe even a bit loose. Buchanan's always holding some kind of festivity or banquet with his glamorous niece running things. You be careful around her," she teased him.

"She's too tall for me — I like petite women, like you Bess," he replied with a smile. He knew all about America's new "First Lady" from his late brother, Elisha. Before she was in the White House with her Uncle James, Harriett Lane had told Elisha she'd be there when he returned from the Arctic, but fate had other plans.

After Thomas finished packing, he spent the next two hours carefully preparing his "brief" for the president. Bess tucked the youngest children into bed and then reviewed his brief and made some suggestions:

"What's this comment about the 'knife and tomahawk?'"

Thomas hesitated: "It's something that I heard from Jeter Clinton."

"Who's that?"

Thomas backtracked a bit: "He's a Mormon leader here in Philadelphia. He told me that Brigham warned him that the government better make peace with the Latter-day Saints or face the 'knife and tomahawk' from the Indian tribes that President Young claims he keeps under control."

"Sounds like a threat that would raise Buchanan's dander — I see you crossed it out," she said.

"I wasn't planning on talking about it to Buchanan, but rather with Van Dyke," Thomas replied.

"If he's an ally, don't make him an enemy; anything you tell

him might reach the president's ears. Brigham is under great stress trying to wear two hats at once, governor and prophet. Didn't work out too well for Jeremiah, and they sawed the prophet Isaiah in half. As you said, once Cumming is governor, President Young would prefer to stick to religion and toss the politician's hat aside."

Then she added: "But the rest of it looks good, I think. One more thing, Thomas: Are you really not planning to ask the administration for any travel expenses?"

Thomas stood firm: "No, Bess, even if he offers it, I'll turn it down. Either I'm an arbitrator or an advocate, either for one side or for the other. I'm not in either President Buchanan's employ nor in President Young's. I'm trying to walk a fine line between the two."

She stood behind him and massaged his shoulders: "I understand. You're awfully tight, Thomas. Too much tension. You do know, don't you, that I'm with you on this tightrope act of yours. Please believe me: I'm convinced that your mission is divinely inspired, confident that you'll return safe and sound."

And, as she was leaving the room to let him rewrite his brief, she added: "And, when you're in Washington, get some warm clothing for your expedition. I think you'll need it."

THOMAS KANE HAD VISITED THE WHITE HOUSE earlier in the year, but it was a private conversation first with Van Dyke and then very briefly with the president. As of yet, he had never experienced the pomp and circumstance of an elaborate event that the president's social butterfly of a niece had organized like this one. Van Dyke stifled a laugh. When he saw Thomas enter the East Room, he greeted Thomas who admitted he felt self-conscious.

"My wife made me bring the tuxedo — I feel like the tiny man on the wedding cake!" They both laughed at that one, and then continued on with the political banter that was continuing all around them. Kane had arrived early, and many of the city's

movers and shakers were making liberal use of the White House's collection of wine and spirits. A string quartet was filling the room with some of the best pieces composed by dead Germans.

Kane wished Elizabeth had accompanied him, but alas, he was the last guest added to the list.

Thomas caught the eye of the "First Lady," Harriet Lane, the bachelor President Buchanan's niece. She was orphaned as a girl and Uncle James, or "Nunc" as she called him, adopted her. When Buchanan was the ambassador to Great Britain, she was the talk of the town — a position she now held in Washington D.C. Rumor has it that she was a favorite of Queen Victoria as well as her teenage son, Edward Albert, later King of Great Britain, Scotland and Ireland. Harriett took Van Dyke aside and asked him if Thomas was the little man in the tuxedo. She made a beeline to him.

"So, I'm sorry we never met. Elisha always talked about you and your brothers. Then fate stepped in ..." she looked away and wiped her eyes, and then confided to Thomas: "Your brother was one of my favorite people, the death of the heroic Elisha Kane was a national tragedy, and for me, a personal one. I wept when I heard about his demise. The whole country did," she said as she grabbed his arm, as she wrestled to compose herself, and then bravely changed the subject:

"I understand you are the Mormons' benefactor. Tell me: I hear they are allied with the Red Man, friends of our native peoples. How is that?"

She led Thomas over to the bar where she grabbed a glass of Chablis. Van Dyke watched them from across the room and buttonholed Senator William Bigler of Pennsylvania: "Does she know that Kane is married?"

Bigler smiled. "Maybe, but she doesn't care. She and his brother Elisha knew each other quite well, according to rumors, but that Judge Kane didn't approve. It's all moot now."

"Well, since you're sitting next to him at dinner, please see if you can find out anything — Kane is important for us to get Buchanan out of the pickle he's in." Bigler headed for the bar.

Harriet had cornered an uncomfortable Kane at a small table near a table arrayed with appetizers. Two large Southern senators were gorging themselves on crabs and crayfish nearby which increased Kane's level of discomfort.

"About your question regarding Mormons and Indians..." Thomas began.

"Yes," Harriet said. Thomas tried to get to the point, answer her question and then slip away; after all, he missed Bess, and he wasn't sure what this young woman had on her mind. Elisha had people talking about their relationship, but that was long before her Uncle James had been elected president.

Thomas answered her as if he were a missionary: "So, you want to know how is it that you and the Mormons, the Latter-day Saints, are both so interested in our native peoples. From what I understand, when the Mormons embarked on their initial missionary efforts, they took their newly printed Book of Mormon, a book they regard as scripture, to the Delaware people who had been relocated to western Missouri. Their Book of Mormon led the Saints to believe that American Indians are part of the Lost Tribes of Israel, and where they can, they evangelize them."

"And, what is it that you admire about these people, these Mormons?"

He smiled and simply said: "Their soft hearts and their hard hands. They're heroic, as I discovered when I first visited them in their camps ten years ago."

"That makes sense," she said. "Heroism runs in your family," Harriett Lane said quietly with some emotion. Thomas blushed.

Harriet took a sip of her wine: "You know we met once on the SS Great Britain on our way to England. I worried about him — watched his many exploits from afar."

"We all did — he was always so 'afar'— when was he ever at home?" Thomas interjected — he was looking to make his escape.

She continued her sentence: "… and I read his book about the Grinell Expedition, but what really caught my attention was when he saved the life of the general's son and refused to allow those Mexican prisoners to be executed."

Thomas was pained by her reminding him of his hero brother, then she asked gently:

"Is it hard to live in his shadow?"

Now he was agitated and wanted to break free from her clutches, but he knew he had an opportunity to further his "divine mission," as he saw it:

"No, Miss Lane: What is hard is to accept the fact that as Americans, we give lip service to freedom of speech, freedom of religion and all the other freedoms guaranteed us in the First Amendment, and yet we allow our bigotry to preclude others from exercising their freedoms. Your work with the Chippewas and other native peoples is a great example, and I hope our desire to fulfill our so-called Manifest Destiny doesn't deny others, whether they are Chippewas or Mormons, the right to live their lives unimpeded by armed men marching on them. Excuse me," he said, then used the occasion to grab an appetizer and escape her grasp.

She watched in amazement as he stood up and left.

Nobody ever did that!

19

LIVING UNDER ELISHA'S SHADOW

Unlike in the White House, appetizers were in short supply at Camp Scott where the soldiers and hangers-on of the Utah Expeditionary force were garrisoned, scrounging for food and trying not to freeze. It was December, Christmas was coming and not much to celebrate — rations were meager. But, appetite itself was doing very well — there was so much of it.

In fact, every night the soldiers were kept awake by the painful pleadings of mules in the throes of death from starvation and cold. Every morning the landscape would be littered from the carcasses of dead horses and mules. In the evening, the mess tent would offer on its menu a new stew available with stringy, tough meat. No one ever dared question the mess sergeant about where his new dish originated. It was better than nothing.

A note from Brigham Young had reached the tent of Colonel Albert Sydney Johnston offering a shipment of grain and other foodstuffs now that President Young believed that the Army wouldn't be marching until late spring. The colonel refused the offer.

What the colonel didn't know, but Brigham did, was that Thomas Kane was coming to the rescue. Perhaps Kane's brothers didn't believe Thomas could accomplish his gargantuan task, but Young hoped and prayed he would. And from hope springs faith, followed by certainty.

Thomas now shared that hope and believed he could indeed persuade President James Buchanan to believe as well. Before his meeting with Buchanan, the Old Public Functionary, Kane sat

down with Van Dyke. They were in a small anteroom in the White House. It was Saturday, December 26th, Boxing Day in the UK and Decision Day in Washington D.C., even if James Buchanan didn't know it yet.

Thomas looked through his leather binder as Van Dyke hung his jacket on a chair and took up pen, ink and writing tablet.

"Taking notes?" Thomas asked.

"No, just checking mine and making notes on my notes. I presume we have the same goal in mind: to get our clients out of the fix they're in," Van Dyke said with a sigh. Kane nodded in agreement then Van Dyke asked:

"Celebrate Christmas?"

"All by myself?," Thomas replied. "Well, I did attend a mass at the Episcopal Church in the morning — even though I am now officially a Presbyterian, thanks to my wife — then joined Mr. Bernhisel, and we shared a goose at a guest house in Georgetown. Oh, and I wrote my wife a letter and double checked my departure time with the steamer company."

"When do you leave?"

"If all goes well with the president next hour, I'm sailing out of New York at noon on January 5th on my way to Panama. Not sure how long that will take."

"All alone?"

"No, I have hired myself an aide, a companion to help ensure my safe arrival, actually a bodyguard, a former slave and now a friend, and I have taken his last name as mine. I am traveling as Dr. Osborne, a world famous botanist. I like botany — so it's not that far-fetched," Thomas quipped. Van Dyke seemed pleased.

"And," Thomas continued, "if from time to time you receive a cryptic message from a mysterious Dr. Osborne, it's no mystery — it's just me," Thomas said with a smile.

It was cold in the White House, and Van Dyke put his jacket back on. Thomas was still bundled up.

As Thomas closed his binder, he took a deep breath, and Van Dyke asked him: "Are you ready to see the president?"

"Any expectations?"

Van Dyke frowned then answered carefully: "He can be…how should I say…"

"Timorous?"

The president's advisor smiled: "Yes, careful, indecisive, but if he doesn't say 'No,' I would take that to mean 'All right, go ahead.' I think he has overall a positive attitude towards your proposal, but I think he has faith enough in your abilities to allow you, to well, 'dive into deep water in hopes you can swim.'"

Ten minutes later, Kane and Van Dyke took off their coats and sat across from the President James Buchanan who was leaning back in his chair behind the desk as if to say "persuade me." Thomas was ready to do just that. Van Dyke had his back — to a degree. But, Buchanan still seemed fearful, fearful that if Thomas failed, or worse died in the venture, that it would sully his already damaged reputation. But, Thomas, Bernhisel and Van Dyke already suspected, and history would record, that James Buchanan would be the stigmatized icon for failed presidents well into the future. The president, on the other hand, had no idea.

After Thomas described his proposed mission and his travel schedule to the president, Van Dyke and Kane waited as Buchanan percolated and then finally spoke:

"Mr. Kane, as you know, your father and I are well acquainted, and I am impressed with your courage to take on such a venture; the heroic nature of your family is well documented, **but I advise you to give all thought of an enterprise [could be perceived] as vain, rash, and foolhardy and promised no other result than the tragic loss of your life which might be added to the to the weight of the public indignation against the unfortunate Mormons."**

"Mr. President, these very same arguments about the risks I am taking I have heard from my own family, from my brothers —

the living ones — and I appreciate your advice to be cautious. As I have told Mr. Van Dyke, I seek no official endorsement from your administration, which I think would damage my ability to speak frankly with Governor Young. All I am asking is that you convey to Brigham Young in a letter which I will take with me that I come to him 'at my own expense and without official position,' and that if he has no objection to the installment of Mr. Cumming as the new territorial governor, that the Army would proceed beyond Salt Lake City to set up their new garrison. I would also like a letter directed to Colonel Johnston and his staff that covers the same points."

Kane and Van Dyke watched President Buchanan ruminate on that for more than a minute, and finally, he replied:

"Thomas, I would advise you to reconsider this risky endeavor, **but if you proceed, may Heaven protect you. The purity of your motives and the energy of your character are beyond all question.**"

"James, if you and I could consult on this proposal for a few minutes, I would appreciate it," Buchanan said to Van Dyke. "And, Thomas, I will have a written reply to you within a week. Godspeed and best wishes to the judge and your whole family."

Thomas thanked the president and Van Dyke, put on his coat, left the White House, and set out for Philadelphia. Did he just waste his time? Was he really like Don Quixote jousting at windmills as his father suggested, or would he actually pull off a miracle? He would proceed as planned regardless as to whatever Buchanan wrote in his letters. In any case, Kane had already determined to reserve his passage on the steamer SS. Moses Taylor departing on January 5th. Little did he know that one of his fellow passengers was William Tecumsah Sherman, a future Civil War general who would wreck havoc in Georgia in just a few years. Sherman was on his way to California to seek a command as an officer to lead a contingent of Californians anxious to fight the Mormons. Kane prayed he would receive the three letters from the president in time to board the steamer in New York. Some things do require divine intervention.

Divine intervention was a common topic of conversation in the very large Young household. The celebration of Christmas as practiced in Great Britain was rather novel in the early years of the 19th century in America. But, thanks to Mr. Dickens and the diffusion of innovation, Puritan traditions were on the wane in the United States and in Mormon Utah. Even with an Army at its doorstep just some 113 miles away, Salt Lake City was doing its best to be festive.

Brigham Young's city residence, Lion House, was filled with members of the Young family and some of its closest friends. After singing some favorite holiday melodies and trying an assortment of pies and other treats, Brigham reminded his family whose birthday they were celebrating.

"It would certainly be natural to wring our hands and be fearful given the threats leveled at us at this season, but let's never forget the 'good tidings of great joy' announced that first Christmas: Glory to God and on earth peace and good will to men."

Then, with his wives and children watching, Brigham sat in front as his brother John gave him a blessing, promising Brigham that "you shall never fall at the hand of an enemy...you shall escape...you shall not only have the power over the United States, but over the nations of the earth. Notwithstanding you enemies may hunt you like a Roe, yet you shall escape as a bird from the hands of the Fowler, and not a hair of your head shall fall..."

Following his blessing, Brigham Young shared his faith and hope with his family from his written text, noting that "this will please Sister Fanny, who is fond of 'text preaching...

We have come here to the mountains, and the Lord has done this, and he had it in his mind when this church was built to plant it in these mountains at a certain time. He knew his mind, and he took his own means and time to bring us here.

"Ten years ago this July when we were down upon that

temple block, and I think by Sister Whitney's house I stated that if we were left alone for ten years, we would not ask any odds of our enemies that we were left alone at that time."

"From the time that the signers of the Declaration of Independence put their names to the paper till this last summer, there has never been an Army or troops of men that have met with a perfect bluff, a perfect snag as has these troops now upon our borders, and never were they made to use up and overdo themselves, and hop up and bite their own noses off…"

Brigham continued to predict or prophesy that the Army's efforts would be in vain and that the time would come that [people would say that] *"there is a people in the mountains called Mormons and that they are in the fastness of the Rocky Mountains, and the United States can do nothing with them, and the time will soon be that their sound, and the pride of the people will be 'I am from Utah, and I am a Latter-day Saint…"*

Then he ended his remarks: *"W.W. Phelps called me the 'Lion of the Lord,' and I feel like a thousand lions. Only get the Spirit of the Lord upon you, have it like a fire within you: That is the way it is with me, whether I speak or not. The power of the priesthood is here.*

So, at least for a season, surrounded by their mighty fortress on Christmas 1857, they took heart. There were still miles to go before they slept, but a lion guarded the gates. How long could they hold out? The enemy was waiting.

"ON YOUR FEET," A VOICE RANG OUT at the opening of the prison tent that served as the tenement for William Stowell and other recalcitrants at odds with the officer corp of the Utah Expedition. From a distance, the assortment of Sibley tents in this corner of Camp Winfield appeared to be an Indian village since the Sibleys were conical enclosures designed to accommodate up to 12 inhabitants who slept inside arrayed like the spokes of a wheel with their feet to the center.

In addition to the hole at the top, ventilation was provided in good weather by raising the canvas up at the edges. In inclement weather, all openings would be covered, and the air inside would get quite stale, bad for men, but just fine for the lice that covered their bodies. Each man brushed off his fellow travelers as he got on his feet, leaving an assortment of tiny critters that looked like grains of rice marching in step.

For those like William who also was shackled in leg irons, standing up was not an easy task, but he was up on two legs faster than most. On this particular day, there were eight men in the "bad boys" tent. What was on their jailer's mind?

"Work detail. If you think it's cold now, just wait a few days now that your Christmas holiday is over, and we move into January. For those of you who are interested, it's a toasty 25° outside now, according to the officer in charge of weather, it was about 15° last night.

"He should be demoted," William muttered.

The sergeant laughed, which also drew muffled chuckles from his fellow tent mates: "Always the comedian, Stowell. We'll put you in front." The sergeant bent down and unlocked his leg irons, which was both a relief and puzzling for the prisoner.

The private behind William asked, "What's up, Sergeant?"

"Firewood, gentlemen. We're going to collect firewood."

"In what?" The question came from Welshman who kept trying to go AWOL.

"Follow me," the Sergeant said.

They walked outside and a small wagon was waiting for them. No, they weren't going to ride in it; they were going to pull it.

The man they called big Dutchman asked, "Why is it we have to be draft animals?"

"Ask William. Then, ask yourself, what is that meat we had yesterday in that soup? That was a draft animal, most likely an old stringy mule. They're dying by the cord, thanks to William's

Mormon friends for burning the grass and destroying the wagons."

Then, William Stowell muttered, "Ask Buchanan why you're all here in the first place."

He got a glare from the sergeant, but he and all the all the other non-coms serving with him had been asking the same question for months. Once in place in front of the wagon, each man found a handhold, a knot or a loop on the ropes and started marching with a wagon in their wake.

Another column of "volunteers" joined them, making two rows each with its own tow line with hand holds every six feet or so. At least it was dry, William thought, as they started on their march with their empty wagon following them. The sun was low in the southern sky, then he realized: It was New Year's Day.

"Happy New Year," he shouted and then added:

"It's a celebration we'll never forget!" Even though he was the only prisoner of "war," he made friends with deserters, slackers and other malcontents. Generally, Stowell was well liked, except for a few officers who wanted to get their revenge on the Mormons — or at least one Mormon: Stowell — for the miserable winter they were suffering through in Wyoming. One of them, the mess officer, watched as the wagon left the camp to go scrounging for fuel:

"Bosworth, I want a special serving of soup for our Mormon friend when he comes back from his duties…one that has been prescribed by the higher-ups."

"What special soup?" the cook asked. The mess officer handed him a scrap of paper:

"Here's the recipe."

For the next six hours, William Stowell and his motley assortment of the two-legged team that was collecting brush, twigs, branches and whatever else they could collect at the edges of the washes and ravines eventually filled up the wagon.

"Time to turn around and go home, boys. Worked up an appetite? Hope so. The idea was simple: Keep you moving so you didn't freeze to death and collect enough wood to keep a small fire going when you're not. You'll thank me for it," the sergeant said, and he meant it. Stowell knew that and appreciated the chance to see the light of day for a change. Later that evening, as the men lined up at the mess tent for supper, a cook pulled Stowell aside: "Hey Mor-mon boy, the commander wanted you to have this, and gave him a large bowl of what appeared to be stew."

William grabbed a hard tack roll, a spoon and walked over to a large log where a couple of other of his tent mates were settling down for supper.

The little Welchman spied Stowell's bowl and looked envious. Neither had yet taken a spoonful of their fare, and William hesitated.

"Wanna trade?"

William considered the offer and replied: "Sure."

Stowell suspected that his soup de jour was simply too good to be true and took him up on his offer. He remembered that he and Joseph Taylor had spent one night vomiting "a special meal" they had been given after they had first been captured. Late that night, the Welshman was retching and woke up everyone. His impression had been heaven-sent, he concluded. What worried William is that his wives and children were suffering even more. The best gift that Cynthia and Sophronia Stowell received for the holidays was a brief note from William.It was simple and to the point, and as they surmised, had been carefully vetted by Johnston's staff before the note was delivered.

He wrote *"I'm fine, kept in a tent, have enough to eat and am staying warm. Read my Bible every day, waiting for my dream to be fulfilled to return to you and the children. Love to you all."* **WS**

20

THOMAS KANE TO THE RESCUE

Riding the train had become a relaxing endeavor for Thomas Kane. It aso gave him time for reflection on his way back to Philadelphia, an uninterrupted opportunity to make sure he was completely prepared for his journey. He was to meet his traveling companion, a former servant and ex-slave Anthony Osborne, at Constitution Hall by three in the afternoon. They had to buy more supplies and fill a trunk with what they needed. Then, there were family matters to take care of which would be the most troubling for Thomas.

But, what gave him the most grief, the one thing he couldn't get out of his mind, was what the "First Lady" Harriet Lane had asked him the night before: Was it hard to live under Elisha's shadow? In the family, Thomas carried the curse of the "man with a thousand unfinished dreams, projects he started but never completed." Judge Kane and Thomas' brother Patrick had that very conversation the night before Thomas returned from Washington.

"Pat, would you please talk to your brother when he returns tomorrow," the judge had tried to talk some sense into Elisha, his oldest sone, and failed. "He hired Anthony…" John Kane said.

"Anthony?"

"You know, Anthony. He used to work in the office and sometimes here and at the country house, a former slave. Very bright fellow, reads and writes," Judge Kane said. "He stayed with Tom and Bess when they were harboring slaves and their family members when he was participating in the Underground Railroad, much to my chagrin."

Patrick was puzzled: "Yes, I remember. Hired him for what?"

"To help Thomas on his journey, to act as his bodyguard for one thing." Patrick and his family were dining with his parents on a Sunday evening. Mother Kane was serving dessert near a blazing fire. The judge liked to have the home toasty warm on such occasions. He threw a Yule log into the fireplace.

Patrick took off his vest. It was too hot for his liking, but he was in his parent's home.

"So, he's going, no matter what we say, regardless of the odds, even though he has two babies to care of? What's he thinking?" Patrick asked indignantly.

"Well, maybe it's my fault — accusing him of starting things and not every completing them. I said, 'why start something an endeavor this huge with all these imponderables, these obstacles that are so life-threatening?'" Patrick agreed with his father:

"Like Thomas trying to finish Elisha's Arctic quest?"

"Exactly." The judge took a poker and played in the fire. It was too hot even for him.

"He has Elisha's fever and is too competitive. I think I said out loud that 'it will pass down as another half-finished scheme, like when he gets the steam up on a favorite hobby, has worked too hard on it and then abandoned it.' I was talking to your mother, but I'm sure he overheard what I said."

Patrick scowled: "That's not helpful."

"I know. But, then last spring, I wrote Buchanan a letter asking him to speak with Thomas, just to kick the door open. Maybe I shouldn't have. It will be interesting to hear what Old Buck had to say. If you speak with Thomas tomorrow, let me know."

Patrick didn't reply. No sense throwing kerosene on the fire; it was already too hot in the house.

TO THE KANE FAMILY, THE WHOLE EPISODE seemed like a repeat performance of Elisha's ventures. His death in February made headlines all over the country. A navy medical officer and Arctic explorer, Elisha Kane participated in the First Grinnell Expedition to rescue or at least discover the the fate of British explorer Sir John Franklin. He even discovered a gravesite on Beechey Island believed to be from Franklin's lost expedition. He led the Second Grinnell expedition to the Arctic but wasn't able to solve the mystery of Franklin's disappearance. He and his party ventured further north than any other group had ever gone before, pointing the way to the North Pole for those who followed him.

Elizabeth had interrogated Thomas more than once about trying to retrace his brother's footsteps. "Don't tell me you're going to go searching for frozen bodies out West!"

He assured her that seeking fame and fortune wasn't his goal: "Making headlines is not what's driving me to stop this madness in Utah. I'm trying to save lives, not uncover corpses!" That seemed to satisfy her then. But now? He wasn't sure.

First, he had to hook up with his travel companion in Philadelphia. Lucky for him, given the weather, Independence Hall was open, and except for a security guard, was empty. He carried his bag inside, found a seat near a pot-belly stove, pulled his hat down over this eyes and cat-napped for a bit. He was expecting Anthony around three. His family's former servant didn't know what Thomas had in mind, but Thomas hoped he wouldn't mind seeing a little bit of the world on Kane's dime.

ABOUT AN HOUR LATER, THOMAS KANE WOKE UP. Anthony Osborne was reading a newspaper at the end of the bench where Thomas Kane had slumped over.

The big African smiled: "Didn't wanna wake you, sir. You was sleepin' like a baby. Been a long time since we seen one another — you growed yourself a nice beard — you looks older."

Thomas rubbed his eyes and stretched his legs: "I feel older, much older, my old friend. How long has it been?"

"I reckon five, six years since we first met, me and the other folks that came up from the plantations. I owes you a lot, Mr. Kane!"

"And I thank you for the kind service you showed our family, especially my parents, and I appreciate your willingness to listen to my proposal, but we can talk about the details later. First I need to get some traveling gear. There's a mercantile at the corner of Franklin and Jersey. Need some saddle bags, some cartridges and powder and wool blankets, cold-weather clothing, this and that," Thomas explained.

"We really goin' to California, Mr. Kane?"

"Yes, and it's a long way, and I need some help getting there. We can't go directly west, not this time of the year, so I was hoping to enlist you to keep me company. Ever been on a ship, Anthony? Ever sailed on the ocean?"

Anthony replied with excitement, "No, sir, can't say I have, but if you need me…"

"I do," Thomas replied. We're going into the mountains, and it gets cold there, but first we need to sail to a place called Panama. Then we travel across to the other side, catch another ship and sail north to California, and from there, we go east to Utah, then on to talk to my friend Brigham Young and then Colonel Johnston. We want to stop a war, help my friends and save the soldiers caught in the mountains. So if you want to go…"

"I do! I remember you talking about your friends in the mountains, the saintly people you helped when they was chased away. And, I been reading about them soldier boys, freezing up on the trail," Anthony said. "So, what's the plan?"

"Keep the Mormons and the soldiers safe. I spent yesterday with President Buchanan who some say was talked into sending the Army there," Thomas said with a worried look on his face.

"But, I'm not certain that he didn't know exactly what he was doing. There could be lots more trouble, more bloodshed."

Osborne could see how concerned Thomas was.

"So we're going to stop a war?"

Thomas nodded and Anthony smiled: "Good!"

"But, we have to be cautious…some people would rather that we don't. For some folks, war is good business. No one should know who we are or why we're going on this journey," Thomas said.

Thomas stood up and grabbed his bag. Anthony folded up his newspaper and put it in his satchel.

"You've been reading my articles, haven't you, Anthony?"

He nodded with pride; after all, it was Thomas' mother who encouraged him to learn his letters. He could read well enough; writing was harder.

"Yes sir, I read about that wicked judge you wrote about," Anthony said.

"Wicked is right," Thomas said. Then, they walked out on the street together. It was windy and cold. As they walked down the street to catch a ride, Thomas admitted to his efforts to tell the Mormons' side of the story as their anonymous publicist:

"Yes, I try to expose lies told about my friends. Wrote some stories here and there. Got them scattered in all kinds of newspapers. It's good to know that the word's getting out, but it's not enough."

A milk wagon sped by, splashing slush all over. Thomas and Anthony had to jump out of the way.

Thomas continued as they dodged piles of snow on the sidewalk. "That's why we're making this journey, to stop a senseless war between Americans before it breaks out all over. I'm afraid the Mormon's prophet, Joseph Smith, was right: I'm certain there will be a war between the North and South before your people are all out of chains. Before that happens, let's see if we can help folks reason together. Before we go, I need to spend a few days with my family, my wife and daughter and new son: They were both born after you left."

"You mean when I was hiding in your root cellar, a couple of years back," Anthony said with a laugh. "Sorry I ate your carrots."

"I don't care. I don't even like carrots."

They arrived at a small Episcopalian chapel. Thomas looked around.

"Let's step inside," he said. They slipped into a small alcove where books and literature were displayed. An old woman at the counter looked up and smiled and returned to her reading. They found a bench and sat down. Thomas unbuttoned his coat, leaned forward and removed a leather case and looked Anthony right in the eye: "Anthony, do you trust me?"

"Yes sir, I do."

Thomas was now whispering: "Good, because I trust you. I need you to do something for me, for the cause. I am entrusting you with a great deal of money." Thomas undid the strap, opened it and pulled out a note. Along side the note was a considerable sum. Thomas explained:

"Here is the address of the dock and steamer schedule to Panama; it leaves next Tuesday, January 5th. from New York on the Steamer Moses Taylor. The note shows the amount for a stateroom on the steamer which will accommodate both of us. You are to book and pay for the passage. I will join you there. It sails at three in the afternoon. I will be there by noon."

Anthony Osborne sat there speechless.

"Is everything all right, Anthony?"

"How do you know that I won't just take this money and leave?"

Thomas smiled: "It didn't occur to me that you would do such a thing. That's what trust means."

With tears in his eyes, Anthony shook Thomas' hand: "Don't you worry about nothin,' Mr. Kane. I will see you next Tuesday at noon, as God is my witness."

Anthony put his hand on Thomas' shoulder and as he turned to leave, Thomas stopped him.

"I have plenty of other things to worry about, Anthony, but not you," Thomas said as his traveling companion walked away.

Kane sat in the small prayer chapel for another ten minutes, to pray and just to get warm. Yes, Thomas Kane was worried. He was really worried about what his parents and his brothers would say, and how his young family would fare in his absence.

He was worried that all the time and money he had spent on behalf of the Allegheny Railroad to acquire land for new lines would be wasted, as Elizabeth had reminded him. And he and many other people were worried about what would happen if his mission to the West failed, worried that it would be yet another great endeavor Thomas started, but never finished. He had to finish this!

Minutes later, Anthony was out of sight, and the hansom arrived. First, he had some shopping to do, kit to buy for his trip. Then he had the most difficult task of all to check off his list, first to say goodbye to his parents and then to his loyal, faithful wife, his three-year-old daughter Harriet and little Elisha, his one-year-old.

When would he see them again? He had no idea.

THE STEAMER S.S. MOSES TAYLOR had made several trips back and forth from Panama to New York, so this journey was nothing novel for Captain Harris and his crew. But for Anthony Osborne, travel companion to the secretive, Dr. Osborne, "a world-famous botanist," the voyage was an adventure. Dr. Osborne was, of course, not the real name of the small, dark man with the bushy beard. It was none other than Thomas Leiper Kane, traveling "incognito." It was a new word for Anthony, and a source of amusement for both men.

"Yes, you may call me "Incognito" Osborne if you wish, Anthony," Thomas said with a laugh. They were up on the top deck enjoying much warmer weather than New York, basking in the sun off the east coast of Florida, not quite halfway to Panama.

"So, does 'incognito' mean 'nobody knows?'" Anthony asked.

"Actually, it's Latin meaning 'nobody knows who you are,'" Thomas explained.

Anthony was puzzled: "Why hide who you are?"

"It's because some people don't want us to succeed; for some, war makes them money, and maybe there are people, especially from the South, who want an advantage in their efforts to secede from the nation."

"How so?" Anthony asked.

"Because they would prefer that Americans would fight with each other over the Mormon problem rather than the real one."

"Slavery?"

"Exactly," Thomas confirmed.

"Then, this is my fight, too…to help you help the Mormons," Anthony replied proudly. Thomas nodded in appreciation.

Far off to the west, they could see the thin line of Florida, just feet above sea level, growing larger as the ship turned in that direction.

The waves were picking up now, and Anthony could see Thomas turn a bit green. He grabbed the railing.

"I'm going down to the stateroom. I thought I had been cured of this sailing disease when I returned from France; I guess not — I better stay close to a privy."

"Yes sir, I'll keep watch. Should I retrieve you when we make land? I like it up here," Anthony asked.

"No, if I can, I'll study my book on botany in case someone asks me a question since I'm purporting to be an expert on the subject."

"Purporting?"

"Either pretending or lying — your choice," Thomas said with a grimace and carefully descended the stairs. He wished he had skipped breakfast; he feared it would soon skip him, and he didn't want poor Anthony to witness that.

THOMAS AND ANTHONY HAD BEEN AT SEA for well over a week when Patrick Kane stopped by to check on his parents. Both he and Thomas, along with the rest of the family, were worried about their father; his health had been failing. Even though he wasn't even 63 yet, in 1858 that was considered "old."

Thomas had expressed his concerns about their father before he left, but Patrick's response was acerbic: "But, not enough to give up your foolish notions about the Mormons."

John and Patrick Kane were sitting at the fireplace, the judge's favorite spot this time of the year.

"Heard anything yet?" Patrick looked oddly at his father.

"Unless he took a homing pigeon with him, then 'No,'" Patrick said, annoyed at the question, but even more annoyed at his Quixotic brother.

"But, he said he'd drop us a note when they landed at St. Augustine — the steamer was supposed to stop there," the judge replied.

"What did you tell him before he left?" Patrick asked his father as he helped himself to his father's liquor cabinet.

"That this whole mess was the Mormon's fault, and if they made war on the Army, the nation would make war on them... that the sentiment of the country will never be sated as long as their community survives on this continent."

"You know, Father, those people were pushed to extreme measures after being driven from place to place; I see Thomas' point of view to some degree.

"And, both he and I are together on our opposition to the Fugitive Slave Act — your jailing him for contempt of court on that issue just hardened his position."

The judge sat up in his seat: "I don't make the law — I just enforce it." Patrick topped off his brandy glass which the judge didn't ignore.

"Go ahead, help yourself, and no, I don't want anything, thank you," John Kane said with a tinge of sarcasm.

"We understand your position, Father, but I also believe that Buchanan is secretly a 'Doughface;' he sympathizes with Southern Democrats…doesn't want to rock the boat."

"Patrick, the boat is already rocking wildly, the Union is unsteady right now, but no, I don't think sending troops after the Mormons was a good idea, but they seem to have taken the bait after that awful massacre," the judge said and then stood up himself to see what refreshments his cabinet might offer to quench his thirst.

"Father, I read the letter John Junior sent you, and I tend to agree with him. There's really not too much any of us could have done "to keep him down on the farm,' not even Bess, and she tried her best," Patrick concluded

"And what was that?"

"… 'that Thomas is never so well as when exposed to what would kill most men of his build, and that hard life in open air agrees with him better than the most tranquil of sedentary existence…he is too great a man to occupy himself with trifles."

The judge agreed and finished the sentence: "Yes, and I second what Junior said, that "his inability to organize an Arctic expedition to finish Elisha's venture was killing him by inches."

Patrick added… "and his big soul was preying on his small body."

Somewhere in the Caribbean, Thomas was experiencing what his father and his brother were saying about him behind his back: He had to get off this damned ship!

CAPTIVITY COMES IN MANY FORMS — IN MANY PLACES: For Thomas Kane (aka "Dr. Osborne") and Anthony Osborne, his man servant (but especially for Thomas), it was a ship at sea. Too far to swim to shore, but still confining. For William Stowell, it was his foul-smelling Sibley tent pegged down in a frozen wilderness.

But, for Carl Heinz Wilcken, it was a campfire not far from Henefer surrounded by Nauvoo legionnaires. And, as far as being a captive, it couldn't get any better than this!

His captor, Jonathan Layne, has just given him a plate of fry bread, or scones in modern parlance, smothered in elk gravy. He smacked his lips.

"*Mensch, das schmeckt! Sehr lecker!*" (That's tasty!), he said.

Before Layne took Wilcken into custody, Carl's English wasn't very good, but the German was learning fast. Jonathan was teaching him, and he was helping him improve his English, but as far as gleaning any military intelligence, Wilcken was still a blank slate. Layne did understand, however, that Carl enjoyed his supper — he hadn't much decent food since Lot Smith burned much of the Army's supplies.

But, interrogation help was on the way. It arrived a couple of hours later, courtesy of Major Joseph Taylor, back in the "intelligence saddle" after his successful escape from the tent that William Stowell still occupied. It was the big woodsman Taylor had brought with him, Christian Holz. The minute the Carl and Holz saw each other, the lights went on (but only if you spoke German).

"*Ich kenne Sie schon,*" Christian exclaimed. "*Wo kommen Sie her?*" (I know you! Where are you from?) They exchanged smiles and handshakes. Then, it was old home week. They had met at artillery school years earlier near Wilhelmshaven in Niedersachsen which would later occupy northwest Germany.

"So, you were captured," Christian concluded.

"Yes, thanks to my new friend Jonathan Layne! My captors need to know that I am happily changing sides. I am here with you today because I actually boarded the wrong ship when I left Europe. I was on my way to South America," Carl explained with a laugh. Soon, Christian was laughing, too.

Their American onlookers were utterly confused. "My friends and I were 'bamboozled' into joining this expedition, but maybe there's a silver lining now that I'm on the right side of this conflict."

Major Taylor was anxious to know what Carl "just confessed to" and Christian translated it and then added, "he's one of us now!"

Taylor then asked, "Ask him about the conditions in their camp, how they are coping with everything, what about Colonel Johnston." The Americans could see from Wilcken's expressions and demeanor how things were up in Wyoming.

"We were on half rations, eating dead mules that froze to death every night, but Colonel Johnston is finally bringing some military discipline to bear with the troops. But, they are a sorry lot, the dregs of humanity, and except for my comrades, ill trained and poorly equipped.

"Most are very bitter and are angry about their situation. Many curse the Mormons and want to burn the city, but anyone with half a brain recognizes that neither the officers nor the enlisted men had any idea why they were there and what they are supposed to do. The whole situation was crazy, pointless."

Christian translated everything for Major Taylor then confided in him: "He is with us, without a doubt. If you need someone to share with him our faith, I'll be happy to help."

Taylor thanked Christian, then remembered a message he was supposed to give him: "Do you know a Caleb…can't remember his last name?"

"Yes, Caleb Rasmussen, my lady friend's brother."

"He was wounded in southern Utah during the skirmish with the Arkansans; he's home recuperating, but he's in a bad way," Taylor said.

"Will he make it?"

"Physically, probably. It was a terrible situation. When you're back in the city, you should see him. He needs a friend. The young man who was with him disappeared."

"Hans?"

"Don't know his name, but Caleb's been asking for you."

Christian looked away, said a silent prayer and muttered:

"I told him so — why didn't he listen?"

WHEN CHRISTIAN WAS ASKED TO ACCOMPANY Jonathan Layne and Carl Wilcken down into the valley, he jumped at the opportunity. Wouldn't it be great to sleep in a bed for a change? And wouldn't it be nice to have a meal and a normal conversation with someone, especially if that person were Winnie Rasmussen? As the three men were exiting Weber Canyon into Ogden valley, Christian was deep in thought when Carl smiled:

"Pleasant thoughts?"

The comment jarred Christian: "Are you a mind reader?"

"No, but I saw how willing you were to take me, 'your prisoner,' and then return to Salt Lake," Carl said, still smiling. "What's her name?"

"Winifred, Winnie. Winnie Rasmussen. And, you don't look like a prisoner; your hands aren't tied — you've made no attempt to escape," Christian said.

Layne gave them an odd look.

"*Auf Englisch,*" (Speak in English) Christian reminded Carl. Then in English, he said, so Layne could hear him: "Brother Layne wants to make sure two Germans aren't talking about him."

"What would I say except 'thank you for making me your prisoner'?" Carl said, then turned to Christian:

So, Christian, why else are you going into the city?"

The three men on horseback were just outside of Ogden, and it was getting dark and the footing, even for well-shod horses, was slippery. Jonathan Layne interrupted the conversation: "Boys, we better find somewhere to stay tonight."

Just as it was almost pitch black, Layne spotted a small inn, and they headed towards it.

Christian turned to Carl: "You're right — I did need an excuse to return to civilization: Her name is Winnie, but now I'm worried about her family," Christian explained.

Layne was puzzled: "Why? Would they object?"

"Her brother wants to see me — he was somehow involved in the Mountain Meadows affair. I warned him and his friend not to follow the Arkansas emigrants south, had a bad feeling about it. I understand the Saints are divided about the whole matter, don't want to take sides."

Layne spoke up: "That's because the people who were there aren't telling what really happened. They're covering it up."

Christian and Carl stopped.

Christian hesitated and then asked Layne: "What happened?"

Even though it was just the three of them all alone on a dark country road, Layne spoke softly: "Because it wasn't just people getting killed in battle, it was murder, pure and simple. Apparently, the leaders mislead the emigrants by raising a white flag, and then when they surrendered their weapons, they were killed, men, women and even children. Only the smallest ones were spared.."

They rode in silence to the inn,.

It gave Christian time to think, ponder and pray. Now he wished he'd just stayed up in the canyon. It was so simple: he knew why he was there, whom he was protecting and who the enemy was. Then, he remembered a scripture, one of the first ones he memorized after he joined the Mormons and came west. He repeated it quietly to himself: *For the natural man is an enemy to God, and has been from the fall of Adam, and will be, forever and ever, unless he yields to the enticings of the Holy Spirit, and putteth off the natural man and becometh a saint through the atonement of Christ the Lord...*

"You say something?" Jonathan Layne asked.

"Reciting a scripture…trying to figure out what I'm going to say to my young friend Caleb," Christian responded. "But, I don't know if I can say anything that will help." They had arrived at the inn. Finally, a warm bed to settle into! But, Christian Holz would lie awake nearly the entire night.

What was he going to say to Caleb?

21

PERILOUS BEYOND COMPREHENSION

Panama would have been more of an adventure for Thomas Kane if he hadn't been so distressed about what lay ahead. For Anthony Osborne, though, it made him nostalgic for a place that he'd never been: Africa. After their steamer made landfall, Thomas, now traveling as "the world-renowned botanist, Dr. Osborne," and Anthony, the real Mr. Osborne, caught the train to travel to other side of the isthmus where another steamer would carry them north to San Francisco. The open-air train cars allowed the passengers to get a first-hand look at the tropical scenery all around them.

"Thomas, do you think Africa looks like this?" Thomas smiled at his traveling companion as they clattered through the Central American jungle watching monkeys and parrots in their natural habitat.

"That is a very good question. I suppose so," Thomas replied. "I've never been there, but I would like to some day, I guess I'm just a romantic."

The big African leaned in closer to hear what his friend had to say. He struggled to hear Thomas due to a cacophony of background noise, a steam engine, the clattering on rails, screeches of monkeys on either side of the train, human conversations and babies crying all around them, but Anthony wanted to know: "What does that mean, a romantic?"

Thomas looked at the former slave, different from him in all ways — in size, color, opportunity and education — and searched for an answer:

"Anthony, things are not always as they seem. The way things are is far different from the way things should be. And, that bothers me. I have come to religious faith somewhat late, but awhile back my wife read me a Bible verse from Matthew, I think, where Jesus said to his disciples that God doesn't judge us by our outward appearance, but rather on what is in our hearts. Maybe that's what a romantic is."

Anthony smiled and put his big hand on Thomas' shoulder: "Thank you, Thomas. I think I am a romantic, too."

Thomas Kane wondered if he was deceiving himself — and Anthony along with everyone else. *Was he just a dreamer? Is a romantic someone who is simply out of touch with reality, like Señor Quixote?* In a few minutes, they would come to the end of the line. The Pacific Ocean waited. There would be another steamer to board. Reality was just ahead, and he had to face it.

THE REALITY OF WINTER IN WYOMING living on half rations with dozens of mules and horses dying every night was ghastly. And if that wasn't bad enough, Col. Albert Sydney Johnston had to deal with some 3,000 enlisted men, officers and bullwhackers trying to stay warm in a frigid winter living in tents. For the past several weeks, he and Captain Randolph Marcy, commander of the 5th Infantry assigned to Johnston's Army, had hatched a scheme to take matters into their own hands, but it was a high-risk venture. They were studying a map spread over the colonel's makeshift desk in candlelight — it was too cold to open a tent flap. A small cast iron stove at least made the interior bearable.

"The big question for which we have no answer is how deep is the snow," the colonel said. "And, I am reluctant to order you or any other men to risk this venture; we are looking for volunteers, and that includes you. You realize, do you not, Captain, that great disaster might befall your command?" Johnston stood back and waited for Marcy's response.

The circumstances in which this band of brothers found themselves had no good point of departure; doing nothing wasn't an option. Doing something was perilous beyond comprehension.

Marcy laughed: "You want me to volunteer, don't you, Colonel?"

"That's preferable to me ordering you, Randolph."

"But, if we were facing a horde of Indians or a Mormon cavalry attack, you would give the order without hesitation, and I would obey," Marcy replied. "What are you afraid of?"

Now Johnston laughed: "Marcy, I am frightened to death to explain to your family that I sent you into the mountains never to return, to be buried under an avalanche of snow when we're not really facing an enemy that's shooting at us."

"Colonel…Albert, sir, I look at this as an exploratory expedition, a chance to conquer the wilderness. I may even write a book about it. So I volunteer. My challenge is to sell this to several dozen other fools to conquer the wilderness with me."

Johnston put his hand on his "brother's" shoulder: "Then, get to it, Captain, before the snow gets any deeper. Take the map, get your volunteers and pack up. When will you depart?

"Next week, Tuesday most likely. If Dickerson believes we cannot pursue our mission without more pack animals, and the shortest route to acquire 2,000 Spanish mules and sheep, as well as salt, is Taos, New Mexico territory. So, we better get started. I'll tell the boys we're going mule hunting. Sounds like fun!. He saluted and left.

Captain Randolph B. Marcy was about to make history — he just didn't know it yet.

HISTORY IS LIKE A STRANGER YOU MEET on life's journey without realizing that someday he will either become a dear friend or a deadly enemy. Little did they know at the time — Thomas Kane and Anthony Osborne were making history, but it wasn't often

pleasant. Sometime after Thomas and Anthony boarded their steamer bound for San Francisco, the wild Pacific made war on them. The waves were many times larger and more ferocious than anything they had encountered on either the Atlantic Ocean or the Caribbean Sea.

Anthony soon became Kane's nursemaid and lifesaver. Thomas could barely stand, and when he did, it was to run to the privy, seasickness doing its deadly business on him. After three days, Thomas called for his loyal aide but could barely be heard. He was in the lower bunk with a bed pan close by, and Anthony tread carefully.

"What is it, Thomas?"

Anthony Osborne could see that Thomas was terrified.

He was mumbling: "I can't see, I can't see!"

Anthony leaned over him to hear better: "You're blind? How can that be?" Thomas was able to sit up momentarily and held his hands out in front of him and tried to focus on them. He turned to Anthony:

"I can't see out of my left eye! Look closely, Anthony, is there anything in it?"

"No sir, they look the same," Anthony said. Thomas pulled himself up and tried to stand, but was wobbly. "I need to get dressed and go up to the galley…"

"Should you eat?"

"No, I need my Bible, my ink and paper. Can you help me, please?"

"Of course, Thomas," Anthony said as he retrieved the items.

"Please remember, don't call me Thomas," he said weakly.

"Mr. Kane, sorry," Anthony apologized.

Thomas managed a smile and whispered, "I'm the world-renowned botanist, Dr. Osborne, remember?"

It revived Thomas ever so slightly who turned to his servant and friend: "You are a godsend, Anthony — how will I ever repay your kindness?"

"You already have — let's go to the galley," Anthony said, and together they staggered upstairs.

A half an hour later the vessel had found calmer waters, and Thomas was looking up verses in the Bible and then scribbling what looked like nonsense. Anthony was puzzled.

Kane smiled and whispered: "It's a secret code, Anthony. The letter's to my wife and father; the Bible is the code book. I write a scripture and hidden in the passage is the message; they have a cipher code. It takes longer, but in case someone else reads the letter, they won't understand, but my family will."

Anthony was intrigued: "So, what's in this message?"

Thomas looked resigned: "Well, there's nothing in here about Jesus healing the blind because I don't want to worry anyone, but in essence, since this journey will take so long to reach first the Mormons and the Army, I just wrote that "I shall probably be too late to make peace, but not too late to stop the spring massacre."

Anthony put his hand on Kane's shoulder who was cleaning his pen, replacing the lid on the bottle and blowing on the paper so the ink would dry. Then, Anthony leaned forward and simply said: "Oh ye of little faith."

"What?" Thomas asked, puzzled,

"We did not come this far to fail. Believe in yourself, Thomas. I believe in you." Thomas put his hand on Anthony's shoulder and smiled. He sealed up the letter. Kane would mail it the next day when they made landfall in Acapulco, Mexico.

EVEN THOUGH HE HAD NEVER YET FOOT IN THE VALLEY nor seen Salt Lake City or its inhabitants, newly appointed Governor Alfred Cumming was taking his assignment seriously. He wasn't about to take orders from Colonel Albert Sydney Johnston. It didn't help matters that Cumming, along with Judge Eckels and other civilian authorities under orders from President Buchanan, were also trying to survive in less than ideal conditions. Everyone was on edge. The new governor was waiting on the great man.

Johnston poked his head outside his command tent:

"Governor, can I help you?"

"Yes, you may. I want to have a word with your prisoner, the Mormon called Stowell," Cumming said.

"That won't be possible, not at this hour," Johnston said, turning away.

Cumming pulled out his pocket watch, and by the dim firelight, could tell time: "It's just 7:30, Colonel. What's the problem?"

"We have to get him ready," he said and turned away.

"You know, I don't report to you — I report to the president, and you report to General Scott. I should send him a letter," Cumming stated.

Johnston pressed him: "And how long would that take, to and from this God-forsaken place, to get an answer, do you think?"

Cumming was now agitated — Johnston was always agitated.

Cumming asked "is there a reason why 'you have to get him ready?' In what miserable circumstances do you keep him?"

"The same miserable circumstances in which we all find ourselves, thanks to his people, those damnable Mormons!"

"They didn't invite us here, and from what I've learned, they actually left the borders of the United States in 1846, and according to your Col. St. George Cooke, they helped you and this country fight the Mexicans, and this is the thanks we give them. Stowell, as I understand it, was following the orders of the current governor of this territory who had said no outside force was to enter without his permission. We are at loggerheads with these people, these fellow Americans — I just want to talk to them. starting with Stowell."

"Fine! I'll have my adjutant come fetch you when Stowell's ready, tomorrow morning; let's say 10:00 o'clock?"

"Ten it is. Good night, Colonel." If Johnston could have slammed the door of his tent, he would have. Canvas doesn't slam.

IT WAS ALSO NIGHT WHEN THOMAS KANE (aka "the world famous botanist Dr. Osborne") and the real Anthony Osborne arrived in San Francisco Bay and disembarked from their Panamanian steamer.

They were standing on the wharf, staring at their baggage, immersed in San Francisco fog and trying to find a street sign. But at least Thomas was finally steady on his feet. Anthony paused and then asked, "Now what, Mr. Kane?"

Thomas looked at the sundry articles and travel gear he had amassed before they left lying at his feet and scratched his head: "I'm not sure…"

Anthony picked up as much of the baggage as he could carry, leaving a duffel for Thomas. "Sir, we needs to get you quarters so you can plan your journey. You is no condition to go off half-cocked tonight."

Thomas protested: "I have to find some Mormons to help me in my journey first…"

Anthony was persistent. "Follow me, Mr. Kane." And he started walking.

They were on The Embarcadero, turned right on Powell, almost crawling to determine exactly where they were in the dimly narrow streets until finally, three blocks later, they found a pension at Grant and Pfeiffer.

After Anthony thought he had tucked his boss in for the night, Thomas was not finished. They said their farewell outside the sorry little shelter where Thomas had left his gear.

"Thank you, Anthony, for getting me safely here, and for your friendship," Thomas said wearily. "I have to find my Mormon

friends tonight — they are expecting me. So, I guess it's good-bye," he added as he picked up his large duffel.

"Thank you, Thomas, but I must say, you is a stubborn man. I don't want to hear that you died in the desert or in a snowstorm," Anthony said and then with unconcealed emotion, he added: "You be a fine man, Thomas, a good Christian man, but don't you go do nothin' crazy!"

Thomas laughed out loud: "Anthony, this whole affair is crazy! My father, my mother and my brothers think I'm crazy and say so to my face! My wife doesn't say it, but she can't hide it. She's likely praying for me right now because I'm crazy. But, sometimes, my dear friend, insanity has its own reward. Crazy got me here, and I pray crazy will get me to Utah. Take this sum; I hope it will help you get started here, a place where as a free man you can make a life for yourself," Thomas said as he took Anthony's hand and gave him a purse full of coins.

With tears in his eyes, the big African walked into the night, glancing one final time over his shoulder at the small man standing at the doorway of a run-down inn.

CHRISTIAN WAITED OUTSIDE THE LITTLE FRAME HOUSE where Winnie and Caleb lived with their mother, a couple of miles north-east of the city center. Finally, he knocked on the door. Mrs. Rasmussen was surprised to see him.

"Brother Holz, it's good to see you, but I'm sorry Winifred is not here. She is working at a small shop…"

"I am actually here to speak with Caleb. Is he here," Christian asked.

She hesitated: "Let me check and see if he's available," she said, leaving him standing at the door. After a few minutes, Christian sat on the stairs determined to leave soon if Caleb did not appear. It was a chilly day, but at least wasn't raining or snowing. Across the street from the small home was the city cemetery, now with small trees — the oldest not more than 10 years old. Christian watched as an older woman and a small child hovered over a headstone. The child, a little girl, had what looked like a single rose in her hand. This time of the year there would only be a few frozen stragglers still on the stem. The girl dropped the flower and then both of them knelt down. The woman held the child close to her bosom, and from his distance, it appeared as if they were sobbing, overtaken by grief. He watched for five minutes at least until he was interrupted by a voice behind him:

"Hello, Christian. I was sleeping." He turned and saw Caleb standing with the support of a crutch. "Come in if you wish."

Caleb looked gaunt, pale and distant. His appearance was haunting, Christian thought. He joined Caleb inside the tiny home. They sat on two mismatched wooden chairs near a small freshly painted table. The interior was Spartan, but clean.

"How can I help you?"

Christian was taken aback by the question and replied: "I was told you wanted to see me."

"Who told you that?"

"Someone up in Echo Canyon who relayed a message about your circumstances, that I should check up on you, so here I am," Christian said. "What happened?"

"I was injured…wounded. The nurse said I'm getting better. I hope so. I need to leave this place," Caleb said matter-of-factly. "California maybe."

Christian studied his young friend, but said nothing.

"Hans left for California, at least that's what he told me…"

Christian leaned forward: "When?"

"After the trouble. He was so enthusiastic about 'teaching those people a lesson' … but when we were told to kill those people, he ran and I followed him. A lot of the younger people did. It was a shameful act," Caleb trembled and looked away.

"What was…killing or running?"

"Both!"

Christian watched him for a moment, and then handed Caleb his handkerchief. "How were you wounded?"

"No idea…bullets were flying around, but Hans wrapped up my leg, helped me on a horse and we made it back to Cedar City; I found a wagon train going north, but he took the horse and his supplies and said he was going south. There were some wagons on their way to St. George, and he joined them. What should I do, Christian?"

Christian studied the boy's face for a moment. He didn't answer right away — he didn't   want to just spit out some pat advice, he wanted Caleb to feel some portion of the Holy Spirit. Caleb needed that more than anything at the moment.

"Get better. That's the first place to start. Then learn from your experience through study and prayer. One verse in Moroni reminds us to *'give thanks unto God that he hath made manifest unto you our imperfections, that ye may learn to be more wise than we have been.'*"

Caleb sat up in his chair: "That sounds like good advice."

Then Christian added: "Isn't that the whole story of the Old Testament, too? The prophet Jeremiah warned the Jews, they gave him no heed and were carried into Babylon. The choice is the easy way or the hard way. The easy way, the plan of happiness simply says 'follow God's commandments. It reminds me of another of my favorite scriptures: *'Wickedness never was happiness.'*" Caleb nodded in agreement. It was time to leave, and as Christian stood, Caleb hobbled over and shook his hand:

"Ask your people if they need help — I'll be back on my feet soon. You're right: Wickedness never was happiness."

"It looks like you're already back on your feet. Tell Winnie I'll be back."

22

JUST FOLLOWING ORDERS

After searching for two hours in the dead of night, Thomas Kane discovered that Mormons were now a rare commodity in San Francisco. Ever since Brigham Young had called the Saints back to "Deseret" — after his declaration of martial law — most of the faithful members had already fled to Utah, however he did find a Mormon "backslider"— or a "Jack Mormon"—at the address that he had been given, one Bill Gaylord, who was willing to freely share his advice with Thomas. Their chance meeting was at a saloon at the far end of the Embarcadero:

"So, Dr. Osborne," Gaylord asked Thomas, "how did you find me?"

"An old woman I met at the address where Mormons had lived said you could be found here, and so here I am," Thomas explained.

"That is quite a coincidence, since I have been hiding from the Mormons as best I can — it seems they feel that I still need saving."

"Mr. Gaylord, don't we all need saving, even botanists like myself," Thomas replied.

Gaylord gave Thomas a slight nod and asked: "So tell me. Dr. Osborne, why would old Brigham seek the advice of a botanist, and what is a botanist anyway?"

Thomas was now knee deep in his own prevarication, his manufactured false identity, didn't want to drown in his own fabrications and felt rather silly, so he improvised by asking a question:

"Since a botanist studies plants and determines their value for human consumption, tell me, Mr. Gaylord, aren't there plants unique to Utah that are deserving of study, plants of some scientific value?" Thomas thought that would stump him for awhile, but he got an immediate answer:

"I can think of one, a flowering onion, a bulb, that the pioneers ate when they first arrived, what was it called...? The Indians introduced it to them..." Gaylord was deep in thought.

Thomas wanted to get out of this conversation, but he still needed some travel advice.

Suddenly, Thomas could see a light go on inside the man, no flash of brilliance, but at least he remembered the plant's name:

"Ah ha! Sego, yes, that's it! A sego lily. Kind of tastes like garlic or onion, and they put it in soup," Gaylord said and then hesitated: "But, I don't think it would merit a sojourn to Utah."

"But, if I did go, should I head east to Carson City; or what other route would you suggest?"

He shook his head: "No, don't go east that is, unless you're a cannibal..." He smiled at his witticism.

"What?"

"You know, cannibals? Remember the Donner Party, the winter of '46? The Sierra Nevada mountains are in the way, packed with snow this time of the year. That's what happened to them, got caught in the snow, California's very own cannibals! They ate each other, well just the ones who died, I should say," Gaylord continued: "No sir, don't go east. Go south, catch a steamer to San Pedro and get yourself outfitted there and then travel through the desert northeast. That's the only way to make it this time of the year."

Thomas was taking mental notes, then Gaylord changed the subject:

"Thirsty?"

"What?"

"Are you thirsty?"

"No, mentioning cannibalism sort of killed my appetite."

"Well, I'm thirsty," he declared, as if it were an order. They were, after all, in a saloon, where Mr. Gaylord spent his nights — and days."

"Let me buy you a drink," Thomas offered, "then I suppose I should make plans to catch a steamer to San Pedro, correct?"

"Yes sir. One leaves every morning."

"From where?"

"Right down at the far end of the Embarcadero…that way," Gaylord pointed west which caught the eye of the man behind the bar.

Thomas nodded to the bartender who brought Gaylord his favorite beverage.Tomorrow Thomas Kane, aka "Dr. Osborne" would be on the sea again.

He cursed, which was uncharacteristic of him.

GOVERNOR CUMMING AND WILLIAM STOWELL MET in the mess tent between breakfast and lunch, despite the fact that nowadays there was just brunch, but by then, all the eating was over. It didn't last long — there wasn't much to choose from anyway. Cumming had been trying to look on the bright side; he weighed close to 300 pounds when he arrived at Fort Scott (which had been near the ruins of Fort Bridger). Now he was probably down to a trim 250 pounds, he estimated, and his clothes hung on him.

Johnston had the sergeant-at-arms clean up their Mormon prisoner a bit before they brought him in to meet Cumming, brushed off as many lice as they could and found him a clean blouse from a private who had disappeared.

There was an awkward silence after the sergeant-at-arms led Stowell to his chair and ordered him to "mind his manners." William watched the man leave their presence then took a breath and relaxed. It wasn't lost on the governor.

"So, Mr. Stowell, I'm Alfred Cumming of Georgia, apparently the next governor of the Territory of Utah, at least that's what President Buchanan said. And I hope you are being treated all right."

"Can't complain, and even if I did, it would probably make things worse," William said. "After all, nobody wants to be here, me included. We just don't understand why it was necessary to send an Army here to accompany you. First, they canceled our mail contract, then we learned that people were marching on Zion."

"Zion?"

"An ideal place where people care for one another."

"It wasn't my decision to send the Army here, but I was just following orders," Cumming said.

"Yes, so were the Roman soldiers who crucified the Savior. Men have been following orders since the beginning. Every once in awhile somebody should say 'to hell with the orders.' I was also following orders of the territorial governor Brigham Young, and here I am a prisoner. That's why my indictment is out of line by the so-called Judge Eckels; he seems to be just like the judges we have already had to endure in Utah. I hope you take that into consideration; I would like to be released to my family. We have a large number of children to care for, myself and my wives," Stowell replied.

"How many children?"

"Eleven, sir. Cynthia and I adopted six, then we 'adopted' Sophronia, and she came with a small boy, then the other four we had naturally, including the twins. My wives have their hands full — they need my help."

William now had Cumming's attention: "Mr. Stowell, I'm happy to share some good news: Your family is awaiting your arrival; they got your note. Here's proof of that." The governor handed him a letter.

"It's from Cynthia…and Sophronia!" William declared. He was

grinning from ear to ear as he read their message. "Thank you, sir! This is most appreciated."

The bad news was that as far as prisoners were concerned only the commanding officer, Colonel Albert Sydney Johnston could release Stowell, and he could discipline him as he saw fit, but now William Stowell had a guardian in his corner: the next governor of the Territory of Utah.

FOR THE NEXT TWO DAYS, Thomas was doing his best to sell the persona of a world-famous botanist, the mysterious Dr. Osborne. But, he felt more like a spy, an undercover agent in the employ of the infamous Brigham Young, the leader of a gang of cutthroat religious fanatics with harems of imprisoned, deluded women, at least that's the way it was being depicted in America's penny press.

Rather than endure more sea-sickness in the belly of the boat, Thomas preferred the view on the upper deck in the open air with a gaggle of soldiers, miners, ne'er do wells of all kinds and other unfortunate outcasts seeking greener pastures.

He found himself on a deck chair next to a small table, where if he felt the urge, could lean over the rail and leave a souvenir in the ocean below. Soon he ran out of souvenirs, but learned that mint tea helped a bit.

There was a card game going on next to him; the players all wore U.S. uniforms. A sinewy man in civilian clothes sat near the officers all engaged in a lively conversation. Kane was eavesdropping:

"They won't make it down to the Salt Lake valley until spring, mark my word," the civilian said.

"Major, how can you be so sure?"

"Alexander doesn't have the respect of his men — like Buchanan, he's just another public functionary; he's lost too many animals and most of his supplies," he explained.

"Major Sherman, why don't you join us?"

"Officers don't enlist — we're invited. I'm waiting for my invitation. In the meantime, I'll sit and wait until the next war."

Who is that man, Thomas asked himself. After sipping on tea for a few minutes, he kept an eye on the game and the civilian who was waiting for a war and watched as a raw recruit had just lost all his earthly possessions and sat there in silence. Black Jack was the game, and it required the ability to add and subtract.

Thomas whispered to him: "Never take a card if you have 16 or more unless you've seen a lot of Jack, Queens and Kings dealt. Watch the old guy with the handle-bar mustache. By the way, who's the man with the steely eyes in the corner?"

"That's Major Sherman. He's looking for an open officer's slot."

"John Sherman? I've heard of him," Kane said.

"No, it's his brother William — made a name for himself in Mexico,"Thomas' confidant whispered, leaned back in his chair and got back in the game, He asked the dealer for another card. It was a ten and that put him over.

The private cursed: "I swear all this sea travel is getting me all worked up to get back on a horse. Can't wait until we get to Utah to teach those old whore-mongers a thing or two, relieve one of those farmers of one of his young wives."

One of his cohorts, the dealer, countered: "She'll have to be blind or diseased to leave with you, Hoskins. Nobody's that hard up!" They all laughed at that one; Thomas was now curious and whispered to the poor private next to him.

"You infantry? Where y'all headed?"

"San Diego. We're dragoons, on our way to get our mounts, then get outfitted and wait for orders to head north. That's the scuttlebutt anyway."

"North?"

"Utah. They say there's a war going on up there, but I'm happy if we just stay in California for awhile. They say it's supposed to be nice and warm there all the time. What about you?"

Thomas held up a small book: "*Desert Plants of North America.* I'm a botanist…I study plants. I want to find out what grows best in dry climates like the West. If people come West, how are we going to feed them? What will they eat?"

The sergeant overheard their conversation:

"Well, Mr. Botanist, sir. If we get to Utah, we're going to feed those Mormons just one thing."

"What's that?" Thomas asked.

"Lead!"

That brought a ripple of laughter from his comrades. Thomas wrote a line in his little notebook to use in future correspondence: *"What kind of a country pays its soldiers to butcher its own citizens?"* Thomas had had enough — he left to find another seat on the upper deck. Seasickness comes in many varieties.

It became apparent to Thomas Kane after he found himself on dry land again that he needed to take a lower profile. The anti-Mormon sentiment was as thick as mud in southern California, and he didn't want to leave any footprints, didn't want anybody following him. The Los Angeles Star's continuing articles about the atrocities in southern Utah were stirring up trouble for the Saints all over southern California. Eyewitness accounts by George Powers and P.M. Warn were described in graphic details under the banner headline of "Horrible Massacre of Emigrants!! Over 100 Persons Murdered!! Confirmation of the Reports." All of the publicity that Kane had garnered over a decade favoring the church was destroyed by the madness at Mountain Meadows. Now the story imperiled Kane's trek to Salt Lake.

He determined to first pass through San Bernardino. It had been an LDS settlement, but after the clarion call to return to Utah, Thomas was worried all he'd find was tumbleweeds and crickets. He reckoned that it was about 80 miles from San Pedro

to San Bernardino, a three-day ride on a fast pony. *How would he locate someone to accompany him to Utah? Was anyone left?*

The old smith spit his chaw at a bucket near Kane's feet, but missed. Thomas saw the sign near the blacksmith's shop that a mustang and mule were available, a "two-for-one special" — both for $250. He remembered the old saying, "never look a gift horse in the mouth," but he did anyway — he checked both animals out for missing teeth. They passed the teeth test. He had his transportation, but how to get there?

"The best way to San Bernardino? Hmmm, maybe Perkins knows." the blacksmith said and walked into the back of the shop.

In a minute, the crusty old smith returned with a rough map sketched out on the back of an envelope. He spat again, this time hitting the bull's eye.

Soon thereafter Thomas Kane, his horse, his mule and his baggage were outfitted and on their way.

The blacksmith did confide in Kane that if he wanted to find someone to guide him to Utah, "let folks know that he felt some kinship with the Saints" and then the local anti-Mormons would obliquely identify who they were — and why they weren't to be trusted.

Still traveling as the vagabond botanist "seeking to find unique species of local flora," Kane continued to arouse both suspicion and curiosity and entered the city limits of San Bernardino to tract out any remaining Mormons.

Ebenezer Hanks was one Mormon who stayed put when the others packed up and left, some at great personal loss.

"You're still here," the portly clerk at the mercantile muttered when Hanks walked in.

"Yes, ma'am, as you can plainly see. My money still good here? Do you prefer I took my business somewhere else?"

The clerk looked around to ensure they were alone and then

confided to him: "Heaven's no, Mr. Hanks. If it weren't for you Mormons, we wouldn't even have a town. You built the schools, the streets, kept gambling and drinking out of here. Before you folks came, all we had was gamblers and horse-thieving Indians. Now we have a right nice town! By the way, did you hear there was some scientist asking around for horsemen; he wants to hire some folks to accompany him to Utah… he's looking for strange plants and stuff."

Ebenezer Hanks, like Captain Andrew Lytle, was one of the first Latter-day Saints who found the verdant area surrounding the small creek that flowed into the Santa Anna River to be an ideal place to settle. With an abundance of water, a dense growth of willows, cottonwoods and sycamores as well as mustard and wild oats, it became home to nearly 1,000 Mormons in a town of a little more than 1,200. They were the heart and soul of the community until 2,500 soldiers and hangers-on began marching on Zion up north. By the time Thomas Kane arrived looking for horsemen, most of them had left.

Besides Hanks, Francis Jessie Clark an ex-wife of Heber C. Kimball, the former counselor to Brigham Young also remained in town. Francis had heard of a "vigilance committee" of the remaining non-Mormons, who were unfriendly to the Saints making inquiries of the strange, diminutive man claiming to be a "botanist." Then, she recognized Thomas outside the mercantile and made a visit to Ebenezer Hanks at his livery stable.

"You may not remember me, Brother Hanks, but I know you," she said when she entered his barn. "I was once a Mormon, I suppose I still am, but I left Utah some time ago."

"I do know you," he said gently. "Aren't you Jessie Kimball, a wife of Heber C., if I am not mistaken?"

Hanks walked out front, took a seat on a bench, and offered her one and asked, "How can I help you?" She was in tears.

"I saw a man in town yesterday at the town hall making inquiries; he was looking to hire some horsemen to take him to Utah. I know him. I first met him in Mt. Pisgah on the Missouri where he became quite ill, almost died actually. His name is Kane," she said.

"Thomas Kane?"

"Yes sir. But, now he's going by the name of Osborne. He's staying at the inn on Hill Street. He needs our help."

"Our help?"

"Yes, help from the members. Would you mind meeting him — I don't want to go by myself?" Hanks saw she was troubled, and if this man really was the famous Thomas Kane, then by all means, he said, he would accompany her.

About seven in the evening, Hanks and Francis Clark appeared at the boarding house. He inquired at the front desk, asking for "the scientist."

"He's registered on the second floor, room 11. I'll send my boy up for him, the woman said.

In a minute, "Dr. Osborne" came down the stairs and was directed to meet his guests in the dining hall.

"It's him! It's Thomas Kane," Mrs. Clark whispered to Hanks as Thomas walked in, looking very much like the "scientist" he was pretending to be.

Ebenezer Hanks offered his hand and introduced Jessie Clark who was now all teared up.

She whispered to Thomas: "We met in 1846 in Mt. Pisgah; I was married to Heber Kimball at the time. You are Thomas Kane, are you not?" He nodded, but then said quietly:

"My presence here as Brigham Young's old friend may not be well received by some, so as far as others are concerned, I'm a 'traveling botanist' in search of some veteran horsemen to guide me, or at least accompany me, to Utah. I carry with me introductory letters from President Buchanan.

"I'm on a peace mission to forestall and hopefully prevent a war."

Hanks leaned forward and shared what he had heard: "There are rumors in town that members of the 'vigilance committee' are inquiring as to who you really are, and if they knew your identity, they would do their best to stop you in your tracks."

Jessie Clark took Thomas by the hands and made a promise to him: *"If by saving you, I could do a service to God's church on earth, I would feel that I did not need a drop of water to cool my tongue when I shall lift up my eyes being in torment."*

And, then she wept.

The two men looked on with compassion, and then Hanks said: "Mrs. Clark, thank you for getting us together. I know people, skilled horsemen who can guide our 'botanist' to safety."

Then Hanks turned to Kane: "When can you leave?"

"Is tomorrow too soon?"

"It's perfect," Hanks answered.

MORE THAN A WEEK LATER, after enduring a hot and dusty 200-mile journey through the desert, Kane and his entourage of Mormon horsemen were making their way to the Spartan settlement of Cottonwood Camp. But, Kane himself, was not on horseback. Given the paranoia of Saints and the spying eyes of their enemies, Kane was hidden under the merchandise piled in the wagon. But, he remained discouraged at his prospects. Before he left California, he sent an encoded letter to Bess admitting that *"the day may be, and is probably past to make peace, but not to save our poor fellows. Have no fear for my life, the cloud and the pillar will be my escort. I swear I will arrive in time."* What else could he do?

AS THOMAS KANE AND COMPANY were making their way northward in Utah, another party was heading south through the future states of Colorado and New Mexico on their "mule hunt." Their trek was fraught with danger and death in the higher elevations of the eastern edge of the Rockies. The commander of the 70-man expedition of volunteers, Captain Randolph B. Marcy, and his principal guide, a Mexican national from Taos, Mariano Medina, slipped away from the group one evening. Medina had the fire started when the captain joined him.

"Gracias, Señor Medina," Marcy whispered. "Good fire. I think we should talk about the mess we're in. We have been misled."

"Si, Señor Capitan, I knew this to be true before we left, but I am the only one to find the fort in Taos. Someday, maybe, we will be in your history books."

"If they find our bodies…"

"If not, we will be the missing soldiers who disappeared in the mountains," Medina joked. "But, that will also be in the history books."

"Why did Captain Dickerson paint such a rosy picture of our prospects? We are on our way to get horses and mules but to make it down the spine of mountain passes, the only way to stay alive is to eat our horses and mules. It's snowing again — let's stay out of the history books. One Donner Party is enough."

"Who were they?"

"You don't want to know, my friend. Maybe you'd like to know why I wanted to talk to you alone," Marcy said. "We can't keep marching through two or three feet of snow when we don't even know exactly where we are. We had rations for 35 days, but most of that is gone. Who knows if they can even find us."

"So, what are your orders, Señor?"

Marcy stood up to get more deadwood, threw it on the fire and then continued: "I have a letter for the commander at the fort. Get a couple more of your best people, probably, Alona, who can get you to the Cochetopa Pass. We need to send an advance party to Taos to get some help.Otherwise, we're doomed. Can you leave in the morning, my friend?"

"We will. I'll pray for you."

"Pray for all of us," Marcy whispered.

23

I JUST WISH HE WOULD HURRY

If Johnston and Marcy thought their mission was a well kept secret, they were mistaken. Brigham Young and his close confidants already had considerable knowledge about of the so-called "mule mission," and they were not inclined to help.

George Watt, Brigham's secretary and stenographer. was tidying up business in the Lion House, reviewing some of the newspaper clippings from George Q. Cannon from his "newspaper war" in California to prepare a summary for the President when he saw one of Brigham's daughters tip-toe into the corner of his office. She waited patiently for him to notice her. He figured she was about 8-years-old.

He smiled. "Lucy, can I help you, darling?"

"Papa asked me to fetch you, Brother Watt. Am I bothering you?"

"Heaven's no! Consider me fetched. Show me the way," Watt said holding out his hand. She eagerly took it.

"He's in the dining hall," she said.

George and Lucy entered the room, and George announced their arrival: "Sir, I have been summoned to see you," he announced for Lucy's benefit.

Brigham chuckled.

"I certainly hope she is well paid," George joked.

"We'll see how she works out, Brother Watt." Brigham gave his daughter a hug, and she skipped away.

"What's happening, President?"

Brigham handed him a note he had just received:

"As you can see George, Johnston has sent his most capable officer, a Captain Marcy, on a death-defying mission to a fort in Taos, New Mexico."

George was astounded: "Are they insane? If they think the winter's harsh up in their flatlands at 6,000 feet, don't they realize what predicament they'll be in, that is, if the map you have here is accurate? Those Colorado mountains are higher than the Wasatch, and the passages between them could be filled with snow up to their heads. What do you want me to do?" Watt asked as he grabbed pen and paper, ready to take dictation.

"So, I need to get this information to Horace Eldredge in St. Louis as soon as possible, President Young answered. Tell him that we do not anticipate that the Army will be able to move in early spring, especially if they have to wait for a fresh supply of animals. We trust that their way will continue to be hedged up and that this and all other attempts to subvert the liberties of a free people, and that our enemies will be confounded and utterly wasted away while this people shall abide in strength and power." George crossed out a couple of words, and then before he left to rewrite the letter, he asked Brigham. "Any news from Thomas Kane? Is he still in Philadelphia?"

"That is the hundred-dollar question now isn't it, Brother Watt? You'd think if I were a prophet, I would know these things, that the Lord would tell me these things," he said. "Directly!"

George knew that his boss was testing him: "But, I believe you are, and so do most of the people in our territory." Now, Brigham became the teacher: "But, I remember what the Lord told Oliver Cowdery, do you?" George scratched his head and attempted a smile: "...that we must study it out in our mind and ask if it be right, then your bosom shall burn within you and you shall feel it's right. President, do you feel he is coming?"

"I feel he is coming, I believe he is coming — I just wish he would hurry," Brigham said.

BEFORE THERE WERE CASINOS, BEFORE THERE WAS EVEN A CITY, practically the only people in what today is called Las Vegas were Mormons. It was then called Cottonwood Camp, farther west than where Las Vegas would eventually arise. It was established to house lead miners and their families. To defend themselves against the Utah Expedition, the Saints of the Latter-day Saints of the Church of Jesus Christ in their vast Territory of Deseret needed lead for their various types of firearms. Buying lead on the open market was difficult, if not impossible. In fact, there was a wagon of powder and lead that the Mormons had sent west that was intercepted and taken by the Army — two can play this game.

So, it was at the Cottonwood Camp where Thomas Kane uncovered himself from underneath the merchandise in the wagon where he had been hiding. He finally saw daylight for the first time in days. And, to his surprise, he discovered that he now had a protector, an advocate who would help ferry him safely up the California trail and through the Mormon settlements to Salt Lake City. His name was Elder Amasa Lyman, an apostle of the Church. Thomas and his party joined several wagons accompanying the apostle and headed north. To all concerned, the small, dark man was a botanist, whatever that was.

Days later, after he and his party passed through the bleak landscape between the settlement of Cottonwood Camp and St. George, he had penned a note to President Young to be forwarded to Salt Lake in advance of his arrival pleading with him *"to postpone any imminent military movement of importance until we meet and have a serious interview."* Rather than add his signature, he simply expressed the hope that "you will recognize my handwriting."

While the weather along the way seemed to be dangerous and threatening, Kane welcomed a huge snowstorm that buried much of the territory as they were plodding northwards, concluding that "if we can't move, neither can the Utah Expedition nor can the

Nauvoo legionnaires." The snow bought him and his mission time. And hope.

More than a week before Kane's arrival, George Watt ran into President Young's office and handed him hope, in the form of an envelope that had just been delivered to the Lion House.

George was smiling: "See, I told you that you were a prophet!" Brigham beamed.

Help was indeed just days away. But, things would never be as simple as Brigham Young and Thomas Kane had wished. There were doubters everywhere, from Salt Lake City to Fort Supply. Outcomes were in doubt.

PEOPLE WERE PRAYING FOR HELP on both sides of the Rocky Mountains. Some 50 miles west of Pikes Peak in what would someday be the State of Colorado, Marcy's party had been "rescued," at least discovered would be more accurate. They had finally reached the Cochetopa Pass which runs along the Continental Divide and sits at about 10,000 feet with peaks on either side rising another three or four thousand above them. Days earlier, Marcy and his packer, Miguel Alona, had climbed a peak to find their objective: a dip in the mountain range to the southeast. He saw it:

"Señor, I am certain that that is the place. Through there we will pass into San Luis valley, and beyond it, the fort. I bet my life on it!"

Marcy smirked: "And mine. And everyone else's. Miguel, mi amigo, could anybody else besides you get us there?"

Miguel simply said, "Nadie." Marcy understood. He hoped Miguel knew that he valued him.

That was three days earlier.

On this morning, Marcy's company awoke in a stand of conifers covered in newly fallen powder snow. The good news was that they had found Cochetopa Pass — the bad news was they were in Cochetopa Pass, and somehow, some way, they had to get through it.

`Captain Marcy yelled for Medina, his immortal pathfinder, but all he saw were moving piles of snow with people inside. Now and then, a head emerged from the powder to look around. It would have been funny, the captain mused, if it weren't 10° below zero.

Medina tried to hurry over to the captain, but he was just 5'5" — the snow was up to his waist:

"Señor Captain, we cannot march through this deep snow. We sink. And the animals, how can we get them through?"

Marcy, Medina and Alona, their other Mexican guide, discussed it for half an hour, attempted to make snowshoes out of pine boughs and other futile efforts until a young enterprising volunteer, just a private, demonstrated his solution.

"Captain, do what we did when were little tykes. Do this!" He then jumped face down into the snow and then did it again, compressing the snow as he did so, compressing it enough that the men following in his tracks could walk on it without sinking up past their knees.

"Let's put two volunteers up front and let them 'leap frog' for a hundred yards then have two others replace them," Marcy said. "It will be slow, but we can move this column. By the time the last 20 or 25 men pass over the track, it will be compacted enough that the animals can follow. What's the command for such an action," Marcy asked.

The enterprising private barked it out: "Fall in, then Forward March!"

A few weak laughs followed, but no one was laughing when they finally exited Cochetopa Pass days later.

PEACE OR WAR WAS A PRIMARY SUBJECT OF A MEETING ON THIS DAY, February 25th, 1858, in the Lion House with several members of the Twelve and Young's counselors.

Speaking as "the General," Young's counselor, Daniel H. Wells, shared with the group his recently acquired intelligence from his

sources within the Utah Expedition that Captain Randolph Marcy was trudging through the snow along the Continental Divide on his way to Taos, New Mexico. "To what end?" Someone asked,

Brigham had an immediate answer: "To get mules and horses to replace the ones Lot and Porter liberated. It's that simple."

Another voice shouted out: "From where?"

And the answer came immediately: "From Taos and their Army fort."

"Fort Massachusetts," someone else volunteered.

Brigham looked around at "the Brethren," took a breath and asked: "So, what are we going to do about it? It appears they will bring more than just draft animals, probably more troops. Can the Nauvoo Legion be stretched that thin?"

One after another, each man bellowed out the same answer:

"No!"

"Heaven's no."

"Probably not."

Then Brigham turned to Wells who suggested, "Maybe it's time to present your idea to everyone, President: The Standing Army of Zion."

"Go ahead," Brigham said.

Wells took a few minutes to describe the plan. It would entail an armed group of Saints including infantry, artillery, dragoons and cavalry and then suggested they could be sent east to stop the reinforcements on the way to Fort Supply. Just then George Watt rushed in:

"He's here! Thomas is out in front with Elder Lyman; they're bringing in his luggage."

Brigham clapped his hands and exclaimed: "Finally. There's still time."

Not all of the Twelve on hand were as excited as Brigham was about Kane's arrival. George A. Smith wasn't; he represented the

southern Saints, those in the so-called "outlying areas," where life was much more austere, where the members who experienced the battle with the Arkansans lived, including those few who slew them. They didn't trust any outsiders, not even the beloved Thomas Kane.

Apostle Wilford Woodruff was also reticent. He had written earlier about the U.S. Army officer who had bragged that "not even Jesus Christ could keep him out of Salt Lake." Woodruff declared that "in 10 days, we can deploy 2,000 men to surround the Army which would soon use them up. I do not believe that they will have 500 fighting men in the spring."

He was one of those Saints who subscribed to the notion that all such commotion was just a sign of the coming of the Millennium. The arrival of Jesus Christ would mean the end of their adversaries, wouldn't it? To many Saints like apostles Woodruff and Smith who doubted the government's willingness to cooperate, Brigham's discourse in August about the "Russian solution" — to lay waste to their own city so as to make its occupation moot — still hung over their heads like a storm cloud. Hundreds heard Brigham's speech, but it was too terrible to consider it as a realistic option. He had begun his "ashes" threat in that talk with a question:

"[How] many is there of the elders of Israel and this community that will go with me...do as I do and take the road I shall travel? I will tell you what it is before I ask you to do it or not. If the Army does come here, and if it is necessary I will tell you what I shall do. I shall lay this building to ashes, I shall cut [down] every tree and shrub in this valley, every pole, every inch of board and put it all into ashes. I will burn the grass and the stubble, lay it waste. and make a worse Moscow of every settlement, and then I guess we will make a Potter's field of every canyon the enemy goes into."

Many would rather take the battle to the Army than to destroy their own homes — it was likely this position that prompted Kane to label those Saints as "the War Party."

But as the "official leader of the 'Peace Party,'" as Thomas Kane described him to President Buchanan, Brigham Young knew all too well that killing U.S. soldiers would bring on the wrath of 40 million Americans. Maybe you win the battle, but you lose the war, along with scores of settlements that you have built out of nothing over the past decade.

"Excuse me, Brethren," President Young said and left the meeting to greet his long time friend. Minutes later, when he set eyes on Thomas Kane, Brigham Young was shocked: "Brother Thomas, let's get you inside," Brigham said and embraced his old friend. "Thomas, you are skin and bones!" Brigham yelled to his sons and other members of the leadership, "Can we get a little help here?" Soon with some assistance, Thomas made it up the steps into the Lion House where he could recuperate, get hydrated and cleaned up after his journey.

That evening, Kane was the guest of honor, but his presence was disconcerting. "He is so pale and worn down," Wilford whispered to Lyman. He nodded. "I know," Lyman concurred, "I don't understand how he was able to make it this far."

After the introductions, Thomas thanked the delegation for welcoming him and for their kindness, and then summarized his reasons for making the journey:

"John Bernhisel and I first met with Mr. Van Dyke, President Buchanan's advisor, to develop a strategy to present to him which we did the following day. I come to you this evening to announce that I am fully prepared and duly authorized to represent the president's position both to the Saints and to the commander of the Utah Expedition. And, from the president, I expect — and asked for — a full pardon for the Saints, all of them."

To an observer watching the reaction of the leadership, one could cut the skepticism with a knife. Kane continued:

"My message to the Expeditionary force is that the Saints will accept and welcome the new governor, and that the Army will pass through the valley and then billet themselves far from the city."

Kane further expounded on his conversation with Buchanan and then added that Buchanan "hoped that the Saints would think of our soldiers who are buried in the snow in the mountains, take immediate measures to ensure their safety, supply their wants and then bid them all a cordial welcome to your hospitable valley."

At the conclusion of his remarks, Kane thanked Brigham, his counselors and the other leaders, including the apostles for accommodating him and then requested a personal meeting with President Young the next day. Kane was exhausted from his travels — that was obvious to his audience. He needed rest, and Brigham and his most trusted advisors needed to assimilate Kane's comments and then consider their next steps.

THE NEXT DAY, THOMAS SAT ACROSS THE DESK from Brigham Young in his office. It was just the two of them. After regaling the president about his harrowing journey down to Panama, then his voyage to California and his overland trip hidden under merchandise to make it through the desert and blizzards to arrive in the city, Thomas waited for the question of the day.

"How did the President react to your proposal?" Brigham asked.

Thomas hesitated, then implied that Buchanan apologized for the mobilization of the Utah Expedition, and said "it was so precipitate as legitimately open to misconception. It's not too late for a remedy between persons of honor and good intentions ."

Brigham furrowed his eyebrows, then relaxed, but let his friend continue:

"President Young, I urge you to believe and accept his assurance that no disrespect had at any time been intended."

Brigham leaned back in his chair and sighed: "Thomas, I should not turn to neither the left nor the right or pursue any course but only the one that God dictated to me. The President's actions have been injudicious and hasty. James Buchanan," Brigham declared, "is a man of straw."

Thomas paused, reached into the satchel he had brought with him and then showed President Young the letters signed by Buchanan,. both the letter to Brigham and the one to Albert Sydney Johnston.

Brigham Young read them both thoroughly, relaxed and finally smiled:

"Thomas, so now that your journey as the world-famous Dr. Osborne has come to an end, will you return to your rank and title as 'Colonel Thomas Leiper Kane/'"

Thomas smiled: "Maybe I will once I reach Johnston's camp, but I only have civilian clothes. Nor uniform yet. But maybe it will garner me some cachet with the boys in blue — we'll see."

After sharing a few personal comments about their wives and children, Brigham and Thomas agreed to enlarge the conversation and include others in the discussion. Later that evening, Kane told a small group of Saints gathered in a chapel that *"you have built a great empire here and your conduct in these affairs has been manly."* Then, he piled on praise for Buchanan which was not accepted very well, claiming that "he is an excellent president."

Elder George A. Smith, who was a bear of an apostle, a behemoth of a man, huffed to one of his fellow quorum members: *"I have warm regards for Brother Kane for his courage and persistence, but nevertheless I perceive he may be a pawn of Buchanan sent here to persuade us not to destroy the soldiers at Camp Scott until he can send sufficient reinforcements here to destroy us"*

Rumors about Johnston's troops stirring up the Shoshones were worrying the Saints, since that tribe was always at war with the Utes, officially friendly with the Mormons. Along with the Utah Expedition's foray to New Mexico to get more draft animals and

probably more troops was yet another reason why many of the Saints were not ready yet to march to Thomas Kane's drumbeat.

After the meeting with Thomas Kane, Brigham Young further documented the Church's stance on the Indians in a letter he wrote to Jeter Clinton, a church leader in Philadelphia: *"for years I have been holding the Indians, the check rein has been broken, and cousin Lemuel is at large; in fact, he has already been collecting some of his annuities. Day after day, I am visited by their chiefs to know if they may strike while the iron is hot. My answer depends on Mr. Buchanan's policies — if he do [sic] not mete our justice to us, the war cry will resound from the Rio Colorado to the headwaters of the Missouri — from the Black Hills to the Sierra Nevada — travel will be stopped across the continent — the deserts of Utah will become a battle ground for freedom. It [is] peace and our rights or the knife and the tomahawk — let Uncle Sam choose."*

This was the mindset of the Saints of the Latter-day in 1858, besieged by all sides, driven from state to state, beginning in 1846 until in 1847, when they left the borders of the United States to what was then called Upper California, ostensibly owned by Mexico, to be left alone. In 1846, Thomas Kane convinced Brigham Young that it would improve the Mormons' caché with the federal government to enlist the Mormon Battalion for the war against Mexico to undertake the longest march in U.S. military history. How did that work out, the Mormons asked themselves?

24

ENOUGH IS ENOUGH

It should not come as a surprise to anyone that these agrarian people, these eschatological city planners and community creators, these millennial anticipators, who were making the desert blossom as a rose would finally rise up and declare, "enough is enough."

They would fight.

That is the situation Thomas Kane faced when he set out again in early March 1858 to convince Colonel Albert Sydney Johnston and his soldiers to back down and peaceably pass through their capital city and billet themselves somewhere else, somewhere far from the Valley of the Great Salt Lake.

But, would he listen?

Before Kane left for Wyoming, there was still more wooing to be done in Salt Lake City. He was a man not easily dissuaded, not when he had come this far, not after his ocean voyages and multiple bouts of seasickness. Problem was, there were still Saints who doubted that Kane could stay the hand of the persecutors — they had suffered so much.

So, he continued his wooing. If Thomas Leiper Kane couldn't persuade his friends, what kind of success could he expect from the likes of General Albert Sydney Johnston?

Apostle Wilford Woodruff, the Mormons' most prolific journal writer, sent Kane a note spelling out the nightmarish scenario that so many Saints feared. The settlements would be filled with "drunken, quarrelsome and licentious soldiers" (not to mention their "hangers-on), Federal judges would "arrest and persecute prominent men." Woodruff took the threats from General Harney and the Yankee editors seriously. He didn't view their diatribes as hyperbole. He had witnessed it all first-hand.

Nevertheless, Kane later reported to Bess that the Saints' feelings had started to thaw — despite Woodruff's influence. The conversations became less apocalyptic and shifted to more pleasant topics, such as reestablishing reliable mail routes, connecting a transcontinental railroad through Utah, and even constructing artesian wells along the southern route. Kane felt encouraged by this change.

The day before Kane left for Wyoming, Thomas was scheduled to meet with Brigham one last time, but the President had kept him waiting for nearly an hour. What had transpired, Kane wondered.

Then, George Watt came into the anteroom.

"Brother Kane, please be patient. There have been a few developments, — President Young will be with you shortly."

Twenty minutes later, Kane was seated with Brigham Young. Thomas saw that Brigham's eyes were swollen — he was visibly upset. Finally, the president spoke:

"Rumors about the Shoshones allying with the Army have been proven to be true. There has been an attack on our settlement in Oregon territory at Fort Limhi, two were killed, and others were wounded. We sent a party north to retrieve our friends and bring them back home. Given the weapons that the survivors saw brandished by the attackers, our people were convinced that Johnston and his people were behind the attack," Brigham said flatly. Thomas could see that his demeanor was shaken. Young was clearly worried, if not panicked.

"At any rate, Thomas, your mission has taken on even more importance to the peace and prosperity of our people, and I think, for the country as well." Thomas nodded and as he did, he sensed a softening of the president's martial attitude.

For Kane, it seemed as though any reticence that Brigham had felt regarding his upcoming meeting with the general was evaporating. That strengthened his hand.

Finally, on March 8th, 1858, Thomas Kane bid farewell to his beloved friends and was on his way to work his magic with Johnston. He was determined to finish his mission and prove to his father that he wasn't Don Quixote, that his venture wouldn't fail. But, before he repacked his baggage for his journey to Johnston, he found a letter that Bess had hidden in his trunk when he was looking for his writing materials — Thomas had a letter to write to Buchanan.

The letter he found was from his father. It was "tough love," difficult to read.

While Judge Kane admitted his "strenuous opposition to Thomas' venture, he wanted his son to know that he loved him and that he carried with him *all the blessing that a father's prayers* can invoke." But, he didn't back down; the judge was still convinced that Thomas would fail, and he wrote *"I want you to prepare for the worst." And, he warned his son "that if the Mormons once assail our troops, the sentiment of the country will never be satisfied while a Mormon community survives on this continent... I have very faint hopes connected with your mission."*

He percolated over his father's letter before he began writing to President Buchanan. His father was right: If the Mormons shed the blood of American soldiers, his mission would fail, but Buchanan needed to understand the awful situation the Latter-day Saints were in. Thomas began writing, describing the fears that the Mormons had about the Army some 113 miles away, hanging over their heads like the sword of Damocles... "that they would have Illinois & Missouri all over again ... that the soldiers would be drunken, quarrelsome and licentious and that the judges would not punish them... that the officer commanding the Army of the U.S. here, would proclaim martial law by which they could be punished summarily… and finally would call on the soldiers to see every man the Saints loved hanged, or they chose to have a mind to…"

His mission could succeed, and he wanted his father to know that, but he'd never have the chance. Judge John Kane had died on February 25th, but the news hadn't reached Thomas yet. It was time to say good-bye and get back on the trail. There would be no welcome mat waiting in Wyoming.

NOTHING WAS GETTING EASIER AS THOMAS KANE and his bodyguards, under the watchful eye of Mormon gunman Porter Rockwell, were getting closer to Fort Scott. If anything, as the elevation increased, the weather grew colder and the snow deeper as did Kane's depression. Nevertheless, he and his party pressed on. Brigham had enlisted several of his most trusted aides to accompany Thomas Kane to Wyoming, including Brig. General Lewis Robinson and Major Howard Egan as well as Porter Rockwell. Thomas later wrote to his brother Patrick that only "his mountaineers [could have guided him through places where the mountain passes were covered in snow drifts up to 25-feet high and that they] "had our foolish herd of soldiers at their mercy."

With his face covered from the blizzard coming straight at him, Thomas yelled to Porter:

"How much farther, do you think, Porter?" The grizzled gunman laughed and grunted, Thomas wasn't sure which. The wind made it hard to make out what he was saying:

"No tellin' where *we* are, never mind where *they* are," Porter yelled back. "If we come to some kind of wind break, we should shelter."

Thomas was relentless: "We have to keep moving!"

They had passed Cache Cave in Echo Canyon maybe a half an hour ago, Porter figured. They were coming to the end of the canyon where they would then be in the gun sights of the Army.

A copse of junipers lay straight ahead in a depression surrounded by boulders.

"Let's stop there," Porter said. "They could be watching us, but since we can't see anything, neither can they."

They dismounted and huddled between the animals — the storm was easing, they assumed.

"I think I have to go on by myself now," Thomas said. "You should return down the canyon and shelter in the cave."

One of the party was worried: "How will we know you arrived safely?"

"I'll release a pigeon," Thomas joked, attempting to lighten the mood — it didn't help. "You won't know. If the Army starts marching down the canyon, then you'll know I failed. I'll find some way to get word to you At any rate, I am indebted to you — your faith and courage will be remembered, even if I'm not."

Rockwell smiled: "Thomas, we both know you'd rather die than be forgotten. Someday there will be a statue of you in Salt Lake City. History will remember your journey, successful or not." In a rare gesture of genuine affection, Porter gave his slight friend a hug: "You stay safe, and try to eat something when you can."

Thomas laughed: "You sound like my mother."

The men climbed back in their saddles and headed out in opposite directions, Porter, Robison, Egan and the rest of the guides south back down the canyon towards the city and Thomas east into the unknown, the unexpected and the unwelcome, clothed in his furs, his buffalo cape with his well-packed mule in tow.

IN PHILADELPHIA, ELIZABETH KANE HAD NO IDEA where her husband was, if he had made it to Salt Lake City or even of he had survived. Then, she received a letter from Anthony Osborne, Thomas' erstwhile traveling companion, who sent Elizabeth Kane correspondence with a clipping from a San Francisco newspaper confirming Kane's arrival in the Mormon capitol.

Soon afterwards, Thomas' brother Patrick came to see her. He had been charged with "checking in on her from time to time." He did more than that; the family knew that Thomas had left her with little more than a hope and a prayer — the last time they met she admitted to Patrick that she only had $9 left and wanted to sell some stocks or bonds, but he advised against that. He made sure she and the children had enough to keep body and soul together. It was evening when he dropped by after she had put Harriet and Elisha to bed.

"Have you seen this?" Patrick showed her a page of a California newspaper.

"Yes, Thomas' friend Anthony…"

"I know Anthony — he worked for us years ago," Patrick said interrupting her.

Elizabeth Kane finished her sentence: "…sent me a clipping of the same paper, but then he must have left for the Army camp, since then, nothing. It can be brutal in the mountains this time of the year."

Patrick agreed, but then proceeded to offer her some encouragement:

"Mother received a letter from John Junior just a few days ago; did she share it with you?" She shook her head: "From Paris?"

"Yes," Patrick replied, "He's still in Paris, apparently still studying, but he took some time to encourage Mother, and he would want me to do the same thing for you. He is an odd creature, Thomas is," he said with a laugh. "We all know it, you know it, but it is nevertheless true. Yes, he is a small man but must possess a stupendous spirit, much larger than the body that encompasses it," Patrick said with a chuckle. Bess smiled as well and leaned forward to hear him better.

"So, John wrote about a trip the two of them took awhile back. I think John described your husband and our brother perfectly. He will be fine, and despite what Father wrote in his letter to

Thomas before he departed for Utah. I have come to believe he will succeed..Did you read the letter?"

"I am ashamed to admit it, but I did, and unbeknownst to Thomas, I put it into his trunk before he left. It will discourage him, but it would have been wrong for me to keep it from him."

"Well, it's a shame that the last correspondence Thomas ever received from his father would have been so discouraging. I wonder if he knows Father died."

"Don't know if he knows — I sent a letter to Salt Lake City in hopes Brigham would share it with him," Bess said.

"Well, if he did get your letter, he would press on just the same, just to prove to the judge that he was right. It will push him, I think. He won't stop."

THOMAS HAD BROUGHT A COMPASS WITH HIM, but with the wind in his face and his eyes tearing up, he couldn't quite make out where he was headed. Porter Rockwell had told him that once he had exited the canyon and crossed the narrow Bear River bridge, he should follow the trail in an east by northeasterly direction. But, the trail was covered in snow, and no one had passed this way in either direction — at least there was no distinguishable trail or tracks to follow. He was the sole pathfinder for miles in any direction. For his mare, it was easy to carry him — he barely weighed 100 pounds. But, his trunk and his saddle bags packed on the mule weighed more than he did. Thomas stopped near a leafless cottonwood, dismounted and readjusted his load. He put feedbags on his animals and filled them with oats — there was no forage whatsoever, not in January, not in this God-forsaken part of Wyoming.

When the animals had emptied their feedbags, Thomas packed them up and patted each animal. And, as he was ready to mount up again, he heard a gunshot. Then a voice rang out:

"Do not move, mister, unless you want to taste my lead!"

Thomas Kane shouted back: "I am on a mission to see your commanding officer with a letter from the president himself! You put your weapon down!" He grabbed his pistol and cocked it.

Two men in uniform on horseback emerged from behind a stand of junipers. The older one asked: "Who are you? State your business."

"I am Colonel Thomas Leiper Kane, and I have come a long distance from Washington D.C. to speak with your commanding officer. As I said, I have a letter from James Buchanan, president of the United States, for Colonel Johnston."

The younger soldier spoke up: "What's in the letter?"

Thomas was now irritated, but exhausted: "Are you Albert Sydney Johnston, commanding officer of the Utah Expedition? This letter is addressed to *him*."

"No, of course not," the corporal admitted.

Thomas steadied himself. He was so lightheaded that he was afraid he'd fall off his horse. The conversation had exhausted him. "Take me to Johnston. I am on the president's errand!"

The older soldier stared at his companion and finally turned to Thomas: "Follow us, it's not far."

Far was a relative term in frontier America in the mid 19th century. Independence, Missouri, was far. Fort Leavenworth was far. San Francisco was far. Wherever Kane and his escorts had met was somewhere in the middle of a blinding snowstorm, but no one knew exactly where that "somewhere" was for sure.

But, after traveling nearly 6,000 miles, Thomas was numb; he hadn't checked his pocket watch when the three horsemen turned north and followed their own tracks back to the camp, but he was certain they had spent at least an hour to get there. Everything was far. It was now dusk, and the blizzard had let up. His escorts led Kane's horse and mule to a gabled tent next to a spruce tree and dismounted. Looking around, Thomas realized Colonel Albert

Sydney Johnston wasn't in the neighborhood. Kane was at Fort Bridger — General Johnston was at Camp Scott, a few miles distant. But, at this point, Kane didn't know and didn't care.

The next thing he recalled was being lifted off his horse and taken to the tent of Captain Robinson, commander of the 5th Infantry. After introductions, Robinson took Thomas inside and deposited him on his couch where the weary traveler immediately fell asleep. The corporal nodded, saluted and left. Thomas needed sleep for what was coming. The captain called for a messenger.

"Corporal, please take this note to Camp Scott and deliver it to Johnston's aide, Major Porter. The nearly frozen man in my tent is Colonel Thomas Kane, brother of Elisha Kane, and he is here at the behest of President Buchanan; he would like an audience with Colonel Johnston and with Governor Cumming.

"Double time this, please."

By then, Thomas Leiper Kane was somewhere else, somewhere dreamy, warm and comfortable. He didn't want to wake up.

25

A MAN LARGER THAN MYTH

Far away in the nation's capital, another storm was brewing. The Mormons' only other friend in high places was working his magic as well: Texas Senator Sam Houston had a bill to kill.... a bill to fund more troops for Utah. Utah's delegate to Congress, John Bernhisel, found Houston outside the Senate chambers:

"Senator, I stopped at your boarding house earlier, but was informed you had already left for the capitol. I spoke with Seth Blair a day or two ago. We have some concerns about the funding bill," Bernhisel said.

"I know where you are going with this," Houston replied.

"Yes, the measure to increase funding for additional troops for the Utah Expedition is bad enough, but it's worse than that."

Houston was perplexed: "How so?"

"In one state after another, first California, then Ohio and now it's Kentucky, there are recalcitrant war mongers who are itching to get into the battle against the Mormons by sending volunteers. There's bloodlust everywhere, so even if we kill Federal funding, who's to say some state or group doesn't decide to go hunting after Mormons on their own," Bernhisel pled with Houston.

"Fill me in," Houston asked. Bernhisel drew closer.

"Do you know an officer by the name of Simon Bolivar Buckner of Illinois? He has recruited some Illinois volunteers, people who already tasted Mormon blood and want more. Another troublemaker is a West Point graduate who is campaigning for a promotion who was apparently on board the steamer with Kane when he sailed to California."

Bernhisel continued: "The officer wants to lead a battalion of California volunteers to Utah."

"What's his name?" Houston asked.

"Sherman."

"John Sherman?"

"No, his brother William; they're both riled up," Bernhisel said. "And, maybe you heard that a General Sargent of Ohio has organized a battalion of Ohio infantry companies from around Cincinnati to join him, plus more from areas farther north."

"Yes, I heard about Sargent. What is your advice?

Bernhisel took a deep breath and looked around as people continued to walk by their cubby hole: "Ask some serious questions. Why all the anti-Mormon sentiments? It isn't just the massacre, because this is nothing new. After being driven from state to state, we still ask 'why.' Why was it necessary to move one-third of the U.S. Army to Utah just to accompany a new governor. Why didn't someone just inform Brigham Young that he was to be replaced? Why all the humbuggery?"

Houston sat back and percolated for a couple of minutes while Bernhisel waited for his response.

"This is an excellent idea, John," Houston said with a smile.

"What is?"

"A commission to answer all these questions, to look into the reasons why Buchanan made his blunder: Who encouraged him to do it? What were the reasons? Why was it justified? Thank you, John, you have given me new purpose.," Houston was ebullient.

Bernhisel was confused.

But Houston continued: "Sometimes it is better to attack than retreat. No, it's always better to attack than retreat. Let's talk again in a few days."

They parted company, promising to meet soon, very soon. For the first time in a long time, Utah's territorial delegate John Bernhisel had a bounce in his step. It was a good conversation.

THE MORNING AFTER KANE ARRIVED, Johnston's adjutant took notice of the newcomer with a jaundiced eye. Major Fitz John Porter had a dim view of the Mormons and anyone like Thomas Kane who would come to their aid. The major called the Saints "thieves and cowards," and like many members of the Utah Expedition, he would just as soon take part in their extermination as spend another day in the frozen hell-hole where he found himself.

The fact that he was the one delivering the news of Thomas' arrival to Col. Albert Sydney Johnston put Kane's mission on a bad footing from the very start.

Johnston read the note from Robinson about Kane's arrival and wanted Porter's opinion: "So, what do you think, Major?"

"Colonel, I'm skeptical," Porter replied.

They were attempting to choke down their sorry excuse of a breakfast which included watered down coffee supplemented with burnt toast drippings. Johnston glared at his cup in disgust and poured it out.

"I'd give up my command for a milk cow," he complained. "And a really strong cup of coffee."

"Then the Mormons would steal it while you were sleeping," Major Porter wisecracked.

"No, because its left rear leg would be shackled to you, Porter. Well, what's your assessment of this Kane and his proposal?"

"We haven't seen him yet, but he should be here later this morning, I assume. But, he's looking for glory, that's for sure. He's a self-constituted ambassador of sorts, smells like a Mormon, some say he secretly is. The proposal he's bringing from Brigham Young is likely as insulting as their offer of salt…"

"Salt. They obviously have a lot of it…" the colonel smirked.

"My opinion is, Kane has nothing to do with us — we have to go forward. Only orders to the contrary will stop us once we're ready." Johnston mulled Porter's assessment for a moment and then replied:

"All right, let's keep that in mind when we meet him. In the meantime, get me some real coffee or shoot the mess sergeant."

"I'll do it myself," Porter said, grinning.

Just then, an orderly poked his head in the tent, irritating both officers, but had a message to deliver: "Colonel, Major, you'll want to hear this: We have a visitor from New Mexico: Mariano Medina has returned from Taos. Marcy and his men made it. Help is coming!"

Johnston beamed and slapped Major Porter on the back: "Finally, some good news for a change! Now get me that coffee!"

AS THEY SAY, SENATOR SAM HOUSTON had his ducks in a row. He was locked and loaded and ready to fire. He and Bernhisel went over all the possible arguments that those seeking Mormon blood might mention, and he was ready. He was the next speaker in the Senate chambers, the last of the day with only a few minutes remaining. Utah's delegate whispered to Houston just outside the entrance: "So, is Blair's intelligence reliable?"

"Absolutely. Johnston and Cumming don't see eye to eye on very much. The governor doesn't want to sit by and watch his constituents murdered by the United States Army, and Johnston, as always, sees combat as his first and only option. Our bad blood goes back to the war with Mexico, as you know — I don't care for him nor he for me. And, if it ever came to secession, he would be among the first to change uniforms, mark my word," Houston said.

"So, he really doesn't care how he came to be in Utah, whether it was a blunder or not," Bernhisel surmised.

"Exactly. That, and I think he wants to get this over with. If he has sit in the mountains and then peacefully post himself somewhere far from the action, he will be furious that he ended his career doing nothing," Houston explained.

The sergeant-at-arms was calling the senators to take their seats, and Houston excused himself as Bernhisel sneaked up into the gallery. Minutes later, he sat down and was as nervous as a bride on her wedding night, worrying and praying. Down below on the Senate floor, Sam Houston was as gussied up as a peacock in season wearing a white beaver hat, a Cherokee blanket and a jaguar-skin vest.

As John Bernhisel had walked up to the gallery he had heard a senator call Houston "that magnificent barbarian." John smiled and muttered to himself, "yes, OUR magnificent barbarian!" Then, he just sat and waited. The barbarian rose to his feet.

"I understand what you all call the Utah War has entered a new phase, which is to increase the regular Army permanently. So, is it your plan to send them out to Utah…to be destroyed?" A ripple and then a rumble could be heard among the Senators, some angered, others bewildered: *"What does he mean by that?"*

Houston waited and then proceeded:

"Rather, since there are so many who have expressed their desire to 'volunteer,' why not let them? Some say this is more expensive, but I think not — the celerity of the volunteers would mitigate this.

"What a calamity would this be for our country: the blood of our fellow Americans spilled in that mountain valley. I am certain that the facts about the situation in Utah have been concealed from the executive — we should have ascertained FIRST what the people there thought and whether or not they even asked if they would submit.

"It seems clear to me that the more people we send, the greater the difficulties we will face. It's 1,200 miles distant — they have to be fed and clothed. When the regiment arrived, it found Fort Bridger in ashes. These people will fight and die before they surrender.

"I have in my possession a lengthy letter from a very respectable man, a former district attorney from Utah who says

that there never has been the least hostility towards the United States and that there never would have been any if we had sent good there in the first place. He says Governor Young would have been anxious to get rid of the responsibilities of his office.

"And as far as how many we send, he says that fifty thousand wouldn't be any more efficient than two or three thousand. Remember that an act of civility was tendered by Brigham Young to the troops — a shipment of salt — and it was sent back. Colonel Johnston had the chance to make peace, and he squandered it.

"Volunteers may conquer the day, regulars not."

It took a man larger than myth to stem the tide, and it was Sam Houston.

The vote for funding for more soldiers to march on Zion failed in the Senate — the Mormons' champion, Sam Houston, killed it.

SENATOR SAM HOUSTON'S DEFIANT STAND against the funding for more troops to march on Zion had made ripples in Washington, but the news had not yet reached the Rocky Mountains. The Saints in Salt Lake were praying that Thomas Kane had made it safely to Fort Bridger and Camp Scott; the hungry, ill-clad troops of the Utah Expedition had other plans for their unwelcome visitor. Kane could sense it.

Saddle-sore and bleary eyed after his 24-hour mad dash up to Wyoming and his long night's sleep, Thomas Kane finally sat up. The captain gave him a cup of something hot that tasted vaguely like coffee, no cream or sugar.

"Thank you, Captain, for your kindness," Thomas managed to say. He found himself in a make-shift dwelling fashioned from canvas, timbers — some of it charred. But, thankfully, with a primitive cast-iron stove blazing in the corner, it was at least cozy…cozier than the last several days had been, in any case. He was still sitting on the make-shift sofa where he had collapsed.

"Kindness, Mr. Kane, is in short supply up here. My mother always taught me that kindness is easy when life is. Sometimes kindness takes effort," Captain Robinson said.

Then, he lowered his voice. "Colonel …"

"You can call me Thomas," Kane said.

"Thomas, you need to be alert all the time. While I am not privy to your plans, I have spoken with Phillip St. George Cooke..."

"I know him…"

"Yes, he told me. There are others around us, and we don't know their intentions, but just keep an eye open…" the captain whispered.

"I've been doing that for two months now, and I appreciate your concern. But, if the Mormons are correct, if I stay the course…" Thomas replied.

"Stay the course?"

"Stay true to my friends — the Mormons don't have many of them. Anyway, they say I'll have divine protection, but you can't be too careful," Thomas said.

The captain had noticed that when Kane rode in. It was easy to see that he was well armed.

Robinson walked to the camp table, grabbed the coffee pot and refilled Kane's cup: "So, will you soon be leaving for Camp Scott?"

"As soon as I take care of some business, if someone can send me off in the right direction…"

"Sure. It's not far."

"I heard that two days ago — far is relative up here," Thomas replied. The captain smiled and agreed. Kane gathered his belongings, grabbed what he could find to eat and then followed the well-worn path to Camp Scott. Even though it was already March, the ground was still frozen.

Thomas was grateful for that. His horse seemed to perk up, but the mule was dragging them along.

As Thomas passed by the tents, lean-to's and other sorry excuses for human habitation along the trail, the hair went up on the back of his neck — onlookers stopped whatever they were doing to watch "the rich young prince" trot out of town. The comparison in their appearances was stark. Amasa Lyman's daughter had fashioned him a cloak out of a buffalo hide after he arrived in the Cottonwood Camp weeks earlier. She said, "Brother Kane, you will freeze to death without something warmer when you arrive in Wyoming."

Underneath the cloak, he was dressed in a fur waistcoat and under that was a bright, red plaid vest. "Maybe I'm overdressed for the occasion," he said to his beasts of burden. For a moment, he thought he saw the mule smirk.

It was supposed to only be two or three miles, but Thomas felt like he was running a gauntlet. Brigham told him to beware of assassins. That's all he saw: assassins to the left of him, assassins to the right.

"They look more like rag dolls than soldiers," he muttered to no on in particular.

About a half hour later, the scenery changed a bit — the colonel's effect on the camp was obvious. This was headquarters, the Sibley tents and the four-cornered ones were standing at attention, dress-right-dress.

There was a sentry of sorts at the check point ahead. Thomas stopped to make an inquiry:

"Excuse me, corporal, could you direct me to Colonel Johnston's whereabouts?"

"Are you Kane?"

"Yes, Colonel Thomas Kane."

"He is expecting you. Keep on — straight ahead; it's the large gabled tent at the far end where you see his colors posted. Are you really Elisha Kane the explorer's brother?" Thomas nodded.

The sentry smiled, saluted and waved him on.

Kane's mule needed some encouragement; Thomas waited and then he proceeded, and as he trotted straight ahead, he felt dozens of eyes focused on him as if he were on parade. A long line of tents on either side lay before him. Enlisted men and officers alike stopped what they were doing. It was like the arrival of "a prince." As he approached Johnston's headquarters, a sergeant hurried over to his side and took the reins, stepped aside and led the way. Following his lead, Kane came right up to the commander's tent, pushed his mare right up to the front of the headquarter's tent, and just as the chief occupant looked out to see who was coming, the horse's muzzle pushed right into the opening — Johnston and Kane's horse met nose to nose. It was an unusual stand-off for a commander of Albert Sydney's Johnston's stature, since he had to bow slightly and push the mare's nose to the side to even see who had dared to enter his holy space.

Johnston bellowed: "What is the meaning of this? Who are you?"

"Colonel Johnston, sir," Thomas said. "I am Colonel Thomas Kane. I have come from Philadelphia bearing dispatches from President Buchanan. I ask your permission to visit Governor Cumming."

Johnston was flummoxed, but assented. He nodded and turned back inside to continue his conversation with Captain John Phelps, his artillery officer, Captain Jesse Gove and Colonel Johnston's adjutant, Major Fitz-John Porter. Thomas called for the man who was leading his mule. Then, they left for the governor's residency..

Porter was shocked: "That was Kane?"

"One and the same," Captain Phelps said. "A flair for the dramatic, don't you think?"

Johnston said little at first, still enraged by Thomas' intrusion, but not wanting his subordinates to acknowledge his humiliation, he called for his sergeant major.

"Bradley, can you summon Cuvier Grover? I have an assignment for him." In a few minutes, Captain Grover would receive the assignment to be Thomas Kane's babysitter, although Thomas would have another name for him: The Spy.

As Johnston counseled with the men in headquartrs, both Major Porter and Captain Gove shared their disdain for the Mormons, but Gove had a nagging question: *"Why is this little man so enamored with these people? Murder is as common among them, to all who do not bow to Mormondom as the sun rises."*

Johnston concurred, adding that *"their insane desire of establishing a form of government so despotic is utterly repugnant to our institutions."*

A minute later, Grover arrived.

"So, Kane left?" Phelps asked.

"Yes, the sergeant led the way; he took his mule in tow and the little prince followed," Grover said.

Fitz-John Porter couldn't resist commenting: "So, the sergeant led the ass…followed by Kane's pack animal…one ass after another!"

The colonel loved it: "Now I know why I keep you around, Porter," Johnston said.

The officers enjoyed a laugh then had to return to the business of the day — trying to find enough food and clothing to keep their brigade alive in their ragtag Army camp. Johnston gave Grover a very direct order: "Captain, just keep the little man alive; I want to find out what Buchanan gave him."

Grover saluted and left to make sure he was able to make it alive to his next stop. After he was gone, Fitz-John was puzzled:

"Colonel, why select an officer to babysit Kane — why not send a crusty old sergeant?" Johnston was still annoyed by the whole business:

"Because John, I want him to feel like he can confide in an equal; I want him to see Grover as a friend." Porter was puzzled: "You know, Kane's probably a secret Mormon anyway.Why would he tell anybody anything? Why Grover?"

Phelps was listening, then interjected himself into the conver-sation after he could see that Johnston was still irritated: "The real question is, Colonel, why did he want to hurry away and see the governor in the first place, before sitting down with you?"

Johnston sighed. thought about it for a minute, then replied. "Phelps, that is the one question we need answered. Please see what you can find out. I fear that this fancy young man will likely be a pain in the ass for some time to come."

26

MAY I INTRODUCE MYSELF?

Thomas Kane's introduction to Alfred Cumming, the newly appointed governor of the Utah Territory and the former mayor of Augusta, Georgia, went much better than his meeting with Colonel Johnston.

Cumming was in Eckelsville, a place named after the judge who presided over the sorry place. It was a ramshackle warren of gabled and Sibley tents of various sizes, and thanks to the sergeant who was willing to take the reins of his pack mule, Thomas was led to a cluster of five tents encircling a large fire pit surrounded by log seating. A ruddy-faced, white-haired man in the shape of a whiskey barrel was dropping logs on a fire. A woman was tending to a Dutch oven hanging from a tripod over the fire. Thomas dismounted his mare. The governor introduced himself.

"Alfred Cumming. I've been expecting you."

Thomas smiled:: "Nice to finally meet you, Governor."

"Come inside." The governor opened the flap to a Sibley tent. Inside, Cumming took a seat behind a desk in front of a bookcase and motioned to Thomas to take a seat. The ground was covered with a wool carpet; a small cast iron stove with a flue extended nearly up to the opening of his "teepee." Thomas appreciated how Cumming had made the best of an inconvenient situation.

"Congratulations for making it all the way here. It must have been quite an adventure."

Kane nodded: "Yes it was."And then as if he were searching for a reaction, the governor got right down to business:

"So, Mr. Kane, you did meet the colonel, correct?"

Thomas weighed the governor's statement and chose his words carefully. He wondered how the two of them got along: "It was a very brief introduction, and I'm not sure how happy the colonel and his officers were to see me."

Thomas was not a card shark — games of chance were not a personal or a family pastime, even though his brothers accused him of having a poker face. Nevertheless, gambling as blood sport was indeed a Kane family obsession, as his family constantly reminded him. And, sometimes, as was the case with Elisha, gambling with your life can be fatal. That's why it was often necessary to be calculating, careful, but still willing to step into the darkness while anticipating obstacles.

Knowing that he was surrounded by men willing to do him harm, Kane asked Cumming directly: "How do you think Johnston and his officers view my being here?"

Cumming turned the question back on Thomas; now he perceived that the governor was playing his cards close to his vest, too. Cumming addressed him by his first name:

"Thomas, first tell me your reaction when you met the colonel."

Cumming waited for Kane's answer, but before he could reply, Mrs. Cumming poked her head inside the tent.

"Mr. Kane, did you have any breakfast?"

Thomas smiled: "Define breakfast."

That drew laughter from his host and hostess. She pushed through the tent's opening and entered toting a Dutch oven hanging from a hook and set it down and then left,

The governor stood up and pulled a rickety folding camp table out and set it in front of the desk next to Thomas. Mrs. Cumming returned with dishes, a pitcher, three cups and tongs and removed a clump of rolls from the cast iron pot and poured three cups of coffee. The governor turned to the bookshelf behind him and grabbed a small honey pot and put it on the rickety table. Mrs. Cumming declared: "Breakfast is served!" And, then she laughed. She was a cheery, short woman who reminded Thomas of the quintessential social butterfly, a delightful person who always looked out for the comfort of others.

"The honey is from the governor's private reserve," Mrs. Cumming boasted in jest. "Sorry, no milk or cream. Mr. Kane, I interrupted you when I came in."

"Well, regarding my initial meeting with the colonel, I didn't have much time to learn anything substantial — we had no real conversation. I may have started things on the wrong foot...too dramatic, perhaps, but ..."

Cumming leaned forward to hear the rest of the sentence.

Thomas continued: "But, it was frosty. Yes, frosty like the weather. No welcome mat."

Cumming nodded: "Well, as you know, when armies march, they generally are heading into trouble; they don't march for nothing. And when they're idle, they're unhappy."

Mrs. Cumming spoke up: "Armies break things. And, this Army doesn't like being here."

"Does anybody like being here? But, here we are," Cumming said. "So, Thomas, what's next? What's in those letters you brought from the President?"

Mrs. Cumming interjected: "First, Thomas, tell us about Salt Lake City."

The governor shot a glance at his wife who gave him "a pirate eye"—the governor backed down. Thomas pretended to enjoy his bland breakfast and then answered Cumming's wife: "Just wait until you emerge from Emigration Canyon and see the community all laid out in front of you. This isn't your normal frontier town with streets snaking out in all directions, mines and mills scattered helter skelter with little hovels and shacks interspersed next to blacksmith shops and what not. All of their settlements are planned cities, every one of them, all through the territory.

The streets are laid out north and south, east and west, with building lots reserved for churches, schools and public buildings. There's even a university, founded in 1850. The streets are wide enough that a wagon pulled by a team of four horses can turn around completely and reverse direction. The homes are set back from the street — each frontage being the same width, with gardens in back. Yes, there were very few trees when the Saints entered the valley, but now..."

"Saints?" Mrs. Cumming asked.

"Mormons is the name other people give them — they call themselves 'Saints of the Latter-days."

"But, now most of the trees are ones they planted themselves — still spindly, but they're growing, some already 10 years old. Although hot and dry in the summer and very cold in the winter, And, the climate is probably more pleasant than in the East, not as humid as in the summer It's a clean, neat city, that reminds me of New England."

Mrs. Cumming seemed delighted as she cleaned up the table. Now the governor wanted his questions answered.

"You can read Buchanan's letters for yourself," Thomas said as he handed him the leather valise. Cumming took out a pair of small reading glasses and lit a candle.

"This is excellent," Cumming exclaimed, as he read the letters. "But, I wonder how Johnston will react to being asked to quarter away from the city. He will want to be in the city, close to conveniences."

"Governor, that is my mission — to keep the soldiers, the teamsters, their gambling, drinking and fighting out of the city and away from the young Mormon women. Johnston must understand that or Brigham will never let them march into the city. They must garrison themselves at least a day's ride away from Salt Lake City and about the same distance from Provo which is some 50 miles further south from Salt Lake"

"That's going to be a problem," the governor admitted.

"Then, we have work to do, you and me."

Cumming agreed. Then Thomas explained his strategy:

"Here's what I would suggest: that you and I travel into the city, meet with Brigham Young, get his agreement and allow you to assume your duties, and then 'persuade him' to accept the terms of the Army's presence in Utah and satisfy the Mormons as to its legitimate role in the territory and its limitations."

The governor scratched his head: "All fine and good. But, will Brigham accept those terms?"

"Oh, President Young will, I believe. He and I are of one mind on the subject. But, despite what the eastern newspapers claim, namely that he is a despot and that all the Mormons follow him no questions asked, that is not accurate. Brigham leads the 'peace faction' among his people, but many others don't trust any outsiders, regardless of how well meaning. These people have been persecuted and driven from place to place for nearly 20 years now that has led to the formation of a 'war faction' within their community that wants the Army to stay away and is willing to fight to make that happen. They are even suspicious of me, and I think the Army is determined to hang all of them, starting with Brigham Young, his counselors and the Twelve."

"The Twelve?"

"The Twelve Apostles. Their church is set up much like the primitive church of New Testament times, with prophets, apostles, and evangelists."

"I see," said Cumming. "And this 'war faction,' it's no doubt very leery of any kind of military action?"

"Absolutely, They believe the ridiculous notion that there are wagon loads of rope sitting by ready to be put to use," Thomas said.

Cumming shook his head: "It's not ridiculous. General Harney ordered several wagon loads of rope for the expedition, but I don't know how many are left since the Mormon raiders burned those wagon trains."

Mrs. Cumming had been pretending not to be listening to their conversation, but nevertheless couldn't help being caught up in it. And, since she had a few items to acquire from the local mercantile, she excused herself — it would give her the chance to help by doing a little "intelligence gathering."

"Alfred," she said as she tied on her cape, "I'm walking down to our sad excuse for a village — won't be long." He nodded and she left. Then Cumming turned back to his guest:

"So, Thomas, tell me what prompted you to make such a long circuitous journey? And why your interest in the Mormons?"

For the next hour, Thomas Kane reviewed his 10-year history with the Mormons, his trip to the Missouri in 1846, his meeting with Orson Pratt and the man praying in the woods and his brush with death in their camps and the blessing he received from Patriarch John Smith. He told Cumming of his meeting with President Polk, the creation of the Mormon Battallion and finally his own battle with his family, specifically, and his father's comparison of him to Don Quixote. But he explained that he had his aces in the hole with the letters he had received from the President of the United States. Cumming now knew the reason why Kane came to be in Wyoming, but not what Kane had in mind for him.

One thing was obvious — Governor Alfred Cumming and Thomas Kane were singing the same song; yes, they had to get Brigham Young to harmonize with them. But, first, Kane would have to work his magic in Wyoming. In the days ahead, the obstacles would be formidable — and they were all in uniform.

One of those obstacles in uniform had dismounted and found himself a seat on one of the logs surrounding the Cumming's fire pit. He tied his horse up to a rail outside the Cumming's compound and sat there whittling. And waiting. Thomas and the Cumming were still inside the governor's tent.

The whittler tried to listen to the conversation, but it was windy, too hard to hear anything. He muttered to himself: *"This is no job for a captain."* Captain Grover suspected that Johnston didn't like him and that this assignment was punishment for something, but what? He kept whittling. At times, he wished he had joined the Marcy expedition to New Mexico to resupply the Army and reconstitute its horses and mules; he could have volunteered, but the outcome was so uncertain. But now with the news of Medina's return two days earlier and his positive report, he wished he had just volunteered. Maybe that's why he was sitting on a log whittling outside's Cumming's tent, babysitting Thomas Kane. A half an hour later, Cumming and Kane exited the tent where Grover was waiting for them.

"Aren't you Captain Grover?" the governor asked him.

"I am, Governor."

"How can we help you?"

"Actually, I am here under orders from Colonel Johnston to make sure no harm comes to you, Colonel Kane," he said addressing Thomas. "There may be some people here who wish you harm."

Thomas attempted a smile: "Probably more than a few. I am leaving with the Governor. We are on our way to meet with Judge Eckels."

Grover stood up as if to block their way.

"We will keep an open mind, Captain," Thomas said. "Nobody even knows I'm here."

"Sir, everyone knows you are here and why you are here, to protect the Mormons, and they wouldn't need protection if they just followed the law," Grover said.

"Actually, Captain, you have that backwards. They are here because others did not follow the law, persecuted them and drove them from place to place. That wasn't their choice. Now if you'll excuse us, we have to go speak with Judge Eckels.

Cumming stepped around Kane and addressed the captain: "You should go tell the Colonel that we're fine, that Judge Eckels poses no risk to Mr. Kane."

They left Grover standing there, not sure where to go: *Should he follow Cumming and Kane or return and report?* Either way, Albert Sydney Johnston would not be happy.

ON THEIR WAY TO ECKELS' THRONE, Cumming and Kane had walked just a few hundred yards down a muddy path between what was once a pasture and corral. Inside the corral the surviving horses and mules were deposited along with a series of battle-worn tents, a three-walled firewood shed and a blacksmith shop.

"That's the prisoners' tent," the governor said, pointing to a muddy Sibley tent just beyond the blacksmith's.

"We should stop there when we're finished with the judge." Thomas made a mental note of it. He had promised Brigham Young that he would look in on the Mormons' sole prisoner-of -war, William Stowell. Minutes later, they had made their way through the mud to the Judge's tent and his sad "courthouse."

Judge Eckels read the letters from President Buchanan that Thomas gave him rather impassively, not giving any clue as to his real feelings. Cumming and Kane watched as the crafty old justice made notes in his journal, not sharing his views on any of the matters regarding the issues at hand. He had begun planning to indict scores of Mormon leaders and members from Brigham Young down to Stowell, the Mormon held in captivity. Ten minutes later, the judge announced his "verdict."

"I am satisfied. According to what is written here, we need to comply with President Buchanan's wishes, as vague as they are, and let Mr. Kane accompany you, Governor, to undertake a mis-sion to meet with Brigham Young and the Mormons so as to avoid any kind of armed conflict. What's your timetable?"

Cumming and Kane exchanged glances and then Thomas said,

"Given the snow drifts in the canyon and more than the 100 miles we need to cover, we will probably want to wait until after the first of April at least — two or three weeks, don't you think, Governor Cumming?"

Cumming nodded and then advised Eckels: "Judge, I think it advisable for you to discuss this matter with Colonel Johnston so there is no misunderstanding on his part. We need to be able to go and return unhindered."

"All right, then," Eckels said. "Let's talk before you leave."

Then, Kane had another question: "What about the other letter, the one instructing Johnston to garrison his troops far from the city?"

Eckels thought for a moment: "That appears to also be genuine, and I assume Johnston will comply."

Cumming stopped him: "Comply? Is there any question he wouldn't follow orders?"

Eckels was cagey: "You better ask him."

Cumming wasn't happy: "Since when do elected officials and their staff take orders from the Army? Who does Johnston think he is, Napoleon Bonaparte?"

Cumming had assumed that Eckels was on board, but was he? Elizabeth Cumming knew better. She always had her ear to the ground and held information close in an effort to protect her husband. She had her husband's back, and she trusted Kane, but certainly not Eckels nor Johnston. When the governor shared with her the conversation he and Thomas had held with the judge, she knew that she had to be Alfred's eyes and ears in the camp after he left to meet with Brigham Young. It was clear to her that in Albert Sydney Johnston's mind, no one would be going anywhere until he said so.

Colonel Johnston kept Grover waiting. The captain was standing outside the colonel's tent, picking gravel out of his horse's hoof — he noticed the mare had been favoring her right front leg.

Then the colonel left his lair.

"Where's the 'little prince,' Captain?"

"Little prince?"

"Kane. Where's Kane?"

Grover hesitated, "He and the Governor Cummming left to go speak with Justice Eckels."

Johnston drew nearer to his subordinate — they were eyeball to eyeball. The colonel wanted Grover to understand "to a T" what he wanted:

"Captain, I told you not to let him out of your sight — I need to know with whom he speaks, where he goes and what his plans are, do you understand?"

Grover nodded — he was irritated, but not as much as Albert Sydney Johnston, who continued: "Kane claims to have letters signed by President Buchanan with instructions for me and for you...for all of us. We have been freezing and starving here for reasons that are above my pay grade and yours. It is imperative that he stay safe — for now."

The captain grabbed the reins of his horse, put his foot in the stirrup and got in the saddle. But, before he rode away to find Kane and follow his orders, Johnston stopped him:

"Grover, tell him I want to sup with him tonight — invite him to dinner. It's not RSVP — it's mandatory, do you understand?"

"RSVP?"

"It's French — it means get him here by suppertime. And make notes of what he does in the meantime. Now carry on." They saluted and Grover trotted away.

His father had told him joining the Army was a mistake. *Fathers always know best*, the captain told himself.

THOMAS HAD A SIXTH SENSE ABOUT PEOPLE, and like Elizabeth Cumming, he felt that Judge Eckels had his own agenda. He and Cumming carefully stepped around the mud puddles and the road apples before they said anything more, no sense sharing with

Eckels their misgivings. so they waited until they were far enough away from his tent to talk. Eckels was no ally.

"I wonder what he means about Johnston not following orders," Kane said.

"Neither he nor Johnston want to leave the field until they have a coonskin nailed to the wall," Cumming said. Thomas looked a little puzzled. Cumming replied.

"Eckels is indicting Brigham and all the church leadership, along with our prisoner for treason, and he wants to leave here with a trophy. Same for Johnston. He wants a star on his lapel. You don't get brevetted in the field for sitting in camp all winter and freezing and doing nothing. And because they are all so angry for what they've suffered all winter at the Mormons' hands, they want vengeance."

That soon was evidenced in Thomas' direction when a stone came flying towards him. It missed, but the message was clear: Mormon lovers are not welcome here!

The little ramshackle warren of muddy tents and firewood sheds could shield dozens of stone throwers. The stares Kane saw directed at him were not friendly, that was for sure.

"The jail is up ahead," Cumming said. "Shall we meet the only Mormon for miles around?"

Kane smiled: "There are more around here than you can imagine." That aroused the governor's curiosity. The Sibley was to the right, below a cottonwood that was now leafing out after the long. hard winter. A guard sat on a stump outside the tent. He recognized the governor and stood up.

"Corporal. we've come to speak with the prisoner," Cumming said.

"Which one?" The corporal picked up his weapon and put it butt down but erect.

"Stowell," Kane said.

The corporal smiled: "He's the Mormon — he entertains folks at night! Go right in." They both ventured into the canvas prison.

"William Stowell?" Thomas said. Stowell looked up.

William was near the front where he had enough light to read his Bible, sitting cross-legged, but shackled. The tent smelled bad, so the governor suggested they step outside, walk and talk. He helped Stowell up and they stepped out.

"Corporal, we'll keep him close by — he can't really run far," Cumming said and the soldier returned to his stump.

"Want to read for awhile, Percy?" Thomas handed him his Bible.

"Thanks, Will," the corporal said.

Stowell was stiff and took a minute to balance himself.

"I'm Thomas Kane," Kane said and extended his hand. Stowell grabbed both of them. The governor put his hand on Stowell's shoulder. "How are you handling things, Lieutenant?" Stowell could only shuffle with his leg irons on, dragging mud as he moved slowly ahead.

"As good as can be expected," he replied.

"How's my family?"

"Brigham says they are doing fine," Kane answered. "They miss you and wonder when you'll return. We're leaving soon for the city — the governor will assume his position. Then, we'll return, and I will stop by in Ogden and tell them you're healthy. You are, right?"

"So far, and I'm not worried," Stowell answered. "You know, I was indicted for treason, along with Brigham Young and all the leaders. So was Major Taylor. Some of my 'keepers' tell me I'll be hanged, but I just laugh, because I saw myself in a dream riding down Echo Canyon after having been released, and I had that dream just days before I was captured. I just hope it's soon," William said.

"We're working on that. We're leaving soon to work it all out," Thomas assured him.

"I suppose you better deposit me back into my 'tent of wickedness' before someone gives Percy a few lashes," Stowell said as he stopped. "He's my guard and a friend."

"Tent of wickedness?" Thomas asked.

"It's in Psalms 84 — you should read it."

"Maybe I should — when I unpack my Bible," Thomas said.

Before they returned to the tent, Thomas filled Stowell in about news from Utah, his journey on the steamers, his overland trip through the winter storms and national news.

"Here's your Bible, Will," Percy said who handed the prisoner his Bible as he returned to his canvas dungeon.

"I have some questions."

William Stowell dragged his shackles into the tent and answered: "That's why I'm here," he said. "Come in later — we'll talk."

Alfred Cumming and Thomas Kane looked at each other.

"I like Stowell" Thomas said to Cumming as the prisoner disappeared inside the tent.

"Everybody does," the governor said.

"It would be nice to be liked — for a change," Thomas said as they walked back to the governor's tent compound and felt the cold stares of men in uniform boring holes into his back. The atmosphere in Eckelsville would soon be even more hostile.

27

NO SALT, NO THANKS!

Captain Grover was sitting on a log by Cumming's fire with an enlisted man, waiting for Kane to exit the tent. Grover knew he better do as Johnston had ordered this time, otherwise there would be even more onerous chores prepared for him.

Cumming and Kane both looked at Grover as if to say, "you still here?".

"Mr. Kane," Grover announced, "the colonel requests you to meet him for supper later this evening." His tone of voice set Thomas off, which surprised the governor:

"He does, does he?' Kane replied. "You arresting me? Putting shackles on me like you have on the Mormon prisoner?"

"Mr. Kane, I'm just inviting you for a discussion with the colonel for supper, that's all," Grover replied. Governor Cumming stepped in and handed the captain a note:

"Captain, this is a statement from Judge Eckels confirming that the letters Mr. Kane received from President Buchanan are legitimate and that we are to visit Salt Lake City. Our duty is to speak with Brigham Young and the other Mormon leaders to work out a peaceful arrangement. Would you be so kind as to deliver this to Colonel Johnston?"

"Governor, I am supposed to keep a perimeter of protection for you and Mr. Kane at all times, I believe that if I ..."

Kane interrupted him: "Captain, we're not going anywhere. I'm staying right here — we still have issues we need to discuss. You're free to return to spy on me when you're finished," Thomas said and walked into Cumming's tent.

"I'm not spying…" Grover said, but by then both men were back in Cumming's tent. The captain climbed up on his horse, hesitated, then turned to the private who was still at the fire: "Keep an eye on that damned Mormon!" Cumming and Kane heard the captain's orders just as they entered the tent, looked at each other — both were now agitated. Kane whispered to the governor: "I assume Grover thinks I'm a Mormon, they all do. I'm going to go speak with that arrogant colonel myself, face to face! Governor, do you have a pen and paper close at hand?"

Cumming nodded and complied with his request. Kane scribbled a note, telling Johnston *that the invitation is an indignity of the gravest order and I require an explanation and retraction,* folded it and walked out to the fire pit.

"Young man," he said to the private who was poking at the fire, "would you be so kind as to take this note back to the commanding officer, post haste?"

The enlisted man was puzzled: "Post haste?"

"Right now — I need to clear some things up with the commander. Will you do that?"

The private nodded. From then on, Colonel Albert Sydney Johnston and Colonel Thomas Leiper Kane would conduct their frosty business with each other using notes sent back and forth when a short horse ride would have been so much more convenient. And quicker.

IN PHILADELPHIA, BESS AND THE BABIES took a hansom to see her widowed mother-in-law. The fact that she had just received a letter from Thomas was good news — but the contents were troubling; she had to talk with someone, and besides, grandmothers like to see their grandchildren. Both of the women were lonely.

She knocked, then opened the door slightly: "Mother Kane, are you here?"

"Back in the kitchen, Elizabeth."

With Harriett by the hand and carrying little Elisha and his "luggage," she waddled in. Grandma rushed over and picked up her granddaughter, kissed her and then grabbed the baby.

"I have a letter from the West. Thomas is safe, cold and hungry, but safe!"

"Praise God," exclaimed Jane Leiper Kane, Thomas' mother, As they shared some tea, Bess took out the letter.

"Read it for me, please. My reading glasses are upstairs," Mother Kane said and then Elizabeth began:

"It's still cold here, windy and not much to eat, but I still have my own supplies, and the Army's commissary is a sorry place, but the governor and I will be leaving for Salt Lake City soon.

"I can only report so far disappointment, wifie, except in having saved our troops, which perhaps I ought not to have done, when I think of the heavy odds against the Mormons, and the fierce spirit of this party longing to assail them.

"I have tested my prowess enough to be sure what is in my blood; and when I come home to hide my head in our beloved obscurity — I will not be a humble one, except in the sense in which you yourself have prayed for me to bow it."

Mother Kane asked her daughter-in-law, "Do you think the Lord is guiding his steps, and to what end?"

"I'm not sure he knows, except that he is the only one willing to risk it all for the Mormons and the soldiers."

"Do you believe he will return safely?"

Elizabeth smiled: "He says the Mormon's patriarch said he would, and if he believes it, that's good enough for me."

"Faith is always the first miracle," Mother Kane said.

"I better change the baby." There's nothing like babies to give grandmothers purpose. Faith, hope and charity. As Paul wrote to the Corinthians, Elizabeth prayed that charity might also touch the hearts of those so far away who would do Thomas harm.

THE DAY AFTER THOMAS' DRAMATIC ARRIVAL, COLONEL JOHNSTON and his officers were occupied with a visitor. Captain Grover who had been posted outside Cumming's compound, was gone. Governor Cumming was curious, and he asked the enlisted man who was still guarding them where Grover was.

"The colonel and the other officers are meeting with a visitor; the mule skinner Medina has returned — mules are coming!"

So now Cumming's suspicions were confirmed; he and Thomas had heard rumors about Marcy's expedition. The guide Mariano Medina had arrived a couple of days earlier, but due to his condition he first needed to rest and recuperate.

After his return from Fort Massachusetts in Taos, New Mexico, he gave Johnston the best news he had heard in a year. The Army would not be marooned for long!

When they heard the news, Johnston and his officers were speechless, especially when they caught a glimpse of Medina after he arrived. They all stared at him for at least a minute before anyone said anything. He was a small man to begin with — now his tattered clothes hung on him. He was a pitiful sight.

"What about casualties," Captain Phelps asked.

"Just one, a Sergeant Morton, Englishman," Medina answered.

"How did he die?"

Medina turned to Phelps and snapped: *"How didn't we all die?* When we arrived at the fort, the soldiers thought we were ghosts, the walking dead they called us. We were wearing rags, Marcy must have lost 50 pounds. In some places, the snow was four or five feet deep. We were lucky we found the pass, otherwise none of us would have made it."

Johnston then asked the question they all wanted answered: "So, when do you think Marcy's party and the mules will arrive?"

"Now that there's enough feed on the trail, probably early in July. To survive, we ate all but 18 of the mules on our way down the Divide. We left the surviving animals there. I think Marcy and the men are driving 1200 to 1500 mules with them. Help IS coming. We need to be patient."

"The Mormons will pay for what they did," Major Porter vowed. "Once we have our animals, we'll rain hellfire on them."

Captain St. George Cooke corrected him: "All the Mormons did was try to survive after being driven from state to state for the last 20 years. If you want to blame someone, blame the ones who always create catastrophes like this — the arrogant men in charge: the politicians. This was their blunder."

Johnston glared at Cooke, but he couldn't really argue with him. Military discipline was necessary to keep everyone marching in step. He would have to remind Cooke of that fact later.

ALBERT BROWNE, CORRESPONDENT FOR THE NEW YORK TRIBUNE heard through the grapevine at Camp Scott about the impending duel between Kane and Johnston. Over the course of a week, notes were passed back and forth while Kane remained in the camp, and the bad blood came to a boil. Kane even challenged the colonel to a duel, naming Cumming as his "second." Within days, Browne had sent the report straight away to his contact in Fort Leavenworth who then had it telegraphed to Mr. Horace Greeley himself at the *New York Tribune*. It was succinct. In Browne's words, *"an orderly was supposed to invite Kane to dinner — no slight compliment where rations were to tightly abridged — but instead defied orders and arrested Thomas Kane."* Within days, it was a sensational tidbit of yellow journalism that made it into the editorial rumor mill all over the East coast, and eventually got back to Johnston and Kane. Truth, as they say, was the victim.

Even Thomas Kane understood that not all publicity was good. Soon reports had filtered back to Camp Scott about the so-called duel, and he knew he better mend fences and try to speak with Johnston's adjutant, Major Fitz-John Porter.

A week later, Thomas rode into Camp Scott to meet with Major Porter after consuming a generous portion of humble pie.

"Thank you, Major, for meeting with me" Thomas said. They were at a mess tent next to the commissary. Porter's contempt for Kane was visible to bystanders, but Thomas didn't care — he knew why he was there.

"Major Porter, I am puzzled why the Army won't accept the supplies that Brigham Young and his people are offering — it's a gesture of good faith." Porter smirked: "Doesn't Brigham understand his precarious situation? We know that his 'peace offering' is just his way of trying to avoid the consequences of his rebellion. We will march into the city and the Mormons will submit to federal authority one way or the other."

Thomas sighed and put on a happy face: "Major, I don't think you appreciate Brigham Young's position. He wants a peaceful solution as soon as possible, but there's a significant portion of his people who don't trust you or the federal government — you forget that they have been driven from place to place for 20 years, and they have heard dozens of promises that weren't kept. Why should they trust you now? Believe me when I tell you that when and if the Army marches into Salt Lake City, the city will already be in ashes by their own hand. Unless Cumming and I can work out some kind of compromise, the Mormons are not going to stand for another attack on their homes, property, and lives. Otherwise, there will be no one there, and all of you," Thomas said, with a sweeping motion of his arm to indicate the camp and its occupants, "will have spent the winter here for nought. There will be no one to take command of, no one to order about and not one person left to hang."

Major Porter sat back, chewed on that for a minute, then he finally replied: "I'll speak with Johnston."

In response, Kane said "I will check with the courier and tell

him that you don't need the salt or supplies. He will see that the note is taken down to Salt Lake."

Thanks to the intercession from Governor Cumming and being aware of how a duel would mar his public reputation, Johnston replied with a note of conciliation to Kane expressing his regrets and admitting that his invitation had been "incorrectly communicated."

It was time to talk to the courier.

LEWIS ROBISON WAS MORE THAN KANE'S SECRET CONTACT. He was also the Nauvoo Legion's quartermaster and led the scouts who watched the perimeter outside the Army's territory. The last time Kane ventured out to relay a message to him, Johnston's men fired on Robison, creating an incident that stirred things up between Kane and the colonel.

Later that day, Kane slipped away to meet Lewis Robison, at their usual meeting place.

"Colonel Kane, I'm over here, behind the dead cottonwood," Robison yelled to Thomas. They met in a clearing of Gambel oak where Robison had a lean-to. "So, Colonel, what's the word?" Robison could see that Thomas was discouraged, but determined.

"Lewis, here's the note to pass on to Brigham. The Army doesn't want any help, no salt, no flour, nothing. They consider the Mormons their enemies…"

Robison stopped him. "Brigham and the leaders have already come to that conclusion; they've decided to move the people south."

"I was afraid of that, but I have a glimmer of hope. I believe Governor Cumming will come around to our way of thinking. Ask Brigham to send William Kimball to accompany Cumming and me down into the valley. I think I can persuade him to meet with President Young and help smooth the transition. Be calm, justice will be done in due time."

Robison thanked Thomas, and he left with Kane's note.

But, then as Kane was returning to Camp Scott, he fired one shot as per agreed upon, and more shots were fired back at him. He was shaken; Thomas' patience was being tested. The camp was in uproar after their near miss. The troops thought a battle had begun, and the shooter was worried about what the brass had in store for him, but Kane came to his rescue and gave the poor boy five dollars. After the smoke had settled, Gove told Fitz-John Porter about it. He laughed: *"He was really astonished…a more frightened individual I never saw."*

Major Porter sneered: "Such a pity they did not rid him of his life — it would have saved us from a fool continually troubling us."

KANE AND THE CUMMINGS WERE OUTSIDE THE COMPOUND. Thomas was ready to climb aboard Phoebe, his beloved mare; Abraham, the mule was ready to go. Thomas was grateful for the only two friends who were there to wish him well, Alfred and Elizabeth Cumming. He thought they were an odd couple — she barely came up to his chin, the one on the bottom, and she was incensed when she overheard the soldiers call him "the whiskey barrel."

Kane had Robison waiting for him who would take him to General William Kimball. He didn't want to give too much away, but Cumming needed to understand what Thomas was planning.

"I have people waiting for me," Thomas said to Cumming who was outside his command tent. He spoke quietly so that Johnston's enlisted man wouldn't hear.

But first, Governor, I have some paperwork to do. I am writing the president to tell him that I cannot advise the Mormons to allow the Army to march into the city given the Expedition's level of hostility — the Saints will most certainly abandon it before the troops march in."

Cumming frowned: "That concerns me, but I am also dubious that Johnston will pay much attention to what I say — if I felt I held any sway over the officers, I would try to convince the Mormons to stand down — but Brigham doesn't know, or trust me…"

"Yet…" Kane corrected him…"doesn't trust you yet, but that trust will come — I trust you."

Cumming smiled: "That's nice to hear for a change."

"It's not only the men in his command, but the bullwhackers and other camp followers that would cause so much trouble. Disorder would follow them everywhere."

"And then there's Young's peace offering of food and supplies," Cumming added.

"Right. Brigham Young will most certainly interpret Johnston's refusal to accept the gift as a humiliation and a grave mistake, even an instrument of prejudice — What's the phrase, a 'Declaration of War to the knife?' " Thomas said. "We certainly have our work cut out for us."

"You are right, Thomas," the governor said. "You haven't come this far to fail now."

"I don't plan to. William Kimball is waiting for me at the mouth of the canyon. I'll be back soon enough and then we can depart together,. but he and I will need to work out the details. Consider me to be your 'John the Baptist' announcing your imminent arrival," Thomas said.

"I'm no one's Savior, that's for sure. But, between you and me, I believe my most important role is to keep the barbarians outside the gate," Cumming said.

"Mine, too," Thomas replied, then added: "I will see you later, Governor."

Elizabeth Cumming nothing, just walked over to Thomas and grabbed his hand, wiped her eyes and hurried into the tent. She had Alfred's breakfast to prepare.

Thomas got on Phoebe, tied on Abraham and left.

Always planning for any contingency, Kane stopped by the camp's post office and left a long letter addressed to President

James Buchanan, Washington D.C., in the postal bag. Its contents weighed on his mind.

In it, Thomas shared with Buchanan that he found the state of affairs at Camp Scott even less favorable than he had feared and promised *"to serve you [best] by putting myself in the witness box."*

He described the camp to be *"a mixed society of about 2,000 womanless men — soldiers, officers, teamsters and camp followers (gamblers etc. and professional anti-Mormons)...who had been compelled to halt within less than the distance between Philadelphia and Washington from the little capital where they had promised themselves a 'Capua' of enjoyment and luxury and compelled [instead] to pass an entire winter in extreme discomfort and a state of idleness and inactivity itself sufficiently shocking to contemplate."*

For pages, Kane described the condition and attitude of the men imprisoned in their own camp, sequestered from the outside world and seething in resentment. Then he wrote, *"it was the eye mark of the world and must therefore consent to settle the Utah question for the world, and then, given the mindset of the Utah Expedition and its leaders...[and] I dare not take upon myself the responsibility of advising the Mormons — as I did a fortnight ago — to admit this Army and its followers within their valley."*

In five minutes, he was outside the perimeter of the campsite where Lewis Robison was waiting for him.

"Thomas, you made it! So far, so good. Is the governor really on our side," Lewis asked.

"I believe so, and so is his wife, which is always good,' Thomas replied. "Seen any sign of Kimball yet?"

"Let's ride and see. The weather may be a problem."

Hours later, Robison was proven right.

"There's a protected spot up ahead," Robison yelled. "Let's

overnight there!" Twenty minutes later, Thomas was wrapped up in a large piece of canvas and a wool blanket. They spent the night and woke up in the morning covered in snow.

They were back on their horses right after dawn, tromping through newly fallen powder. But, the skies were now clear, and after some small talk, Kane was concerned:

"I was told that General William Kimball would meet me further down the canyon. How much farther?"

The answer came almost immediately. A shot rang out ahead. Kane answered with one of his own, then three riders emerged from a copse of Gambel oak. Behind them was Thomas Kane's old friend, General William Kimball.

Minutes later, Kane and Kimball got down to business: how to plan Governor Alfred Cumming's safe arrival into Salt Lake City.

Lewis Robison was happy to take on his new role as "postmaster" and return to his family.

Kane handed him a large canvas bag: "Inside are letters to be forwarded onto California," Thomas said. Then he handed him the letter for President Young. "And, this one is to be delivered directly to Brigham Young. He's expecting it. And, thank you, Lewis, for protecting me and getting me this far."

Lewis revealed his emotions: "No, we thank you…all of us do, don't we, General?"

"Indeed we do. Let's feed you something, Brother Kane, then let's figure this out." Kimball and Kane retired to a campsite and sat by the fire. Lewis Robison left. He had mail to deliver.

DOWN IN THE CITY, BRIGHAM YOUNG AND THE LEADERSHIP waited for Thomas Kane's report from Camp Scott. George Watt brought it into the meeting:

"Well, George, what's the verdict?" Brigham asked.

"Why don't you read it for all of us?

Brigham put on his reading glasses, took a moment, frowned,

and then summarized it: "The note from Thomas says Johnston would rather 'starve like a beggar than take supplies from their enemies' — us." One of the members of the council spoke up: "President, perhaps we may have to abandon the city and prepare to send it up in smoke, or at least give that impression. There's a lot of blood lust up there, I fear."

"The fact that we burned the grass and destroyed their wagons and pushed them into a corner made them stick their heels in," somebody else said. The prophet agreed with both statements. But, then he reminded everybody what was common knowledge among the Mormons but never occurred to the Eastern press:

"The editors forget that we were pushed into these mountains while we had to bury our dead by the hundreds on our way here. And, if we had done nothing to defend ourselves, old Harney or his successor, the blood-thirsty Colonel Johnston, would have all of us hanging from trees by now," Brigham said and continued:

"We need to give our friend Thomas Kane time— I have faith in him and faith in the Lord. However, I agree: We should prepare for the worst and make plans now to abandon the city when we hear the Army is marching this way. Let's pray that we will soon see Brother Kane and the Governor Cumming emerging from Emigration Canyon."

28

STILL A JOURNEY AHEAD

After his second night sleeping under a quilt of snow, Thomas Kane awoke with a start. In this part of the country, calendars had very little sway over the weather. It was the 25th of March — just a couple of days after the first day of spring — but at over 7,300 feet, spring came when it was darned good and ready. It wasn't ready. Once Kane was alert enough to carry on a conversation, he saw that General William Kimball had a nice fire going. Kane put on his boots and joined him at the fire. Kimball had been waiting for him and gave Thomas a letter.

"It's from the president — there have been developments," Kimball said.

Thomas sat a little closer to the fire, both to read and to warm himself. He looked over his shoulder and saw that his animals had their feed bags on.

Then, he saw the bad news:

"So, it's true — Brigham is really evacuating the valley."

Kimball nodded: "Everyone from settlements from Salt Lake Valley north is being relocated. For those who have their own teams and wagons, they're loading up as much as they can — even lumber, nails and other building materials they might need to reconstruct their lives farther south. After all, wherever you are, you need a privy!"

Thomas was shaken, and Kimball and the others saw it.

"I had hoped that Brigham would wait until Governor Cumming arrived. He's following me down, just waiting for the snow to melt."

Thomas continued: "I sense he's on our side — he and Johnston do not see eye to eye. I am certain of that,"

He read one paragraph out loud: *"What do you think of the policy? Which is the better, the plan or fighting? And will our enemies keep off and let us alone while we are removing, or are they so bloodthirsty that they will not be satisfied short of doing their utmost to destroy our lives?"*

This news weighed heavily on Kane. Cumming's arrival in the Valley could change everything, but it sounded like Brigham and the others weren't willing to place all their faith in one gentile outsider from Georgia, whom they knew nothing about. Thomas was beginning to realize that he and Cumming's plans might need to change.

"I was planning to come with you General Kimball and prepare the way for Governor Cumming, but I need to return to Camp Scott and persuade him to get to Salt Lake as soon as possible, not wait for the snow to melt, but to leave now," Thomas admitted.

Kane read the balance of the letter to himself, and in response to one question regarding William Stowell, he said:

"Tell the president that the governor and I met with Stowell before we left, and believe it or not, he is in good spirits and has impressed his captors with lively stories and entertaining wit, but we need to see him set free," Kane said and then continued, "General, my work is not done here — my letters from President Buchanan are explicit — Colonel Johnston has read the one that was just for him: It calls for the Army to pass through the city and garrison itself at least a day's ride away from Salt Lake or Provo or any other settlement. Brigham's comment that he fears Johnston will post himself in the city to act as a posse will only be realized if Governor Cumming and I fail. I can assure that the governor is committed to keep the military where it belongs: under the direction of elected officials and its representatives." Kimball listened and then replied: "It's not that we don't trust you Thomas, it's that we don't know Cumming and don't know if he can control the horde marching on us. Brigham Young and the leaders don't want to take that chance. Neither do I nor my family."

They spent much of the rest of the day dodging snow drifts and fallen rocks as they approached the entrance to Echo Canyon. Night was beginning to settle on the group and Kane needed to retire. He wanted to mull over these new developments and discuss them further with General Kimball the next day.

THE NEXT MORNING COLONEL THOMAS KANE, GENERAL KIMBALL and his Mormon posse woke up to sunshine, and as they entered Echo Canyon, spring took over from winter. The lower the elevation and the further they rode, the more civilized their surroundings appeared. Kane's animals seemed rejuvenated, but he was not. Brigham Young's letter had been weighing on him. He caught up to Kimball.

"Can we put a little distance between ourselves and the rest of the men?"

"Of course, what's on your mind?"

"The new governor — we need to give him a chance: He's the key to a peaceful solution to all of this," Thomas said.

"Maybe so, but that won't stop the Saints from moving south," Kimball replied.

The trail had turned into a road, still rutted and a little muddy in places, but the scenery was impressive. They were now coming into Echo Canyon with its grassy environs, Gambling oak brush and quaking aspens beginning to bud. The crimson cliffs overlooking them gave a traveler a sense of security and protection. Then General Kimball looked up and exclaimed:

"I never get tired of the 'mighty fortress' protecting us. We were not just driven here to some wasteland — this is more picturesque and magnificent than Missouri, Kansas and Illinois put together! God reserved this place for us, and I'm willing to fight for it."

Thomas leaned over so he and Kimball were eyeball to eyeball: "You won't have to fight for it. We'll win without spilling blood — there will be compromises, I'm sure. Yes, Judge Eckels muddied the water with his asinine indictments of Brigham young, the Quorum of the Twelve and even William Stowell — now he's trying to prosecute the Mormons for polygamy, but that's a local institution. That beloved Democrat party watchword — *popular sovereignty* — makes his point moot. Plus, the slave-holders in the South don't want to kick over that lantern. There's no federal law prohibiting that," Thomas said.

"Not yet anyway," Kimball replied.

"True," Thomas agreed. "Besides, they don't really care about polygamy. They care about this," he said making a sweeping motion.

"This?"

"They want the gold that's in these hills, and they don't want anybody stopping them from turning this beautiful place into ugly mining towns and all that goes with it," Thomas said.

"That's their 'Manifest Destiny' they're always crowing about."

Kimball was stunned by the remark and then he added: "And, we all know what those 'good Christians' like to do with all their 'surplus women' and the 'gentlemen's clubs' they occupy."

They were now far ahead of the men and their wagons. Kane and Kimball stopped at a stream feeding into the Bear River. "Let's stop here and fill our canteens," Thomas said.

The animals refreshed themselves and partook of the new spring grass. The two men found a ledge to rest and continue their conversation.

"May I put a couple of questions to you, General?"

"Certainly," Kimball answered.

Thomas leaned back and looked around. A mountain jay flew by and found a perch to listen in. A hawk circled way overhead checking out the landscape for a clueless chipmunk.

"General Kimball, how old were you when we first met on the Missouri?"

"I was 20, was married just the year before in Nauvoo before we were chased out, and then they burned the temple."

"I thought you were younger than that. So, I'm just four years older than you. So, here's my first question: Don't you think it's important to gain some time?"

"Gain time?"

"Yes, is there anything to be lost, any position to be waived, by admitting Cumming and recognizing him as the official territorial governor?"

"Well, as you know, President Young, rather Governor Young, in this case, has told the militia to arrest him if he set foot in the territory," Kimball replied. "But..."

"But what?"

"That was before...all this," the general admitted.

"Exactly," Thomas countered. "Consider the key role that Cumming could play in establishing peace. If the Saints accepted and recognized him without any insult or indignity and without doing so at the point of a bayonet, but rather welcomed him and gave him the respect due a man of his stature, what reason would the Army have to be a 'posse'? There would be no rebellion and certainly no cause for Colonel Johnston to establish a military dictatorship, would there?"

Kimball smiled: "Certainly not — no rational reason, assuming you can reason with Johnston."

Kane summarized his argument: "The Mormons could choose war, burn their cities, give up everything they've built over the past 11 years and be refugees again, or they could welcome Cumming, show him respect and choose peace. Is this too difficult for even the likes of George A. Smith?"

"No."

"Well, that's what I'm fighting for, and why I've come so far. Can you help me convince Brigham to accept Cumming and choose peace, and can you make sure he is safely escorted into the city?"

"Yes. I better hurry, then, don't you think?" Kimball asked.

They refreshed themselves in the stream and as agreed, Thomas would return to Camp Scott to retrieve the new governor and Kimball would hurry back to prepare for Cumming's arrival.

WHEN THOMAS RODE BACK INTO CAMP a few days later, the only people who seemed happy to see him were Cumming and his wife, Elizabeth. "What is he doing here?" several infantrymen and officers complained. But, the officers at Camp Scott, on the other hand, were all hot and bothered that Kane and Cumming were planning a trip to Salt Lake without a military escort. Where's the glory in that?

Captain Jesse A. Gove questioned why Thomas Kane would be so naive as to defend the Mormons in the first place, claiming that *"murders are as common among them, to all those who do not bow to Mormondom as the sun rises."* The day before Cumming left, the officers were conferring in Johnston's command tent.

Johnston spoke up: "Governor Cumming assured me that Brigham Young wishes for peace, and that he finds it difficult to rule his people, that the people were expecting him and that he had nothing to fear from them."

"But, I opposed it," Johnston added, telling him that unless he had some invitation or impression from them that his presence was desired, that he shouldn't go."

Jesse Gove snorted in disbelief, saying Cumming was acting childish: "If Governor Cumming has been so far fooled by this nincompoop of a Mr. Colonel Kane, he is a bigger fool than I thought him to be." Johnston's adjutant, Fitz-John Porter, was even more skeptical that Cumming's mission would amount to anything and heaped criticism on Kane:

"This whole notion of a division in Mormondom is a fabrication created by the little colonel. He is hiding his game — Cumming is in no danger by going there. It's all theater. The Mormons may even be playing the part of being at odds with Brigham to gain sympathy and to hoodwink us."

Then a lieutenant asked: "Well then shouldn't we worry about Governor Cumming's safety?"

"No, we don't," Gove snapped: "Lieutenant, we have enough to do just by worrying about our own safety." Johnston's officers continued their complaining and listing of grievances as if that could change anything. They were still miserable, and the return of Thomas Kane to gloat over his meeting with General Kimball was even more intolerable. When the military learned that the Saints were moving south and abandoning the city, and worse, preparing to burn it to the ground if Johnston tried to stay there, it drove them mad. There was no upside for them.

AS THE GOVERNOR PREPARED FOR HIS JOURNEY south in one tent, assuring his wife that all would be well, Thomas was in an adjoining tent writing letters, one to President Buchanan and a letter to his wife and his brother Patrick. One common trait of the Kane family was their shameless proclivity for self-promotion. When Thomas Kane wrote a letter, his audience was much larger than just Elizabeth, his wife, or Patrick. He hoped — no he planned — that what he wrote would be widely distributed in the hungry eastern press. And, before he left, he made sure that he took the opportunity to have a "one-on-one" with Greeley's correspondents, especially Albert G. Browne Jr., and the stringer for the New York Times. *What would it hurt?*

Thomas was using paper and ink as fast as he could, worrying he would run out before he left, when Elizabeth Cumming poked her head inside the tent:

"Thomas, am I bothering you?"

"Heavens no, Mrs. Cumming. I think we're all in this together," he replied.

"I know, I know, and I'm worried." He put his pen down and listened, motioning her to take seat on a stool. She looked behind her out the tent flap to see if there was anyone listening, then continued: "This is not a safe place. The things I hear!"

"I know. What have you heard?"

"Backbiting, defaming and not just directed at the Mormons. Some woman, an officer's wife — I don't know her name — accused Alfred of making a 'dishonorable compromise with Brigham Young' and that Alfred was foolishly marching into imprisonment in Utah.' And, they've said some unflattering things about you, too. But, it's what people *don't* say that worries me — the looks I get, the murderous looks." Then, her emotions got the best of her: "Please get my husband unharmed to Utah and bring him back safe and sound to me. He's a good man with a good heart!"

Thomas walked over to the door flap and looked out — he also wanted to make sure they were alone.

"Mrs. Cumming …"

"You may call me Elizabeth…"

"Did you know that my wife's name is also Elizabeth? It's a wonderful name for a loyal woman of character, and Elizabeth…"

"Yes?"

"I should have never made it here. I have nearly died of seasickness, been almost frozen in blizzards, nearly shot by sentries and fallen sick to all kinds of diseases. I barely weigh 100 pounds. I'm no larger than a child. But, even though I'm no religious man — I don't study the Bible nor go to church very often, but, I can't deny that I have been protected, watched over. I was nursed back to health in the Mormon camps on the Missouri River some 12 years ago and given a blessing by their patriarch. It's worked so far. I will keep your husband close by," Thomas promised Elizabeth Cumming.

"And, if I indeed have some kind of divine umbrella protecting me, I promise I'll do my best to see it covers him as well."

She stood up and took Thomas' hand in both of hers and said simply, "Thank you. That satisfies me." Then she left to help Alfred pack for his trip.

And, Thomas returned to his mission: writing letters that would change the outcome of the so-called "Utah War."

He wanted President Buchanan — and his reading public — to know of the bellicose attitude of Johnston and his troops. They indeed want to "hang a coonskin trophy on the wall." Johnston and his officers knew that they wouldn't earn more stars or bars simply by sitting in their tents all winter.

He compared Cumming's bravery and manly character to forge ahead amidst threats and dangers to the Army's "bragging, parading, bugle playing and musket-firing of bravos by profession by whom he is surrounded."

Thomas finally finished his communications, put stamps on the envelopes and tried to slip by onlookers to take them to the camp's postmaster. On his way back, he inquired as to the "press room" of Horace Greeley's chief correspondent Albert G. Browne, Jr., the man Jim Bridger dubbed "Doc."

"Try the commissary," the private said. Since it wasn't mealtime — there wasn't much on the menu, anyway — he hoped there wouldn't be a crowd, just a few of the lower ranking soldiers condemned to "KP." Then, he thought: *Is there a gift I could take 'Herr Doktor Professor Browne' to soften him up? Hmmm.* Thomas knew that the governor had brought with him an ample liquor cabinet.

He did what publicists have been doing for journalists ever since Gutenberg's invention and that was to ply them with liquor. *Don't politicians do that all the time? Or is it the other way around?* Thomas wondered.

A half an hour later, he left the governor's tent with a bottle from Cumming's collection disguised in a nondescript container to find the correspondent. Browne was talking to a young officer, so Kane waited, and then when Browne was alone, he took a seat at the other end of the table and started reading a newspaper, a copy of the *New York Tribune*. Five minutes later, Browne couldn't take it any longer and walked over and introduced himself.

Kane and Browne had a lot in common, and Thomas Kane knew it. Both came from money. Both knew people in high places. Both dressed better than all the other common folks around them. And both had studied and lived in Europe. Why hadn't Kane made the connection before now, he wondered? He hadn't had the opportunity, and frankly, why deal with a lowly correspondent when Kane dealt directly with the editors? But, this lonely, well-educated young man had no peers among the rank and file members of the Utah Expedition. He needed a friend.

And a bottle of cognac.

And, Thomas Kane? He needed readers around the country to know who the good guys and bad guys were in this cold war in Utah. He changed seats to one closer to Browne, who took notice of him. Then Browne moved towards Thomas.

"Are you Thomas Kane?"

"Yes, I've seen you in passing. You're Doctor Browne. You making a house call?"

Browne smiled. "Not exactly. Do you see a house?"

Thomas laughed. "Not for a long time now, but I'm going to sleep in one soon."

"So, it's true. So, are you and the governor on your way to see old Brigham and his wives."

"He's not that old — maybe you should meet him sometime," Thomas said, ignoring Browne's snide comment.

"That would be interesting, but aren't you worried about the governor's safety, or yours?"

Thomas leaned in closer to him: "The only danger we're facing is right here, given the hostility from Colonel Johnston, his officers and men."

"From what I hear, the real danger is the Mormons," Browne said.

"As a journalist, Mr. Browne, you should check your sources. If all goes well, sometime soon, you'll have the opportunity to ride into the Valley of the Great Salt Lake and see for yourself, and I guarantee you'll like what you see. I got a first-hand look at the Mormons some 12 years ago when they were refugees — some 20,000 of them then — camped along the Missouri River.

"I discovered a people who were willing to sacrifice for what they believed in and help others often at a great cost to themselves. They have been misrepresented in the press. You can help correct that misrepresentation. If you have the chance to meet Brigham Young, you'll make acquaintance with a man with a soft heart and hard hands. It's a unique combination."

Thomas then reached for the gift he had brought with him and handed it to Browne: "Since you've suffered along with the soldiers up here, thanks to my Mormon friends, here's something for you to salve your wounds. Let's talk later — there's more to share."

Kane handed him his "truth serum" and left.

Browne watched Thomas walk away, sat there a bit puzzled, looked inside the bag and then smiled, telling himself that he could still be impartial, but at the same time, enjoy some long overdue liquid refreshment.

29

PEACE HAS ITS PRICE

It was April 2nd, and it was snowing. Governor Cumming looked at Thomas Kane and frowned: "So the Mormons call this the promised land, and it snows in April!"

Thomas laughed: "That's a question for you to ask of Brigham Young. Maybe it only snows on us."

After leaving Camp Scott some four days earlier, Kane believed they were still a day away from Echo Canyon where Thomas had hoped once again to meet their Mormon guides.

Then, he corrected what he had said earlier about their whereabouts: "Governor, I believe we're still actually in Wyoming, still technically Utah Territory, but not quite the Promised Land. It's right around the corner," he smiled.

Cumming laughed: "That's good. Because as governor, I want to designate myself what's promised land and what isn't!" So far, the two were enjoying themselves. A few snowflakes couldn't ruin the trip. Encountering snowdrifts was still possible — and they did worry Kane, but so far so good.

Later that evening, that ended. A new crop of snowdrifts had taken the fun completely out of their road trip. Deep snow had forced Kane and Cumming to leave the servants with the buggy and the cargo wagon and go ahead on horseback with Thomas' mule in tow. They were making better time than the servants with the heavy load, but by nightfall they regretted it. By the next morning, the wagon and the governor's servants, his driver and his cook, were reunited, even though were still moving slowly.

Crossing a creek, the carriage got stuck and in the attempt,

Thomas fell in and Cumming laughed: "You can't deny it any longer, Thomas, you've been baptized, as I am your witness! Your friend Brigham will be happy to hear that."

By nightfall, however, their fortunes were reversed. As the carriage and riders approached the beginning of Echo Canyon, they were welcomed by General William Kimball, the legendary Porter Rockwell and Howard Egan.

"Governor Cumming, it is my pleasure to welcome you," said General Kimball.I hope you and Brother Kane have worked up an appetite. May I introduce you to O.P. Rockwell and Howard Egan?

Each man took the opportunity to shake the governor's hand. The group then moved very slowly down the wagon road and soon cliff tops illuminated by campfires came into view. Cumming would later report to Elizabeth that "the works were brilliantly lighted by bonfires and much parade." Mounted Nauvoo Legionnaires led them to a reception where tables were spread around a bonfire, and one of Salt Lake City's premier chefs had prepared a banquet for them.

General Kimball then introduced Alfred Cumming to the two dozen or so guests who had enjoyed the meal with him:

"Welcome, Governor! We wish you the best in your new assignment and believe your presence here will settle any misunderstandings that the American people and President Buchanan's administration may have had about our community. If you would like to say a few words, we would welcome that."

Alfred Cumming, being a politician and a master of prose, did his best to pacify his audience and reassure them of his peaceful intentions. His words were received with applause and hurrahs. He then repeated this up and down the canyon to assemblages of Saints eager to hear from their new governor, but who was not aware that the very same group of lively listeners had moved along with him. It was a Potemkin-like parade created for Cumming's benefit.

The next day, as Cumming's party cameto the end of Echo Canyon, they were met by a merchant, Abel Gilbert, who had spent some time with Brigham Young on his way from California to Missouri. He also shared some chilling details about passing through Mountain Meadows with Cumming and Kane.

Several days later, Gilbert told Johnston and Eckels of Cumming's acceptance by the Mormons and of the Saints' exodus from the Salt Lake Valley.

That news spread east...news that did not set well with Colonel Albert Sydney Johnson.

The night before Kane and Cumming rode into the valley, Thomas and the governor were sitting around a bonfire at the top of Emigration Canyon. After nearly a week fighting snowdrifts and getting baptized in mountain streams, Thomas penned a few words in his journal: Cumming looked over his shoulder to read his scribbling: *"Hope, Adventure, Mountain Air, a Good Horse and Liberty! What Fun! So Near Happiness!"*

"Sorry if I was peeking," said Cumming, "but those are my thoughts exactly. I am sending Johnston a letter about our recep-tion, once I see that Brigham Young is as welcoming as the people in the canyon. For the first time, I am genuinely optimistic about our chances for peace."

Kane closed his journal and smiled. "I am, too." But, in the days to come, Thomas Kane would not only worry about how well Johnston and his horde would accept peace when they thirsted for war, but also how the Mormons would accept Cumming as their governor, because at that very moment they forming a 20-mile long wagon train to leave Salt Lake Valley, heading south, taking everything they could put intheir wagons.

DESPITE THE EXODUS, THE WELCOME WAGON WAS ROLLED OUT for Governor Cumming. The entertainers who had stage-managed the extravaganza and had illuminated Echo Canyon left ahead of

Kane, Cumming and his aides to set up another cliff-top celebration. After crossing the Bear River and exiting Echo Canyon, Cumming's entourage faced Big Mountain and snaked through the narrow road that eventually turned right into Emigration Canyon. After they passed the hamlet settled by the Henefer brothers, Cumming was able to see the layers of peaks and valleys laid out before them, much greener and spectacular than what they had seen earlier.

"This doesn't look like a desert to me," the new governor exulted. "What a magnificent sight!" Later, as they finally emerged from Emigration Canyon, they stopped to view the scenery of the Salt Lake Valley laid out before them.

"Neat as a pin," Cumming exclaimed as he took in the view of the valley.

But as they descended closer to the city, they saw that the streets were filled with wagons filled to overflowing with children and household goods with animals following in their wake.

Cumming was astonished: "They really are leaving!"

Kane nodded: "Unfortunately, Governor, yes. It was not empty talk. If the Army were to march into the valley, and afterwards Johnston decided to gather up the leaders and hang a few, then there would be bloodshed. They don't trust that the government will keep its word, not after Ohio, Missouri and Illinois. I suppose you and I have to earn that trust, and I'll help you. They certainly don't trust Albert Sydney Johnston, and after all the bad blood we both witnessed at Camp Scott, neither do I."

"Between you and me, Thomas, I'm of the same mind."

At the top of a hill overlooking the city, they stretched their legs before Major Egan and his staff bid them farewell. Cumming thanked him for delivering them safely into the city, and as he was saying good-bye, Egan could see how upset he was.

"What's wrong, Governor?"

"Major Egan, it appears to me that this exodus is madness, unnecessary. Tell President Young that the people won't be hurt — I wouldn't countenance such a thing: I will not be governor if the people don't want me. Tell him that, please!" Egan nodded, shaking Cumming's hand, and mounted his horse to ride down into the valley to relay the message to Brigham Young. Kane and Cumming's group then began their decent into the city where they were paraded through the streets on their way to the Staines mansion.

That night, for the first time in a long time, they would sleep indoors, get a hot meal, a hot bath, and all the luxuries the 19th-century could offer. Kane was delighted — so far, so good, but Cumming was stunned. Now what?

BRIGHAM YOUNG, GEORGE A. SMITH, WILFORD WOODRUFF and other leaders, including General Daniel Wells were meeting in the Lion House in Salt Lake about moving more than 30,000 people out of northern Utah south to Provo and beyond. The tension in the room was thick.

Then Brigham Young's stenographer, GeorgeWatt, rushed in, interrupting the meeting:

"President, excuse me, but Major Howard Egan is here:"

"Show him in, George," Brigham said. And then Watt added:

"And Kane and Cumming are already at the Staines mansion."

"Thank you, Brother Watt," the president said.

No one said anything for a moment. No one needed to remind his brothers that the Lord once told the early apostles, "if ye are not one, ye are not mine."

So, Brigham Young reminded them: "Thomas Kane has come here at his own peril and expense to prevent bloodshed, to be a peacemaker."Someone else posed a question:

"What about this so-called Governor Cumming. We already have a governor…a governor we can trust."

Brigham laughed: "I don't recall being called to be the Utah

Territorial Governor by the Lord — that was just the President of the United States who gave me that responsibility. My calling to be your prophet wasn't from a man."

"Fight or flight is not a good option," another member offered.

"Neither is surrender or die," said another.

Wilford Woodruff still was skeptical of anyone sent from Washington. He was counting on someone of a much higher stature to visit the Saints and save them — but when would He make His appearance? Woodruff's view of the United States government had already been expressed, but this moment seemed apropos to repeat it again:

"I have always believed that the United States — in a national capacity and under the form of law — seeks to destroy the Church and the Kingdom of God from off the earth...Whenever the rulers of any nation trample their own constitution and laws underfoot and oppress and destroy the weak because they have the power, and the people love to have it so, they sow the seeds of their own disillusion, and they will reap their own destruction."

Brigham then spoke: "Thank you, Wilford. But, in regards to Cumming, maybe we should meet the man before we judge him. Thomas says he is "our fish to cook.'"

That comment added a little levity, but it was gallows humor.

"Brother George Smith and I will pay him a visit in the next day or so. I'll send for Thomas and have him arrange things," Brigham concluded.

Someone else asked: "But, can we trust Kane?" Brigham tried not to take offense at that remark after all his friend had done for the Saints, and replied: "There's no one else here now is there?"

The topic then reverted back to their original topic, moving 30,000 people 50 miles or more as soon as feasible. They had an army on their doorstep that had spent a winter of discontent thanks to them, and now the Utah Expedition had their mules.

WHILE KANE WAS FEELING A SENSE OF SELF-SATISFACTION about Cumming's arrival and how he had been received in Utah so far, other events were unfolding in Washington D.C. about which he knew nothing and which neither he nor anyone else, anywhere, could do anything about.

In fact, only the Old Public Functionary was aware of what was happening because he was the only one "functioning" in these matters — not even Van Dyke — except for the First Lady, his lovely niece, Harriett Lane. Harriett was engrossed in putting the finishing touches on her spring ball, she had the invitation list all ready but "Unch" had to first sign off on it. She knocked on his office door.

"It's just me, Uncle James," she said.

"Come in, but close the door," Buchanan said. It was Saturday, even though only a few servants were in the White House. Van Dyke was out of town, and Old Buck didn't trust too many other people, but he did trust her.

"I have the invitation list, and I hoped…" Harriett began, but the president waved her off.

"Never mind about that — invite whom you will. I have another matter I wanted to pass by you."

"What other matter?" Harriett was puzzled, but Buchanan motioned her to sit.

"Utah and this 'Mormon thing.'"

Harriett was worried: "Have you heard from Kane?"

Buchanan sighed: "No one knows where he is or what he's doing. Van Dyke has no idea. Van Dyke has people watching his house — he's nowhere to be seen, but I have to reply to the House's demand that I explain why we sent the Army out there and how we're going to pay for it."

"Well, it was to get the new governor there — what's his name?"

"Cumming, a Georgian," Buchanan said in frustration, then continued: "The Mormons didn't even know he was coming, Bernhisel did, but there wasn't any way to tell them. No telegraph wires extend that far."

"Uncle James, I don't understand what you want of me," Harriett Lane admitted.

"I need someone to tell me that my proposal is fair, makes sense, and you're the only I trust, and frankly the only person who really cares about…about me," Buchanan confessed.

"Sometimes I wish that arrogant Fremont had won, and I didn't have to deal with this, all this…"

"Mess, this mess," Harriett said as she walked over squeezed his hand and took a chair closer to his desk. "All right, tell me your remedy."

He thumbed through his notes, pulled out his draft — the one with all the corrections — and summed up his proposal: "Now first, I believe Kane could already be in Utah, and although he has no official status because he didn't want one — he wanted to appear neutral, I hope he's there. Anyway, in the beginning I summarized how the Mormons, particularly Brigham Young, have been in state of rebellion, that the judges we sent there were rebuffed and run off mor abandoned their posts and left, and that Utah is a territory, not a state. But then," he hesitated.

"Well?"

"Well, then per the request of Kane when we met, I am granting amnesty for all of them, from Brigham Young down to the least of them, the paupers who live like John the Baptist on wild honey and crickets — barely surviving. It's all here — what do you think?"

She reviewed the document and wondered what to say. But, she trusted Kane and had loved his brother, and then smiled: "You know, Uncle James, there are so few heroes these days." He waited,

and finally, she walked over to the window, peered out and then turned back to her uncle: "What a beautiful summer day; it's a great time to start over. Declaring amnesty shows you to be a man who sees the good in people, believes in forgiveness and mercy."

She paused and then declared: "Uncle James, it's brilliant! Now you, like Kane, can be viewed as a peacemaker!"

Her uncle stood and gave her a hug. "I don't know what I'd do without you here in the White House with me."

"Thank you. So now can I proceed with the invitation list?"

"Absolutely my dear," Buchanan proclaimed.

THE PAUPERS — THE MORMONS WHO BUCHANAN thought lived on wild honey and crickets — were refugees once again, unaware that they were about to be granted amnesty for their rebellion, despite the fact that they had no idea that they had rebelled in the first place. Many had experienced forced evacuations before, first from Missouri and then Illinois. so they weren't going to stand for another one… they would leave before they could be forced out again. Thousands were on the road south. Mormon settlers from Ogden to the far south end of the Salt Lake valley were now being accommodated by others or looking for places where they could live in their wagons and where their horses and cattle, and sometimes even pigs, could graze.

William Wagstaff, his stepson Willy, his two wives, their babes in arms and toddlers had relocated along the Provo River with hundreds of other Mormon families. It was organized squalor, with new privys set back of the wagons, along with temporary corrals where beasts of burden and the occasional milk cow could be cordoned off. But, the children viewed it as a holiday with parents worried to death that the fast-moving river might claim another innocent life.

William was sorting through his "seed chest," one of his most prized possessions, to ensure that his inventory had not been disturbed on their trip south. His stepson William Richard, or Willy, looked concerned:

"Papa, I'm worried."

"About what, Willy?"

"The orchard, what if the trees die because we didn't water them? What if the deer eat them?"

William pointed to his collection of seedlings wrapped in burlap and arranged in boxes in the big wagon: "We have replacements."

"But, you sold some."

"Yes, we did, but now the people here in Provo can grow fruit, too."

"I like it here…they have pretty mountains," Willy said, pointing to majestic Mount Timpanogos looming over their heads. It was early evening, and even in June, snow still clung to the tops of the peaks. "Papa, when are we going home?"

William Wagstaff hesitated then told the boy: "Only when they tell us it's safe to go back, only then."

His wife Maria called to him: "William, we have supper ready," she said as she pulled a large cast-iron pot out of the fire and set it on a plank table supported by sawhorses. As he set down his shovel to join the family for dinner, there was a loud cry further up the river.

"Help, my boy fell in, my boy…somebody grab him! Anybody!"

The Provo River in June was still swollen from the spring run-off, and it was doubtful if even a grown man would have an easy time of it, but William ran to the river anyway. A small blond head was bobbing up and down, arms flailing trying to reach a branch at the river's edge. William Wagstaff ran to the bank, jumped in, grabbed a branch so he wouldn't be swept away and stuck out his right leg and the boy, who was maybe three or four grabbed his pant leg. William bent down and grabbed him by the collar, lost his balance and fell in, too, but with some help, got hold of a tree root that extended into the river and both he and the boy were pulled to safety.

Wagstaff was drenched, and the boy was coughing, but safe. His mother ran to the scene, picked up her son and hugged William who looked embarrassed. Soggy, but happy, he slogged to the covered wagon, climbed in and changed his clothes.

"Save me some supper," he said to Maria Stubbs, his fifth wife — three had already died on the way to Zion, along with all of his own six children plus three of his other wives.

But, on this day, one small boy was alive, and another was very proud of his step-father: "Papa's a hero, huh, Mamma?"

She smiled: "I think you're a hero, too — just like Papa."

THOMAS KANE, THE MAN WHO MANY MORMONS considered to be a hero, met Brigham Young and George A. Smith at the Lion House the day afer he and Cumming had arrived in the valley.

"Want to take a walk?" Brigham said to Kane. They went out in the garden in back, and sat on a bench while Smith and Cumming went inside. The apostle knew what Brigham was about to share with his friend. He thought they ought to be left alone.

"Thomas, I don't how to tell you this, but I received a note from Elizabeth a month or so ago while you were traveling here: Your father passed away on February 25th. I am so sorry."

Cumming and Smith watched President Young break the news to Thomas — he buried his face in his hands as Brigham put his arm around him and comforted him.

Later that afternoon, Cumming inventoried everything in the territorial office while Brigham, Thomas, John Taylor, George A. Smith and Wilford Woodruff returned to the Lion House. Woodruff and Smith still had questions.

"Cumming has discovered for himself that despite claims to the contrary spread by that old curmudgeon Drummond, all the documents, the law books, the seal are all in good order," Kane explained. "And, now that he's there, he can organize his office."

That seemed to please Brigham Young, but Apostle George Smith, like Apostle Woodruff was still unconvinced.

"Yes, but how do we know Cumming won't let the colonel loose on us," Smith said.

Kane was irritated, but kept it in check.

"What do you think I've been doing for the past couple of months, Elder Smith? I've helped Cumming see the light — he and Johnston are not close; there's bad blood there. In his eyes, our friend Brigham here is leading the 'peace faction,' and it only makes sense for Cumming and eventually Johnston will come to that conclusion as well, especially after Johnston follows his marching orders …to keep marching far from here."

Brigham listened, turned to Smith and Woodruff and declared: "I think the people should meet; they should see their new governor — let him know that they recognize him as such."

Smith asked, "Do you mean like an invitation-only event somewhere, like a political meeting, an open house — is that safe?"

"No, George, at the tabernacle, a church-wide conference. Thomas, can you please float that idea by him — the new governor will speak to his people, and then, Elder Taylor, can you follow him with a talk reminding the Saints that 'we believe in being subject to kings, presidents, rulers, and magistrates, in obeying, honoring, and sustaining the law.'

"In other words, we're not rebelling?"

Taylor asked: "When?"

"Sunday, a morning and afternoon session. Let's get the word out to the people."

AFTER AN OPENING PRAYER, A HYMN AND SOME INITIAL REMARKS, President Brigham Young introduced Governor Alfred Cumming to some 4,000 congregants.

Cumming got off to a good start, noting that Brigham Young had introduced him and said that *"it is a source of pleasure to me that I have the pleasure of the friendship of the gentleman who*

introduced me to this stand." Then he admitted, to the pleasure of his audience, that *"I am not ignorant of the gross misrepresentation that has been made by the enemies of this people with regard to you.'* Then he hit upon a theme that the leaders had been preaching for years: self-government. He said *"I hope you will soon be formed in the grand galaxy as an entirely independent state."*

With that, he ended with a comparison of himself with his predecessors, the judges and other officials who ran off for one reason or another, noting that *"I desire this people to understand that I am not here to represent that miserable set of office seekers who are constantly prowling around the administration, neither am I here to have an office which I have declined."*

Elder Taylor then spoke frankly about the Mormons' feelings about the Army's reasons for coming to Utah—"it wasn't for our protection," as Cumming had said, but admitted that *"prejudices have risen against you and I have come to disband them."*

In the end, Cumming stated that he had come to investigate what the Saints felt were injustices made against them by previous officials. Before the meeting concluded, Brigham asked by a show of hands how many of those present felt that Cumming's appointment "restrained their liberties." Only four hands were raised, two of which were from nonmembers.

Cumming had won round one.

30

A LAND OF FABLE & MYTHOLOGY

Once trust is lost, it is often difficult to reclaim, even if peace is officially declared. Thomas Kane and Alfred Cumming had to accept this harsh truth, even though they had spent the last month diligently proffering Cumming as the solution the Mormons desperately needed to keep the U.S. Army in its place and out of their valleys.

Church leadership had seemed to accept Utah's new governor — after all, he had all the accoutrements of his office, and he had the title. There was constantly heard a *"Welcome Governor,"* here and a *"Good Morning, Governor,"* there. And the cordial *"How do you like Utah, Governor?."* But when Cumming declared to the Utah Territory citizens, *"Don't worry about the Army — they'll be far away from the city. You won't even know they're here,"* it was a different matter. The Latter-day Saints were still streaming out of the valley as fast as their animals could take them.

Cynthia and Sophronia Stowell, William's young wives and a dozen or so children — both theirs and the orphans — did their best to load up a wagon, fill it with offspring and bedsprings, hitch four steers to it and leave Ogden for Provo, nearly 100 miles away. A week before they left, Cynthia gave birth to Rufus.

That left pregnant Sophronia as the bullwhacker.

"Good morning, Sisters," a friendly voice said as the family traveled along. Cynthia was breastfeeding and had concealed herself under a quilt as she sat atop the wagon seat, but managed a smile for the man on a horse who had greeted them. Sophronia had a tight grip on the reins — she never went to bullwhacking school and had her hands full, too busy to pay notice to the man.

It was mid morning on their second day of migration, and they had just passed the little hamlet of Farmington, some 20 miles north of Salt Lake.

"Are you the Stowells?"

Finally that caught Sophronia's attention.

"Yes, why?"

"President Young wanted you to know that Brother Kane and Governor Cumming spoke with William a couple of weeks ago, and they believe he'll be released soon…that is, as soon as Kane and Cumming return to Fort Bridger. It seems that Brother Stowell has become quite well known in the camp and well liked by the soldier boys — they find him quite entertaining. He wishes you well and hopes to see you all soon. Thought you'd like to know."

The rider tipped his hat and trotted away. The two young women looked at each other as tears streamed down their faces. Cynthia grabbed Sophronia's hand and then a long overdue smile crept over Sophronia's face, the first one Cynthia had seen in days.

They now had a glimmer of hope.

AFTER A MONTH GETTING CUMMING INSTALLED AS THE GOVERNOR, Thomas Kane and Alfred Cumming, realizing that the Mormons would likely not stop their exodus from the Salt Lake Valley until they had settled things with Johnston and the U.S. Army once and for all, Thomas and Governor Cumming determined to return to Fort Bridger and Camp Scott to deal with the matter.

The two men hitched up the horses, loaded the carriage and got ready to roll. They stopped by the Lion House on their way out of the city to say good-bye to Brigham and to try to gauge Young's intentions for how long he would continue moving his people south. As they entered the home, Brigham and George Smith came down the stairs and Brigham Young reached out to shake their hands:

"Governor, is there anything else you need?" Brigham inquired. We're looking forward to meeting Mrs. Cumming."

Cumming smiled: "No, we have everything pretty well in hand for the move out here; Elizabeth is a pretty independent woman — I'm sure she's getting everything packed up. I imagine you'll see me again in a fortnight. Thank you for your accommodations so far."

"Glad to hear it," said Brigham. "On another note, I understand you and Thomas spoke with our prisoner, William Stowell…" he said as he gave Cumming a letter. "This is from his wives. Please give it to him, and if you could get him released and bring him back to his family, that would be much appreciated and…a miracle."

"I will do what I can," Cumming said.

"We're counting on it.'

Kane enjoyed listening to the conversation, but wondered whether in his absence if everything would go as he had planned, would Johnston comply with his presidential order and garrison his people far from the city? Did Brigham mean what he said to the governor? Kane hoped so.

Then, Young gave Kane a double-fisted handshake.

"When will I see you again, my friend?"

"Not for awhile, but I know someday Bess wants to see Utah firsthand. We'll see. I have to be the breadwinner again, find some way to compensate her for my absence."

"I hope it may be some consolation, however, for you to know that your sacrifice for peace and for this people and for those poor boys in Wyoming, will long be remembered," Brigham and then added: "The Saints of the Latter-days will never forget you. Godspeed to both of you."

"President, there's one more thing," said Thomas. "How can we persuade you to quit this migration south? With the Governor here and in charge, I see no reason *not* to let the people return to their homes."

"Thomas, I appreciate your concern — you are our dearest friend, and we are grateful that we have a good man here to serve as the governor. But, until we see with our own eyes that Johnston and his horde moves far away from our cities and can't rule us with an iron fist, we are moving on. I'm sorry."

"Then, let's hope the Army can find a place far away from here to garrison themselves," Kane said.

FOR THE BOYS IN WYOMING, maybe the weather had improved, but nothing else. Colonel Johnston had grown even wearier than his men because they just wouldn't shut up!

Even his best friend, Major Fitz-John Porter had worn him out. Any hope of glory had been snuffed out upon hearing that two "Presidential Emissaries" were on their way to "settle matters once and for all." No opportunity to teach Old Brigham a lesson for his civil disobedience. Johnston was feeling the noose tighten around his neck and realized he would likely have to acquiesce on the matter of the Mormons more than he was comfortable with.

"Colonel, I don't know what General Scott or the president has in mind for us, but I'm not optimistic," Major Porter said.

"Really?" Johnston had heard it all before so he continued walking to the commissary to see if the expected shipments, especially coffee had arrived. He had heard that wagons did roll in yesterday.

Porter continued complaining: "Maybe our illustrious Indian agent Mr. Forney believes that Cumming is some paragon of courage for braving it, risking his life to travel down to Mormon town to be their governor, but I doubt he was ever at risk at all."

"Why so, Porter?"

"Little Kane fabricated the whole thing — there was no division at all among the Mormons, Whatever Brigham says, goes. We see through Kane's game — Cumming's no hero, just a fool for taking the bait."

"Fitz-John, put a muzzle on it!" Johnston finally retorted. Porter was getting on his nerves. "Let's go get some coffee, good rich undiluted coffee."

Just then, a rider came galloping towards them: "Colonel, they're back!"

"Who's back?"

"Cumming and the little colonel. The Mormons have welcomed him — our problems are over!"

Fitz-John profaned and then added: "No, they just got worse!"

ELIZABETH CUMMING HAD MIXED FEELINGS — she wanted to escape the foul place where she had been quarantined for the last few months, but she was also very worried about how she and her beloved Alfred would be received in the Utah Territory. The rumor mill had poisoned her about the way the Mormons would treat them:

"No one will speak to you — there will be constant threats against Alfred's life."

"The men will desire to add you to their harems."

"You will have no one to talk to…it will be a lonely experience."

Such demoralizing gossip was weighing her down. It had been nearly a month since Alfred left, and now that he had returned, she could finally leave this purgatory, her penance fully paid. but she also worried what kind of hot, sweltering hell she might be headed for in Utah. Even though the weather was cooperating, she brooded over what lay ahead. And, she had to pack.

She called for her little, black servant, Dundee.

"Is all the silver wear and china packed and secure? Make sure it's wrapped so it doesn't break. Got all the bedding, pillows, towels and such?"

"Yes' um." They filled the wagons and then waited for the governor to share with Colonel Johnston what had transpired in Salt Lake City.

An hour or so later, Alfred returned:

"Sorry I'm late. I had to share with Thomas what I told Colonel Johnston, that when the presidential emissaries arrive they will order the Army to do exactly what's in the letter that Buchanan gave Kane, to move through Salt Lake City, billet themselves somewhere far away and let the Mormons live in peace. He just grunted and I left. Now is everybody ready to go? Then let's get out of here!"

Elizabeth smiled, and he bent down and kissed her on the forehead. She grabbed his hand as he lumbered away and let her fingers fall through his.

In a moment, another servant came riding up bareback on a painted pony: "I got your ride, Mrs. Cumming; he's young, but gentle, perfect for a lady. I'll saddle him up.So sorry about your other horse, ma'am. I hope he finds his way back,." the young man said, referring to her horse that had been lost after a violent storm.

"Me too," said Elizabeth. "I miss that animal. That was a terrible storm, a terrible day." Although she was nervous, the wife of the new governor of the Utah Territory was ready for a new adventure. A granddaughter of the Revolutionary War hero Samuel Adams, Elizabeth Randall Cumming, was from Boston, but would soon make Salt Lake City her home. There was no time to waste. The Mormons were waiting for her.

But, by the end of the day, she was spent. Then, she made the mistake of letting her "chef" prepare her "Last Supper."

THE NEXT MORNING, CUMMING WAS UP EARLY packing everything onto the wagon. Mrs. Cumming was nowhere to be seen — probably still asleep, he thought. She had complained of a stomachache the night before. Oh, just let her rest a bit, Cumming concluded.

He called for his chief aide: "Labrum, when can we depart?"

"As soon as we load up your boxes from your tent and pack up the tents. Just load the two big tents — leave the others. I have to go free the prisoner."

"What prisoner?"

"The Mormon, Stowell. He's coming with us. Please secure him a mount and saddle. Can you do that?"

"Yes sir, but people wanted to hang him," Labrum objected.

"Who wanted to hang him?"

"Some bullwhackers, I think. They're still sore about their wagons and stock that was burned."

"Murderous thugs," Cumming said and charged off.

A half an hour later, he was in Eckelsville, first to see the judge to get a writ of habeas corpus, then grab some clothing from the quartermaster and deliver the good news to Stowell.

Back at Camp Scott, Cumming approached the guard on the stump who challenged him:

"Halt, who goes there?"

"I'm the governor, and I've come for the prisoner."

"Which one?"

"William Stowell, the Mormon," Cumming said. "I am here to have him released into my custody. Here's the writ from Judge Eckels," Cumming said and gave the guard the paper.

"The colonel told me to keep him safe and keep other people away," the guard said, clearly confused.

"Corporal, the Army follows orders from the government, not the other way around. So, you go in and get him, remove his shackles or I will have to bring Colonel Albert Sydney Johnston himself or another officer here to issue you those orders, and if I do, you'll be the one wearing the shackles, do you understand?"

"Yes sir."

"Here's some new clothing — see that he gets a bath, and I'll be back shortly; a man's coming with a horse." Cumming declared and gave him a bundle.

"Bath?"

"Take him to the river and get those lice washed off!"

The governor walked into Stowell's "tent of wickedness" and was assaulted by the stench of unbathed, shackled men.

"William, I have something for you. Come with me," he said and helped him up. He turned to another guard who had heard about Stowell's release. "Sergeant, this man needs his shackles removed."

Stowell was more surprised than his captors. The sergeant told the corporal to get a hammer and a spike who returned minutes later. As the sergeant squatted down to remove the shackles, Stowell volunteered to do it, grabbed the hammer and knocked the pins out himself.

The sergeant was puzzled: "Governor, what's happening here?"

"I have a writ of habeas corpus — this man is released into my custody; he's coming with me…after you clean him up." He tossed a bundle to William who was still too stunned to speak. "Hope they fit," he said to Stowell. "I think there's a towel in there, too."

The sergeant was perplexed: "What?"

"Read it," he said and handed him the writ.

"I'll be back in an hour — we're getting you a horse. Wait here," he said to Stowell.

William was crying, laughing and trying to speak all at the same time, but managed to thank the governor. Cumming got on his horse and rode back to his compound

ELIZABETH CUMMING STAGGERED OUT OF HER TENT, finally dressed for the journey. Alfred was irritated with her but only a little bit after she told him how sick she had been the night before.

"I fired the cook — he wasn't a 'chef,' by the way," she said. "I think he tried to poison me. I'm ready now. I'm fine."

Three wagons, the buggy and an Army ambulance (with its glass windows and fancy seating) were all lined up outside what was once the gubernatorial compound — all that was left were three ratty tents and a privy — an unsightly mess.

"I feel like Eve," she said with a grin.

"What?" The governor was confused.

"You know, when she was driven out of paradise. Let's get the you-know-what out of here!" She laughed. Just then, a well-groomed rode up on a big bay . The governor introduced him:

"Elizabeth, this man is a Mormon, in case you've never seen one before. This is Mr. Stowell — we are breaking him out of prison."

"I don't know what to say, except thank you," Stowell stammered. And, thanks to the judge and the enlisted men who've been guarding me, they raised $50 for my going-away present."

Cumming smiled: "Well, good for them! You must have been a good prisoner. And, William, as my first act as the governor of the Territory of Utah, I'm setting you free! I think I'm going to like this job. Let's go!

IT WAS JUNE — SUPPOSED TO BE SUMMER. But, when Cumming's train left Camp Scott and headed southwest, it was suddenly winter again. As those who had lived in the Rockies for a time all knew, the weather could change in an instant, from sunshine to storm, but to these Southerners, this was something they hadn't quite gotten used to yet.The train consisted of wagons, carriages and an ambulance (a weather-tight carriage with windows and roofs)—with Alfred and his driver in the first one, Dr. Forney, the superintendent of Indian affairs and his driver and cook, Elizabeth Cumming, and her servant Dundee and Stowell were next. Saddled, but riderless horses were strung behind. These mounts were used whenever someone needed to scout ahead or in case of an emergency.

Elizabeth later wrote home about the trip that *"first it blew cold, then it snowed, then it hailed, then it was as cold as winter. The road was dreary until we came to a descent called Cobblestone Hill (a very good mountain though). "Here,"* she wrote, *"everybody chose to walk — so steep and precipitous was the place...more than three-quarters of a mile in length.*

"It was a long and stony walk, but I found some flowers and mosses which rejoiced my eyes and heart. In spite of the fierce wind, I gathered many new plants for my herbarium."

The next day, Stowell and Elizabeth chose to go on horseback. Along the way, the wagon train was followed by Indians, likely Utes (or "Utahs") who had overtaken all the good camping spots forcing the Cumming party to *"encamp in a desolate place because the comfortable places were filled with very fierce Indians — in numbers — who might steal our mules were we too near."*

For the next few days, Elizabeth regaled her sister about her adventure, *"that filled my heart to aching as we advanced…in Echo Canyon…when it was my good fortune to see the grandeur and beauty such as I can never forget. On my right were copper or orange-gold cliffs, said to be over 2,000-feet high in places… [hanging over] our path in many places, [making it] dim in broad daylight…with a mass of the densest, richest foliage… shrubs, vines,. small trees, wild fruit trees in blossom…imagination was thrown far away into the land of fable and mythology…"*

Such was the experience of the First Lady of the Utah Territory, who in a few days would be surprised again, not just by the beauty and grandeur of the scenery, but by the people she would meet, who had been dehumanized, defamed, vilified and reviled as no other people in American history, except perhaps Blacks or Indians. It would be the adventure of a lifetime for Elizabeth Randall Cumming. On her thrilling journey through canyons and for-ests to the Valley of the Great Salt Lake, Elizabeth Cumming found a new friend, William Stowell. Stowell was even more joyful than she was, reveling in the fact that he was no longer shackled in a tent wickedness, but instead on his way to Zion to rejoin his family.

Many times, he had offered to set up Elizabeth's tent and help her with the fire, but she would have none of it.

"You're as independent as a Mormon woman, Mrs. Cumming," he joked. "But, in our family, we have more to do than we have hands to do it."

"How so?"

"Well, when I was captured, there were 13 of us, me, my two young wives and 10 children, but while I was a prisoner, according to the letter the governor gave me yesterday, there are now 15, myself included, since two more babies have been born since I was captured."

"But, you are so young, and your wives, how old are they?"

"Cynthia is 21 and Sophronia 19, I believe," he admitted.

They were gathering wood and rocks for a fire; it was a little chilly just before the ascent over Big Mountain.

"You have some explaining to do, Mr. Stowell. I know you Mormons are 'unusual,' but this seems more like 'strange," she said, pressing him.

"Well, I was a father before I was married…"

"That's not hard," she ribbed him.

"I adopted an orphan, and so I needed a wife. So, I married Cynthia." Now he had her undivided attention.

"Then, my half-brother died — his wife was already gone, and he had five children. By then, Cynthia had twins, and she knew Sophronia, who had a baby. And while I was gone, two more were born, one to each wife, but I have never seen them. Anyway, with me, it adds up to 15. So, I need to find them since everyone's moving south."

"Moving south?"

"To stay away from the Army…I hear they're threatening to burn the city if the Army stays. Ask Governor Cumming. Anyway, I think all will turn out all right — the fact that I'm here and we just passed through Echo Canyon is an affirmation," he said.

"An affirmation of what," she asked.

"Before I was captured, I had a dream that I had been released and was returning home with a man I didn't know — I believe that man was your husband."

"So my Alfred is a fulfillment of your prophesy?"

"Mrs. Cumming, he's a fulfillment in more ways than you know!"

Later, Elizabeth Cumming would write to her sister how she had enjoyed her horseback ride down the canyon with her "new friend" — the Mormon POW, William Stowell, whom her husband had just released from captivity in his first official act as the new governor of the Territory of Utah.

31

SWEET REUNIONS

Once Kane arrived at Council Bluffs, Iowa, he and his traveling companions — his unofficial bodyguard, Howard Egan and two of Egan's enlisted men — accompanied Thomas to the Missouri docks. They had made it just in time to get tickets on the paddleboat steamer, the *Emigrant.* It was a sticky summer day, filled with travelers heading west and others like Kane and Egan returning to the East. After spending weeks bouncing along the dusty, and in some cases desolate plains of Wyoming territory, Thomas Kane witnessed how water can change a landscape.

After they had loaded up Kane's luggage, Thomas, Egan and their traveling companions were on top of the paddleboat on its way to St. Louis. Rich Iowa farmland stretched out before them filled with corn now nearly waist high.

Did Howard Egan read Kane's mind? He smiled.

"Imagine, Brother Kane, how much easier life would be for us back in Utah if water just fell out of the sky. No irrigation canals necessary!"

"But, where are the mountains?" Thomas asked. "Where are the barriers, the fortress to keep unwanted guests out?"

Egan could see that Kane was a bit melancholy. "I hope I can return to your mountain home, this time with Elizabeth and the children," Thomas said.

"I hope you can return in more peaceful circumstances," Egan replied. They had found seats with a good view near the front of the paddleboat, and for a long while, they just watched the scenery pass by. Thomas began scribbling notes with a stubby pencil.

His little notebook was now nearly full, and his pencil needed sharpening if he were to write any smaller — he only had two full pages left. He stood up, put the notebook in his pocket and leaned over the railing. He figured they were now traveling about 10 mph. He recognized a fellow passenger off to his right reading a newspaper: It was Horace Greeley's correspondent, Albert Gallatin Browne Jr. Browne saw him out of the corner of his eye.

For a few miles, they rode in awkward silence. They weren't exactly friends.

Browne, the journalist, knew there was a story standing just a few paces from him, and Kane, the publicist, saw an opportunity to correct "the fake news" that Browne had been spewing. It made sense to bury the hatchet. Thomas walked over and found a seat across from Browne.

"So, it's over, you're going home," Browne said.

"No, the drama may be over, but there are still details to be settled…"

"Like the Mormons' rebellion?"

Thomas tried not to take the bait — it would be a long, unpleasant trip to St. Louis if he did.

"As I told you the first time, the Mormons didn't know they were in a state of rebellion until they heard an Army was marching on Zion," Thomas corrected him. "Brigham Young told me that if there had been telegraph wires strung to Utah beforehand, none of these troubles would have happened — no Army, no Move South, no massacre at Mountain Meadows."

Browne nodded: "So you're close to Brigham Young?"

Thomas looked out the window, a little misty:

"We are like brothers," Thomas almost whispered.

"How did this all come about?" For the next several hours as they steamed southeast, Albert Brown learned more about the Mormons, their persecution and their flight to the West than he had ever learned while holed up at Camp Scott.

When they finally arrived in St. Louis, Kane and Browne were now better acquainted, certainly not friends, but at least they learned to respect each other. They had both discovered that they shared a passion for abolitionism, that both had been jailed for their opposition to the Fugitive Slave Act and that Judge Kane, in fact, had even put his own son Thomas in jail. Kane made sure that Browne understood how other newspapers, particularly in New York, had unfairly criticized Kane for manipulating a "naive" Cumming, accusing both Thomas and the governor of being under the spell of Old Brigham. With all that new information, Browne saw an opportunity to "get a scoop."

At the train station, Thomas caught a train to Philadelphia and Browne one to New York.

When Albert finally walked into Greeley's office a couple of days later, he had a story about the Utah Expedition ready to print. He just made the deadline, but hardly anyone noticed him, especially in the heat, humidity and the competitive atmosphere of a 19th-century newspaper. Greeley finally saw him.

"What have you got?" Greeley demanded.

Browne was as proud as a peacock:

"Mr. Greeley, here is my report on Thomas Kane's remarkable venture," Albert declared, handing his article ceremoniously to Horace.

"And furthermore, I am planning to return after the Army 'marches into Zion' and arrange for an interview with Brigham Young himself."

Greeley took a minute to read it, made a couple of notes and yelled, "Copy!"

A minute later, a slavish-looking young man rushed in and grabbed it.

"To typesetting, tell them — page three — top."

Then Horace Greeley leaned forward in his chair to laud his young correspondent:

"Albert, it's more of an editorial than a standard story, but I think you've captured it well. And in regards to the interview with Brigham Young…"

"Yes?" Albert replied, his eyes lit up.

"Face-to-face interview with Brigham Young — what a wonderful idea! In fact, since I'm always preaching 'go west,' I'm going to follow my own advice. When all of this settles down and peace is secure, I'm going west myself and meet the man 'mano a' mano.' What do you think about that?"

Albert was crestfallen, devastated, but tried not to show it. "Great idea, sir."

"Browne, that's because it's your idea! Thank you! And, mark my word: we'll make it happen," Greeley said, then stood up and left for lunch.

On Saturday, June 19, 1858, Greeley printed Albert Gallatin Browne's story without an attribution in the *New York Tribune*:

Col. Thomas L. Kane arrived at Philadelphia yesterday, after an absence of little more than five months. During this period he has traveled from New York, by way of San Francisco and San Bernardino to Salt Lake City in the depth of winter in the surprisingly short time, if we are not mistaken, of forty-seven days. In San Bernardino, he was arrested as a Mormon agent and escaped with great danger, losing all the furs he had provided for the tedious journey between that place and the Mormon settlements in Utah. This journey, as we have heard, was attended with much peril; he was repeatedly compelled to conceal himself under merchandise conveyed by his companions, in order to avoid falling into the hands of outlying parties of Mormons, who would have killed him as a secret agent or spy of the Federal government. What difficulties he encountered after his arrival at Salt Lake City, or how he finally induced the Mormon leaders to make peace and submit to the Federal authorities, will very probably in due time be communicated to the public. Then came the extraordinary ride from Salt Lake City to the camp of the United States Army, where as our readers will remember, after 26 hours continuous exposure to the inclemency of Winter, most if not all the time in the saddle, he arrived in a state of speechless exhaustion. Finally, he accompanied Gov. Cumming to Salt Lake City, and saw him inducted into his office; and then, his mission accomplished, he came home. The Government having disavowed all connection with Col. Kane's efforts, the credit and making of the success with which they have been crowned belongs entirely to him. In our judgment they constitute a claim upon the esteem and gratitude of the company which can never be disputed. He has avoided the effusion of blood; he has saved the expenditure of millions; he has substituted peace for war in which glory was impossible. A private citizen, he has done what all the power of the Government could not accomplish. Honor to the patriot and the peacemaker!

Elizabeth Kane loved it, got copies for everybody; she wouldn't let Thomas out of her sight. His safe return was an answer to prayer.

Cumming and his party emerged from Emigration Canyon as the sun was setting on a beautiful summer evening. The western sky was a brilliant coral pink with streaks of turquoise all set against the shimmering blue of the Great Salt Lake below it.

"Oh my!" the new First Lady of the Territory of Utah, Elizabeth Cumming, exclaimed. "I think I'm going to like it here."

And, the Governor added, "I think we will, if we can sort out all the politics and petty prejudices."

Soon, a welcoming party rushed up the hill to greet them, and within a few minutes, they were making there way slowly through a quiet deserted settlement.

Galloping up to the front to speak with the hosts came William Stowell, almost panicked.

"So, it's true — they've abandoned the city, literally just pulled up stakes and left!" Stowell exclaimed.

The uniformed young man stopped him: "Yes, didn't you know? Who are you?"

Governor Cumming spoke for him: "This is William Stowell, the Mormon prisoner we were able to wrest away from the Army."

"You're William Stowell? Well, may I shake your hand? I'm Randall Smith, sergeant Nauvoo Legion. You've made a name for yourself. Welcome home. How can we help you?"

"I need to find my family — we're from Ogden."

The two legionnaires looked at each other, speechless for a moment: "Your best bet would be to speak with Brigham Young himself, but he's in Provo. You should find some place to sleep tonight and then leave in the morning."

Cumming interrupted the conversation: "Young man, there's likely room in the Staines mansion — that is where you're taking us, right?" Their hosts nodded, but William was adamant.

"No, Governor, I'm going to find some food for myself and my horse and ride all night if I have to."

Elizabeth spoke up: "You should stay in the mansion."

"They have been waiting for me for nine months, not knowing whether I'd live or die. Thank you all for your help and consideration, but I'm leaving now."

Just then, Major Howard Egan rode up to officially welcome the new arrivals. After some initial introductions, Egan turned to William:

"So, you are the famous prisoner of war and entertaining story teller. There are some people in the city who want to meet you and to hear how you were treated."

"Who are they?" Stowell asked, still anxious to leave.

"President Buchanan's official peacemakers and his emissaries; they've come to grant clemency and amnesty to both the leaders and all the Saints, and that, Brother Stowell, includes you."

The Governor was adamant, too: "Stay in the mansion tonight, William, as our guest."

"No lice?"

They laughed.

"I doubt it," the governor said.

"I hope not," Elizabeth Cumming countered.

"It will take some getting used to," William relented, and they made their way down into the city."

As they rode along, the horses' footsteps seemed to echo, and the wagons creaked. Every cough, ever word uttered seemed amplified. They were nearly alone in a ghost town.

Occasionally, they would see a young man on a porch or a stump or sitting under a tree with an unlit torch, ready to set the city ablaze if they got the order. If the Army marched in and de-cided to stay, all they'd inherit would be smoke and ashes.

But, Governor Cumming and the president's commissioners, Ben McCulloch of Texas, and Lazarus Powell of Kentucky, couldn't allow that to happen — they were scheduled to meet tomorrow. And, William Stowell was invited.

BUCHANAN'S PEACE COMMISSIONERS HAD ARRIVED several days before the Governor and had already met with Brigham Young and other church leaders who were grateful for the declaration of amnesty, nevertheless continued to maintain their innocence.

Major Egan had escorted the commissioners to the territorial headquarters where Cumming's assistant, Theo Benson, managed the office. They also discovered, contrary to the prevarications spread by Drummond and others, that the law library, deeds and other legal documents were all in order, right where they were supposed to be After the commissioners had left for their boarding house, Cumming buttonholed Egan.

"Major, do you have a few minutes to talk, just you and me," Governor Cumming asked.

"Certainly, Governor."

"Now that Thomas is gone, my confidant has flown the coop! It's just me and Elizabeth, but there are some nagging issues that I need to resolve. First of all, the Move South. It's not only a problem of physical security and safety for the Mormons who have fled the valley, but it sends a message to Johnston and to Buchanan."

Egan was puzzled: "How so?"

"Because, first, it tells the government that the Mormons don't believe that Thomas Kane succeeded...that he failed — that the peace he tried to broker between the Mormons and Colonel Johnston won't hold."

Now he had Egan's attention.

"Second, it emboldens Judge Eckels. It will also give teeth to his move to indict you, the rest of the presidency and everyone else who matters. That's what Johnston wants. He takes orders — he won't do anything rash. It was a blessing that the Squaw Killer Harney was replaced — Johnston is a dedicated officer. We don't get along, and he and Senator Sam Houston have been rivals for years. Nevertheless, Colonel Albert Sydney Johnston will follow his orders, no question about it."

"Third, the powers that be, especially the 'cabal,' Missouri Senator Benton, Robert Tyler and others who want the Mormons gone are also emboldened. They've heard that Brigham has been talking to the British, looking at the Indies, anywhere else where the Mormons can't interfere with their 'Manifest Destiny.' And, that's fine with the 'cabal.' They want this beautiful valley and those magnificent mountains all for themselves...to dig out all the gold they can find. And last of all, I trust Thomas Kane, and I've come to like and admire Brigham Young. That, Major Egan, puts me on the chopping block. I don't want to leave this place until my job is done..."

"And, what's that, Governor?"

"To see that you can have what Thomas Jefferson promised all Americans: 'life, liberty and the pursuit of happiness.'"

Cumming hoped he had just made a friend and appealed to Major Howard Egan.

"Major, please keep me informed," Cumming said, "because there will be efforts to replace me with someone less friendly to your people. You have to start trusting somebody. You can trust Thomas Kane, and you can trust me."

Egan may have not recognized the truth of Cumming's statement, but over the next five years, the Mormons would gradually come to appreciate the former mayor of Augusta, George, the portly man that the soldiers in Fort Bridger referred to as "the Old Whiskey Barrel." Cumming had proven his commitment to act in their behalf, even if they didn't yet realize it.

THE DAY AFER CUMMING'S PARTY HAD ARRIVED IN SALT LAKE CITY William Stowell had relented and stayed in the city to answer questions from the governor and the Buchanan's commissioners. These men who showed genuine interest in the way William was treated while in captivity, which was gratifying, but Stowell was pressed to find his family; he was in a hurry, but did his best to answer all their questions:

Q: How were you treated?

A: As best as they could, I suppose, under the circumstances — we were in a tent and were short of food like everyone else.

Q: Were you mistreated?"

A: Well, I had to wear shackles and have sores on my ankles; even though we had a small cast-iron stove in the tent, it was pretty cold in December and January.

Q: Were there threats against you?

A: All the time, but it was just talk, except when we were leaving, but the governor stepped in and that stopped it.

Q: Anything else?

A: The judge did indict me along with church leaders like Brigham Young, but it never got to trial, again thanks to Governor Cumming. But, I did make a few friends among my captors — they raised a few dollars for me. I have a lot of mouths to feed.

This part of the questioning aroused the governor: "You know, gentlemen, this whole indictment is entirely improper, especially because of Eckels' new charges," Cumming insisted.

Commissioner Powell was curious: "What new charges?"

"Polygamy," Cumming said. "That is a local matter — the whole concept of local sovereignty flies in the face of that. It is a local custom, and you will see as I have that Mormon women are not kept in harem-like conditions. In Mr. Stowell's case here, as he explained to me, he adopted…what six orphans…?"

Stowell nodded.

Cumming continued: "And add to the children he has had with his wives, he brought a second wife with her own child into the family to help care for a very large family. Plus, I think Eckels is just trying to make a name for himself at the expense of people like William here."

Commissioner McCulloch thanked William for his testimony and excused him. William was in a hurry: He had a manhunt to conduct — wives and children to find.

IN THE TABERNACLE, BRIGHAM YOUNG PRESIDED over a public meeting with the peace commissioners in attendance. The prophet accepted the blanket pardon that was granted by Buchanan "for any and all offenses" that he and the rest of the Mormons may or may not have made, but he insisted *"we are guilty of nothing."*

Elder George A. Smith noted the "slanderous" nature of President Buchanan's accusations against the Latter-day Saints and that they "would incite" anyone to rebel, in fact, he charged "the proclamation contains 42 separate charges."

When asked publicly about what the government had ever done about persecution of the Mormons in Missouri or Illinois, peace commissioner McCullough said he knew nothing about it. Smith then pointed out that he was forced to leave his home (due to persecution) five different times.

Smith admitted that *"I was in favor of stopping the Army last fall; we gained by that means a winter's quiet."* Then he added, *"You know a sick patient would pay a large sum of money to physicians to lengthen out a miserable existence a little while…"*

Smith then explained how he came to embrace Cumming, noting that when he came with Thomas Kane down to the city, despite warnings from the Army and elsewhere that he could be in danger, *"he broke out from the forest and threw himself into the midst of the settlements unescorted (by the Army) and declared that he did not want to govern a people who did not want him, but was ready to fulfill the obligations of his office."* At that point, Smith declared *"I began to respect him…I see in him a manly, free generous spirit; he said 'I come not to govern you as a military despot, but as a fellow citizen."*

Then, with Cumming and the peace commissioners listening, Apostle George A. Smith then summarized the Saints' position about an Army in their midst:

"If Mr. Buchanan actually means …that the citizens of Utah should have the same privileges as other citizens of the United States, all right … [then] withdraw your armies, and that act would cry louder than a thousand proclamations and promises…it is hard for me to believe that peace is intended when you point your cannon at our houses."

As Brigham Young and the other Saints who were assembled in the old tabernacle heard Elder Smith state their case so clearly, one could wonder if President Brigham Young reflected on the letter he had received months earlier written by Captain Stewart

Van Vliet, the quartermaster who first visited Salt Lake City the previous fall. Van Vliet and Young had a friendship of sorts, certainly they respected one another. The captain gave the letter to peace commissioner Ben McCulloch to deliver to Young. Van Vliet's argument was that the government had no desire *"to interfere or meddle with the Mormon religion in any way. If your religion cannot withstand the contact of the world, it cannot be true. If the presence of a thousand U.S. troops quartered in Rush Valley can shake the faith of your people that faith can be of little value."*

What would Brigham Young's response have been? Perhaps it would focus on the word 'contact.' For Brigham Young, George A. Smith, Wilford Woodruff and thousands of other Mormons that word meant being driven from your homes, your property being taken and a forced march from settlements that you had built, and even more hastily dug graves marking their trail. And for many Mormon women, it meant rape and abuse.

If history taught the Mormons anything, it was that it cannot be repeated — never again would they allow their enemies to persecute, scatter and destroy them. If Thomas Kane and Alfred Cumming weren't successful, there would only be two options for the Latter-day Saints:

Fight or Flight.

32

DREAMS DO COME TRUE

In the summer of 1858, William Stowell was getting closer to his objective — finding Cynthia, Sophronia and the children. But, first he had to seek out Brigham Young who now had an increased layer of security surrounding him. So, he sought out the one friend in high places who could help him: his former cell-mate who had shared a canvas prison with him — Major Joseph Taylor.

Taylor was supposed to be with a contingent of legionnaires who were camped along the Provo River in the canyon near Bridal Veil Falls, one of the most picturesque sites in all of Utah. William rode up the canyon late in the afternoon. A half a dozen men were cutting and notching logs. William got off his horse and stopped one of them:

"Excuse me, I'm looking for Major Taylor. Is he nearby?"

"Who's asking?"

"Lt. William Stowell," he said growing impatient.

"Did you say Stowell?" William nodded.

"Really? The major didn't think they'd ever let you go," the foreman said. "It's really you?"

Stowell nodded and smiled.

"Brady, get the major — tell him William Stowell's here!" Then the foreman held out his hand in welcome. "Come on down — we have some cider cooling in the river!"

Then Stowell saw his old comrade wiping his hands on a towel hurrying to him. Taylor shouted to the men: "Come meet the man who helped me escape — he's quite the story-teller!"

In ten minutes, a group of legionnaires and loggers all shook Stowell's hand and wanted to see him in person.

"The major has told us all about how you stayed behind and entertained the troops so he could escape," a young logger said. "How did you escape?"

"The Governor got me out."

"You mean Brother Brigham?"

"No, his replacement, Governor Cumming. He's no friend of the Army. He's on our side. Listen, Major, I don't know where my family is, so I came looking for President Young, but his whereabouts are closely guarded."

"The Germans know — they're cutting timber up the river. They're about two miles up the river and are floating the logs down. Ask for Holz or Wilcken; they work as bodyguards for Brother Brigham," Major Taylor said.

"William, I can't tell how happy I am to see you made it out. Was it like your dream, your liberation and return?"

William smiled: "To a 'T'— Cumming was the man I returned with."

"Well, how about that!"

A half an hour later, William found the Germans. He recognized Christian Holz right away.

"You are back!" Christian said and almost shook his hand off. "This is my countryman, Carl Wilcken."

The Provo River was running higher than usual for July, but still offering up some pretty good fish. Across the river Wilford Woodruff had just snagged a good-sized cutthroat and was pulling it in.

"It's called 'fly-fishing,'" Christian said. "That's Elder Woodruff — he picked that up in England, along with several congregations of Englishmen and Welshmen he caught there as well."

Wilcken held out his hand: "Carl Wilcken — I think I saw you when they brought you in," Carl said in his thick German accent.

"You saw me up at Camp Scott? How is that?"

Christian answered the question: "He changed sides. he was a reluctant U.S. Army recruit, now he's an enthusiastic Latter-day Saint," Christian answered for Carl.

"Come on, we'll take you to the president. He's in Provo."

As they rode down the canyon, William Stowell was struck by the beauty of Bridal Veil Falls.

Wilcken was in awe: "Looks like paradise, don't you think?"

"It won't be paradise until I find my family," Stowell said.

BRIGHAM YOUNG WAS PUTTING UP FENCING around his family compound when the Germans and Major Taylor brought William through the front gate. The prophet saw them, dropped his tools and hurried over to greet them.

"Well, I know my bodyguards and Major Taylor, so you must be our 'prodigal prisoner,' William Stowell," Brigham Young declared and shook his hand. "God does watch over us and answer prayers, does he not?"

"Yes sir, He keeps His promises!" Stowell affirmed.

After a few minutes of Stowell summarizing his nine months in the "tent of wickedness," Brigham watched Stowell give his horse a nudge and leave for the foothills south of Provo. Later that afternoon, William was sitting on a log near a fire with children hanging all over him. Cynthia sat right next to him with her head on his shoulder. Henry sat right next to him, monopolizing that real estate. There were mostly toddlers around the little campsite where Cynthia was caring for most of the brood.

"Papa, did your dream come true?" Henry asked William.

"It sure did, Henry. Did Aunt Cynthia tell you about it."

The boy nodded and added: "She had a dream, too."

William held a small bundle in his left arm. It was Rufus, his two-month old son. With tears in her eyes, she turned to her husband and pointed to Rufus: "This is exactly what I dreamed of...

— you were holding our son! And, tomorrow, we should all go to see Aunt Sophronia and meet Rufus' sister," Cynthia said and then added: "She's in Pondtown."

"Where is Pondtown?" William said.

"Not far. Let's go surprise her tomorrow. I told her what President Young told us about your release. But, we didn't know when you'd be coming," Cynthia said.

"Let's leave first thing in the morning — we've waited long enough for this reunion,"

FOR THE FIRST TIME SINCE JOHNSTON'S ARMY HALTED in the Wyoming wilderness, there was jubilation. Captain Marcy and his contingent had returned, but not alone — they arrived on June 8th with 1,500 mules. Captain Jesse Gove came galloping into camp and nearly was thrown from his mount as pulled back the reins and skidded in front of Colonel Johnston's tent:

"Colonel, colonel, Marcy's back!"

Major Porter rushed out first — the colonel was engaged elsewhere (the privy): "Where are they now?"

"The first group is trickling in now, but the bulk of them will be assembling soon. They have to find a place to corral them, where there's enough feed," Gove exclaimed.

Johnston appeared shortly after Gove's dramatic entrance:

"Gove, go inform all the officers to assemble here in half an hour. And see if you can find Marcy."

Later that afternoon, Captain Randolph Marcy and his sergeant major dismounted near Johnston's command tent and was greeted by the colonel. They saluted. Johnston was speechless:

"Captain, I hardly recognize you — you are half the man you used to be," he said and extended his hand.

"Colonel, you should have seen us when we crawled into Fort Massachusetts. I think I lost about 60 pounds, but I'm fit now, thinner but fit. Even have a new uniform. So, Colonel, when do

we march into Salt Lake City and take over that place? We have a score to settle!"

"Come inside. We've had visitors, sent here by President James Buchanan. Our orders have changed."

Two weeks later, Colonel Albert Sydney Johnston addressed his men, all at attention and awaiting his command. Johnston's orders to his men were explicit as they had cleared out their kit from Fort Bridger, Camp Scott and Eckelsville:"Men, the Mormons called us a horde, murderous thugs and all kinds of names. We have specific orders from the president him-self. We may not like those orders, we may feel we have some pay-back due us, but we are not a rabble. We are the United States Army. So, we are marching in good order into Salt Lake City, but we will not garrison there. The Mormons have evacuated their city in fear of us — if we try to stay there, they will burn it to the ground. I want to see excellent military bearing in all ranks and files. Do you understand?" The men answered in unison. "Yes sir!" The next day Johnston's Army finally began mar a week, they would exit Emigration Canyon and make their entrance into the Valley of the Great Salt Lake.

Bringing up the rear of his regiment, Captain Jesse Gove was shocked. Unlike the 2,000 or so enlisted men, Captain Gove was mounted, and he had a great view of men in step and the orderly city laid out in front of him. It was June 26th, 1858, and like most June days in Utah, it was clear and beautiful. The captain was shocked at the site before him, the beautiful valley with rows and rows of neat, orderly homes and church buildings. Gove had been expecting something much different. One of his lieutenants rode along side: "Captain, so this is Salt Lake City, such a beautiful place, so clean and neat."

The streets ran north and south — the avenues east and west. Street signs told them exactly where they were: Salt Lake City!

The entire column, ranks and files, wagons and horses and marching men all made a 90-degree turn left onto South Temple Avenue.

All the cottages and bungalows were set back equally from the street, with gardens in back with coops and small barns.

But, the city was nearly vacant — hardly a soul in sight except for teenagers with torches, all awaiting the order to burn everything. Captain Gove finally replied to his comrade:

"Much better than I expected — this hardly looks like a place inhabited by lunatics."

A couple of miles ahead, drummers had picked up the pace. "They must be passing by Brigham's castle," Gove's aide said.

As they came to Seventh East, they passed a series of mansions, some under construction. On the porch of one, General Burton with an aide observed the parade from a balcony:

"Makes you almost proud to be an American," his master sergeant said.

"Almost," Burton replied.

"Johnston has drilled some discipline into them."

"Good thing, too, that is," the sergeant said. Down the street on the steps of the Lion House, Howard Egan and two of his aides stood in silence as the colors passed by, the drummers setting the beat. Capt. Philip St. George Cooke turned and doffed his hat to his former Mormon Battalion members.

A corporal turned to Egan: "Who's that?"

"I believe it's our old commander, Philip St. George Cooke," Egan said.

"Where are they headed, Major?"

"West of the Jordan River — the pasture out there, I reckon; they'll have to blaze a new trail. I understand there's a site in Cedar Valley that has enough water. But, its dusty and desolate, hardly a tree anywhere. We had to plant ours!"

The column was still moving at steady clip. Egan smiled. His aide looked at him curiously.

"Opportunities will abound," Major Egan said. "They'll need building materials. Jobs are always a good thing. Might give the Cahoon brothers some work to do."

The corporal was curious. "How so?"

"They make bricks." Later that evening, Burton, Egan and others met at the Lion House.

"The governor wanted a count. Who has it," General Burton asked.

"I do," a lieutenant offered. "It's right here: Our best estimate is 3,000 men, both infantry and calvary, 600 wagons and 6,000 head of animals, horses, mules and feedstock, sheep and cattle."

"That's another good reason for them to leave the valley," Burton said, their work is cut out for them, and with all those animals and men, they will need time to get set up out there before the snow flies. And they'll have to employ quite a few Saints."

AS JOHNSTON'S ARMY WAS MARCHING SOUTH, a vanguard of Saints was coming north now that it was confirmed that the Army's garri-son would be built out of their sight, if not out of their minds. At a point the Saints call "the Jordan Narrows," the two columns were on either bank of the meandering Jordan River, traveling in oppo-site directions, the Army south, the Saints north. Like the Holy Land's Jordan River which also connects two lakes — the fresh-water Sea of Galilee and the saltwater Dead Sea (the Jews' "great salt lake"), the similarity in geography was obvious to the Latter-day Saints who also viewed their home as "the Promised Land." After camping along the Provo River for a few weeks, the Wagstaffs were more than eager to return to their various projects, particu-larly their stubby little trees,. Willy, Maria Stubb's 8-year-old son, who now simply called William Wagstaff "Pa," was worried.

"What if they dry up, Pa?"

"Will the deer eat them?"

"When can we eat the apples?"

"How many apples do you need for a pie?"

The questions kept coming.

'How long before we're home?"

"Shouldn't we go to the orchard first?"

William just smiled. Willy's questions didn't bother the good-natured horticulturalist. The big woodsman Christian Holz was traveling with the Wagstaffs. He was still unattached and longed to be with Winnie, but he had heard a calling to serve a mission back in Schleswig-Holstein would soon be forthcoming, and of course, he would go… there was never a question about him continuing to answer the call, whatever it might be, to build up Zion. But he had to first get things in order — at least get the walls and roof on his house finished.

Finally, their little caravan reached the Salt Lake Valley with the immense Lone Peak looming over them on the right, with the beautiful little town of Draper snuggled up against it.

Christian had been enjoying listening to Willy question his father.

"Willy sure has a lot of questions — I admire your patience," Christian said.

"That's because I learned patience the hard way," William said. "Everybody has a breaking point. A lot of Saints have had enough persecution, name-calling and outsiders calling them names, running their cattle through their gardens like the Arkansans did.

"Maybe you saw the wagons leaving the valley, going north or east — I did. When you were up in Emigration Canyon, did you count all the wagons returning to the East?"

"I saw a few. Many Saints had had enough," Christian said.

"A lot went west to California, too," William said. "This move south has been harder on some folks than it was traveling here from Winter Quarters. The tests keep coming. Some just can't endure it."

"Well, I don't know much about others, William, but you seem to be holding up pretty well," Christian said.

"Christian, I left England with my little seed chest and a collection of seedlings to plant in the New World. My first wife and I started out with six children — one died at sea.

"When we landed in New Orleans, another couple got the cholera — we lost them. Finally, when we arrived in St. Louis, the rest of our children died, along with my second wife, and I had to beg to get wood for her casket. Then, they put me in the hospital, convinced I would die. I didn't.

"On the journey to gather with the Saints, I met a woman whose husband had died; she had two children and soon all three of them passed on from cholera, too. Finally, I arrived in Winter Quarters as a childless widower, and there I laid eyes on the cheery little Maria Stubbs Wiseman with her tiny dancing feet and the most beautiful singing voice you ever heard.

"She brought her son, Willy, with her into our union. I love him like my own flesh and blood. I still have my seed chest and my seedlings but that's about all I have left from England — I want Willy and his little brother and sister to help me start a nursery — Willy can't wait. So, you see, every question he asks is like a hymn to me, a chorus of angels. I never tire of it."

Behind the Wagstaffs were miles and miles of wagons, hundreds of animals and at least 20,000 Saints of the Latter-days. Governor Cumming and Utah's First Lady, the adventurous Elizabeth Cumming, were cheering them on. Soon the homes, the gardens and streets would come back to life, but things would never be quite the same.

Time doesn't heal all wounds.

As a former mayor, Governor Alfred Cumming knew all about shaking hands and kissing babies, but that was years earlier when he was campaigning for office, and people actually voted for him. None of these people had voted for him. Instead, he was foisted on them by a blundering president.

And, now that there were people back in their homes and walking the streets, the Governor had some repenting to do on behalf of the president who sent him there, much of it not his doing. First, because he had been the superintendent of Indian affairs for the Upper Missouri Agency and had been branded a Missourian as a result — in Utah "M" was a scarlet letter. And they would easily forget that, in his initial proclamation in accepting his new position, Cumming had employed the same litany of official descriptors about Mormons that had been used in Washington: "Rebellion, Traitorous Acts and Treason." Alfred Cumming had some fences to mend.

So soon after arriving in Utah, he had learned that he'd have to wash his mouth out with soap and water. Finally, there was his drinking problem: He was described as "a whiskey barrel in the morning, but a barrel of whiskey at night." But, then the politician in Cumming took over. And so did his charming, plucky wife, Elizabeth Cumming.

Alfred soon learned to liked these "peculiar people." So did his wife. He liked their leader, Brigham Young, and Brigham liked him back. And, after being treated badly by every other Federal official who abused them and then left, denouncing them, calling them all kinds of names as they did so, the Mormons expected more of the same. But Cumming did none of those things. He and his wife soon won them over. Cumming did the one thing that always gets to a Mormon: He repented and asked for their forgiveness.

Far away in Philadelphia, the man who had created the new Alfred Cumming, Thomas Kane, had visited Buchanan days after he had arrived home. His purpose was to establish amicable relations between the administration and Brigham Young and the Mormons, but to no avail — the ruling class, those Yankee editors, still held the Mormons, and by extension, Cumming in disdain.

The Sunday after Thomas' return, the Kane family was dining with Elizabeth's parents. Her father, William Wood recognized how discouraged Thomas and asked, "So, how did the president take to your proposal?"

Thomas sighed, proclaiming how corrupt the administration was and how little they cared for the Constitution.

Then Wood gave Thomas the praise that he didn't want nor expect, but deserved: *"Thomas, perhaps depression is only what ought to have been expected after all the high-strung enthusiasm which you carried out so triumphantly through your Mormon mission. You attained your object of preventing bloodshed fully. Therefore thank God for having been the instrument in his hands of effecting that good. Think how much you have had to go through during the last 10 months, including as they do very extraordinary illness and your father's death. Who would have ventured to prophecy in September 1857 that you have passed through the trials you have undergone and been alive to tell the tale. Yet God has spared you and for some good."*

Elizabeth smiled: "Thank you, Papa," and then turned to Thomas: "It wasn't a waste of time, you'll see. Just remember what the old Patriarch said. At least the Mormons will never forget you."

Neither would Governor Cumming. He had been wooing the Saints to stay put, but it was too little, too late. As he witnessed ill-clad refugees moving south, he tried to comfort them and talk them into staying. Brigham and the other brethren saw how he was moved by their suffering, and that increased his stock in their eyes. Of all the apostles, George A. Smith, likely the most bellicose, confided to others that although *"his memory is frequently at fault due to his inebriety, he is evidently the most generous, whole-hearted & upright man of all the officers sent to Utah."*

And, the crowning accolade that helped him atone for his earlier sins was how jubilant he and Elizabeth Cumming were when the Saints came marching home. It didn't take Elizabeth long to mix in with Mormon women, learn that they weren't slavish, downtrodden members of harems. The governor and Brigham Young both learned that they were stronger together than they were separate.

Without Alfred Cumming as governor, how the Mormons would have fared with an Army on its doorstep is anyone's guess. It's too nightmarish to consider.

IN PHILADELPHIA, THERE WAS A FAMILY REUNION. Thomas Kane's daughter Harriett was no longer toddling, and little Elisha looked like he'd doubled in size. Bess could barely contain her tears for joy. Patrick was convinced that hardship makes Thomas get stronger: Bess agreed:

"Thomas, you're so tanned and fit. Just look at you!" She pulled her husband to her side, and he welcomed the affection. It had been a long time. His mother hung back — little Harriett clung to his leg.

They had all gathered at his parents' home, the family and a few close friends. Patrick was carrying Thomas' packages and duffel into the house, but set them on the porch. "Bess, Thomas' clothes need a good washing — you might want to send them out."

In addition to the several copies of the *New York Tribune's* article which Bess had set on the dining room table for guests to read or take home, she also had received just the day before a copy of the Deseret News via post. Bess had set out hors d'oeuvres, small sandwiches and other finger foods for her guests — it was supposed to be celebration for a hero, but the hero wasn't happy.

"Anybody read what the *Herald* said or the *Inquirer*? Or how about the Times? Since he hadn't been home to massage the editors and give them pre-written articles to save them all the trouble of doing actual research, most of the papers were continuing to spread the same old "manure," in his words.

"The *Tribune* and the *St. Louis Republican* actually took the risk to tell the truth," Thomas said. "But that's about it."

"I have a copy of a Los Angeles paper," Patrick said, "it goes after the Mormons, but you got good press, Thomas."

"But, Mr. Greeley's *Tribune's* article was still the best," Mother Kane said, holding it up.

"That's because the reporter shared a carriage with Thomas — got it right from the horse's mouth," Patrick pointed out.

"But, the people who really know him and love him had the best things to say," Bess said. "A Mormon poetess, Eliza R. Snow wrote these verses:

"You plead the rights of man — you fain would see
"All men enjoy the sweets of liberty
"Goodness is greatness — knowledge, pow'r and thou
"Perchance are greatest of your nation, now.
"And while that nation sink beneath its blight,
"You like the constellation, cheer the night."

"I met her, you know, a very graceful woman. She's one of Brigham's wives, but suffered greatly from the mobs in Missouri — and is the sister of one of their apostles, Lorenzo Snow. Thomas continued, "Thanks, Bess, I appreciate all the kind words from everybody, but..."

"But what?" Patrick seemed irritated.

"I'm not changing minds — there are still people who don't seem to understand what the First Amendment guarantees all Americans," Thomas complained. "Did you read what the Times wrote, that Buchanan and Cumming have colluded with and are taking orders from the Mormons' High Priest and that Buchanan sent me to trade an amnesty for the their sham obedience to get Old Buck's fingers out of the fire."

"Maybe so, but what can you do about it?" Patrick was growing weary of his brother's obsession.

"I have contacted the New York Historical Society to deliver a declaration of facts — to go on the record so that hostile forces don't undo everything that we've accomplished," Thomas said.

Bess was puzzled: "How could they do that?"

"By removing Cumming — he's the key. But, now that Johnston's Army is garrisoned and away from them, things may appear that they are working for now — but mark my word, the forces of darkness will do their best to sully him, damage his reputation or anything to first get rid of him — and then the Mormons!"

Maybe it was an obsession — but once again, it ended Thomas Kane's hiatus and renewed his desire to defend his friends, "come hell or high water." And, even though the Army was building Camp Floyd more than 40 miles distant from Salt Lake City where they would be billeted until the Civil War began, hell was never very far away whether measured by miles or time, as the Saints' most prodigious journal writer and future church president, Wilford Woodruff, would write after the firing on Fort Sumter.

He noted in his journal that *"whenever the rulers of any nation trample their own constitution and laws underfoot and destroy the weak because they have the power to do so, they sow the seeds to their own dissolution, and they will reap their own destruction."*

33

EPILOGUE

Thomas Kane was back in the ring after hiding away in Philadelphia for a season. The occasion was his address to the New York Historical Society. Elizabeth Kane had joined her husband for the long-awaited trip to the city. Grandmothers welcomed the opportunity to watch the two little Kanes, Harriet and Elisha. The Kane family had assumed that after returning from Utah a year ago that his obsession with all things Mormon would be over once and for all. They were mistaken.

Yes, peace seemed to prevail in that high desert country, but only on the surface. Kane's iron would have to remain in the fire. Dark forces had their eye on Governor Cumming — he was just too accommodating to Brigham Young and the Saints.

For those intent on finding the gold and silver buried in Utah's mountains, that impediment to their Manifest Destiny would have to be dug out. Alfred Cumming had to go!

But, Thomas Kane wasn't going to just stand by and let that happen. Elizabeth Kane stood by her man as he read his notes before leaving for the historical society. The Kanes had spent the night in a cozy little New York pension walking distance from the lecture hall:

"Do you know what irritates me about your address today?"

"That it's raining?" Kane answered distractedly.

"No, Thomas, we have a hansom waiting for us. And, we could share an umbrella. No, that's not it."

Thomas was trying to focus on his speech — she was like a bee buzzing in his ear.

"Then, what is it?" He asked.

"That you have to give a speech at all! After all you did, your five-month journey, sleeping in the snow, getting almost shot and then Buchanan and his 'peace commissioners' getting all the credit. Your name is hardly mentioned. And it drives me mad!"

Thomas chuckled: "I know. But, remember, Buchanan is no George Washington, he's not even Martin Van Buren. And the people around him, they pull his strings like puppeteers."

"I understand that, but Thomas, don't you think the Mormons bring this on themselves, like polygamy, for example?"

"Maybe, and certainly Mountain Meadows is a tragedy they have to own up to. But, look at their history: When they were chased out of Ohio, then Missouri and finally Illinois, it wasn't because of polygamy — that wasn't even an issue then. It wasn't until 1852 that it even became public knowledge. **They weren't persecuted because of polygamy — they practiced polygamy because they were persecuted!** If there were fifty or sixty thousand Mormons sitting right there in the mountains — and soon there would be that many people and even more — there would be too many of them to persecute, drive like cattle or certainly not kill. My purpose is to help people understand that the First Amendment offers protection to all people."

"I agree, but what about slaves and Indians," Bess argued.

"Bess, let's just win one battle at a time — according to Joseph Smith, their prophet, that's coming, too."

"What is?"

"A war, Bess...a war between the states."

Bess gasped. They'd talk about that later. It was time to go. Their ride was outside and a theater full of people was waiting for Elisha Kane's brother, Thomas. Horace Greeley had another correspondent at the theater ready to cover the speech of the man that the *Tribune* had called a hero the previous year.

The New York Tribune provided the highlights for its readers, and from Thomas Kane's perspective, it would illuminate the merits of keeping Alfred Cumming the governor of Utah Territory:

"It has been stated, Mr. Kane said, Gov. Cumming proceeded to Salt Lake assured that his safety was provided for in terms by an agreement with Brigham Young. To this assertion he not only gave an emphatic denial, but he devoted a large portion of his lecture to a narration of facts connected with the Governor's journey to the valley which he justly said negatived such a supposition. There were few men, he said, who would have dared to expose themselves in the face of so unanimous a protest of opposition as was raised against his taking that step; still fewer who, as he did, would have reposed their confidence in persons against whom was raised so unanimous a voice of warning. Mr. Kane's narrative of the real circumstances of Governor Cumming's journey to Salt Lake was very happy; he showed up admirably the cool intrepidity for which Governor Cumming is of all men one of the most remarkable.

At camp there was but one opinion on the subject of his venturing outside the lines. It was not merely that the Mormons had forbidden, under pain of death, all intercourse between our people and theirs. From the time of the first rupture Gov. Cumming was singled out as the especial object of the animosity and invective of the Mormons, rendering him the very bull's-eye of the target for any of their hundreds of free rifles, who lay out watching the movements of our troops, and prowling out among the windings of the mountains.

Had the head men of the Valley been ever so much disposed to spare him, who could guaranty the good conduct of the wild soldiers upon the outposts? A shot from one of these, or any wandering Mormon hunter, might have laid him low before he could attain the main body of the rebel troops.

"But, beside this danger and the more ordinary Mormon purlo thrumbos, there was another form which, as things turned out, there was quite as much serious ground for apprehension as any. The whole country lying between the Mormon and American lines was infested by bands of marauding savages — Indian Cowboys and Skinners — who occupied the neutral ground, prepared to rob and murder in the name of either party, as might best promote their purposes. About three weeks before they had succeeded in lifting several hundred head of cattle from the enemy in the name of the United States, killing and scalping two frontiersmen in the course of the transaction. Within ten days they had carried off as many as a hundred horses in another levy of the kind... "Arriving in the vicinity of the Spring, which is on this side of Quaking Asp Hill, after night, Indian campfires were discerned on the rocks overhanging the valley. We proceeded to the spring, and, after disposing of the animals, retired from the trail beyond the mountains. We had reason to congratulate ourselves upon having taken this precaution, as we subsequently ascertained that the country lying below your outposts and 'Yellow' [Creek] is infested by hostile renegades and outlaws from various tribes. "By this brevity on subjects involving self-laudation you recognize the true man," said Mr. Kane.

The editor summarized what Kane's purpose was in appearing at the historical society: *"...he would confess, simply for the purpose of doing justice to an individual whose means of usefulness were seriously menaced by the assaults upon his character.*

He thought it was time for the public to know something about one man in Utah who had enemies in Washington."

Kane's praise for Cumming had its intended effect: Until the Civil War ended Cumming's assignment in Utah, and he returned to Confederate Georgia, the Mormons in Utah continued to benefit from the work of a governor who cared for and looked out for them.

Thomas Kane had helped the "old whiskey barrel" keep his job. And, the Latter-day Saints benefited, even if they didn't know it.

MORMONS WERE IN THE NEWS AGAIN after an unofficial truce was declared with the United States Army, and true to his famous slogan, "Go West, Young Man," Horace Greeley made his overland trip to Utah before the railroad's arrival in 1869. Brigham Young received his request for an interview and replied in the affirmative. An uneasy peace existed in Utah in the summer of 1859. Occasionally on official business, people in Salt Lake would see an officer accompanied by an enlisted man call on Governor Cumming at the territorial office. And, at Camp Floyd some 40 miles southwest of Salt Lake City, Mormons found work. There was a garrison to construct, and lacking local timber and a miller willing to cut wood to length, the Army was buying locally produced adobe bricks, which required labor to form, dry and kiln. Horace Greeley arrived in Salt Lake City and was invited to sit down with the prophet, seer and revelator of the Church of Jesus Christ of Latter-day Saints, even Brigham Young. Here is much of Greeley's report as later printed in his *New York Tribune*:

"My friend, Dr. Bernheisel, took me this afternoon by appointment to meet Brigham Young, president of the Mormon Church, who had expressed a willingness to receive me at 2:00 p.m After some unimportant conversation on general topics, I stated that I had come in quest of fuller knowledge respecting the doctrines and policy of the Mormon Church and would like to ask some questions bearing directly on these if there are no objections. President Young avowed his willingness to respond to all pertinent inquiries. The conversation proceeded substantially as follows:

H.G. Am I to regard Mormonism (so-called) as a new religion or simply a new development of Christianity?

B.Y. We hold that can be no true Christian church without a priesthood directly commissioned by immediate communication with the Son of God, and Savior of Mankind. Such a church is that of the Latter-day Saints, called by their enemies, Mormons; we know no other that even pretends to have present and direct revelation of God's will.

H.G. Am I to understand that you regard all other churches professing to be Christian as the Church of Rome regard all churches not in communion with itself — as scholastic, heretical and out of the way of salvation?

B.Y. Yes, substantially.

H.G. Let me now be enlightened with regard more especially to your Church policy I understand that you require each member to pay over one-tenth of all he produces or earns to the Church.

B.Y. That is the requirement of our Faith.

H.G. What is done with the proceeds of this tithing?

B.Y. Part of it devoted to building temples and other places of worship; part to helping the poor and needy converts on their way to this country; and the largest portion to support of the poor among the saints.

H.G. Is none of it paid to bishops and other dignitaries of the church?

B.Y. Not one penny.

H.G. How then do your ministers live?

B.Y. By the labor of their own hands like the first apostles. I am the only person in the Church who has not a regular calling apart from the church's service.

H.G. Can you give any rational explanation of the aversion and hatred with which your people are generally regarded by this among whom they have lived and with whom they have been brought directly into contact?

B.Y. No other explanation than is afforded by the crucifixion of Christ and the kindred treatment of God's ministers, prophets, and Saints in all ages.

H.G. How general is polygamy among you?

B.Y. I could not say. Some of those present (head of the Church) have each but one wife, others have more; each determines what is his individual duty.

H.G. What is the largest number of wives belonging to any one man?

B.Y. I have fifteen. I know no one who has more; but some of those sealed to me are old ladies whom I regard rather as mothers but whom I have taken home to cherish and support.

H.G. Does not Christ say that he who puts away his wife or married one whom another has put away commits adultery?

B.Y. Yes; and I hold that no man should ever put away a wife except for adultery — not always even for that. Such is my individual view of the matter. I do not say that wives have never been put away in our church, but I do not approve of that practice.

Such is, as nearly as I can recollect, the substance of nearly two hours conversation. President Young spoke readily, not always with grammatical accuracy but with no appearance of hesitations or reserve, and with not apparent desire of conceal anything. He was very plainly dressed in thin summer clothing, and with no air of sanctimony or fanaticism. In appearance, he is a portly, frank, good-natured and rather thick set man of fifty-eight. Seeming to enjoy life and be of no particular hurry to get to heaven. His associates are plain men, evidently born and reared to a life of labor, and looking as little like crafty hypocrites or swindlers as any body of men I have ever met.

By 1859, Camp Floyd was well under construction and proved to be a boon for Mormon workmen lumberjacks, masons and brick-makers. By 1860, the camp had grown to 7,000 inhab-

itants with 3,000 officers and enlisted men, along with civilians and support staff, altogether the third largest city or town in Utah Territory. Here soldiers, staff and the local population met and intermingled. It was here that Patience Loader, the young woman who had buried her father along the Mormon trail and one of the 1856 Willie Company handcart survivors, met a soldier, John Rozsa; they were then married by her Mormon bishop.

Even though Rozsa had joined the LDS Church, his commanding officer didn't recognize the marriage and refused to give Patience the status of a soldier's wife, so they had to be married again by a chaplain stationed at Camp Floyd. Together, they had three boys, but then Patience had another tragedy — her husband died of an illness during the Civil War. She later remarried.

At the outbreak of the Civil War, the fort was renamed Camp Crittenden due to Secretary of War John Floyd's resignation; he had worked so hard to push for the Utah Expedition to "put down the Mormon rebellion" and then rebelled himself and joined the Confederacy. Once hostilities began after the firing on Fort Sumpter, Camp Crittenden was closed. Within a year, only 17 people remained at the site. Within a couple of years, Mormons and other local inhabitants were able to acquire the assets left by the Army for cents on the dollar. The Army left, and the Mormons prospered.

The federal government's continuing "Reconstruction" of Utah continued even longer than it did in the Confederate South. Mormon men in polygamous marriages were pursued, harassed and many of them jailed, including George Q. Cannon, counselor to Brigham Young, editor and publisher and close confidant of Thomas Kane. The tragedy of the massacre at Mountain Meadows did not disappear — it haunts members of The Church of Jesus Christ of Latter-day Saints even to this day. Instigator of the massacre, John D. Lee, was the only participant who was ever tried and convicted of his crime, although many others had gone into hiding. He was executed by a firing squad in 1877.

Suffering and persecution continued for another generation among the Latter-day Saints, despite an official peace declared with Johnston's Army. For William Stowell, his wives Cynthia and Sophronia, they did have a few months together before they would be tried again. In the late summer of 1858, they made their pilgrimage back from Payson and Pondtown to their tiny residence in Ogden. It was a hot and dusty journey, some 100 miles northward that took them several days.

Then in October, tragedy struck. First, Cynthia's little boy, Rufus, who was born when William was in captivity — the same baby Cynthia saw in a dream in her husband's arms — died on October 14th. Then, three days later, Sophronia's infant daughter Mary passed away. The two Stowell babies were buried in the same grave.

In the coming years, Cythnia would have five more children as would Sophronia. But, they couldn't stay in Ogden nor any-where else in the United States. Targeted for their polygamous marriage by Federal officials, they fled with many other Mormon families — including Carl Wilcken and his family — to Colonia Juarez in northern Mexico. There William became a mill owner and a church patriarch. He died in 1901, then free from political pressure, the Stowell widows moved back to Utah. Their offspring today would number in the hundreds.

DURING THE CIVIL WAR, LOT SMITH BECAME A CAVALRY OFFICER with other troops who were assigned to protect the telegraph lines from the Great Basin to California after they came to Utah; however, Lot's service was of short duration.

Governor Cumming and his wife Elizabeth returned to Georgia and were loyal to the Confederacy. However, Senator Sam Houston, a Texan, resigned his seat in the U.S. Senate (since Texas joined the Confederacy), left public life, returning

to Austin, embittered that his state and even his son, who became a Confederate officer, had aligned with the South.

When Thomas Kane learned of the bombardment of Fort Sumter, he became the first Pennsylvanian to volunteer for duty, raised a regiment — *the Pennsylvania Bucktails* — and eventually earned his star as a brigadier general. He fought and was wounded at Gettysburg and suffered from his wounds the rest of his life.

After the Civil War and the end of slavery, the U.S. Government and the ruling Republican Party turned its attention back to its remaining obsession, the other twin relic of barbarism: polygamy. It became a federal crime, and Utah like the South, experienced its own version of Reconstruction. Then, in 1869, the transcontinental railroad was completed with the Union Pacific and the Central Pacific railroads meeting at Promontory Point, Utah, where the legendary golden spike was driven. Utah's isolation was coming to an end.

And, with the driving of that spike, Thomas Kane was able to keep the promise he made years earlier to Elizabeth when, in 1872, he took her to Utah to meet his dear friends. Always wary of polygamy, Elizabeth made the long train ride to Utah with some reservation. She and Thomas then traveled with Brigham Young on the long road from Salt Lake to St. George staying at 12 different Mormons homes where she met many Mormon women who were living in polygamous marriages. In 1874, she wrote and published a small book titled *Twelve Mormon Homes*. Not only did she have her eyes opened, but Elizabeth Kane, like her husband Thomas, also made some new Mormon friends. An all too common occurrence in the 19th-century was the number of women who died in childbirth. Marrying another wife was the only cure for a helpless widower, as she wrote in her book: Describing a conversation she had had with a plural wife about her husband who had lost his first wife, Elizabeth Kane wrote that the woman had endured *"three bereave-*

ments since we were married...[his deceased wife] left four chil-dren. I thought I could never have any children of my own...but, dear me, I found there was quite a new love for them...I brought up my own little brothers and sisters, too, my mother died when I was thirteen." Mormon women, Elizabeth wrote, *do not regret the birth of a daughter as a misfortune,* rather *"they honestly believe in the grand calling their theology assigns to women, 'that of endowing souls with tabernacles that they may accept redemption.' Nowhere is the 'sphere of women according to [their] gospel more fully recognized than in Utah."*

When the Kanes spent the winter of 1872 and 1873 with Brigham Young in St. George, Utah, it brought back memories of his trip north 15 years earlier. When he was traveling through southern California as "the botanist, Dr. Osborne," in 1858, he met the Cocheron family and their 13-year-old daughter, Augusta.

In St. George, he paid them a courtesy visit. Later that evening, according to Elizabeth Kane, *"it had grown very dark, and it was raining. . . . Looking from the doorway on the light within and the stormy night without, he said: 'This looks like our political horizon. Stay you in camp, eat roast beef and rest. I will go out in the storm and stand on picket guard for you.' He extended his hand, repeated thrice, 'goodnight,' and was gone."*

It was the same Thomas Kane, the peacemaker, playing the role of the romantic. Brigham Young had invited Thomas and Elizabeth to come to Utah, telling Thomas that *"there is not one among the thousands who will cross the plains this season whom the Saints who would rather extend the hand of warm welcome... [than to you]—"* Kane had even said that he wished to write Brigham Young's biography.

So, Kane accepted the invitation. Bess was skeptical, but when she arrived, she was immediately impressed by the Mormons' affection for him. She wrote to her daughter, *"he is like another man here! It would delight you to see how the people worship him here."* He had arrived sick, but once again, the Mormons — and the dry, warm climate of St. George — worked wonders with Thomas. And, it endeared Elizabeth Kane, as it did Thomas in 1846, to the Mormons. She wrote that *"I never saw so great a change in anyone in so short a time...I am indebted for the recovery to the kind and able nursing of the Mormons."*

That was Elizabeth Kane's only journey west, but she was enthralled by the Latter-day Saints, their devotion to Thomas, the climate and the scenery. Thomas Kane returned one more time, in 1877, to attend the funeral of his beloved friend, the Mormon prophet and colonizer Brigham Young. Kane's weak constitution, combined with his war wounds, eventually caught up with him, leading to his death from pneumonia in 1883.

Today, very few Americans — or Utahns for that matter — know anything about the Utah War or who Thomas Kane was, and yet there's a statue of Thomas Kane on the Utah State Capitol grounds and a county in southern Utah named after him.

Fading into history seemed to be fine with Kane. But, it's not to those who have come to know and appreciate him:

Thomas Kane deserves our acclamation.

THE END

BIBLIOGRAPHY

Recollections of Past Days: The Autobiography of Patience Rosza Archer By Sandra Alley Petree, Digitalcommons@USU (2006) *pp. 11 & 13*

Discourses of Brigham Young, Compiled by John A. Widstoe Deseret Book Company 1978 pg 480 © 1954 Church of Jesus Christ of Latter-day Saints | Salt Lake City, Utah 84111 USA   pp. 143-146

Popular History of Utah By Orson F. Whitney Salt Lake City, Utah © 1916 The Deseret News pp. 503-505

"I Was Not Ready to Die Yet": William Stowell's Utah War Ordeal — Compiled & edited by Kenneth L. Alford, Ph.D. Brigham Young University — Utah & R Devan Jensen, Brigham Young University, BYU Studies Quarterly 56. no.4 (Fall 2017) pp. 143-146

"Lion in the Path: Genesis of the Utah War" by David L. Bigler pp 4-21 | "And the War Came: James Buchanan, the Utah Expedition and Decision to Intervene" By William MacKinnon, pp 22-37 | Utah Historical Quarterly Winter 2008 Vol. 76 #1

Liberty to the Downtrodden: Thomas L. Kane, Romantic Reformer, By Matthew J. Grow © 2009 Yale University

At Sword's Point, Part I: A Documentary History of the Utah War to 1858 By William MacKinnon | Volume 10 of the Kingdom in the West Series — The Mormons and the American Frontier © 2008 W. MacKinnon The Arthur H. Clarke Company

At Sword's Point, Part II: A Documentary History of the Utah War 1858-1859 By William MacKinnon | Volume 11 of the Kingdom in the West Series — The Mormons and the American Frontier © 2016 W. MacKinnon The Arthur H. Clarke Company

Twelve Mormon Homes: Visited in Succession on a Journey through Utah and Arizona By Elizabeth Wood Kane Pantianos Classics, first published in 1874

AUTHOR

G.M. "Jackson" Jarrard is an adman, who at the suggestion of his father, a newspaper editor, studied that crass subject in college. For more than 50 years, he worked as a copywriter, creative director and then ran his own ad agency while also working as a copy editor at a daily newspaper. Then in 2005 graduated to a more respectable occupation: book publishing.

For the past 20 years, he has been editing, designing (or "paginating") digitally printed, limited-run personal and family histories for his clients. What was an occupation became a "preoccupation" which led to his appreciation for the sacrifices and lifestyles of his forebears, most of whom were Mormon pioneers and who lived their lives in poverty compared to the lap of luxury most of us find ourselves in today.

He lives today with his wife Christie in South Jordan, Utah, surrounded by a mountain fortress to remind him every day of his pioneer forebears who bounced down canyon trails and made the desert "blossom as a rose."

This book was written as an expression of gratitude to them.

*For ongoing commentary and facts about rhe real people and real events found in Marching on Zion, please visit marchingonzion.com — send an e-mail to preservationbooks@icloud.com or drop a note in the post to >>>
Preservation Books | PO Box 95274 | South Jordan, Utah 84095-0274*

William Richard Wiseman with his grandson Joe Garland, circa 1920. *William was my great-grandfather, born in London, England, in 1849 and came west with his mother, Marie Stubbs around 1853. She married William Wagstaff who had already lost two wives and all of his six children before he ever arrived in "Zion." Wagstaff adopted William and the two of them later founded a nursery and planted some of the first fruit trees in East Millcreek, southeast of the city. He and "little Willy" are both depicted in Chapter 1. Wagstaff's personal journey is one of the most poignant stories of personal loss and triumph I have ever read.* **The Author**

And the Lord called his people Zion, because
they were of one heart and one mind, and dwelt
in righteousness; and there was no poor among
them.

(Moses 7:18 — Pearl of Great Price)

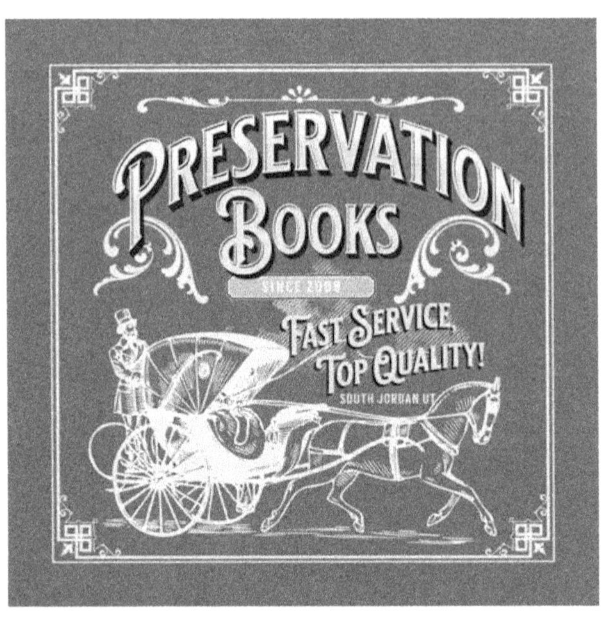

PRESERVATION BOOKS

South Jordan, Utah

Marching on Zion
© 2025 Jackson Jarrard